“I am dead,” he said.

Scowling, I narrowed my eyes. His complexion was paling, dark blue veins appearing in his face like a gruesome cobweb of decay.

“Don’t be absurd,” I mumbled.

He gripped my shoulder, black and cracked fingernails digging into me. “The young man is innocent, Ebenezer!” he urged.

I shrugged out of Fezziwig’s grip and noticed that his hand had withered. Panic rose in the pit of my gut.

“I see shadows of the past, present, and future, and exist within them all,” he whispered. “Not all is known to me, Ebenezer. But he is innocent. Of this much I am certain.”

He drew a pained, rattling breath. Before my eyes, his clothes became dust and fell from his decomposing body. Then his terrible gaze held mine once more.

“Many more will die. And then you, Ebenezer Scrooge. Though still a young man of thirty with much potential for good or ill, you will die, too.”

AN
EBENEEZER
SCROOGE
MYSTERY

The
HUMBUG MURDERS

L. J. OLIVER

POCKET BOOKS
New York London Toronto Sydney New Delhi

Pocket Books
An Imprint of Simon & Schuster, Inc.
1230 Avenue of the Americas
New York, NY 10020

First Pocket Books paperback edition November 2015

POCKET and colophon are registered trademarks of Simon & Schuster, Inc.

For information about special discounts for bulk purchases, please contact Simon & Schuster Special Sales at 1-866-506-1949 or business@simonandschuster.com.

The Simon & Schuster Speakers Bureau can bring authors to your live event. For more information or to book an event, contact the Simon & Schuster Speakers Bureau at 1-866-248-3049 or visit our website at www.simonspeakers.com.

Interior design by Estelle Leora Malmed

Manufactured in the United States of America

10 9 8 7 6 5 4 3 2 1

ISBN 978-1-4767-9234-7
ISBN 978-1-4767-9239-2 (ebook)

This book is dedicated to the memory of Scott Ciencin.
You were gone too soon my best, beloved one, my soulmate.
You taught me everything I know of unconditional love, writing, and never giving up on my dreams.
I will miss you every day for the rest of my life.

Denise Ciencin

For my dear friend and co-author, Scott Ciencin, who truly believed. And for Jane Wilson, an exceptional historian and even better mum.

Elizabeth Wilson

CHAPTER ONE

Monday, December 19th, 1833
Cheapside, London
Six Days to Christmas

FEZZIWIG WAS DEAD to begin with. Had I known that, had I been among those first few to discover his bloodied corpse and seen the brutal, rage-fueled manner in which he'd been murdered, I would have been far more alarmed when he walked through the door to my office only a few hours after his demise. Instead, my focus was on the annoying drone of Christmas carolers battling the howling winds of winter, which was mercifully silenced as he shut the door. Brushing newly-fallen snow from his shoulders and hat, he caught sight of what I was doing and slinked into the shadows by my bookshelf as I addressed my would-be client.

It was early in the morning, the meager light of the sun not yet fully penetrating the foul London smog. Yet only a single small lump of coal added its glow to my office. Darkness is cheap, and I liked it.

"Mr. Greville, sir, the time is now. I need not remind you of the pressing nature of this investment: the project governors leave for York by the morning." I indicated the leather chair once more, but Mr. Greville remained standing. "And as you know, I have little patience for anything other than *profit*."

He grunted an unintelligible reply as he flicked through the papers of our agreement, squinting to see the inked words through the hazy light of dawn.

"Very well, I'll give you a moment to see that all is in order." While Mr. Greville continued thumbing through the documents, I strode to Fezziwig, eased beside my former mentor.

"Let me look at you, boy," Fezziwig said, in a voice dustier than I remembered. He straightened my lapels. "Smartly dressed, of course. Brass buttons, freshly polished. Good. A suitably handsome jawline and a full head of healthy, dark hair add to the necessary scintilla of authority. Subtle wrinkles in the crook of your eyes and high upon your forehead. No matter. They counter your youth with an air of gravitas and experience. Merry Christmas, Ebenezer!" His eyes darted round my office, from my client to me and to the dark corners. "Now then, where's the *girl*?"

What an odd thing to say. Fezziwig knew that there had been no one in my life since Belle broke our engagement five years earlier. True, I had made some half-hearted attempts at engaging in conversation with mindless young women at society parties. But since Belle had told me, with ice in her voice as glacial as her eyes, that my love for profit had smothered my love for her, my heart had withered. I slipped my hand in my pocket, where I kept a secret: a little locket, smooth and shiny. Safely hidden inside was a tiny cameo portrait of my Belle, with her perfect ringlets and starched lace collar. Between finger and thumb I stroked the metal. It gave me comfort. Perhaps Fezziwig thought one of his granddaughters was meeting him here.

"Merry Christmas indeed," I replied with a cheerful smirk. "You'll be happy to know I've come around to your way of thinking on the season."

The old man's eyes brightened. "Really? You no longer consider Christmas a humbug?"

"Absolutely not! 'Tis the season in which I may charge ninety percent interest on loans, and these poor fools are so desperate to put on a spread, they'll gladly pay it. God bless us, everyone."

Sighing, Fezziwig nodded to my pale and trembling client. "Ebenezer, you have the same look as Ralph, my tabby, when he comes upon a rat sitting on an as yet unsprung trap."

I raised an eyebrow. "This man has cost me time, energy, and hard-earned cash. There will be an accounting."

Returning to my desk, I faced Greville and waited for him to speak. My unswerving gaze unsettled him; he made a strained effort to avoid eye contact.

Still, with a shaky voice, he mustered up enough courage to spit out, "I shall be candid."

"Of course."

"I am not sure about you, Ebenezer Scrooge."

I sat down behind my desk. I've found it is almost impossible not to trust a man willing to sit down before his aggressor. "That remains entirely your prerogative."

He was leaning on his cane, which, as had been

pointed out by my paid investigator, was a few inches too short. He stood at an acute angle as he pounded a fist on my desk.

"These conditions! Steep, no? I am a grief-stricken man, Scrooge. You are aware that my mother died recently? I have no desire to see her inheritance defrauded through your exorbitant interest rates. I came to you in good faith, despite the fact that your practice has been operating a mere six months, because I was assured of your reputation as a cutthroat businessman. But I didn't expect mine to be the throat that suffers!"

He was willing me to falter, challenging me to succumb with his narrowed eyes and puffed-out chest. I looked to old man Fezziwig. There was an urgency in Fezziwig's eyes and stance that suggested the old man was here on pressing business.

I peered up at Mr. Greville and opened my hands solicitously. "I will be investing in rail with or without your stake; such is my confidence in the project. Naturally, the inclusion of your funds will render the return significantly more bountiful for both of us. So, considering my *callous* terms, as you put it, ask yourself this: would you rather own forty percent of the greatest endeavor of our century, or a hundred percent of nothing? No, don't concern yourself with the mathematics, I can see it is overwhelming you. The time is now, sir."

Mr. Greville pulled his pocket watch out of his jacket's breast. He stared at it for a minute, then started rubbing the smooth side against his other hand as he hummed a song better suited to a church choir. Then he froze as he caught me looking at him. His face darkened.

"Look, Scrooge. You were the one who advertised for an investment partner, not me. I don't need to sign any terms I'm not happy with."

"Indeed you do not, Mr. Greville."

Though he stood as calm and solid as St. Paul's, I could see his fingers twitching. I let the potent silence hang between us like a gaping crevice demanding to be filled. Mr. Greville's fidgeting intensified, spreading to his feet with little spasms of energy.

Then it finally happened. He lunged for the pen. I smiled. The trap had at last been sprung.

"Ah, not so fast, Mr. Greville."

My would-be client froze, jaw opening and closing like a gasping fish, one hand clutching a too-short cane and the other my fine pen. His eyes met mine and widened. The faintest shimmer of sweat on his forehead reflected the flames in my fireplace.

"Did *you* write to me in response to my advertisement for an investment partner? Claiming to be able to pledge the funds against the security of these?" I waved at the papers on my desk. "Certificates of your late mother's estate?"

"Don't be so damned impertinent, Scrooge! Why else would we be here?"

"I see. That's a *terrible* shame." I pushed the papers away and folded my arms.

"What in the devil—"

"There is a young reporter chap I met recently. We'll call him Charles. He's damn near as greedy and grasping, as hard as flint as me. I had him follow you. Investigate you. According to him, *you* didn't write to me at all, did you? I am told that Mr. Greville is left-handed. But see here, all these unsightly ink smudges on your right cuff." He gulped and glanced at my ivory pen, firmly clasped in his right fist. I stood up and walked to the coat rail, where I pulled his heavy wax coat from its hook. It still dripped horrible grey sludge onto my expensive carpet; sludge that had been pure white snow before it was trodden down by the boots of thousands of Londoners racing about in frantic anticipation of Christmas though the day was still a week away.

He took the coat without expression.

"You dragged snow and slush into my office. That is not very gentlemanly. And that is not your cane. It is too short. My investigator also caught you cavorting with some unseemly types of both sexes. Gambling, whoring, drinking, the holy trinity of vices, yes? And a trip or two to the opium dens for good measure. Surprising for a man of Greville's reputation and a short leap to unmasking you as an imposter." I snorted. "That you were not even aware that the true deadline for the rail deal is Friday, four days from now, shows you're lazy, too. Can't be bothered to do your research. Well, I do not know who you are or where the real Mr. Greville is, but judging from the dark stain that looks very much like dried blood on your trouser leg, I judge that he is not in a fine condition."

The imposter just stood there, his face ablaze despite the chill. The warbling of carolers in the distance did nothing to soothe his fury.

Without taking my eyes from him, I snatched a lump of coal from the brass shuttle by the fireplace and tossed it on the flames. I loathed the expenditure, but it was necessary to place my hand within inches of the poker without attracting his notice.

"My reporter friend has been paid for his silence. It is my duty as a citizen of London to inform the police of my suspicion of fraud, and who knows what else. Though, honestly, you strike me as a lazy and cowardly man, I don't see you as the type to commit murder. So I would return to wherever you have Mr. Greville bound and gagged and free him this instant. Then perhaps catching a ship to the colonies might be prudent. As you've probably heard, I don't appreciate being crossed and I forget nothing. In fact, I would say that if I do not receive a visit from the true Mr. Greville by lunchtime that I will happily set the wretched hounds of the legal system upon you."

The imposter stood before me, boiling in his own pudding, so to speak.

"But there is yet a way I might recoup the time and expenses you've cost me. When you speak to Greville, tell him the name of his savior and advise him to bring his checkbook when he pays me a visit to thank me for his liberty and even his life. After all, I do have a business to run. Good day, sir!"

The imposter's arms were pulled slightly out to the side, he had lifted his chin and his eyes were darting from me to the door and back again. I could tell he was calculating whether or not to attack me. I felt my hand close around the poker, and my nostrils flared despite my efforts to control them.

"You're a devil, sir," he told me. "You'll pay for your sins."

"No. Today I mean to collect."

Then, eyes glazed, he nodded once, turned, and bolted towards the door at the same moment it opened from the outside, a woman's gloved hand clutching the knob. With a tinkling crash, he thudded into the door and nearly collided with a snow-covered female visitor. She stepped back and held the door as the angry gentleman vanished out into the cold London morning.

"Mr. Jasper!" she called out. "Are you quite well?" With a sigh, she entered and hung her umbrella on the hat stand. She stomped the snow off her tightly-wound black boots and straightened her coat. The straight edge of a plain but craftily hand-sewn burgundy dress poking out under her coat betrayed a simple background, yet a high regard for quality. She was a true English rose, the hair tucked under her snowy and simple hat a rich and dark chocolate, her skin so velveteen it was like poured cream. Unwinding her crocheted scarf, she smiled and sent me a quick glance with her sparkling emerald eyes. Then, with delicate hands encased in smart but inexpensive gloves, she discretely applied a pomade to her pink peony lips and checked her timepiece with a snap.

"Young lady," I said, intent on drawing her attention so that I might dismiss both her and Fezziwig and get on with more pressing matters.

But now she was digging into a satchel, rummaging about for papers, from the sound of it. "One moment, sir," she said with a polite exuberance.

"Whatever charity it is you represent, I can assure you I want none of it," I told her. "Be on your way, you're wasting your time—"

"One moment," she said again, her smile cheery and beguiling as she continued rustling about through her papers. "Almost ready . . ."

I breathed out and turned to my friend. "Pardon me for extending our conversation to a later date, Fezziwig, I must make ready in the event that the actual Greville pays me a visit wishing to reward his true savior—me."

Fezziwig's brow crinkled. "And for that possibility of profit you let a criminal loose?"

"Call it a calculated investment."

"I call it cause for immense regret, as should you," Fezziwig groused as he retreated back into the shadows, his eyes narrowed and glued to the woman who had swept in from the cold. Was that recognition in his eyes? I heard the rustle of his fingers twitching nervously against his pocket. My friend was eager to speak with me—but as he had taught me, business always comes first.

"Have I the honor of addressing Mr. Ebenezer Scrooge, sir?" asked the young lady, one hand outstretched to shake mine and the other clutching a packet of neatly tied papers. Delicate yet strong handwriting marched across the sheets.

"I am, and—hold on now. Do you *know* that gentleman who just left my offices?" I asked.

"I believe so, yes," she said. "Did he not give you his name?"

"Jasper, you called him?"

"He bore the look and untoward demeanor of a choirmaster I have seen here and there, a certain John Jasper, but I could be wrong. He did not turn when I called after him."

"I see, I see. Well, what is it you want? I've already told you, if it is a charity—"

"I have come to speak with you in regards to your advertisement. My name is Adelaide Owen." Her voice was soft yet her tone determined, and surprisingly, it sent a tingle of pleasure up my neck.

"Advertisement?" I frowned. I couldn't recall advertising for the services of any woman. Her hand was still stretched towards mine, so I shook it. "Are you certain you have the right address?"

"In your window, sir, you advertise the need of a clerk."

I stared at Miss Owen, and then at my window. True enough, the paper hanging there against the frosted pane announced an immediate opening for a junior clerk, against a payment, which I thought far more generous than ideal, of one hundred pence a week. In truth, it had been so long since I had seen a single applicant I had forgotten it still hung there. I have a bit of a reputation among clerks, it seems . . .

"Here are my papers." She withdrew her hand and laid a series of crisp white sheets out on my desk, jabbing at one of them with her gloved finger. "As you can see here, I have excellent references, particularly concerning my outstanding eye for detail, a skill which I am sure you value most highly in any clerk within your employ."

I stared at her in confusion. "You mean to say you know someone who might be appropriate for the job?"

"Of course!" she said with a smile that seemed to illuminate my office all the way to the dark corner where Fezziwig waited. "Me! Why else would I be here?" She leaned forward again to scrutinize her own papers, and a strand of her chocolate hair tumbled down her forehead. She blushed and hastily tucked it back. "I can begin immediately, and I shall require some initial instruction and training, but I'm sure you'll agree it'll be worth the investment of your time. As you can see from my papers—"

"Surely you don't mean to say that *you* are seeking employment as a *clerk* in *my* office?" I said, emphasizing the words I felt certain would highlight the absurdity of what she was proposing.

Her shoulders tightened and drew back, her spine straightened just a touch, but her polite smile never wavered.

"What I mean to say is, ah, well," I sputtered. "I've simply never heard of such a thing. You have clerked before?"

"In an unofficial capacity." Her confidence and resolve were impressive.

My eyes drifted from hers to Fezziwig, still looming in the dark corner, and despite the shadows, I could make out a mild grin spreading across his wrinkled face. "Perhaps she is a devotee of that Mary Shelley woman, who espouses equality between the sexes. You might put her to 'the question,' yes?"

I quite liked the idea. Glancing at more of her papers, I said, "You have a head for numbers, it says here. You are used to balancing accounts?"

Her smile widened. "Certainly, Mr. Scrooge. You will find evidence in these papers of my experience working both in the city and in the country. I'm sure you'll agree the post will require the ability to relate to and conduct discourse with a wide range of types, and you'll find me just the right person to build mutual relationships with any client, old or young, rich or poor."

I laughed.

"Do you think me foolish, Mr. Scrooge? Applying for a position normally held by a man?"

"I would have reacted so no matter your sex," I told her, and it was true. "It seems you have my needs all figured out. So I say to you, sit down at that dusty desk in the corner and remove the red leather folder. You have ten minutes to balance the spread within. Do so, and I will seriously consider awarding you the position."

"What if I don't need ten minutes?" she asked, taking herself and her crooked smile to the little cell, as I jovially called the cramped work area.

A dusty shuffle sounded as my old master emerged from the shadows, the sound competing with Miss Owen's grunts of displeasure and the scratching of her quill as she attempted to work with the hopeless ledgers I used as a test for prospective clerks.

I looked at my former master in surprise. He was paler than usual. "Fezziwig—are you well?"

"No, no. This is not about that," he said. "This is more urgent. More urgent."

"I doubt your business can be more pressing than the railway deal. I have very little time. But I could meet with you tomorrow afternoon perhaps." I lowered my voice to a conspiratorial whisper. "Miss Owen will be done in just a bit. Perhaps you might walk her out of the district?"

"You must listen to me, you and this girl—"

"I cannot, Fezziwig. You have my word, tomorrow afternoon. Good day." I rose from behind my desk, went to his side, and gestured to the door, where I wished to lead both him and the girl. As I touched his elbow, a wave of icy dread fell down me. The room darkened as a thick cloud moved in front of the morning sun outside. "We will speak . . . soon," I whispered.

Miss Owen sprang to life and hastily gathered her papers, stuffing them in her satchel with less care than she had extracted them. "Mr. Scrooge, I have come to you with the utmost respect, but you and I both know the test you have put me to has no solution. Any one of those ledgers might be balanced in and of its own, but together they are mush. I think it is time for me to do as you desired from the start and take my leave."

The hurt in her voice was palpable, but unimportant. I cared for profit, not feelings.

"Why are you looking at me like that?" she asked, brow furrowed, taking a step back. Then I smiled, and she shared in it. She was right: there was no balance to be found; that was the whole point, and in all my years, no other prospective employee had ever deduced that, let alone with such blinding speed.

I can't say what I might have done next. The idea of hiring a female clerk was so audacious and attention-generating that I might have given in to it for the sheer perversity of seeing my competitor's scandalized looks at the Exchange. But a wretched dark working was setting upon my counting-house. I looked to her as she approached. Her face was pale, her lips parted in a silent

"O." As she turned to the door, the flames in the fireplace flickered and died, leaving the candle on my desk the only light.

She froze.

"Peculiar," I muttered. A physical chill seeped through me. The temperature within my office seemed to have fallen several dozen degrees in the blink of an eye.

Fezziwig stood as still as a corpse, his eyes as wide and white as marbles.

"Ebenezer," he whispered. "Listen to me now. You have both been chosen to glimpse beyond the veil of mortal men. Together you must protect the innocent."

I stopped, suspended in a sudden overwhelming unease, and was only barely aware of Miss Owen standing beside me, her chill hand brushing mine. Fezziwig's words came out as white steam in the cold, darkened office. I dropped my grip of his elbow and held my breath.

"I am dead."

Scowling, I narrowed my eyes. His complexion was paling before my eyes, dark blue veins appearing in his face like a gruesome cobweb of decay.

"Don't be absurd," I mumbled.

"Such things are not possible," whispered Miss Owen. She shrieked as Fezziwig flung himself at me.

He gripped my shoulder suddenly, black and cracked fingernails digging into me, ice creeping into my blood through his touch. "The young man is innocent, Ebenezer!" he urged. I glanced at Miss Owen, who was staring back at me.

I shrugged out of Fezziwig's grip and noticed that his hand had withered. The bluish skin was cracking, revealing grey muscle beneath. Panic rose in the pit of my gut. Desperately searching for something logical and tangible to bring my mind back to reality, I spotted a ring on his finger. He had never worn that before. Ostentatious, a gleaming ruby-red stone in a gold setting; not something he'd be likely to wear, yet there it was.

"Innocent," he whispered once more, and Miss Owen gave a quiet whimper, almost inaudible, because he was looking at her now. Was she the "girl" he had expected to see when I first greeted him? Madness!

Then, his once thick hair wilted and fell, revealing a cracking scalp beneath. His breath was putrid, and I recoiled. "I see shadows of the past, present, and future, and exist within them all. What may be . . . what must be . . . Not all is known to me, Ebenezer. But he is innocent. Of this much I am certain. And you are in danger!"

My mind was reeling. I could not accept the evidence of my senses. "Forgive me, Fezziwig, I think I am unwell. Indigestion, perhaps. A blot of mustard, an undigested bit of beef. I'm certain there is more gravy than grave about you." I backed from him to leave my office. My imagination was playing tricks on me.

But as I inched my way towards the door, Miss Owen grasped my arm so tightly I thought her nails would bite through my jacket and into my flesh. Before us, Fezziwig's throat split open and deep, black gashes appeared in his face and chest. He drew a pained, rattling breath. Before my eyes his clothes became dust and fell from his decomposing body.

Miss Owen and I dashed for the door, but despite our combined strength, it would not open. Fezziwig approached, shuffling slowly as if to avoid completely disintegrating. The girl squeezed between him and the wall and dashed to the window: it too was stuck.

Fezziwig was upon me. Once more he gripped my shoulders, sending dark daggers of ice into my bones. My legs weakened, a ball of nausea rose in my gullet.

"Leave him!" Miss Owen cried. And when the grim specter would not release its grip, she snatched a heavy book from a nearby table and raised it as if to strike the withered apparition. One hand sweeping from me, he brushed it over the air separating her from him and she froze, bewildered, shaking, unable to take another step.

Then his terrible gaze held mine once more.

"Many more will die. And then you, Ebenezer Scrooge. Though still a young man of thirty with much potential for good or ill, you will die, too." His flesh began to rot, his eyes became solid grey and shriveled into his skull. "Remember 'Chimera,' Ebenezer. It may save you. And remember that I chose *you*, and think long and hard upon why . . . and the consequences of volunteering a blindness to what you know is right."

Horror gripped my very soul. Was this real? I glanced at Miss Owen to ascertain whether she was witnessing the same phantasm that I was, but she was pressed against the window, standing as stoic as a pillar. Her expression betrayed nothing.

I struggled to control my breathing, to focus on something logical. That heavy gold ring on his skeletal finger, the ring was not decomposing. Gold, at least, would always be a comfort to me. I squinted and focused on it.

A confused look appeared on what was left of Fezziwig's face. It was as if he saw something not in these rooms. "A *humbug*?" he asked with a putrid whisper. "Do you think I would deceive you, Ebenezer?" Then he screamed the word so loudly that the walls and windows shook. It echoed in my skull, lacerated my thoughts. *Humbug, Humbug, HUMBUG*—

And then his skeleton collapsed. Legs first, then the rest of him, until a yellow skull was crumbling on top of a pile of dust. The ring spun on the floor, then disappeared into the carpet's thickness.

I clapped my hand to my mouth in dread and stared in revulsion at the dusty remains on my office floor. What by God had happened here?

CRASH! The door swung open and a gust of icy wind sent the pile of Fezziwig swirling into the air and away. My legs finally buckled and I sank to my knees. My hand darted to where I had last seen the ring, but it too was gone.

"A humbug," I whispered. "A humbug!"

Heavy booted footsteps fell across the wooden floor, one clunk at a time. I lifted my eyes, and the constable who'd burst inside spotted me. His lip curled. I recognized him from some function I'd attended a month ago. Crabapple was his name. The politeness he'd shown that evening had altogether faded.

"Ebenezer Scrooge, the calculating and controlled businessman, is trembling on the floor," he said with a snarl. "The demeanor of a guilty man sentenced to hang." He strode over to me and hoisted me to my feet. "A man has been murdered, Mr. Scrooge, the word

'Humbug' written in blood beside the body. The very word you were just mumbling. You, sir, are required to come with me for questioning." As I was being dragged across the floor, the sun once more streamed through the window, a solid beam of light catching flecks of dust as they settled in my office.

"And who is this?" said the constable, as he spotted Miss Owen by the window. She was trembling, arms crossed over her chest. "An accomplice? Or another would-be victim?"

She managed a subtle shake of the head before she took a deep breath and composed herself. "I have seen . . . no, no . . . My name is Adelaide Owen. And, and this man . . . he may be many things, but a murderer, no."

"I'll be the judge of that," the constable said as he continued dragging me to the door. I heard her footsteps quick and light behind.

"Who has been murdered?" I managed.

"Your onetime master, Mr. Reginald D. Fezziwig."

CHAPTER TWO

FEZZIWIG'S WORKSHOP IN the tight streets of Spitalfields was normally fairly calm and quiet, but this morning it was bustling with police. The bracing cold on the ride here and the sharp-as-a-tack nerve-piercing shrieks of Christmas carolers had helped revive and focus my thoughts. I could no sooner explain the vivid and horrible dream (or visitation or moment of madness) I had experienced any more than I could reasonably accept that the man who had been more of a father to me than that of my own flesh was now dead. But I was a rational man, and I stood accused of a crime. Only calm and reason would keep me from the noose, and so I vowed to apply them.

Only . . . the presence of Miss Owen beside me on the ride here had upset my claims to reason. One look into her dark, shocked, and quite literally haunted eyes and there was no denying that she had seen what I had. And that made the visitation *real*.

"You, Missy, I have questions for you," Crabapple had demanded of her. "I think you're a witness. To what, I'm not exactly sure. But I come into the moneylender's lair and what do I find? You, a pretty, young thing, pressed up against a wall, terrified; and him looking half out of his gourd. I mean to get at the truth of things!"

And so he had "invited" her along.

Constable Crabapple now sat in Fezziwig's chair by the rudimentary fireplace, muddy boots unceremoniously plopped on my old friend's mahogany pedestal desk. Miss Owen had been taken away, presumably to be questioned elsewhere, apart from me. He was twiddling a calling card, and a ghost of a smirk was playing at the corner of his mouth. I scowled at him.

"Let us cut to the chase, Crabapple. What's your purpose in bringing me here? Is there perhaps some . . . arrangement . . . you seek? I understand a constable's salary is far from enviable."

Crabapple said nothing but used the calling card to pick something out of his teeth. He swung his legs from off the desk and leaned forward, sliding a single sheet of crisp paper towards me. Frowning, I took it, and read:

> *Sir,*
>
> *'Tis the season for generosity, and I simply must repay you for your earlier kindness. This time you shall receive in kind a gift no less life-altering than the gesture you once paid me, a symbol of my most profound gratitude for what you have done for me. I shall not accept a refusal!*
>
> *—An Admirer*

"I know nothing of this," I barked, crumpling the paper and tossing it back at Crabapple. "It's not even in my hand." The inspector caught the paper ball and smoothed it back out.

"Handwriting is easily forged," he smirked, holding up the card he had been twiddling. "And I wonder why Fezziwig was clutching your calling card when he died?" he said, looking at it.

"How the devil should I know? We are men of business who knew each other exceedingly well: he has no need for it."

"Don't you sell me a dog!" he growled.

I sighed. "I can assure you, I am *not* lying."

"Perhaps you *did* know each other, Scrooge, but certainly no longer. Did he have business with you recently?"

"He may have been intending to pay me a visit, I really could not say. I last spoke with him on Thursday. He seemed well."

I heard angry voices and knocking coming from the back room, and another constable called out, "Keep it down, back there!"

"Your accomplices," said Crabapple, twiddling the calling card again. "An eclectic mix of characters, but no doubt they each had a use to you. You're all cut of the same cloth, now ain't you? But perhaps your cut ain't quite so fine as theirs, so blackmail is what I'm thinking. Moneylenders learn all kinds of secrets, now don't they?"

"You have a mind like a steel trap, Constable. Anything entering gets crushed and mangled."

"You done him in, didn't you?"

I knew there was no point in arguing that I had no idea what he was talking about. I remained silent, simmering with suppressed anger. "Where have you taken Miss Owen? Far from this place, I should hope."

"Worried about her, yes? About what she might say? Confess now, before she spills all your secrets."

I chuckled. "I would confess that I find your manners appalling, Constable. But first you would have to have some."

"I see. Let's discuss this upstairs in the workroom, shall we?" Constable Crabapple got up, strode to the fragile staircase, and turned, waiting for me to follow. Clearly, he would tell me nothing of Miss Owen's whereabouts. He had another card to play.

My stomach was heavy with dread. I'd been informed that Fezziwig's body was up there. I could already smell the rot. And there Crabapple stood, grinning as he waited patiently for me to take the first steps. The last thing I wanted to do was go up that narrow staircase and through the trap in the floor. But I was not a coward.

The workroom was spacious, approximately the size of both the front and back rooms downstairs, lined with cases holding books and ledgers. Three looms and several spinning wheels cluttered the floor. Here Fezziwig would conduct his business, with a team of boys weaving fabrics and materials for trade across the country. The familiar smells of wood, velvet, and sweat lingered. But there was another smell: sweet, pungent.

A long, narrow window spilled light into the room, slashed across the floor like a laceration through the air.

Then I saw the body and froze. Fezziwig lay sprawled under the window, drenched in a harsh winter light, a gaping black wound in his throat. At first glance, his face looked peaceful, as his powdered wig lay askew across half his head. Then I spotted deep stab wounds that opened his face and chest, his velvet waistcoat in shreds. His cheek had been sliced to the ear. As promised, the word, "Humbug" was scrawled in blood on a nearby wall.

Suddenly my heart stopped. I spotted the heavy-set gold ring on his finger. The ring I had seen only once before, on a rotting corpse in my office. My head swam and I doubled over and vomited.

"Terrifying sight, ain't it? Did you cut his throat before or after you sliced his face open?"

A prickling dizziness spread across my face as I struggled to clean myself with my handkerchief. Grief threatened to unbalance me, I felt it forming in the back of my throat, but there was too much to process to succumb to it. I couldn't help staring at the cut in his throat and the black pool of sticky, coagulated blood spreading from it.

"He must have been unconscious when he was attacked," a calm and familiar voice said, fragrant tobacco smoke sweeping in behind me. I turned and was surprised to see my young "investigator" entering the scene. Thin but well-dressed, scowling, sketchbook at the fore with pen poised, his usual cigarette hanging at the corner of his mouth. He didn't so much as look my way.

"What the . . ." Crabapple began. "Dickens!"

"Judging from the color of the old man's skin, I'd say

he died late last night," the sometime reporter added. He was rarely without his sketchbook, and he often added drawings to his articles and observations. If Dickens—or Charles, as I had referred to him earlier—was correct, then Fezziwig had been struck down around the time I was making my nightly "collections."

"And how did you achieve that?" asked Crabapple, turning back to me, his voice calm and inquiring, as if asking me whether I used a rag or brush to polish my shoes in the morning.

I stared at the constable, anger rising. That damned smirk was still playing at his mouth; he was toying with me.

Dickens began sketching both the room and the body. "That sweet smell, Constable. I'm sure you have noticed it. The killer used chloroform, and plenty of it."

"Enough out of you," Crabapple said. "We pay you for a rendering of crime scenes, not your commentary."

"You don't pay me at all," Dickens muttered, wincing as he pinched out his smoke between finger and thumb.

"You get no money for your exclusives?" Crabapple chided. He looked back to me. "The old man was drugged first. So you showed your friend some mercy. You have a heart after all."

I had had enough of this trumped-up thief-taker and his attacks on my good name. "If Fezziwig met his violent end late last night, then I'm as innocent of this crime as you are of knowing which fork to use at a formal dinner, you oaf!"

The constable started to reach out for me with his large callus-covered hands.

Before he got to me, I pointed at something that had been bothering me about the gruesome business. "Good Lord, Crabapple, you couldn't find your way through a maze even if the rats helped you. There's no *blood* on his *hands*. Think. What do you make of that?"

The young reporter jumped in. "No struggle, see? He didn't clasp at his throat when it was cut."

Crabapple smacked the top of Dickens' head as he began to pace. His venomous words were for me alone. "He was not expecting to be murdered when you called upon him; I doubt he even had time to resist you."

"I'd agree with you, Crabapple, but then we'd *both* sound like idiots. If this attack happened late last night, then I have a dozen tenants who can confirm my exact location. I was collecting weekly rents until the wee hours of the morning," I said as I turned away from Fezziwig's bloody remains.

"You got witnesses for the *whole* night?" Crabapple barked. "Otherwise, shut your gob!"

"He's right, it doesn't add up, Constable," Dickens supplied. "I've read many case reports similar to this. I'd say he was attacked from behind, and then spun round and laid on the floor. See the marks on the floor here from where he was moved to the window?"

Crabapple shuddered but kept his gaze on me. "Was he heavy?"

"The killer would not have had to use much strength, judging from the angle of the body," Dickens declared. "He simply laid the unconscious victim to the floor. There is very little blood around the stab wounds. They were inflicted after he bled to death."

Staring right at me, Crabapple added, "Got a might annoyed that he went so quick, did you? Needed to vent your anger? And what's this 'humbug' you wrote on the wall, presumably in your victim's blood? A humbug is a liar, a fraud. What did he lie to you about, Mr. Scrooge? How did he defraud you? Is that why you butchered him?"

Gold glinted in the sunlight. I pointed at Fezziwig's right hand. "I have not seen him wear that ring before."

"Yet you didn't steal it. You had another motive, perhaps. Mrs. Fezziwig? No, she is far too fat and old for you. One of his delicate daughters, perhaps."

Fury blinded me. With a lunge, I spun round, grabbed Crabapple by the throat and slammed him against a bookshelf. "Damned be you, Crabapple," I growled through my teeth. "You know perfectly well I didn't do this. You are just trying to find out what I know. Well, I know nothing about this, do you hear? So stop wasting my time!"

He was startled, but not afraid. "Assaulting a constable is not a wise move given your circumstances, Scrooge." With cold hands he moved my grip from his throat. "And perhaps you've a point after all. What need would you have of Fezziwig's daughters when you have that fair bit of crumpet I found you with? What *does* she do for you, Mr. Scrooge? *Really*?"

This time I refused to be baited. Though I did not know Miss Owen well, she had earned my respect with her quick thinking and brave acts. The best way I could think to see her reputation left untarnished was to give the constable absolutely nothing.

At length, he turned from me, growling with frustration. "I am a simple man. I like things simple. Simple crime is proper crime. For example, only last week a man was found murdered quite to death next to some anonymous lady. Never identified his bit of crumpet, but a London theatre owner was he! Both slashed to smithereens. Obviously a crime of passion. Obviously an enraged missus. I like those types of cases. Husband opens his wife's neck for cheating on him. Business partners fall out over money and one ends up stabbed. Simple!"

Dickens shrugged. "I believe we have a position open in the mail room, if you'd like to apply for that. It's simple work. Perhaps it would suit you?"

"Humperdink!" Crabapple called, his face red, his hands balled into fists. Long seconds passed in silence before the heavy, slow steps on the staircase began. A ruddy-faced constable appeared at the trap in the floor, wheezing and reeking of gin as he climbed the last steps. "Escort Mr. Scrooge downstairs, detain him in the back room with the others. And you, Dickens. You make sure I get the credit for all this in your article. Not Inspector Foote. You hear me?"

I glared at Crabapple as I followed Humperdink back downstairs. Behind me, Dickens issued a sharp cough. When I glanced his way, his fingers not-so-subtly described a brisk rubbing of the thumb against forefinger and middle finger, a motion universally signaling that payment would be expected for services rendered.

I didn't dare reply in any form, but it wasn't a concern for either of us. He knew that unlike most of the thieves and rotters populating this foul city, I always, begrudgingly, paid my debts.

As Humperdink unlocked the door to the back room, a cacophony of protests rang out from behind it.

"Now see here!"

"Do you know who I am?"

"I demand to be released this instant!"

"Humperdink, really," I said as the rotund man reached for the door. "What is Crabapple playing at here?"

With a shrug, Humperdink hauled the door open. A forceful shove to my back sent me stumbling into the middle of the room where not only Miss Owen waited, but also three men and another woman. Everyone except Miss Owen scrambled out of my way, then immediately took up challenging positions against me.

"For the love of God, Humperdink," I said, shrugging off his rough treatment. "We all spring from apes, yet you did not spring far enough!"

Three well-dressed men of business, one heftier than the other two, one a stuffed-shirt member of the aristocracy if ever I'd seen one, the last a hard-eyed Asian fellow. The woman was very young, barely over twenty, I guessed. Quite beautiful, yet slight, and certainly able to awaken a protective instinct in any male caught in her orbit, judging by the way all three of the men stationed themselves between me and her. She wore a burgundy dress with a gold partridge pin over her breast. An impeccably crafted chain of holly sprigs adorned her felt hat.

Opposite me, Miss Owen surveyed their faces intently, then cast me a look that was equal parts warning and exasperation. Warning of what, I had no notion.

The back room normally served as a joint kitchen and privy, so the four characters staring at me looked deeply uncomfortable and out of place. Subtle conspiratorial looks passed between them.

The door was still open. Humperdink stood framed there, shifting his weight from one foot to another as if the mere act of standing were a challenge considering the amount of alcohol in which his brain had been soaked.

"So what is it you want me to do in here?" I asked the constable, my hand sweeping round to the tiny space. "Teach them to waltz?"

"Um, ah, no, Mr. Scrooge, sir," Humperdink said. "You lot are supposed to be proper refined gents and whatnot. Introduce yourselves to our new guest or you'll be without a pot to piss in, and I mean that quite lit'rally!"

"First things first," the closest man said as he looked up at me. He was short in stature but vast in presence: mighty black whiskers and dark eyes blazing. He wore a gold silk cravat stuffed in artful folds into a deep-orange quilted waistcoat, buttons shining. "Who might you be?"

"I'm Ebenezer Scrooge," I said. "A former associate of poor Mr. Fezziwig. I handle investments."

"Did you receive an invitation?" asked the young woman.

"Only from the Constable," I admitted.

Humperdink wobbled a bit and steadied himself on

the door frame. "You see, Mr. Scrooge, sir, this lot had an audience scheduled with the deceased, or so they claim. They says they arrived at the, ah, how would you say, sir, appointed time this morning, only to find Mr. Fezziwig unable to receive visitors, so to speak, on account of being a deader."

"And so," Scrooge said, "following what I would guess is standard police procedure, you then pressed on with locking them in a closet."

"We did, sir! We did indeed!" It took Humperdink a moment to note the sarcasm. "Ah, well, it was just that they was being quite rowdy, sir. Rowdy and disruptive, eh? A murder investigation is a serious business and here's this lot, refusing to answer civil questions such as 'Why'd you butcher the poor old sod?' and 'What kind of blade did you use to turn that sweet old man into sliced meat?' and so on and it got a bit wearisome for us, didn't it. Out of their mouths it was all, 'Call my solicitor, I don't have time for this nonsense.' Well, who has time now, eh? You're a gentleman, Mr. Scrooge. See if you and your lady friend can get them to talk. It might slip that noose off your necks and onto another!"

With a snide laugh, Humperdink slammed the door shut. After a moment of silence, the four settled into different corners.

"I suppose we should introduce ourselves," said the fat little man.

He looked familiar.

"Ah, then you *do* know me," he said flatly, noting the flare of recognition in my gaze.

I nodded. Now that my initial upset had passed,

I identified him as a businessman who moved in loftier circles than I might ever dream to, a merchant and builder said to be the true power behind George Hudson's railway scheme.

But before I could speak, Miss Owen surprised me by surging forward and presenting her hand for him to kiss. "Mr. George Sunderland," she said, smiling sweetly. "I am Miss Adelaide Owen, and I'm quite the ardent admirer of your recent ventures in India!"

"Why, why—how delightful!" he said. And kiss her hand he did. Then he gestured broadly towards the stuffed shirt next to him. "To my left is Lord Rutledge. He numbers princes and moguls of a higher station than even myself among his intimates."

Rutledge nodded, fingering the monogram embroidered on his fine glove, and eagerly took Miss Owen's hand, kissing her fingers, but with something more of a lecherous look in his eyes. She seemed to stare past it, and the man's ardor instantly ebbed. He straightened up, displaying only a flicker of shame, and adeptly fixed his mask of aristocracy back in place.

From the corner of my eye, I caught the Chinaman staring at the little woman in the burgundy dress. His stare was piercing, and she turned from it, hugging herself uncomfortably.

"Charmed, Miss Owen," Rutledge said. "And my apologies at, well, ignoring you until now. This whole matter has been most confounding."

"Yes," I interjected, "it has been a most shocking and confusing time. For instance, Humperdink's assertion that Miss Owen is my lady friend—"

"Couldn't be further from the truth," Adelaide assured him. "I'm actually considering an offer of employment from Mr. Scrooge, even as we speak."

I tossed a thoroughly vexed look her way, which she caught and deftly returned with a sparkle in her lovely eyes.

"In what capacity?" the other woman asked. The woman's delicate complexion was blotched from tears, and her wide blue eyes were red from crying.

"Domestic, of course," she said quickly. "Though I do dream of one day owning a business of my own. A millinery, I should think. I do so adore hats. Yours is truly enchanting for this Christmas season!"

"Yes, Miss Pearl," I added. My onetime associate, Jacob Marley, had been quite taken with her and had dragged me to several of her performances a few years back. I'd stayed awake through at least one. "Nellie Pearl, charmed to meet you in person. Yes, I recognize you, of course. The *Lady of Shalott* posters are all over town."

"But you have not seen it yet?" she asked.

"I—"

"I will have tickets sent to you." The actress curtsied politely and sat down on a small wooden stool, still eyeing me uneasily.

"And Mr. Shen Kai-Rui here is with the House of Liu," said Sunderland. "He is a powerful lobbyist within the East India Trade Company."

Miss Owen smiled and delivered a half-curtsy, all one might manage in these cramped confines.

The handsome Chinese man turned away disdainfully and would not meet my gaze. "A moneylender? I do not associate with common *muck snipes*."

I bristled at the accusation that I was a person of low morals or a vagrant but let it go. I was more interested in the intense gazes Shen cast at the clearly unreceptive Nellie Pearl.

Sunderland threw open his hands, a born orator. "What the drunkard said is true. Each of us, separately, as we did not personally know one another before this morning's unpleasant events, received a summons from, ah, the deceased. He asked us to meet him here at seven precisely on a matter of great importance. I have no idea how many of these summonses he may have sent throughout London, but we four were respondents. We arrived, we found him, we called the constable. And from the moment they arrived, we have been treated like criminals."

I could not restrain a smirk. Crabapple's tactics were consistent, if nothing else.

"Is this funny to you?" the foreigner asked.

"Certainly, it is not," Miss Owen rushed in to assure him.

"May I see the summons?" I asked.

Sunderland cleared his throat. "I'm sure the summons is back at my office. A viewing could be arranged."

"Do any of you have the letter on your person now?" I asked. "I'm sure that producing it would go some way to substantiating your tale."

Miss Owen smiled kindly and nodded encouragingly. I could not fail to notice that they looked at her for cues more than they did at myself.

Interesting. Perhaps she might have a place in my dealings after all.

If she had the stomach for it.

Not one of them had the invitation with them. Before I could ask another question, Rutledge's stool shattered and he fell, shouting and smacking at the wall beside him as he attempted not to go down with it. The stool must have been nursing a wounded leg.

A shriek and a scrambling sound from the other side of that wall caught my attention. It was followed by a mad scratching, like a sharp instrument striking and dragging along it. Rutledge stumbled from the wall in fright, then quickly recovered. Shen brushed Nellie behind him protectively, and stood with one hand near his belt. Had he a weapon secreted there?

"Did you hear that? A scratching?" Miss Owen asked.

"Rats, I'm sure," said the frustrated Sunderland.

I ignored the businessman and drew closer to the wall. "I recall this room from when I was an apprentice here. Fezziwig let us play games. He encouraged it."

"You, playing games," Miss Owen said with a twinkle. "I should like to see it."

I reached up to the corner of the embroidered tapestry tacked to the wall. The moment my hand touched its cold threads, I heard a ghostly sobbing echoing from the other side of the wall. I glanced at Miss Owen, who nodded at my unspoken question: she had heard it, too.

Then she looked down and I with her. Together we spotted the footprints in the dust matting the table, noted the items that had been swept from it: a pair of candles, scissors, a piece of cloth. Empty spaces among the dusty surface marked where each had been.

The scratching and the sobbing intensified. Nellie

gasped in fear at the sounds, and the portly Sunderland tossed a protective arm about her shoulders.

The sound echoing from the other side of the wall rose from a man's throat.

The young man is innocent, the spirit had insisted.

Could he have meant the poor creature secreted in a cubbyhole we adolescents used to play hide and seek? Perhaps this was one of Fezziwig's current apprentices, a child who witnessed the brutal events of last night?

Ignoring the strange lightness of the scurrying and the plaintive sounds, I shook off the unsettling memory of Fezziwig's apparition. It would not be Bedlam for me. I smacked at the corner of the embroidery and a panel popped open, just as I recalled. I pried it open, stuck my head inside.

Had I been wrong in my conclusions, I might well have been attacked by rats. As it was, I saw, in the dim light from the outer room, a sight nearly as frightful and ghastly as Fezziwig's spirit. A young man—though no child, perhaps of the same age as Miss Owen, two and twenty—with wild hair and wilder eyes clutching a carving knife. He was covered in blood. It matted his hair, dark, dried flakes peeling off his cheeks. He trembled, raising the blade defensively, but made no attempt to strike.

The young man is innocent.

"Call for Crabapple," I said. "Tell them the murderer is ready to confess."

With that, the man in the hole's sobs turned to shrieks and he lunged at me with the blade.

CHAPTER THREE

"BUTCHER!" THE MAN howled as he struck at me with the bloody knife. I fell backward off the small table, narrowly evading the crimson blade's terrible arc, I collapsed onto my back on the floor as Rutledge and the others pressed themselves to the walls in shock and terror. The maniac sprang from the hidey-hole, pouncing on me, his weight enough to drive the breath from my lungs.

The blade sliced towards my face and stopped suddenly, an inch away from striking. For a moment, his dark eyes seemed to clear. Then his lips drew back in a snarl. "Not me. Not me, hear? You won't have *me*!"

"No!" Miss Owen screamed suddenly, and then made a move to rush towards the man, but the foreigner held her back.

My attacker drew the blade back—and something swept from the darkness to his left and clubbed the side of his head. The blade clattered to the floor as the blood-drenched man collapsed in a heap beside me. Miss Owen stared at the fallen man in horror as the foreigner firmed his grip on her struggling body. Then she looked away and began to sob.

Lord Rutledge stared at the rolling pin in his hand with wide-eyed amazement. He looked as if he might faint. Behind him, Miss Owen glared his way.

"I thought I was about to take a loss," I said, my right hand protectively covering my throat. "Seven or eight pints' worth, at least!"

Not long after, I stood outside Fezziwig's establishment, watching as three policemen dragged my semi-conscious assailant through the light snow drifting about me. Crabapple was beside me. He should have been pleased, but he was not. The four who had discovered the body had been dismissed and evaporated from the scene quickly, but not before the constable and Shen exchanged odd hostile looks. Perhaps Crabapple didn't like foreigners? Or was there more to it?

The murder suspect was being led towards Crabapple's wagon, and soon he'd been done up in chains on the cold floor of the prison. Miss Owen stood at the edge of the crowd, shivering in the icy cold, watching the scene intently. Somewhere distant, carolers sang a merry tune, a mocking chorus to the dark proceedings of this day. Snow lazily whirled about us, carried on the indifferent breeze.

"Case closed," mumbled Crabapple. "You and all

your cronies may return to your lucrative businesses, yeah? To hell with answers. Or justice. Or the truth."

I smiled thinly and hugged myself against the chill. "I thought you liked things simple, Constable. Murderer. Knife. Blood. Hang him. How could it be any simpler than that? Or is it that you don't believe he's guilty?"

"I'd like to. And as things sit now, he'll surely hang for it. But he's ranting and raving like he's afraid he'll be the next victim, and that just doesn't sit right. Those four Humperdink introduced you to . . . I stood listening at the door as they went on a fair while. There's quite a bit they're hiding, I'm certain of it. And you've hardly been forthcoming yourself! Nor that little lady of yours."

"Miss Owen is not my 'little lady.' But no matter. You can take heart that our reluctance has nothing to do with your courteous and efficient manner, Constable. You have a way with people that I believe is second to none. In fact, I'd wager you have a great number of well-wishers. They would all like to throw you down one."

He glared at me. "Get out of here before I charge you with obstruction. But remember: innocent people tend not to spin wild stories or to hide the truth the way you lot did. All of you. There was something strange about the way I found you and that woman at your counting-house. And you saying 'humbug' like that, the same thing scribbled on the wall beside the corpse. I'm not done with this, Mr. Scrooge. And neither are—"

The constable stopped short as a hundred paces ahead, a bulky man in an expensive coat opened his arms before Dickens and the flock of reporters who had glued themselves to his sides. The man brushed his neatly trimmed mustache and began to hold court for the crowd.

"Ah—damn!" Crabapple snarled.

"Inspector Foote, I would assume?" I asked. But Crabapple wasn't listening. He stormed off towards the ring of reporters and the inspector who was surely taking credit for the young man's arrest.

Crabapple stopped suddenly. "Hey now, what's this here?"

Miss Owen burst from the crowd just as the policemen slammed the gate on the wagon and clanged the lock. "Tom!" she screamed, and pushed past me, racing towards the wagon just as its horses neighed and the vehicle jolted into movement. "Tom, I'll help you, I know you're innocent!"

The face of the accused appeared in the back window of the wagon, his hands clutching the bars. He grimaced and yelled, "Be gone, wretched woman!"

Miss Owen began to run after the wagon as it trundled up the uneven road. I frowned, staring at the hands clenched around the bars, and before the wagon turned a cobbled corner, I noted a circle of pale skin about his ring finger. It looked about the size and shape of the peculiar ring Fezziwig had worn in both his final "ghostly" and earthbound states. But I wanted no more of this. I was a man of reason, a man of business, and I needed to be far from here.

I walked away, towards the river. I needed time to compose myself, order my thoughts . . . and banish the specter of my dead friend, which now haunted my reason.

It wasn't long before I saw that I was being followed. Miss Owen trudged after me, her boots sloshing in the snow, and her gaze locked fiercely on me each time I chanced a look over my shoulder.

I stopped and allowed her to catch up when I had reached a quiet alley in a derelict maze of damp brick-work. There was little evidence of Christmas approaching in this part of town, neglected by all but the most wretched. The bone-chilling December wind and the whipping sleet it carried were the only hints of the season.

Nobody would hear us in this shadowy spot.

"Mr. Scrooge, sir, please . . ." she began. "I know I have no right to ask, but will you help me?"

A pained sigh escaped me. "Miss Owen, I don't know what you would have of me. Employment is not a topic I wish to discuss now. Nor your evident connection to the man taken into custody for murder. Your . . . Tom."

She flinched at the mention of his name but otherwise remained not just resolute, but hard as flint. It was difficult not to admire her strength. Yet I had been through much today.

I went on, "My oldest friend—a man who was more father to me than the wretch who sired me ever was—is murdered. I would have time, alone, to mourn. If that is not too much to ask?"

"Clearly it is," she said insistently, taking my arm. "Considering your dead friend didn't wish to stay dead. Considering the warnings he came to deliver."

I could not meet her gaze. "What is it you think you saw?"

"Everything you did. And I heard everything you heard. He said, 'The young man is innocent.' Have you forgotten? It is my Tom he was speaking of. How can you have any doubt? And what could he have meant by 'humbug'? He screamed the terrible word so frightfully that it still haunts me."

"Humbug? No doubt that the killer is an imposter, a fraud of some sort. Or, more likely, that the whole ghastly situation is a setup. You ask me how I can have any doubt. Well, I doubt many things," I said, shrugging from her grasp. "Most things," I added, looking into her pleading eyes. "Including you."

"Me?"

I felt hot anger rise in furious prickles up my face and walked briskly from the alley, towards the great bridge in the distance. "What we—what I experienced this morning was impossible. The only rational explanation is that something happened, yes, but not what I have been duped into believing. This city is crawling with charlatans and crooks. Those who prey on the living in the name of the dead. Table rappers. Fortune-tellers. Mystics and more. All done with mirrors, illusion, sleight-of-hand. Yuletide is the worst season for such tricksters. You recognized that scoundrel I ejected from my office. You share some bond with the man who threatened to kill me at Fezziwig's. Perhaps I have been drugged and hypnotized. Made to believe what you lot would have me believe so you might fleece my pockets and—"

We drew up suddenly, myself and Miss Owen, because next to the bridge was Fezziwig. Large as life. His back not bowed by the horrible toils of time, his hair grey, not salt-white. He was laughing, smiling, tolling a Christmas bell and holding a pail for charitable donations. The morning light ringed his ill-kempt locks in a way that never failed to bring a smile to me. A bit of drifting snow fell into my eye, startling me, and when I wiped it away, the bridge was empty once more.

I didn't realize how I was shaking until Miss Owen boldly took my hand.

"Mr. Scrooge—Ebenezer—if truly, in your bones, you believe I am nothing but some opportunist, if you think your mind and will so fragile they could be manipulated as you have described, then I will leave and you will never have to suffer my presence again. I would not displease anyone so. Let alone . . . suffice to say, a man of deep character, as I perceive you to be."

I drew my hand away slowly. Adjusted my waistcoat and shawl. "I may know a barrister. I fail to see what else I can do for you. For your . . . for this Tom." Was there a hint of jealousy in my tone? Absurd.

Miss Owen lowered her voice and leaned up to my ear. "There is more to it, and you know it. You heard what Fezziwig said," she whispered, and my heart stopped. "He said that more would die." She pulled herself away and stood tall, lifting her chin, and said, "Including you."

Chills crept down me like thin cobwebs of dread. "And of the four suspects in Fezziwig's pantry just now? Did you believe the tales spun by any of the four in that room?"

"Not in their entirety. And you?"

"Not at all. Apart from the actress, I would say every one of them is lying."

She raised her eyebrows. "I would not be so quick to accept Nellie's tale either, Mr. Scrooge. There was a tangible unease in her eyes. I sense it, you see—woman's intuition."

"Woman's folly. Members of the fairer sex are so quick to condemn their sisters. Don't forget the gravity of the situation, Miss Owen. This is not the time for idle accusations."

Miss Owen took a deep breath and her eyes drifted to the falling snowflakes. The icy wind blew a gust and she pulled her shawl tight. "And there was something more, this Chimera business," she continued. "What do you make of—"

Gasping, Miss Owen stopped suddenly as a man who had more in common with a wall than with flesh and blood slipped in front of us with a quietness and sureness that made me start.

"Apologies, sir," he said in the deepest, most gravelly voice I'd ever heard.

"You can make the attempt to apologize," I offered, "but I'm not sure apologies come in sizes large enough to suit the likes of you!"

Despite herself, Miss Owen could not restrain a snicker beside me.

The man's enormous girth filled my vision. Yet his ridiculously muscled bulk had been poured into one of the finest tailored suits available in London. And the particular way he ordered his cravat marked him as an Oxford man. He remained unmoved by my barb. "My employer, Mr. Sunderland, wishes to speak with you further."

"Does he now?" I asked warily. "Is it about a business matter, or about the awful affair we were both caught up in this morning? As you can see, I am in the middle of a discourse."

The man glanced at Miss Owen and grinned. "I wouldn't ordinarily interrupt a man in the middle of a . . . discourse. But I believe it is about an advertisement you placed, looking for investment partners?" he said. "You are Ebenezer Scrooge, the investment banker, are you not?"

I tipped my hat. "A moneylender, in point of fact. But I will be more, and soon. Have no doubt."

"Well, my employer takes great pleasure in helping others achieve their aspirations."

I laughed. It was very close to a line I had used myself on many an occasion. Still, George Sunderland, despite the terrible manner in which we had met, could prove just the ally I'd dreamed of enlisting. "Very well. He can make an appointment to see me at my office—"

"It is urgent. He requests your presence now. And in a place of privacy." The big man nodded to London Bridge—where George Sunderland now waited in the exact spot I thought I had spied Fezziwig's spirit.

I nodded and exchanged glances with Miss Owen. She smiled and crooked her arm.

"Perhaps this lovely gentleman would deign to walk with me for a time?" she asked warmly.

The giant's knees buckled as he tipped his bowler to her and allowed her to take his arm. I frowned, not particularly fond of the idea of Miss Owen going off with some man I didn't know, but business was business. And if he worked for George Sunderland, well, that was recommendation enough. They strolled towards a spot off to one side of the bridge, while I climbed it eagerly.

Not one of us was aware of the malevolent shadows detaching from the alley far behind us.

Or the weapons they carried.

The stink of rotting fish and the clanging of ropes against ship masts helped me navigate through the thick orange mist. The wooden docks were slippery under the December sludge, so I kept my distance from their edges, blurred above the black Thames below.

Sunderland was waiting for me alone under the bridge, his cigar adding heavy grey swirls to the polluted air. As I approached, Sunderland gave an almost imperceptible nod towards the shadows, where his burly bodyguard was leaning with arms folded against the brickwork of the bridge, Miss Owen chatting away beside him.

Together Sunderland and I ascended the steps to the bridge, and as we reached the top, the wind blew cold and bitter. I heard slow, almost silent steps following behind; heavy boots placed carefully on cold stone. Sunderland's ever-present shadow. The Oxford Man. And next to his, the light graceful steps of Miss Owen.

"Thank you for meeting with me, Scrooge," said Sunderland as we reached the middle of the bridge. I looked back to the bodyguard, who was nearly hidden at the end of the bridge, and the lithe form of Miss Owen beside him.

Sunderland appeared to guess my thoughts. "Rest easy, Scrooge. I raised that man up from nothing. He would give his life in my service. Miss Owen is quite safe, I assure you."

"But it's hardly proper—"

Sunderland laughed and guided me ahead. "Surely after what we have shared today, and considering the spot we are all in, propriety is the least of our concerns, yes? Besides, look at them. I'd be more worried about my man than Miss Owen should he even think of doing or saying anything untoward. Wouldn't you?"

I nodded and said flatly, "I consider the expenditure of my time as an investment. Are there dividends to be reaped from our discussion?"

"That depends on you. But it's distinctly possible, yes."

"Then the pleasure is entirely mine, Mr. Sunderland. Your commercial acuity built you a veritable empire of industry, and I am still looking for an investment partner. Need I look any further?"

"Not if your eyesight is worth a damn." Holding his thin cigar, he pointed out over the Pool of London and at the vast expanse of ships, docks, and warehouses. "A fine sight, isn't it? And beyond, to the city. So many buildings that only exist because I had vision, I had will and strength. I have built so much and, naturally, I must protect it by considering only the most lucrative business proposals. But this horrible bit with Fezziwig, it casts a damper, does it not?"

"You knew him, then?"

Sunderland looked away. "I wish I could say that I did.

From the tales the others told this morning, he sounded like a saint, not a sinner deserving of such treatment. I answered his summons only because I wanted to know if there was truth behind his legend. The wealthy look for novel ways to entertain themselves."

"At least the culprit has been found."

Sunderland sighed. "I must say, I'm not generally the type to concern myself with matters such as this, but when a man is gone, who is there to protect his legacy, his reputation? I saw what was done to him. You?"

"A ghastly business."

"And now he will be remembered as a weak old man who must have been involved with God knows what to deserve such a fate. I can't help but think: if it were me found like that, if tales were being concocted out of convenience that destroyed my good name and ruined the reputation and future of my family, would I not wish that someone would do something? That someone would stick out their neck a bit and say that couldn't possibly be true? Yet I see four people: Rutledge, the actress, the Chinaman, and yourself, and when the press is scurrying about looking for a story to tell, not one of you is there to be found to speak to the character of Mr. Reginald Fezziwig."

My gaze narrowed. He raised a valid point. I would need to give Dickens something about Fezziwig's death in order to keep the newspaperman—and, hopefully, his contemporaries, who often did little more than copy his take on things—from inventing provocative and slanderous fictions to fill the void left by a lack of facts. It was indeed something I should have done rather than slinking off when the wolves were chewing on other meat.

He offered me a cigar and I took it. "What is it you have in mind?" I asked, hiding my eagerness behind the flare of sulphur as I lit the tobacco.

"I have a secret, Mr. Scrooge. Can you guess what it is?"

"I am no detective, sir."

"You sell yourself short, I think. Are you not a keen observer of any who might provide money or advancement? Do you not study the slightest tick, the faintest hint that what a man says to you may be only one lie in a house built on them? I do."

"I employ others to ferret out such details."

"But only after your instincts flare and tell you something is not as it seems. Do that with me, now, and if you succeed, I will know beyond any doubt that you are the man for the job I have in mind."

I looked at him closely and could see nothing amiss. Nothing obviously amiss, in any case, though . . . yes, perhaps it was simply because he had planted the seed in my mind, but there was *something*, was there not?

"I'm no miracle worker," I told him. "I cannot sniff a man's tobacco and effortlessly reconstruct his every movement of the past day as I've heard that Frenchman Dupin supposedly can. But human nature . . . its baseness, its crass, grasping desires . . . with these I am familiar. From these I have learned how to profit. And your eyes have a melancholy, your voice a note of defeat that is entirely at odds with everything one would think to associate with you. It's not loss born from grief, not from a loved one dying; I know that look all too well.

But your talk of how Fezziwig will be remembered . . . you're dying, are you not?"

As soon as I'd brought up death, an image of a crumbling Fezziwig flashed in front of my mind's eye, but I blinked it back out. Even in the icy chill, the Thames seemed to stink a little fouler.

Sunderland shuddered. "Indeed I am, sir. And I wish to hire you to safeguard my legacy."

"Me? As you said, I ran from the chance to do my mentor and his survivors a good turn."

"True. Because you did not stand to gain from the act."

"You make me sound like a monster."

"Just what may be needed. And before you volunteer it, worried as you may be that anything less than full disclosure may change my mind about you, I am well aware of the unpleasantness with your employer of just a year ago. A certain Mr. Marley?"

"He was never my employer," I said firmly. "More a trusted referral source."

"But trusted no longer."

I said nothing. The wind's deep growl was response enough.

Sunderland warmed his arms. "My legacy is all I have left to me. I have no one I can trust. Ensure for me that when the name George Sunderland is spoken of in decades to come, it is with appreciation."

I frowned. "Is your promised investment in the rail deal contingent on my accepting these other duties?"

"No, Mr. Scrooge. They are, what is the phrase? Fish and corn, you see?"

I nodded and turned away to think it over. Why would he want me for this task? I was not a solicitor or an estate specialist. Was it because of my association with Dickens?

I looked over and was about to ask that very question when I heard a rasping beside me. Sunderland was covered in sweat, shaking, eyes wild. He clutched at his stomach and a thin line of blood ran from his nose. Sharp stabbing pains seized him as he convulsed.

"You need a doctor," I said.

Suddenly, Sunderland was stony calm, a statue gathering snowflakes. Then, in the distance, a foghorn sounded, and just like that, the fat man's calm demeanor crumbled. His face flushed red with rage, he grabbed my lapels, thrust me towards the steel railing. "Enough of these games! What did Fezziwig tell you, Scrooge? How much do you know?"

"What?" I snarled. "Are you mad? Unhand me, or I won't care that you are a sick or a wealthy man, I will—"

Then, even in the mist, I could see the color drain from his face. I followed his stony stare to the end of the bridge. Facedown, with the butt of a knife protruding from the base of his neck, lay the shadowed bodyguard.

Miss Owen was nowhere to be seen!

Three figures were swiftly moving towards us, one in the lead and two close behind. The unmistakable silhouette of a gun glinted wet through the smog. Sunderland clutched my arm and spun me round to start running the opposite way, but just as we turned, two more figures appeared at the other end of the bridge.

We had no escape. The men were closing in on us.

I caught Sunderland's eye. Reason had returned to him. A sharp clarity needed for survival. We looked at the black water below—but I hesitated, thinking of Miss Owen.

"She's escaped, surely," Sunderland said. "My man must have fought and given his life to give her that chance."

The men neared.

"What is it you think Fezziwig knew?" I asked. "Sunderland, what have you done?"

"We can do nothing for them if we're dead!" shouted Sunderland.

With a swift leap, I hopped up onto the stone ledge and braced myself for the jump. Then Sunderland cried, "Scrooge!"

I looked over my shoulder: he was struggling to heave his vast bulk up onto the ledge, and the men were just yards away on either side. My lip curled at him. There was no time, I had to jump. I grabbed his arm and he grabbed mine. I hauled his weight onto the ledge and just as a snarling, scarred beast of a man reached out for us with a cry, we both went hurtling down towards the frozen pit below.

Weightlessness, for just a second.

Then a sharp pain split my body in half as I struck the water and the river wrapped its frigid fingers around me and held tight, pulling me down. Ice pierced my skin, and I felt the shock tugging at my lungs. I knew I would have ten minutes or less before hypothermia weakened my judgment and core motor skills, but to save myself I first needed air. Kicking forcefully, I swam towards the surface. Preparing to break, to my horror I realized a thick, frozen film of pollution separated me from that gasp for air, sticking to my face and hair like tar.

I burst through, managed a desperate gasp of the sulphuric air, and heard the angry voices above. They had already turned and were running back across the bridge. They would reach the shores soon. I glanced around for Sunderland.

He was nowhere to be seen. He would no doubt have had a heart attack by now and was sinking to his horrid death.

Many more will die, Ebenezer. Then you. You will die, too.

Battling the uncontrollable shivers that my body had activated to keep warm, I made it to the docks. My fingers were too numb to grip the slimy wood, so I used my elbows to haul myself up the jagged sides. A protruding nail gashed my arm open. I'd need to stem that bleeding soon.

Gasping, I lay on the pier for just a moment to regain some strength. Peering down through the cracks between the planks, I saw the reflection of a figure loom above and behind me. I scurried to roll off the pier, but something flew at my head and—

CHAPTER FOUR

I WOKE ON my side, shivering, my clothes soaked. A cloth had been fitted over my face, tight as a birthing caul. My wrists were bound tightly behind my back, my shoulders ached a hot pain—the only warmth I felt. I moved my head ever so slightly, and a thunderous agony exploded in my skull. Memories of nearly drowning flooded back. I had been struck down and taken—

Where?

I could hear the eerie clanging and clinking of ropes and pulleys against ship masts. The unmistakable waft of fish drifted to my nostrils through the cloth. I smelled seawater. A blood-curdling scream rang out nearby, making my heart skip a beat.

"Damned seagulls," a man said. "Pests. Fish-eating, squawking, arrogant pests. Aren't they s'posed to migrate in winter?"

"Unless it was Roger and Jack, finishing off another one before startin' here!"

They laughed.

It was widely but not *officially* known that the Colley brothers, Roger and Jack, operated from the fish market under the stealthy veil of night. Was I in their tender care now? And though I knew my life was in danger, all I could think was: Miss Owen. Had she truly made it to safety? Or was she similarly bound and close by?

I tried to sit up, but I only succeeded in flopping around like a gasping fish. I had a sense that I was not on a ship, yet the slightest movement made me seasick and elicited white-hot lances of searing pain from my bruised head.

"He's moving."

"I can fix that."

A heavy boot smashed into my stomach, and I doubled over onto my side once more, vomiting into the hood. My mouth was full of foulness; I couldn't swallow or breathe!

Someone crouched beside me as I flopped about in panic, a strong hand pinning my shoulder in place while another yanked at the hood.

"Baldworthy, whatca doin' there?"

"It won't do if he chokes on his own puke."

The hood tore free and I spilled the rest of what had been in my guts onto the floor.

"You get any on my shoes, I'll kick you again!" shouted the scarred man standing over me, the hood clutched in one hand. Baldworthy, I took it from his shiny pate. The man with him was slightly hunched over, and the right side of his face bore a bright red claret mark. He sneered angrily when he caught me staring and I looked away quickly.

I was locked in a dark warehouse, a wide river on one side and a brickwork hell on the other. My chest and ribs were on fire, my head throbbed and burned. Still wearing my clothes drenched in icy river water, I shivered like a newborn fawn, my teeth chattering uncontrollably. I imagined that the stench of my sick was nothing compared to the putrid odor of the Thames, which wafted from me.

I heard footsteps. A handful of others joined us.

The vertigo I'd been experiencing finally subsided, and this time when I attempted to sit up and take in my surroundings, no one stopped me. I saw a ramp on the far end leading into the dark and chilling Thames. There a crane might be led to the side of a boat to unload crates of cargo. Industrial rails, chains, and hooks furnished the expanse. But most interestingly, directly before me sat two men at a rudimentary desk made from barrels and crates. They talked between themselves and paid me no attention for several minutes as I caught my breath and gained my bearings. Large bulldogs of men huddled in dark corners.

I finally recognized the objects the brothers were scrutinizing: they were the contents of my emptied pockets.

At last, they turned to face me.

"Good evening, Mr. Scrooge. I trust you are having a hitherto jolly Christmas season," said the shorter of the two. "The name is Jack Colley. I expect you're wondering why we've brought you to our, ah, temporary offices."

I nodded, hating that I could not stop shaking.

The older brother looked over his shoulder at me. "I'm Roger Colley. By the way. Can't say I'm pleased to meet you."

Jack snorted. "Roger, Roger. Don't be discourteous to our honored guest. Please excuse my brother, Mr. Scrooge. He ain't far evolved beyond beast, and some disturbing recent developments within our trade"— his eyes flashed at me—"have rattled the beast's cage. But don't you fret, I won't let him loose quite yet. Not until I've properly made your acquaintance. We've heard so much about you, Mr. Scrooge. You're what some call a legend in the making, you are."

I wanted to refuse their bait. Whatever "developments" they were alluding to sounded dangerous, far beyond my desired involvement . . . but something within me snapped at it anyway. "Why is that?"

"Because you're what we are on the inside. Us, then, we're all men of the people on the outside, all thief on the inside. Did you know we pass out Christmas turkeys to the poor throughout these neighborhoods? And children's toys. We help others to pay off debts and keep themselves from the streets. Oh, we take our pound of flesh for it, just as you do. But we make them love us for it, unlike you, you greedy miser. You're the type if you owned a rundown building and the tenants complained of rats, you'd charge them for the meat. Still and all, Mr. Scrooge, we have much in common, you and us. Much indeed!"

But I didn't terrorize or murder those who refused to play my game. A slight difference I elected not to mention to these grinning lunatics.

"Roger and Jack Colley," I murmured. "Top of the criminal food chain. So it's true what they say."

"What's that, Mr. Scrooge?" Jack obliged.

"The cream rises to the top. So does scum."

Jack laughed and put a steadying hand on his brother's arm. Roger looked ready to gut me on the spot.

"I don't understand why I'm here," I said. "Have I done some injury to one of you?"

Roger frowned. "I'd say the injury's more what's going to happen to you. Unless you tell us what we want to know. You're the only one left we can ask, is how it is. My boys got a little overeager. They done in that bruiser Sunderland had with him, and didn't see no value in chasing after that fair bit of crimp that went running. A pricy piece, she looked like, but what would a woman know of business, yeah?"

I kept stock-still, willing my face to betray none of the emotions surging through me. They assumed Miss Owen to be a well-dressed prostitute, a bit of afternoon delight for Sunderland. She lived. She was free. Somehow, that made all of this easier. My life, and mine alone, I would be bargaining for. And I was an expert deal-maker.

"What is it . . . you want to know?" I managed.

"It's simple," Jack said reasonably. "Where is it?"

"Where is what?"

Roger rolled his eyes. "Oh, no. It's going to be like this, then."

"Wait, wait, give him a chance. He's probably still waking up from that little nap Baldworthy gave him." Jack looked my way. "Now take a moment and think,

Mr. Scrooge. George Sunderland, that enormous fat bastard that you were fraternizing with on the bridge, didn't deliver certain goods that were promised and paid for. We are extremely angry. Our clients are extremely angry. There is a whole network of extremely angry people on account of that stolen shipment what we no longer have. Quite the humbug Sunderland turned out to be, yeah?"

I flinched at that. *Humbug*? The word scrawled in blood beside poor Fezziwig's body.

Jack Colley was still ranting. "We want to know where he took it *to*. Simple as that. You know or you don't know. You tell us the truth, or you lie. The choice is yours. Helping us will gain you great rewards. Do you like whores? Opium? Boys, whatever? We can supply any need or desire."

"That we can," said his brother. "Or . . ."

"Well, it puts me in mind of a little tale our father used to tell, back before we smothered him in his sleep, then cut off his head."

"We are given to our passions."

"We are, we are . . . He wasn't very helpful, our dear old papa. What about you?"

"Well, you're kind and likable chaps," I said. "Why wouldn't I want to give you the shirt off my back?"

"You'd smell a damn shade better if you did," Roger said, laughing. "The devil only knows what diseases you might have caught in that water. Perhaps we should hose you off?"

"With the hose jammed down your throat," Jack promised.

I faced two widely-feared gangsters and a handful of thick and expendable soldiers. They wanted information, and once they had it, their promises of reward would mean nothing. I had to sweeten the pot, if I could. "In fact, I can think of many ways I could help you and your enterprises. And vice-versa."

The Colley brothers said nothing but exchanged a glance between themselves.

"This one's a cheeky monkey, ain't he?" said Roger, his froglike sneer taunting me. "Worse'n that stinkin' mutton shunter you shanked last week. Tell us and be quick about it."

Jack twiddled a knife and then used it to poke between his teeth.

"I *want* to help you," I said. "But I can't. I don't know what you're talking about. Sunderland said nothing about a warehouse or goods. Now if a sound investment is to your tastes, I happen to be on the cusp of—"

Bang! Jack slammed the knife into an upturned crate and it quivered where it stood. He stood up slowly, glaring at me. The brothers looked at each other, and although they kept their expressions stony, the atmosphere changed noticeably. The bulldogs were more interested now, openly staring at me. Was this entertainment for them?

"Trying to make a stuffed bird laugh," Jack said.

"It's not preposterous," I said. "I can make you money."

The brothers regarded each other—and burst into gravelly guffaws. The sneer lodged permanently on Roger's face sent a repulsed shiver down my spine.

"Oh, but bless your little cottons!" said Jack suddenly with a grin. Looking around his beefy entourage, he laughed. "He hasn't heard!"

Coarse and dark laughter followed.

"*Never*?" grunted a jovial voice from the left of Jack.

"Hasn't he ears?" barked another, laughing.

"What a terrible shock for him, very terrible, hate to be the one."

"Sad news, Mr. Scrooge, sad indeed." Roger had moved beside him and was breathing stale breath down the side of his neck. He nodded at Baldworthy, and the brute's scarred and disfigured mouth twisted into a mocking grin.

He gave a curt nod. "Right you are, sir!"

Baldworthy hauled me to my feet as Jack approached.

"As I said, very terrible," Jack sneered.

"What is?" I asked at last.

"That if we don't get to the bottom of this mess, our kingdom, London's dank and putrefied underbelly, comes falling down. You might think that's a good thing, Mr. Scrooge." Jack was eyeballing me, his nostrils flared, but I could tell from the shaking of his hands that some fearful desperation was fueling his attack on me. He continued. "Trying for another business deal, when, in truth, you should be bargaining for your life? Even if you make it out of here alive, your business will topple within weeks without the creeping, crawling, criminal network what keeps your clients in the need. You need us to like you. And right now, we don't."

Roger jerked my scarf back and painfully crushed my

Adam's apple into the back of my throat. With a blow, he slammed me against the wall and held me fast.

One of the goons quickly pulled a large crane hook along its rail by the chain, the clanging and clattering filling my head. I tried to speak but choked. A punch to the face and a knee to the stomach, I was doubled over before I realized it.

Roger Colley hooked the cold metal around my scarf and tightened the knot, quick as a flash. Choking, I struggled and kicked. With a heave, Roger and his bully friend yanked the chain, and I was lifted into the air by my neck. My legs flailed.

Desperately, I reached for the chain above my head and lifted myself up slightly to relieve the pressure. A blow to my stomach blasted the last of the air from my lungs, but I had just enough strength to kick my assailant in the face. I heard teeth crunch. A good sound.

"Listen here, Ebenezer," said Jack quietly. "I don't have time for polished toffs with scarves and coats withholding valuable and necessary information, no, I do not. Have you no thought for me and me lads here? They all need feeding, don't you, boys?" Another punch landed on my side, but even as I pulled again at the chain, I recognized that I was fading. "Where is our shipment?"

It was then I saw the golden glint on Roger's finger. A ring exactly like the one Fezziwig had been wearing.

They were connected to his murder. I had nothing to go on but the glimpse of that ring and a feeling deep within me that I could not ignore.

I choked, I felt my eyeballs pressing threateningly at their sockets, the pain was indescribable—then they released me. With a crash, I fell to the floor, gasping for air. My heart stung and my tongue swelled in my throat. I rubbed my neck.

"Would you like to do that again?" Roger asked.

I shook my head violently.

"Then tell us what we wish to know." He produced a blade, placed it at my throat, over the scarf. "Or I'll slit you ear-to-ear. After."

I didn't want to ask, but the silence spilled out for so long I could not help myself. "A-after what?"

"Bring the gravel, Baldworthy. And the spoon. Mr. Scrooge needs to be made to see reason. And I'm thinking he only needs one eye for that."

I went mad. I twisted and jerked and fought, but there were too many. They beat me down, subdued me, and held me while Baldworthy approached with the instruments.

I began to babble. I told them I knew exactly what they were talking about. I gave them locations where I knew grain was kept, precious imports, and more. The Colleys tsked tsked with every lie, and my coat and shirt were stripped from me. I told them how I could help them hide their income through legitimate enterprises, how I could launder their money, disperse their illegal goods throughout warehouses stocked with legal trade so that none would suspect what they were up to. But it was no use. They were after something else, something far more critical than what my wildest promises could deliver.

They worked at me with their knives, which they first salted. Tiny burning cuts that bled copiously. And all the time, Baldworthy stood holding the spoon over a candle, heating it like a red-hot iron, smiling as he waited his turn. He would use the spoon to dig out my eye.

Finally, Jack said, "I don't think he has anything to tell us. Nothing of substance. No value to him."

Baldworthy looked crestfallen. "So I don't get to . . ."

"Hang it all, take both eyes before you kill him, do whatever you wish," Roger said. Then he looked down at me . . . and at something lying beside me. "Hold on, now. What's this?"

Roger bent down, his knees clicking, and then rose again gripping my locket. He held it before me. He popped it open and inside I saw a cameo portrait of my beloved Belle. And despite the horrid way we had left things when she released me from our engagement, I would not, and could not, ever stop loving her.

As I was choking and kicking, my brain on fire from the agony of hanging, I heard them describe the vileness they would perpetrate upon Belle. Things they would do together or taking turns. A "party" for all their happy lads.

I could not let that happen. I would not. I scoured my mind for all the ghostly Fezziwig said to me and shouted, "Chimera!"

The mockery came to an abrupt silence. Roger and Jack paled.

"Cut him down," Roger commanded.

"Cut him down now!" echoed his brother.

Roger advanced on me. "Tell me what you know. End this. Be straight and we'll forget about the girl. We're not monsters, Mr. Scrooge."

And just then, while I was sprawled on the floor, panting, spitting, coughing, the warehouse erupted into a hellish crescendo of activity. The doors burst open and men with lanterns flooded the place. Cries of "*mutton shunters*" exploded from the criminals. A warning that the police were here. Roger ran off even as Baldworthy and the man with the claret mark bested a handful of constables and scattered into the darkness like cockroaches. The other thugs fell or surrendered, wishing to keep all their teeth. And their knees. Jack sprang from the darkness.

"I'll kill you!" Jack screamed. "Kill you!"

Then a baton clipped him at the base of the skull and down he went. Crabapple stood behind him, that faint smile I'd seen earlier today playing on his rough-hewn face.

As Jack was dragged to his feet, he screamed. "Where is it, Scrooge? Where's our shipment? *Where is it*?" Crabapple's men led him away, screaming. "When Roger finds your woman, he'll make what was done to that old bastard Fezziwig look like a mercy a thousand times over," Jack promised, as he was dragged past me. "Then Baldworthy can have her eyes, put them in his fun jar. His pickled pleasures. His—"

I was on my feet by then. And somehow, Crabapple's baton had found its way into my hand, as if the man had slipped it there himself.

I made good use of it. And down went Jack, falling in a heap.

And for the first time ever, I heard Constable Crabapple laugh.

On the dock, beneath the stars I found Miss Owen waiting for me. There had indeed been a hose in the warehouse, and after stripping off my clothes, I had used it thoroughly to wash the hellish stink of the Thames from me. A policeman who'd served in the war as a medic and always carried his doctor's bag had seen to the cuts, disinfecting and dressing them. One of Colley's goons who was about the same size as me had been stripped, his dry if ratty clothes given to me. His shoes were a size too big; I moved clumsily, which made Miss Owen smile.

"I owe you my life," I said. Crabapple had told me how Miss Owen had doubled back, watched as I went into the river with Sunderland, saw his men take me from beneath the docks, and followed me here. Then she'd made her way back to the precinct and convinced Crabapple to stage this raid. He wouldn't have given the woman's pleas credence had it not been for her precise descriptions of so many of Colley's "soldiers," particularly the man with the claret mark. Crabapple had returned here with her, and when he saw the mountains of stolen goods in the warehouse, he sent one of his men to round up enough strong fellows for the raid.

"I owe that poor fellow who worked for Mr. Sunderland mine. He fought so that I might go free."

"I don't have much time," I cautioned her. "There are arrangements I must make."

Crabapple had pledged to send men to watch Belle's home on the chance that Roger might make good his threats against her. But he would not keep them there beyond morning. By then the villain's rage would have cooled, Crabapple assured me. And the man would be on to more pressing matters. I was not so sure.

"I expect nothing to be given to me," Miss Owen said. "My entire life, I have earned what little I have received. You are in the midst of a business venture, I believe? Suppose I had information that might prove useful to you in securing investors. Would you not consider partnering with me under those terms?"

"I would certainly be interested to know what you consider 'useful information.' But first, what nature of partnership are you proposing?"

"Partner with me in the solving of Fezziwig's murder, Mr. Scrooge. So that my Tom might be set free. I shall make certain your investment deal benefits."

"Yes . . . your Tom."

She held out her hand like any gentleman might when proposing a business deal.

I frowned. "You will receive the bitterly disappointing wage I had reserved for a clerk. You will perform the duties of a clerk but out of sight, and you will not speak of this; you will receive no letter of recommendation from me. This is a finite arrangement, is that understood?"

Her hand did not waver. And as a chill wind rose off the river, I took it—and found in it a warmth I had not felt in many a year.

"And as your first order of business," I told her, "I want you to investigate something called Chimera." She knew that Fezziwig's spirit had spoken of it, and her eyes widened as I described the strange effect that single word had upon the Colleys. "I'll need to know things about George Sunderland and what Fezziwig might possibly have known about him to cause the businessman sleepless nights. I also must know about this Tom fellow. Any reason you might conceive why he had been at Fezziwig's in the first place."

At the far edge of the warehouse, I saw Dickens and his fellow reporters arrayed before Inspector Foote, who had arrived just in time to take all credit from the fuming Crabapple once more. I knew the ways of London's press. There would be fear-mongering and mass panic brewing in the vile cesspools on either side of the city's class divide unless I could have words with Dickens before this night was over. Miss Owen caught my gaze.

"What I tell you about Tom . . . it will be in the press?" she guessed.

"It will. I must preserve Fezziwig's name. It is all I may do for him now. And I cannot guarantee that what's written will help Tom's case at all."

"But you will try?"

I did not need to reply. She saw in my eyes how all of this benefitted me, and how the night's events had strengthened my resolve to circumvent the ghost's terrible prophecies.

She nodded and promised she would be forthcoming. But another matter weighed on her as well: "We have to know why Fezziwig summoned those people. I know of a gentleman who might be able to help you squeeze that arrogant prick Rutledge. Of the four we met in that room this morning, he struck me as the weak link. Something about him was simply not as it seemed."

"Then squeeze him we shall, but not right away. There are other more pressing matters to deal with first."

Like keeping a dead man from visiting me once again, I silently added.

CHAPTER FIVE

ONE CAN REASONABLY assume that dancing at the end of a rope can leave a man proof against further shocks to the system, but the vile swill that passed for dinner at the Cock and Egg challenged most assumptions. I leaned back in my seat barely two hours after the incident at the warehouse and closed my eyes. I wanted to wish away the bitter tang and thick oppressive odor of the seasoned egg and cheese slop Dickens greedily slurped and swallowed. The din and clatter of the pub crashed over me, Christmas songs merrily slurred by those full to the brim of mulled cider and whiskey pressed me like an inquisition's victim. It pushed down on me with the thick smell of stale beer, rotting straw, sickly sweet perfumes, unwashed bodies, and urine. Shuddering, I opened my eyes and reached for the flagon of spiced rum I shared with my guest and drank. I couldn't wait to be far from this bristly underbelly of Whitechapel and the stench of beer batter. But first I had business to conduct with the young reporter seated across from me.

Dickens smiled thinly as he pushed the scraped-clean

plate away and mopped at his chin with a worn handkerchief. An air of confidence settled about him as he withdrew a small notepad and pencil from his jacket and set them down between us. "Right we are then, Mr. Scrooge. Tell me all there is to know about your secret association with Mr. Sunderland and how it ties to those wretched Colley boys. And what business dealing were they and this Tom fellow mixed up in that led to poor Fezziwig's horrible demise? Mr. Scrooge, imagine the publicity this story will get you. The people who will line up at your door to do business with the final confidant of George Sunderland. That's what I will make of you."

A hot flush burst in my cheeks. "Dickens, you always have your ear to the ground. So what's life like in the gutter, anyway?"

"My theory is, the Colleys took you because of a kidnapping gone terribly wrong," he went on, ignoring my slight. "The big fish, as it were, got away, drowned in the Thames, and the Colleys thought to make do with you. See what gold they might squeeze from you in return for your miserable life. And perhaps find out if you knew where Sunderland keeps his cash."

I leaned across the table, brushing his notepad aside. I felt a throbbing in my temple that had nothing to do with the rum. "Mr. Dickens, I did not ask you here for this. You know what I am after. You promised to write a favorable article on Mr. Fezziwig, extolling his many virtues. I would see him remembered as he was in life, not death."

I shuddered, remembering the ghastly sight of the

man's body disintegrating before me as his voice echoed in my ears. *Humbug, Humbug, HUMBUG—*

"I'd have done that anyway," Dickens said. "He was a good man who did not deserve such a miserable end."

"Beyond that, though, you said you could assist me, as you have done on previous occasions."

"Yes, and as to that, what you failed to consider is twofold: first, this is different from running some minor line of inquiry into someone's background. And second, why should I even consider such an undertaking? What do I get from it?"

I thought of the threats Roger Colley had made against my fair Belle, and Crabapple's only mild interest in helping to keep her—and by extension, her new family—safe. I had to arrange reliable protection, and Dickens knew his way around the darkest corners of London. "A young mother and her family are in danger and here you are with your hand out? And they call moneylenders cold-hearted and tight-fisted. Fine. Name your price."

"I already have. Information."

"You won't get it."

Shrugging, he gathered up his notepad and made to stand up.

"Stop," I said wearily. "There must be something else you want."

The reporter's smile grew as he eased back into his seat. Suddenly the smell of cloves turned a switch in the reporter's head, and he couldn't concentrate. He looked up. A curly-haired vixen in an emerald dress planted a black-gloved hand on her hip. She grinned at us with an infuriating familiarity. Worse, she had a girlfriend with her. With thick ginger curls and slightly parted cherry lips, her bosom heaving as she breathed, the girlfriend was absolutely stunning.

"Move off," I warned the prostitutes. "There's no trade for you here."

"It's a free country, sir," said the lady in red. "I 'ave a mind to take me supper 'ere tonight in the company of my nice friend Miss Piper." She leaned over the merrily distracted Dickens, almost spilling out of her corset. "'Ave you met my nice friend Miss Piper, Mr. Dickens? You said to keep me eye out for persons of interest and talent."

"And in saying that, Irene, I meant those whose abilities lend themselves to the arts. The wealthy are always looking for talented types to reward with their patronage. Painters, dancers, musicians, of that type. I sense quite the story in it."

Irene shrugged. "Well, Miss Piper 'ere, she's ever so talented. And that's drawing a great deal of interest!"

Dickens reddened and smiled broadly. "Irene, thank you. Very obliged to meet you, Miss Piper." He held her hand a little longer than convention.

Miss Piper fluttered her eyelashes. Looking directly into Dickens' eyes, she bit her lip. "Up for a bit of nanty narking? I could sing you a song . . . or do somethin' else with me mouth."

"Ho, ho!" He smiled and kissed her hand. "Now I bet *you* have a tale to tell, don't you?"

"Damn it, Dickens, will you focus! Be gone, women. Leave us to think. Eat your supper somewhere else, I'm sure there are other gentlemen who would welcome the two of you slopping your soup down your busts as they attempted to conduct a negotiation, but we are not they!"

"Oh! Well, we ain't wanted 'ere, Miss Piper. Let's go somewhere else." She linked arms with her friend and sashayed away. "Ta-ta, Mr. Dickens, sir. See you round the corner!"

Laughing, the women were swallowed up by the crowd.

"A journalist," I groused. "I feel that I'm supping with the devil. Or a vulture."

"I'm feeling much the same, sir. But I'll sit with anyone who has an interesting story. Even you." Dickens tapped his chin. "Tell you what: I am curious about the mechanics of your enterprises. How things work, vis-à-vis, in the world of moneylending. And how it feels to put desperate, hopeless, and helpless families out on the street."

I shook my head. "When would feelings come into any of it? It is a matter of business, nothing more."

Dickens strummed his fingers on the wooden surface separating us. "Mr. Scrooge, it seems you leave me no choice. What price would you pay for my services?"

I named a generous sum, a pitiful one I knew would make his blood curdle. I'd make that vulture of a pen-pusher squirm for every farthing he bled from me.

"Yes, now, that is quite fair, surprisingly so. I would have thought your opening bid would be far less, and that—"

"That's my number," I told him, stabbing the table with my forefinger. "Not a farthing more. And I'll have no more of you wasting my time. I asked you here to hire you for a job of work, that is all. I need a capable man to handle the discussed matters with speed and discretion. Are you to work for me or not? I would have your answer, Dickens."

The reporter's upper lip twitched. I knew something of his background. With a father who lived far beyond his means and ended up hauled off with his entire family to debtors' prison, Dickens believed he would be raised a fine young gentleman. He got the shock of his life at the mere age of ten when he was taken to the blacking factory to help work off his father's debts. Yet still, that twitchy sense of entitlement, despite it all, that grasping, grubbing desire to be well off and accepted in the world of his betters. At odds, surely, with his painfully earnest desire to see change done to what *he* considered the corrupt and unjust mechanisms that made this city what it was: mine for the taking.

"I'm quite gainfully employed already."

"I can see the markings of your success from your ratty sleeve, worn shoes, and pitiful excuse for a razor." I nodded at the thin reporter's stubble. His lean stomach growled. "And from your full to overflowing belly."

"I'm interested in truth."

"I'm interested in protecting a woman's life."

Dickens glanced down at his wiry, unthreatening frame. He was anything but a hard man. "If it's hired muscle you require, I'm afraid I'm apt to disappoint. My weapons are my brain and my quill, not—"

"But you know such men, yes? You prowl the city streets night after night, acquainting yourself with all manner of vermin and scum. I've seen you as I've made my rounds. I doubt there is a rat in London you haven't named and fed a bit of cheddar."

Dickens sighed. "It may be as you say."

"So you know those who might be trusted. Former soldiers, fallen on hard times, perhaps, but not fallen far from the ways of duty and honor."

"I've met more than a few."

"I know. I've read your accounts."

Dickens was clearly pleased at this turn, but he attempted to hide his smile behind the flagon as he took it from me and tipped it back for a scorching swallow.

"So you'll do it?"

"Go on, then," Dickens promised. "I know a few I can contact before the dawn."

"Good. And while you're at it, there are a few others I would have you make discreet inquiries about. Well-to-do types."

"The others who answered Fezziwig's summons," Dickens ventured. "The lord, the actress, the Asian?"

"And Sunderland himself," I said, recalling the industrialist's mad fit on the bridge.

"Tell me what's going on, Scrooge. I can do far more for you if I know the full truth."

I looked away. I had no doubt that it was just as he said. And what did I know of poking about in matters generally left to the police? An investigator of his caliber would be a near priceless boon in solving this mystery. There was just one problem: "How do I know I can trust you, Mr. Dickens?"

He smiled. "I have no answer to that. I only hope that you will."

I thought about our many conversations, and one in particular exploded into my thoughts.

"Dickens, you told me that you want out from under the yoke of your publishers, did you not? That you dreamed of becoming a publisher yourself, so that you held the editorial reins and none might censor or change your words unfairly."

A light came into his eyes. One of yearning and hope. "The kind of money that would require . . ."

"What if I pledged to help you raise it? In return for a vow of absolute confidence concerning all I might reveal?"

Dickens raised his chin and blinked with interest. "And if you failed to live up to your end of the bargain?"

"Then you would reveal all. This pact benefits us both."

"Very well. Just keep in mind, Scrooge, that the tip of my pen is sharper than any sword. Of course, you'll have no need to fear its ability to create new realities in the minds of the readers of its words, my good man. But if you prove yourself dishonorable, then you will find all your unsavory business practices revealed for all of London by my pen—in copious detail. So, then, all that remains is to discuss the method of my payment."

"Cash when I see results."

"Oh, no," Dickens said, amused and taken with himself. "You won't be paying *me*."

"Who then?"

Dickens outlined a series of charitable contributions he would see me make. I held my tongue at how useless I found the "good works" of each of them. I did not wish him to see how his machinations rankled me, but I could tell from his growing good cheer that I was failing miserably in this.

"You'll wish to remain anonymous, I imagine," Dickens said. "When making contributions."

"I wish to be left alone by those who come looking for donations, yes. If word spreads of my giving money to the societies you've named, I will never hear the end of it."

"That's a shame. Without a name, how may I verify that you have done as you've pledged?"

"You have my word, sir," I said indignantly. "What more do you need?"

"Receipts, of course, my dear man. We shall have to devise a name for you. How about Tip Slymingstone?"

"Preposterous."

"Jem Knavelet? Gibby Squallindkind? Ely Crotchinary? Oh, yes, that, *that* I think—"

The muscles beside my right eye twitched. "A sharp tongue is no indication of a keen mind, Dickens. I'd say make a mental note of that, but you're clearly out of paper."

Before he might resume his ridicule, he was interrupted by a raucous round of applause from a table across the taproom. A crowd had gathered about the two prostitutes, and one was nodding her head, smiling, and waving for the men to settle down as she got on with her story.

Dickens stole a glance, appreciating the full bouncing bosoms of the boisterous ladies, then fixed his dark eyes on me. "Now let us get back to the matter at hand. Tell me, all, Scrooge!"

Nearly a quarter of an hour passed as I recalled all that had happened to me on this grim day. No, not all. Knowing how it would sound to someone who had not been there to witness it, I said nothing of the ghostly Fezziwig. Instead, I claimed to have received an unsigned letter in which my life had been threatened, I had been instructed that the young man was innocent, and the word "Chimera" had been mentioned. I also said I tossed the letter in the fire, thinking it all a nasty humbug from some angry debtor whose deed I held.

"It's hard to imagine George Sunderland having anything to do with the Colley Brothers," Dickens mused. "But it does all seem to fit, now doesn't it? Sunderland fears Fezziwig knows something about him that might mar his legacy, and so he hires the Colley Brothers to put the fear of God in the old man. They go too far and butcher him instead. Sunderland withholds their payment, the Colleys rush to grab him and force him to hand *it* over—whatever it is he promised to give them in return for their efforts—but he drowns and they get you instead."

"But whoever killed Fezziwig showed him mercy," I said. "He was unconscious when his throat was slit and dead before all the terrible wounds were inflicted. I was put to the question by those boys tonight and can assure you, mercy is not in their repertoire."

"Ah, but I have a theory on that. The Colleys are very small men, are they not? Fezziwig was six feet tall and then some. The chemicals may have been necessary because the killer could not overpower the old man otherwise. That is *if* they got their hands dirty with the task personally, and with all those tall strapping goons, why would they? Hmmm . . ."

I shook my head. "And what is this 'Chimera'? Why did that word have such an effect on those criminals?"

Dickens nodded. "And if all this is related to the threat—or promise—made to you at your counting-house, that three more would die, then you . . . you're right. There's something there, but it doesn't all fit properly. Not yet. I say that we should—"

The bells above the pub's front door jangled and a red-nosed newspaper boy rushed in with a cloud of swirling snowflakes holding up a late edition. "Humbug Killer strikes! George Sunderland drowned! Beloved businessman murdered! Suspect behind bars! Hang him now, cries the public! Read all about it!"

The lad was crushed by enthusiasts who stripped him of every paper he held. Moments later, he left with coins jingling in his pocket. Dickens snatched up a newspaper and had more spiced rum as he skimmed the front page.

"The Humbug Killer. They already have a name for him." Dickens sighed. "Well, Scrooge, the public doesn't know about your connection to Sunderland just yet, and all mention of Shen, Nellie Pearl, and Lord Rutledge being at Fezziwig's this morning—with you, Sunderland, and Miss Owen—has not been reported, either. Let me get you in front of this. We need to know what Sunderland feared Fezziwig might have on him, and what better way than to link you to the man in the minds of the public at large, eh? That way, when you ask questions, doors aplenty will be opened ahead of time.

Otherwise, as we both know, less scrupulous types than me will simply make it all up."

I held out all manner of objection to this, but in the end relented, giving him statements with which he could do what he liked. Dickens took it all down eagerly, like a drunk who had been dry at least a month. I also told him what little information Miss Owen shared about "her Tom."

"Thomas Malcolm Guilfoyle, Piermont and Piermont Acquisitions," he muttered, scratching madly at his notepad. "A history of floundering from one menial position to another despite a fine upbringing at good schools, parents long-deceased. Tasked with securing a number of properties in Fezziwig's neighborhood, including the one his shop had been built upon. He'd made considerable strides with adjoining properties, but Fezziwig refused to sell."

"Fezziwig never mentioned any of this to me," I said.

Dickens frowned. "This makes it look all the worse for Miss Owen's young man. It gives him clear motive."

"I know. All I ask is that you keep Miss Owen's name out of this."

"Of course. But I will need to speak to her further, to better understand—"

Just as we were finishing, an explosion of laughter rocked the tavern. I massaged my temples and caressed my sore neck. "We should—"

"Wait!" someone yelled. "He gave you as much as that for no slap and just a cuddle?"

"That he did!" Miss Piper said, tossing back her ginger locks. "And believe you me, a cuddle's a lot less work than all the rest we lot get up to!"

The men in the crowd guffawed and cheered.

"They call their sort fallen women," I whispered. "I doubt *they* had far to fall."

The women sat close together, Irene with her arm about her companion's shoulders. Miss Piper wiggled her shoulders and gave her onlookers a bit of a bounce. "Well, you know what I always say. If some fool punter wants to throw his money away, I'd just as soon he'd throw it away on me!"

Irene shook her head. "Oh, Annie, you're a wicked one."

"Perhaps you're right. Poor lad fancies himself in love. Pays for the 'ole night, not just for a little knee tickler. But the opium . . . no friend to his arched back, if you get me drift. Spent 'alf last night listening to him blubber that he's not even a man."

A man in a worn waistcoat said, "Wait now, this isn't the same bloke—"

"Yes, the very one." Miss Piper—Annie to her friends—rolled her eyes.

"They've got him right fitted up for murder!" the man said.

"They got it wrong. They always get it wrong. Oh, he went there all right, but he arrived after the dawn, just ahead of those fancy-fancy types. Had to have, my poor Tom. He was with me until then. He couldn't have done the wicked-wicked with that knife to that doddering old man."

"You've got to tell them."

"Hah! They'd send me down as his accomplice. I don't need me neck stretched, thank you. It's quite swan-like as it is, wouldn't you say?"

An icy hand gripped the space between my shoulder and neck, and I felt a ghostly breath upon me. *The young man is innocent.*

"They're talking about Mr. Guilfoyle," I said.

"An alibi," Dickens agreed.

Together we sprang to our feet, the dizziness gone, my world solid as my will and resolve. But an obstacle literally stood in our way. One of considerable girth and, judging from his wine-soaked breath, considerable merriment as well.

"Bless my old chestnuts!" said the happy fat man as he adjusted his spectacles. "If it isn't Mr. Ebenezer Scrooge I see before me, large as life and twice as pleasant. How are you tonight, my good sir?"

"Mr. Pickwick, we do not complain about your shortcomings, but your long stayings. If you will excuse us?"

"Nonsense. And you, Boz—or should I say Mr. Dickens—don't you move a muscle. I have quite the tale for you!"

They tried to skirt the portly man's generous girth, but escape proved impossible. An exodus had begun all about Pickwick. Those he had trapped into conversation now swarmed about them as they tipped their hats and fled. The prostitutes and their audience lay beyond the stampede.

"I've heard that you may have some kind of investment opportunity, is that correct? I just might know someone. Well, bosh, that is to say, I know most everyone, now don't I? But in this most singular regard I may be of considerable value to you. Do you know my good friend Nathaniel Winkle?" Pickwick looked about, his brow furrowing in confusion. "Winkle? Winkle, my fine chap, where are you?"

Pickwick waddled past me, so I grasped Dickens by the arm and rushed for the side exit.

"Winkle? My dear Winkle, where are you going? I was just about to have them bring out the grouse pie!" Pickwick called behind them.

We spotted an opening and ran for it. But the gathering around the painted ladies had evaporated and only a splash of crimson hair heading for a far exit gave any hope. We raced for it, and the burly bartender eased out before us, blocking the way to the shadowy corridor and the door opening on to pools of moonlight glistening in puddles formed by broken bottles in the alleyway beyond.

"Forgetting something, gents?" the barman asked.

Cursing myself, I dug into my pockets, found the necessary coin, and dropped it into his palm—making sure I shot him my nastiest look. He receded and we ran down the narrow dark corridor, slammed open the far door, and came up quick in the darkened alley beyond, a gathering spot known locally as a marketplace for prostitutes. Laughing whores were lining the alley walls, waving mistletoe at passersby, but there was no sign of Irene and Miss Piper.

On the bustling street beyond, I surveyed the sinister mass of fellow Londoners at midnight. I looked away as we passed a clutch of tattered and tired beggars with outstretched and blackened hands. Each pleaded for coin to buy a bit of "Christmas cheer."

"I don't make merry myself at Christmas, and I can't afford to make idle people merry, either. Be off with you!" I turned from them, towards the probing stare of the reporter.

"She's right, you know," Dickens said. "Even if she went to the police, no one's going to believe the word of some slag. Though perhaps Mr. Guilfoyle shared more with her about his dealings than he did with Miss Owen. Opiates tend to loosen the tongue, I've heard. That ring is of considerable interest, I would say. How would such a poor man acquire such a rich item as that? And might he know something of this Chimera? Perhaps it is a person. Or a place . . ."

The ghostly voice whispered, perhaps at my ear, perhaps only on a shallow tide of memory: *Remember that I chose you, and think long and hard upon why . . . and the consequences of volunteering a blindness to what you know is right.*

"Find those men to protect the woman in the brief and then find the prostitute. Her name is Annie Piper, yes. Your girl knows her. Start there."

"Oh, is that *all*, my lordship?" Dickens practically spat.

"That's all for now."

"And what will you be doing?"

"Don't be impertinent. You're in my employ now. But if you must know, I have work to do and I must give my statement to that wretch Crabapple in the morning.

And while I am there, perhaps I might gain an audience with this Tom fellow. Good evening to you, Mr. Dickens. I will expect frequent reports!"

"Remember your pledges, Mr. Scrooge," he called after me. "I have expectations as well, and they are great indeed!"

CHAPTER SIX

Tuesday, December 20th, 1833
Five Days to Christmas

I SKIPPED BREAKFAST the following morning, feeling uneasy and troubled. Mrs. Doors, my landlady, stood in the doorway with a hurt expression on her face. She clutched a bowl of uneaten porridge and a pot of tea as I hailed a cab to drive me to Scotland Yard. I was dreading the interview with Constable Crabapple, fully expecting him to treat Miss Owen and me with the sensitivity and common decency of a feral pig.

The cab turned up an alley into a little paved court in which a number of great-coated policemen ambled to and from the front doors. One tugged at his coat's high reinforced collar, designed to help prevent garroting, a common concern. Crowds had gathered outside, picketers bundled against the Christmas chill held up signs that read, "HANG HUMBUG!" and "LET JUSTICE BE DONE!" Chants and shouts erupted whenever a policeman even glanced their way. Disgust threatened my composure. Even though London's most notable businessman had met his watery demise purely of his own doing, the press knew very well that murder sells more newspapers than accidental drowning. The so-called Humbug would no doubt remain a headline for weeks while London's economy crumbled around us.

I approached a dock, the walls behind which were littered with police notices. One of the posters illustrated a portrait of a wanted pick-pocket. The police artist had even taken care to draw dirt and smudge on the young boy's face, his top hat askew. He'd been given the colorful nickname "The Artful Dodger."

A short discourse with the sergeant behind the desk revealed that Crabapple was expecting me within an inner office. I thanked the officer and went to relive the torture of Crabapple's gentle and respectful "questioning."

Forty-five minutes later, furious and on the brink of throttling the smug constable, I signed the witness declaration and slammed Crabapple's pen on the interview table.

"Just doing my job, Mr. Scrooge, sir," hummed Crabapple, picking up the pen and sliding it into his breast pocket with a smile that did not reach his eyes.

"The hell you are," I shot back. "You're so crooked, you swallow nails and spit out corkscrews."

Crabapple snorted and gestured for me to hold even as I made to rise from my chair. "One thing. Regarding your statement, are you *sure* you want to leave in that bit about the Colleys naming George Sunderland?"

"It happened."

"Sure of that, are you?"

I tapped down my fury. "What are you implying?"

"Just this, *sir*," he said. Each time he used that word I believe he meant for me to substitute the nastiest phrase I might conceive. Clearly, Inspector Foote had dressed Crabapple down for his handling of gentlemen like myself, who should ever be treated with respect, and so he had found a less direct way of being disrespectful. "You say the Colleys were after Sunderland and you were an innocent bystander. That they tortured you on the off chance you knew the whereabouts of something Sunderland had promised to the Colleys. Doesn't quite sound right."

"It doesn't, does it?" I asked.

"Nah," Crabapple said. "But if you flip it about, see, and say Mr. Sunderland was the innocent bystander and the Colleys were after you, a money-lender up to who-knows-what, well . . . that has quite the ring to it! And it doesn't have you throwing dirt on a dead man's name and reputation in order to gain more attention for yourself."

With that, he scooped up a newspaper from the chair beside him and slapped it down on the table. It had been opened to Dickens' article which positioned me as Sunderland's secret advisor.

"Do you ever stop with this?" I asked.

"Maybe when you start to tell me the truth. Why 'Humbug,' eh? When I first stepped into your office, you saying that very word, that woman, terrified of you."

"Not of me."

"Of who, then?"

"You waste time with me when there are villains on

the loose," I said, exasperated. "Roger Colley the worst of the lot, and he and those other two, Baldworthy and the man with the red mark, are free, having escaped *your* net last night."

"I think the words you're searching for, *sir*, are thank you again for saving my life."

"Roger Colley vowed vengeance on me and those I care about. I barely slept last night for fear of waking with that grinning gargoyle arched over me. What say you to that, Crabapple?"

"I say there's a lot of reasons a man might find it difficult to sleep. A guilty conscience being one. Do you have one of those, Mr. Scrooge?"

I shuddered. "The Colleys own the London docks and their empire grows by the day, from what I've heard. I'd urge you to press the brother you have in custody."

"Ah, well, it's so good you're assisting us, sir. Never would have thought of that on our own, now would we? As to their 'ownership' and whatnot, well . . . the raid on their warehouses yielded thousands of pounds of contraband, literally thousands. Took my men hours to extract the goods. Illegal trade, of course, no paperwork. The case against them is solid, even more so now thanks to your testimony, *sir*. Whatever stranglehold they might have had over the criminal elements in that part of the city is well and truly broken. Roger Colley, well, he's just a rat left with a couple of mates and few options. If I was him, I'd be on a boat to the colonies by now."

"And in the matter of the protection of Belle Potterage?"

"Colley didn't show there last night. As I told you,

limited manpower, sir. I've had to recall Humperdink and the more senior bobbies I assigned so they can run down leads on the villain's whereabouts. If he ain't already long gone, as I suspect."

"You believe he would abandon his brother?"

"Rats don't have such loyalties."

"Well, if that'll be all, Crabapple, I'd like to thank you for your time and utter contempt." At least knowing Dickens had his men stationed round the district where Belle and her useless husband lived brought me some relief.

I allowed Constable Crabapple to show me out—there may have been a shove or two—and I knew the mistake I'd made. I needed something from Crabapple and had hardly left things on good terms between us.

"Now, unless I may be of further assistance . . ." began Crabapple, pointing to the door.

Just then, Inspector Foote strode by—and stopped as he saw me. "Why, if it isn't Mr. Ebenezer Scrooge. Why, I was just reading about you!"

Foote smiled, shook my hand, and asked if there was anything, *anything*, that his men could do for an illustrious fellow like myself. Clearly Dickens' plan to raise me up by association to Sunderland was working.

"You may," I said. "I'd like to gain an audience with Fezziwig's murderer."

"Would you now?" said Crabapple, his eyebrows raised high into his hat. "On what account?"

"He has murdered my friend. I wish to ask him why."

"Lot of good that'll do you, sir. The bastard hasn't said a word, nor will he. But no matter, the evidence against him will qualify a trial, have no worry, with a verdict all but assured. So if you'll excuse me . . ."

Inspector Foote flushed. "Please excuse Crabapple. He's *studying* to become a half-wit." He placed a hand on Crabapple's shoulder. "Constable, I believe we talked about this. Politeness to the public we protect, that is the watchword of the day. If Mr. Scrooge wishes to speak with the suspect, I can see no harm in it. It's Christmas, after all! That woman has already been to see Mr. Guilfoyle, has she not? In fact, here she is now!"

I turned to see Adelaide, her face tear-stained and blotchy, walking up the corridor from the cells towards me.

"Ah," sighed Crabapple, stopping. "It appears the murderer's schedule has just opened up."

Adelaide strode up to me, her full skirts swishing on the stone floor. "Are you to speak with Tom?" she asked me, her big eyes gleaming.

"Miss Owen, like you, insisted on visiting the suspect," said the inspector, with more than an air of superiority. Foote turned to her. "I cannot imagine how difficult this must be for you, Miss Owen. Men sometimes hide double lives. A dreadful business, simply dreadful. Thank you for all you revealed in your statement. Crabapple there couldn't even get his name out of him!"

"Thank you, Inspector," Miss Owen said softly. "If Mr. Scrooge is going to see Tom, I'd like to come along."

Foote spun on Crabapple. "Show Mr. Scrooge the way. Mr. Scrooge, you should stop by my club sometime. We can talk of this and that. There are many crimes we simply do not have the manpower to follow up on as much as we'd like. Look here!"

He pointed at several documents tacked to the wall. Missing-persons notices. Attractive women, housewives, mothers, daughters. A half-dozen spread over the past few months. "If some generous benefactor might step forward and help us to hire more men, we might be able to get to the bottom of cases like this."

"I'm handling those," Crabapple said, crossing his arms over his chest, his body tensing. "Nothing to 'em. Young women run off with their sweethearts. Wives get tired of running the household and go off to communes like the one that Shelley woman keeps talking about forming."

"Or maybe their bodies just haven't been dragged from the Thames yet," Miss Owen said. "Like poor Mr. Sunderland."

"Well," Foote said. "Crabapple, extend these two every courtesy." He looked my way. "I want to hear about it if he does not, yes?"

I smiled and delivered an amused nod.

When the inspector had gone, Crabapple walked us down the hall. He sneered at Miss Owen. "Did you enjoy your congregation with the killer, Miss Owen? Fitting, is it, for a young woman to be cavorting with dangerous criminals? Pulled yourself up from hard times, haven't you, miss? Humble beginnings. Difficult to fully scrape off the filth of life on the street, though."

"You misunderstand me, Constable," Miss Owen said, sniffing and dabbing her nose with a silk kerchief before folding it neatly away and raising herself up with dignity. "I have never suffered so. But I have done all I could to help those who have. To be in such an entrusted position that you may help and protect Englishmen from the dangers of the lawless, well, you are most lucky indeed." She smiled at Crabapple through her tears.

Crabapple groaned. "Maybe that's what I smell on you. A do-gooder. Even worse than a common trollop. At least whores see this world for what it is. Not what they delude themselves to think it could be."

"Funny," I said. "*You* lecturing about delusions. They're the foundation of every one of your piss-poor conclusions in this case. You should watch what you say, Crabapple. One word in the right ear and a man like me could end your career."

"The prisoner is down the corridor, Scrooge. You may see yourself to his cell. I'll return in a few to show you out, and I expect your report imminently, though I shan't expect any use for it. And *do* wish the doomed boy a very merry Christmas from me, won't you." Crabapple turned his back on us without saying good-bye, strode across the open atrium, and vanished into an office.

I looked at Miss Owen, her eyes still fixed to mine, gleaming with hope even behind the stinging hurt from Crabapple's cruel jibe.

"Perhaps I should speak to Mr. Guilfoyle alone," I suggested. Miss Piper would feature heavily in the subject of my interrogation, and I did not wish her to hear any of it.

"No, I can tell that you've learned something. Whatever it is, I must know. I must know all of it." She looked straight into my eyes, her gaze unfaltering, her brow set in a firm expression. The subtle scent of rose drifted to me from the nape of her neck, and her grip of my arm tightened. "Please."

"As you wish."

She led me back to the cells further in the building, down a corridor through a suffocating stench of unwashed crooks and unemptied chamber pots. Behind the bars of the furthermost cell, Tom was curled up on a bench. He tried to cover his face with the rough rug that was his only bed-furniture.

"Tom," said Adelaide, gently.

"I told you before, go away!" came the bitter response. The rug slid off his face, revealing tangled hair and bloodshot eyes. Those eyes landed on me, widened in surprise, and then narrowed under a frown. Did he know me from somewhere? How odd.

He wiped his nose on the back of his sleeve, and I noticed, with a flicker of curiosity, that the cuff of his sleeve was adorned with a mother-of-pearl button. Not something I would have expected to see on the cuff of a man of his station.

"Tom, this is Mr. Ebenezer Scrooge," she said. "He can help us."

"Go away, Adelaide," said Tom again, standing up and stuffing his hands into his pockets. He turned his back on us and kicked the wall. His whole body twitched; beads of cold sweat had formed on his pale neck. The threat of hanging may have been weighing heavily on his heart, but so, it seemed, was opium withdrawal. His hands and face had been washed of Fezziwig's blood, but Crabapple had seen fit to leave him in the same blood-soaked clothes in which he'd been arrested.

"Tom, I'm trying to help you—"

"What did you tell them?" Tom demanded, rushing at the bars and gripping them so violently Miss Owen gasped and darted from them. He pressed his face between the bars, his eyes those of a wild dog. "Did you really think it 'helpful' to tell them about my dealings with Fezziwig? You've handed them clear motive. *Clear* motive for why I might have done this thing. Damn it and damned be you!"

I clanged my cane against the bars, making him jump and dart away. "Enough of that. She loves you. Any fool can see that."

Tom stared at me with piercing bloodshot eyes. "And *you're* a fool if you believe anything she says." He looked back to Miss Owen. "He will come, he will deal with this. All of this."

"Tom . . ."

He began to pace in the small cell, his feet sweeping frantically before him. He smacked the walls, the bars, twitched and shook. "The less said the better. He'll be here. He'll be here . . ."

I wanted to ask whom he was talking about, but Miss Owen's warning gaze stopped me.

"Tell me where you were two nights ago," I demanded. "When Fezziwig was murdered."

Tom remained as he was, hands solidly hidden in his pockets, back facing me.

"I know something of you, and soon, the world will as well. I've spoken to the press, and they were keen indeed to hear what I had to say. The gambling, the opium. It doesn't look good for you. Unless you have an alibi, which I think you *do*."

Tom stopped pacing and glared at me again.

"Adelaide," he whispered.

Miss Owen took a sharp breath and turned to me, her hand moving back to the very spot on my arm that she had previously gripped. I felt the pressure of her not-so-gentle squeeze through the rough material but went on anyway.

"Oh, is it true?" she asked me, then turned back to Tom. "Is it true, Tom? Whoever saw you, whoever you were with, you simply must tell Crabapple. I'm begging you, surely the alternative is worse?" Her voice broke, and her chin started to wobble, but she pressed her hand to her mouth and calmed her breathing.

The alternative was worse. Tom's legs kicking wildly as his vertebrae separated, one by one, all his blood forced into his head until his eyes popped, soiling the inside of that black bag. I peered at Adelaide. She would not like what was coming next, but compared to the alternative, my revelation would hardly harm a string in her heart.

"Do you know a Miss Piper, Tom?" I asked. "Pretty woman, ginger hair tightly wound in curls, blue eyes, five foot four or thereabouts? She was overheard at the Cock and Egg testifying to having spent the night with you when the murder was taking place. Laughed about it openly, in front of a pack of drinkers and whores." I stole a sideways glance at Adelaide, but instead of crumbling into heartbroken sobs and accusations of infidelity, she was clutching the bars and her face was beaming.

"We must find her," she urged. "Her account could set you free!"

"Don't be hasty now," I cautioned. "The evidence still weighs against him. But Tom, I urge you to explain yourself."

Neither sound nor movement came from the cell. I turned to Miss Owen and shrugged; she was shaking her head.

"Where did you meet with her?" she asked through the bars. "Where can we find her? Tom, I can bring her to Crabapple; her witness statement must count for something." Apart from an involuntary spasm of the head, betraying a painful withdrawal, no movement came from Tom.

With a sudden *clang* she slammed the handle end of her umbrella against the bars. "Curse you, Thomas Guilfoyle! What can it be that has made you so bitter that you are prepared to meet your death in silence? Here you have the key to your freedom and you will not take it?" Tom flinched but did not turn round.

"Do you know who the real murderer was?" I pressed.

"Tom, dearest, sweetest Tom," whispered Adelaide. "Speak to us."

"What were you doing at Fezziwig's, holding that knife, if not to kill him?" I continued. When he did not answer, I ventured, "I think you arrived, found the door open, and went inside to make sure all was well. You smelled something foul upstairs and found poor Fezziwig dead. Perhaps you slipped in his blood, perhaps you sought to check if any life yet clung to him. Then you heard something and realized his killer was still there. You took the blade to defend yourself, and all manner of blood ended up on you in the process. Might you have even written 'Humbug' on the wall so others would know this wretchedness was not of your design? Perhaps, perhaps not. But you fled and ended up in that cubbyhole. How did you know of its existence? Did you know someone who was once apprenticed there?"

Tom was staring at me now, and his startled expression told me that I had gotten at least some of it right.

"Was it laudanum you carried? I know of your opium use."

I waited for Adelaide to respond, but she did not. This was not news to her.

"No, you would not have wanted oblivion and sleep, far from it. Whatever it is you use to get your blood pumping again, you took that, perhaps that white powder I've seen people mix in their drinks, yes? And I'd wager you consumed all you had, because you knew you'd be fighting for your life if the true killer found you. Is that right?"

Tom was quaking now, casting frantic looks first at me, then Adelaide, and back again. "He has to come for me, Adelaide. Or he'll send someone. He will!"

I straightened my back. "Your acquittal is within reach, Mr. Guilfoyle. If life is of no interest to you, then by all means squander it in the murky depths of vivid dreams of midnight oil in the hell pits of London. If you are ever free again to do so. But by allowing yourself to hang, you are condemning not only your own wretched soul, but Miss . . . but Adelaide's, too. Think what torture her grief will be. I have met many selfish men in my life, Guilfoyle, but you are by far the darkest."

He turned slowly, hands still in his pockets. Glassy eyes, deep set and tired, met mine. He took a few shaking steps towards us, until he was so close I could smell the gruesome mixture of stale opium smoke and sweet, coagulated blood. His jacket rustled as his hands were finally extracted from its depths, and he gripped the bars.

"What," he said quietly, "what if I had seen something? Someone?"

"Tom, you must tell us," Adelaide pleaded.

"You'd never believe me."

"Tell us," I urged.

He darted away, clawing at his own chest, and stared at the ceiling as if appealing to the almighty Himself. "A black veil. A shroud or cloak. Hands like bones, sharp, terrible fingers. A wretched thing that should not have lived. Killed by the dead, he was. A spirit. A dead thing so like the angel of death itself. Killed by the dead! A humbug. Humbug!"

A chill swept through me like a ghost. Adelaide held her breath, her sparkling eyes flashing from Tom to me and back again. *Many more will die. And then you.*

"No, I can see you would not credit it," Tom whispered as he drew close to us again. "Not that I'd blame you."

His fists were closed round the bars, gripped so tight his knuckles were white as bone. And there, on the ring finger, was the tell-tale band of pale skin that betrayed a missing ring.

"Where's your ring, Thomas Guilfoyle?" I asked. He jumped, startled, his eyes wide and darting.

"W-what ring?" he stuttered, and his hands vanished back into his pockets.

"Don't play the fool," I said, then lowered my voice. "Heavy, gold. Red stone set deep in the middle." The very same that had been spinning on my office floor amongst a pile of cadaver-dust.

"No," he murmured, his voice coarse and dry. "No, I know of no ring." His breathing became irregular and panicked, and he retreated to the back of his cell, wildly wringing his hands.

"Of course you do," I said. "You wore it regularly. Daily, for months. You must have noticed such a permanent element of your attire?"

"Answer the man, Tom," demanded Adelaide.

"It wasn't my ring! I had nothing to do with that ring, or any of the locks it opened!" He was blathering wildly, loudly, his pleading voice echoing up the corridor. "My wearing it was nothing more than an accident, you hear? It shouldn't have come to me, it wasn't mine to use in the Royal Quarter, not mine! Don't tell Smithson Adelaide, you won't, will you?" He was on his knees now, tears streaming down his cheeks, clutching at Adelaide's skirts through the bars. She fell to his level and held his hands, soothing him with gentle coos.

"Who's Smithson?" I asked. "What's the Royal Quarter?"

"Killed by the dead, Adelaide," whispered Tom, his face pressed against the bars and the desperation laced in his voice like poison. "By the dead!"

She hushed him and peeled away a strand of hair that was sticking to his sweaty forehead.

"And Annie Piper?" I asked.

"Save her," Tom begged. "Save Annie, please, you must save her . . ."

I froze suddenly. Heavy booted steps reverberated up the corridor like a rhythmic countdown.

"Constable Crabapple!" called Adelaide, rushing to him. "We have made some progress, indeed. There is a witness, a Miss Annie Piper. She was with Tom on the night in question."

He ignored her. "What's this of a ring?" he demanded. Tom sank to the floor in the corner of the cell. "This ring?" With a flourish, Crabapple produced the mysterious ring that Fezziwig had been wearing when he was murdered. Tom's opium withdrawal reached its zenith and he doubled over, heaving and vomiting like a poisoned dog.

"He has an alibi, Constable," Adelaide pressed. "He could not have murdered Fezziwig!"

"Miss Annie Piper, you say? A known prostitute. Not a very credible witness. But the ring—excellent work, Miss Owen, Mr. Scrooge," said Crabapple. "This new connection will expedite the sentencing. We'll have this butcher hanged within a fortnight."

Dickens met us at a newsstand a few blocks from the precinct. We told him all that had happened, and he shook his head. "Every paper has informants within the police. It won't take long before that hallucination he described is relayed to one of them. If he keeps talking about it, that is."

"But what if that's what he truly saw?" Adelaide asked.

"How could it be?" I said.

Her look reminded me of the ghostly vision we had shared. And if one such creature might exist . . .

"A madman running about in a costume meant to strike fear and obscure one's identity. I could see such a thing," Dickens said. "The Japanese once wore terrifying masks into battle. Others have done the same."

"The Royal Quarter and this Smithson," I said. "Mean anything to you?"

"The Quarter, yes. A cesspool of sin, and that's putting it mildly. He said the ring was a key that opened locks in that place? I must learn more. But what weighs on me most heavily is this person Mr. Guilfoyle was certain would swoop in and save him. To whom was he referring?"

We watched Adelaide's face as she turned from us, struggling.

"I understand not wishing to betray a confidence," I told her. "But you do him no good by holding back."

"His father," she said at last.

"You said his parents were dead."

"Yes," she said. "Drowned like Mr. Sunderland. And like him, their bodies never found. It's haunted him. And when he is . . . like that . . . he becomes convinced that his father will return and rescue him."

I tried to envision a version of Thomas Guilfoyle who could possibly have won the heart of a woman like Adelaide Owen. But I could not.

"Didn't it bother you?" I asked. "His whoring?"

"Of course it bothered me!" she snapped. "But it is hardly of the moment now, is it? But if that woman is his only chance for survival, so be it."

"Well," Dickens said. "I have further inquiries to make. I will see you both at the wake?"

"You shall."

Tipping his hat, he bid us a good day.

Miss Owen maintained her composure and waved him off, then instructed me to meet her at Fezziwig's home. She had to return to the hovel in which she rented a room and secure appropriate mourning attire.

It was a flimsy excuse, but I said nothing and only watched her go, her silhouette illuminated as the winter sun glaring over the icy streets of London. She was nearly halfway down the cobbled road before I saw her clutch at a streetlamp and break into what looked like racking sobs.

She reminded me of my dear sister Fanny, whose strength had also been severely tested, and turned away, giving Miss Owen the only boon I might provide: her privacy.

CHAPTER SEVEN

FLOCKS OF PEOPLE gathered outside Fezziwig's home: scores of weeping women and somber-faced men, all dressed in black rags and clutching baskets of holly and roast chestnuts or other humble gifts for the widow. My friend and former mentor had touched many hearts, by the look of it. My stomach clenched painfully as I realized with sadness that I, clearly amongst the wealthiest of Fezziwig's friends, had brought nothing but Adelaide and my own guilt. Mrs. Fezziwig had once been like a mother to me, and I had shamefully prepared to offer her nothing more than my condolences. For once, I was ashamed of the tight-fistedness that had built my career.

With Adelaide by my side, I stood at the bottom of the stone steps leading up to Fezziwig's wide-open front door. An iron dread suffocated me, pressed on my lungs and heart. Taking a deep breath, I checked my nerves by holding my trembling black-gloved hand out, steadying it, and gripping my cane tighter than necessary.

"Please, sir," came a hoarse voice, and I felt a tugging at my jacket. I turned to see a filthy wretch of a woman. Her hair was matted like flocks of wool, poking from underneath a ragged mourning veil. She lifted her syphilitic eyes, deep set and dark from want, squinting through a film of tears so thick she looked almost demoniacal. The skin on her face was blotched from crying and grey with cold and lack of nutrition. But she seemed to have forgotten to be shameful about her appearance as she beseeched me.

"Please, sir, are you visiting Mrs. Fezziwig? Are you, sir? They're only admitting close friends and family, they say. Ain't lettin' none of us lot in, close as we were to dear Fezziwig . . ." The beggar woman's voice cracked and she pressed her lips together. Blinking tears away, she continued. "Would you give this to her, sir? To Mrs. Fezziwig?"

She handed me a silk kerchief, a delicate thing adorned with a tiny embroidered partridge in one corner. "S'all I 'ave, sir, me mother gave it to me. I want Mrs. Fezziwig to 'ave it, can't give her nothin' more."

My hand went to my purse—there was some coin left, but I had not attended business since Sunday and my money was dwindling. Still, if this miserable woman was to gift her only possession of value . . . I reluctantly resolved to give Mrs. Fezziwig two pounds towards the funeral.

"Will you pass it to 'er, sir? She'll know me name, it's Rosie, and tell her Fezziwig was a good man, a very good man, will you, sir?"

I took a deep breath, but just as I was about to turn away from the wretched woman, Adelaide squeezed my arm, leaned forward, and kissed the woman on the cheek.

"Of course, we will, Rosie," she said, her voice as soothing and safe as warm milk. "Fezziwig was a good man, indeed, and Mrs. Fezziwig shall be so comforted by your kind thought."

When Adelaide had carefully folded the kerchief and tucked it safely away to the comfort of the weeping beggar woman, we ascended the steps, rising above the crowd of grieving paupers. I felt Adelaide tense beside me. Was Fezziwig waiting for us inside? His decaying body, would it be standing there, pointing at us with its black fingernails, demanding a resolution to this gruesome mystery?

I tapped the head of my cane against the open door, and a man appeared in the doorway.

"Bless you, Ebenezer," he said, shaking my hand. "Thank you for coming. And thank *you*, miss. Please, do come in."

My heart lifted when I saw that it was Dick Wilkins, a former friend who had studied alongside me in the days I apprenticed with Fezziwig. A good man, his face betrayed sorrow and anguish, but his manner demonstrated none of his own pain, simply compassion for mine. He took my hat and Adelaide's cape, and led us into the main drawing room where a number of visitors loitered round the table of refreshments.

"Mrs. Fezziwig asked me to attend to the visitors," Dick said. "She is simply too weak. Terrible business, Ebenezer. What do you suppose could have driven a man to do such a thing?"

He went to a waste-paper basket and retrieved a crumpled newspaper. "Look what was delivered to poor

Mrs. Fezziwig this morning." He smoothed out the front page and thrust it at me. "Have they no decency at all? Our poor friend."

The headline was no worse than those run in the late edition that boy had peddled at the pub or the pickets held up outside the police station. Thomas Guilfoyle was cited as the murderer, his name printed in capitals next to a fairly accurate sketch of his face. I tried to fold it back up before Adelaide spotted "her Tom's" name, but she snatched the paper from me.

"Oh!" she exclaimed. Her eyes welled up, and with a sudden flourish, she screwed up the paper and tossed it back in the wastebasket.

"Quite," mumbled Dick, his voice somber and his eyes deep with sympathy. "The press has no shame. Well, at least they didn't get wind of what happened to poor Arthur."

"Arthur?"

"Arthur Greville. First, his mother passes, then some ruffian had him tied up in his own home for days for heaven knows only what purpose as he came and went. Suddenly, wonder of wonders, the man freed him and fled. At least Arthur is well, though we live in mad times."

I nodded. The moment Fezziwig's ghost had appeared and Crabapple had come to take me, I had let slip my vow to set the constables on Greville's impersonator if I did not receive a visit from the true article, who I hoped would come by to reward me for saving him.

So much for gratitude.

Dick shook his head. "Do excuse me, but please, make yourselves at home."

My friend bowed and turned to receive another visitor, and I glanced at Adelaide. Her chin was wobbling and she was biting her lip so hard it had turned white. Her eyes were fixed on the crumpled newspaper in the waste-paper basket. I knew she had seen the police statement next to the portrait of the "Humbug Killer," promising justice and a speedy hanging. She took a deep breath and pulled herself up, but her anguish was palpable. I reached out and gave her shoulder the slightest pat.

"Thank you," she whispered, her big emerald eyes locked on to mine.

"Yes, well," I began, when a thunderous voice interrupted.

"Ebenezer Scrooge!" it boomed.

It was Pickwick. I sighed.

"Shocking, shocking!" he wheezed when he had pushed past the mingling mourners and stood before me like a rosy-cheeked golem. "What a shock for us all. But why didn't you say last night? To think, there I stood, harping on about this and t'other, and all along . . . but where's Boz?"

"Dickens is on to another story by now, I'm sure," I said. "Besides, I hardly think the press would be welcome here, all things considered."

"Quite right!" he roared. "But what luck they caught the monster red-handed, eh! Word has it you nabbed the man yourself!" He slapped me on the back, and I felt the welt spreading. "I'm quite the detective, too, you know. Why, when I was in India . . ."

"India?" said Adelaide suddenly. She had seen my

growing frustration, linked arms with Pickwick, and began leading him away. "Why, you must tell me all about India!" She turned and nodded towards the corner of the room. I followed her gaze, and there, at the far end of the room, his head barely visible over the sea of black hats and veils, was Lord Rutledge. She walked off with a very happy Pickwick, listening and nodding to his verbose tales.

I moved through the crowded room towards him, and as I approached, I noticed with confusion that he was rummaging through a rolltop commode. His fingers were quickly flicking through papers, darting about the little drawers, opening and closing them as if he were conducting some strange symphony. Whatever he was searching for remained hidden, and his desperation was growing.

"Good morning," I said politely.

"Nothing!" He slammed down the lid of the rolltop and winced as it caught his finger. His eyes darted round the room for a split second, then rested on mine, and his face softened into a smile. "I'm glad to see you, Scrooge," he said. "In fact you found me at a most coincidental time, for I had just placed an envelope on the surface of this desk and momentarily lost it amongst the papers, but have now retrieved it."

He was lying, of course. He had not retrieved a thing before he slammed his own finger in the lid. Sunderland believed Fezziwig knew some secret of his . . . did Rutledge share that belief?

It seemed that Adelaide's instincts about this fop were dead on.

"Rutledge, the more I think of you, the less I think of you," I said jovially.

"Pardon?" he asked, not really listening. As I'd expected.

"What was your connection to Fezziwig?" I asked bluntly, raising my voice and speaking slowly and clearly.

He leaned in conspiratorially. "There wasn't one, really. Not as such. My father, you see, he served with Fezziwig during the war. Owed Mr. Fezziwig his life. It was a debt of honor my father never had the chance to repay, and so along with his estate and holdings, it was a debt I also inherited. Not that I saw it as such. I introduced Fezziwig to the shawl wool traders of the Punjab for an important partnership. I have quietly funneled funds to Mr. Fezziwig's accounts over the years when his business was ailing. But that hardly seemed payment enough. When I received his urgent summons, there was no question of attending in person."

"What happened to that summons? I would like to see it."

"Lost," Rutledge said, one finger absently tracing the monogram on his opposite glove. "Try as I might to find it."

"And you truly never met Sunderland, Shen, or Miss Pearl before?"

"Oddly, no," he mused. But a muscle twitched at the corner of his eye and his body tensed when he said it. "But from what I read in the papers, it seemed you knew Sunderland quite well!"

"You can't believe everything you read in the newspapers," I assured him. "Often they don't know the half of it!"

Beaming with smiles that didn't quite reach his eyes, Lord Rutledge searched his breast pocket and pulled out a cream envelope, a thick red company seal firmly pressed onto the flap. He did not extend it to me, just held it tight.

"Listen, Scrooge," he said, his voice lowered. "Some friends of mine are throwing a party tomorrow night, a seasonal thing, you know. At Lord Dyer's place. I'm sure you know it."

I didn't. I was not one of the fortunate few who would ever step foot in such circles. "Splendid."

"A number of high-profile politicians, of course, other personalities of worth, you know, investors . . . Quite the opportunity for someone seeking to, eh, further their business acquaintances." He gave me a look from under a darkened brow, and I nodded. Then he smiled and handed me the envelope. I turned it over. *Ebenezer Scrooge* in stunning calligraphy already decorated the front.

"Why?"

"It's terrible business all this, such a shame the likes of you and I have been dragged into this mess. Such a shame. Feel a sort of solidarity, I suppose. We can all do with a celebration, I think. In fact, bring your, uhm . . ." He nodded towards Adelaide, who was listening intently to something Pickwick was laughing about too loudly for a wake, at the other side of the room. "Your, eh, your . . ."

"Miss Owen. You've clearly forgotten her name."

"Yes, yes, Miss Owen. Precisely. And mind you bring the invitation; security will be fairly tight, of course. You know how savage the riff-raff get so close to Christmas, hah!"

"Indeed," I said, and a painful twinge nudged my conscience as I thought about the grieving riff-raff outside, carrying their humble possessions to give to the widow of a man they had loved.

Rutledge strode off, giving a matronly woman just the curtest condolence before swooping past Dick at the door and vanishing into the frosty morning.

It was Mrs. Fezziwig! My heart leaped when I saw the woman. She spotted me, and her eyes lit up, she opened her arms, and I rushed to her. She enveloped me in an embrace as she allowed herself to weep into my chest. I patted the back of her head, feeling her soft curls bounce under her black veil. The familiar smell of her talcum powder warmed my heart.

"I'm so sorry, Jane," I whispered, my lip shaking and my breaths short and pained. Sorrow burned in the back of my throat like acid, so I straightened my back and cleared my throat.

Mrs. Fezziwig blew her nose on a handkerchief, which she tucked up her sleeve. "Oh, you foolish boy," she soothed, and I realized with humiliation that my eyes were wet and red. I cleared my throat again. "Old Mr. Fezziwig would not have you in such a state!"

I mumbled something, but as I was about to protest that I was most calm indeed, my heart stopped. A figure was drifting through the room wearing a dark shroud. I felt my breath shortening, the blood draining from my face. Were those thin, bony fingers stretched out before it, feeling their way through the deathly atmosphere? My body became lead. My mouth was dry and I couldn't swallow. Could this be yet another cruel spectral trick? Could it be the Humbug Killer?!

A glass smashed somewhere behind me, and the figure turned, revealing its face. I evaporated into relief. The figure was no Humbug Killer at all, but Dora Fezziwig, my friend's oldest daughter, her shoulders hunched under her grief and her black veil falling about her face like Death's own shroud. I pressed my eyes closed and felt the hot redness burst like stars in my mind. I was exhausted.

The pressing matter at hand shot back into my consciousness.

"Jane," I said. "There were four summonses sent by Mr. Fezziwig that night. Do you know what they contained?"

"No, dear," she answered. "Reginald minds his own business these days. I barely know what he sells. *Sold*, of course." Once again her face twisted into sadness.

"What of George Sunderland? Was there some spark of friendship between him and Reginald? Were they in business?"

"Oh, that poor man who drowned. No, not so far as I am aware. I can't say I recall Reginald ever mentioning him."

"Jane, do you know of anyone who might have wanted Reginald . . ."

"Dead? No, as I said to the police, I can't imagine why Guilfoyle wished him harm."

"Guilfoyle, yes. Or anyone else for that matter?"

"No, Ebenezer. No more questions now. I read Mr. Dickens' account of Mr. Fezziwig, and your kind, kind words about him. How we all cherish his memory; all that is left to us now. Come and let's toast to Reggie, my husband . . ." She fell into sobs, and I pulled her back to my chest.

"He was most ardently admired by many influential people," I tried, but it sent her into more tears.

"Oh, they *admire* him certainly," she cried, her eyes and nose streaming. "But his friends, the people outside, the ones he helped, they *love* him!"

"Although you can't see their faces," came the soft voice of Adelaide, "their hearts can still reach yours." She was standing next to me, unfolding the silk kerchief she had accepted from the beggar woman, which she handed to Mrs. Fezziwig. My friend's widow took it and beamed. She glanced between us, her tear-stained cheeks bulbous in smile.

"It's from Rosie," Adelaide continued. "She wished me to pass on the message that your husband was a good man. There are scores out there who have come to offer their warmth."

"Oh, thank you, thank you so very much, Miss . . . ?"

Adelaide held out her hand. "Owen. Miss Adelaide Owen. Oh!" She was suddenly startled, and as I followed her gaze back to Mrs. Fezziwig, it became clear why.

The widow's face was white, set in an expression of fury and thunder, nostrils flared and lips pursed. "Well! Adelaide Owen indeed!" she snapped.

Then I saw a blur as her arm swung and her open

palm smacked me across the face. The pain burst into stars behind my eyes and acute heat spread over my cheek. My ears were ringing. Adelaide moved to calm the woman, but Mrs. Fezziwig pushed her away.

"How *dare* you come here with this trollop?" she shouted, shaking. The visitors all hushed and turned to me and Adelaide. "She is campaigning for the monster who killed my Reggie!"

The crowd took a collective gasp, and Adelaide held her hands out.

"No, no," she implored. "I assure you that's not the case at all! The evidence is damning, I know, but there is a witness, an alibi, and she can prove my Tom did not do this thing!"

"You admit it," cried Mrs. Fezziwig. "The police gave me a full report—you are seeking to free the demon who *murdered* my Reggie!" She sank to her knees, so I stooped down to help her up, but instead of taking my hand, she slapped it away.

"Get out now, Ebenezer!" she sobbed. "You have betrayed his memory! Oh, how could you mock me so, Ebenezer? I am so disappointed in you, so very hurt."

Dick rushed to her, his eyebrows raised at me as if begging for an explanation, but all I could do was shake my head. Adelaide was frozen. The sadness and grief were tangible and intense, and Adelaide stood like an iron chasm between me and the woman who had been like a mother to me. The place was heavy, hot, and aggressive so I had no choice but to take my leave with Adelaide in tow.

"I'm so sorry," she whispered to the room.

Dick cradled Mrs. Fezziwig in his lap as we made for the door and rushed outside.

"Foolish of me, so very foolish," Adelaide said when we were blocks away, the icy winds blowing snow and sleet about us as a nearby street hawker laid out his wares on a fold-up table: sloppily crafted tin soldiers and wooden toy carts. He was about to call out to us when I shot him a warning look.

"It will be fine," I promised, barely aware that I was holding Adelaide, comforting the weeping girl much as I had Mrs. Fezziwig.

"Why should anyone believe my Tom is innocent? If—if we had not seen and heard for ourselves . . . if Fezziwig's spirit had not . . ."

"No," I said forcefully. "Even without the haunting, you would never have believed him capable of this. Never. And we're going to prove it. What did you say the name was of that man who might help us squeeze Rutledge? I think it's high time I paid him a visit. . . ."

CHAPTER EIGHT

IN THE HEART of London, I found the narrow sign leading to the narrow stairs and the narrow man who was the sole employee of this minor branch of Shopshire, Shopcraft, and Shoplift, a legal office I'd had occasion to frequent. The main offices, several blocks from here, were spacious, lavishly appointed, a bit like a museum display. Ideal for wooing clients. But the true labors of legal representation took place in this and another additional office. There a dozen lawyers and their dogsbody found ways to make cases drag out as long as possible to accrue the highest legal fees imaginable. Here was the dump, a wretched place of unappreciated toil and misery. In this place, old cases came to die, and those unsound and in need of hiding were bricked up behind row after row of filing cabinets.

I found the young clerk Miss Owen had told me about buried within an alcove brimming with precariously balanced, madly stacked packets of files and letters. Papers were piled from floor to ceiling behind him, beside him, before him. He'd carved something of a snaking path through the paperwork to one side of him, and burrowed out a kind of teller's window before him. He scratched away, pausing only to dip his quill in a bottle of heavy liquid, his ink-blackened fingertips moving in a blur. His hair was ink-black, as were his trousers and vest. He was, head to toe, as neatly polished as his shoes.

That was how I found Billy Humble.

When he spoke, it was with the melodious voice of a born actor. "Oh, joy. Oh, misery. How you walk hand in hand in your cruel, wicked way. Beside me ever you travel. An imp. A gimp! One leg bold, one leg twisted. Oh, would that I had but a window. Would that I had the torturous means to see that there is a life outside the towers—the incendiary towers of toil—oh, but for a flame, a light of righteousness, of truth. Just a flicker, perhaps, to know that Christmas is upon us! What yuletide joy for me? Forever in faith I am, faith and belief, and what does it get me? It gets me fresh stacks of misery and pain to keep me shackled here forever. But there is a light. There is joy. I know her touch. I know her scent. Elsewhere, elsewhere . . . elsewhere."

I cleared my throat. He leaped, knocked over a tower of haphazardly piled papers, shrieked, squealed, squeaked. He set to all fours, piling it up again. I sighed. "Really, sir, I do not fancy speaking to your derriere."

"Oh, no sir, no, of course," he said, leaping nimbly to his feet. The clerk smiled, bowed, greeted me with a flourish, one hand fisted behind his back, the other making a motion I had made many times when I meant to convey "get on with it." But I knew it was his best attempt at formality and respect. "How may I assist you, sir? I'm sorry to say my master is not present. He infrequents this place, you see. I am left like a prisoner, my chains are papyrus and India ink. This is what is referred to as a secondary office. A morgue. A repository of miserable endless toil."

"Then we are completely alone?" I asked.

"Order, sir, a point of pride," the clerk went on. "Deceptive it is. Looks like a mad mess, it does. That's the trick of it. Things aren't always what they look like, are they? Ah, but this miserable place. Some days I fear I will see nothing but this. The rest of my miserable, sure to be short-lived existence will play out here. But to you, sir, a merry Christmas! Very, very merry!"

Miss Owen warned me that Mr. Humble took a bit of getting used to. Had this poor sod gone mad in this place?

"The horror of it is I have pals, see. They have my look, my height, my competence," said young, narrow Billy. "Why, if I had the money I could pay them to take my place here a few days a week. That I might see sunlight. That I might know love. I have a girl, you see. I yearn! I ache! I waste away! Oh, to have time to spend. But time is a precious coin. To spend with my Dolly. Dolly Dally, we say, jokingly, for there is nothing I'd rather do than dally with my Dolly. Oh, sir, have you ever felt such longing, and been so thwarted?"

"Mr. Humble, if I may—"

"But poverty is the other chain binding me here. Oh, forgive, sir. And I pray, keep this between us. I see so very few other souls that when I do, I run at the mouth, I do. I—you know my name?"

"Indeed. And what you've said is a pity, for I was hoping to find one in your position who could be counted on for discretion. Quietude. At least about certain delicate matters. For that discretion, I would and could pay handsomely. Enough to have you rid of this place for weeks or more. But perhaps I've come to the wrong man . . ." I turned, as if to take my leave.

"No, no, no!" he cried. "No! I could be all those things, sir. I was just, ah, surprised. At the company. At *any* company. But yours is an august company, I would take from your appearance. A fine gentleman, honored and true. Pray, how might I be of assistance?"

I told him that I wanted to see certain documents pertaining to his client Lord Rutledge and proposed a hearty sum.

"Gracious, sir. Bless you, sir. Yes, sir!"

"And you would be bound by an oath of silence?"

"Yes, sir! By the lady of goodness and the mother of mercy, yes! What is it you would seek to know about his lordship?"

I smiled. "Nothing less than everything at all."

I arrived early at my offices and was surprised to find the front door unlocked. A stab of cold reached between my shoulder blades as I clutched the door handle and thought of Roger Colley, Baldworthy, and the man with the claret mark on his face, all three still at large. Would they be waiting for me within?

Instead, I was treated to an astonishing sight. Miss

Owen had taken down and laid out a series of ledgers and assorted documents which she had set before a certain Mr. Benjamin Bungily. Bungily had been a nuisance of high ranking lately. He'd come to me seeking financing for a mad venture, but his capital was all too enticing for me to turn down. He was what many would call a remittance man, a Frenchman whose wealthy family paid him a generous allowance simply to reside far enough away that his "exploits" would not reach the ears of anyone who might be embarrassed by his dalliances. But when his venture failed, I'd been unable to track the sod down. It seemed he lived with a series of friends and accomplices and was always on the move—as were they. I'd promised Humperdink and his cronies a fair commission if they tracked down the wretch and brought him to me.

And now—here he was, and Miss Owen had somehow reduced the man to tears.

"Here, here, take this," the Frenchman said, yanking off one expensive cufflink, then its mate. His rings followed, then an expensive set of chains he wore about his neck. When he had divested himself of a silk tie and tie clip and was on the brink of abandoning modesty altogether to deliver literally the shirt from his back, he saw me and thought better of it. The man flung himself at my feet, took my hand, and showered it with kisses. I drew back as he gestured at Miss Owen and blubbered, "This one, she is an angel of mercy, she saves me, saves me from my sins. Mr. Scrooge, I will be back, yes, I will, you have not the doubt, I beg of you, return I shall, au revoir!"

He flung himself to his feet and ran for the door.

"How in the deuce did you manage that?" I asked, as the front door slammed behind the Frenchman.

"I said that I would help you with your rail scheme, Mr. Scrooge," she said brightly. "How better, or more reliably, to infuse your concern with fresh capital than to call in some of your more egregious debts?"

"You didn't answer my question," I said.

"So I didn't," she agreed. "But as you might have gathered from your meeting with Mr. Humble, I have made the acquaintances of many colorful characters in my day. One knows another who knows another and very quickly, when tracking down a known rogue like Bungily—voilà! And don't think I've forgotten my vow to find you more well-monied investors. That, too, is in the works."

"But, but—he paid! How did you get him—"

"There is value in secrets, I find. Now, before our next visitor arrives, here is all I have learned about this 'Chimera': but I warn you, it isn't much."

The dossier Miss Owen had prepared informed me of the mythical Greek creature associated with the name: part male, part female. A single beast with attributes taken from a lion, a snake, and a goat that breathed fire.

"As you see, I have cross-referenced any mention I could find of criminal enterprises composed of three elements, such as the Asian Triad; interesting considering the pedigree of one of our suspects. Beyond this, I cannot shine much light on why that word seems to carry so much weight in underworld circles. Perhaps it refers to a person, a place . . . perhaps it is a key that opens locks, like that ring my Tom somehow acquired. But we'll get to the truth. We have to."

"And Sunderland? Have you uncovered any ties to Fezziwig?"

"None. I can see no way that their circles overlapped."

"This Piermont and Piermont Acquisitions that employed Mr. Guilfoyle. Was it owned by Sunderland or one of his affiliates? There *has* to be a connection."

Adelaide shook her head. "I'll keep digging, but I warn you, there seems to be precious little to find."

Scowling with frustration, I asked, "How did you get in here, anyway? I didn't give you a key, and I'm certain the place was locked tight as a drum when I left."

Miss Owen's smile widened. Pride crept into her eyes. "That may be your curse, Mr. Scrooge. Always underestimating people."

"Infuriating woman."

"Well, at least I have your attention."

I walked over to the desk where she had splayed open my ledgers. I had told her to stay hidden, and she had done anything but. Despite my annoyance, however, I was intrigued. "Miss Owen, you have the mind for this work, of that there is no doubt. But do you have the stomach? I am attempting to grow my business more in the direction of investment banking, yes, but I have a long road ahead of me before that is my sole focus. Until then, this is a counting-house, and I am a moneylender. This work is not for anyone. It can, in fact, be grim indeed."

Miss Owen sat before the table and flipped through my accounts. "Mr. Scrooge, I have spent my years dealing with what is, not what may be. These are numbers in ledgers. Signatures of agreement. Balances. Imbalances. They do not have thoughts. They do not have feelings. I deal with them as such. As to the misery often laid at the doorstep of counting-houses like this one, I say, I see no evidence of deceptive or unfair business practices here. You do not engineer the miserable state of affairs these people find themselves in. You do not force or entice anyone to knock on your door. Every possible term and contingency is addressed in your contracts. You ensure that your clients read them, do you not?"

"Aloud," I added.

"Well, then. However would I be shocked?"

"There are nightly collections. It is not always a pleasant experience."

"I should wager not. But fair is fair. One owes what one owes, and payment must be made, in one form or another."

I smirked. "Then you would not find it disagreeable to seek out a moneylender in a time of trouble?"

"I would sooner leap in the Thames."

I choked on what I was about to say next and returned to my labors.

"Wait," Adelaide said. "This is interesting."

I went to her. She pointed at an entry as if all would instantly become clear to me. It did not. The names were not familiar. There had been so many through my doors.

"Ezra Scrimp and Cyril Shillet," Miss Owen said, beaming. "Tom knew an Ezra Scrimp. We laughed together over the name."

I nodded. Yes, I remembered now. I had privately mused that if Mr. Scrimp had lived up to his name a bit more where his spending was concerned, he wouldn't have found himself in such a bind. "I remember him very well. He also used to call me 'the hog grubber' and never by my name. Fine by me if clients want to see me as a mean, stingy fellow. Certainly they should never see me as their friend!"

"Little chance of that, I think," Adelaide said melodically, her smile unfaltering.

"Perhaps that solves the mystery of why my face was familiar to your Mr. Guilfoyle. He probably saw me trying to get my money out of his friends. But I don't see—"

"Tom is a gambler. He won something of great significance from this Mr. Scrimp. In fact, it is listed here, among his assets. Do you see?"

I ran my finger down the entries until I came to the item she meant. A ring identical to the one found on Fezziwig's finger. And the one Roger Colley wore.

"Look at this address he gave you," Miss Owen continued. "The one for his solicitor, should he die before his debt is paid."

"What of it?"

"It's a warehouse district. No one lives there, let alone has law offices there."

I sighed. Yes, it was an early arrangement, when I was eager to sign any client. My error had proven quite the embarrassment. Yet there was a darker turn to it. "Scrimp and Shillet are dead, I'm afraid. Fished from the Thames. We'll gain no information from them unless you number 'medium' among your many talents."

"I still don't see—"

Adelaide flicked a finger across my skull and stabbed at the journal again.

I read aloud the address above her finger. "King's Head Lane. What of it?"

"Don't you understand? 'King's Head? *The Royal Quarter*! This is what Tom was on about earlier. This is where we find Smithson and perhaps get to the bottom of this."

"That ring was the last of Fezziwig. You saw that, didn't you? As he crumpled, it remained. The Quarter is at the heart of this. It must be."

"So it's where we start!"

I nodded, then thought it over. "No," I declared at last. "It is not."

"But why? It must be investigated. And if this is a place where all manner of sin may be sated, would it not be the logical place to seek Miss Annie Piper, the prostitute?"

"It will *all* be investigated. But not by you. I will question Dickens about the place and go there with him. It sounds like the ideal place for that rake Roger Colley to be hiding, and if I am correct, I will not see you subjected to his tender handling."

"But this Annie woman, her friend Irene said she'd gained a great deal of interest. The Royal Quarter—"

"What part of 'no' is challenging that brain of yours?"

Miss Owen drew in a deep breath, centered herself, and smiled pleasantly. Her words, however, did not match her calm and lovely demeanor. "I saw Sunderland's man murdered. I have, as Constable Crabapple deduced, seen my fair share of wretchedness, sickness, and even death in my time. I am no delicate flower for you to protect."

"But you are my employee, are you not?" I asked.

Shuddering, her smile firmly in place, she said, "I am."

"Then," I said, rising and reaching for my coat, "do what you are told and stay here!"

CHAPTER NINE

I WAITED UNTIL dusk before braving the so-called Royal Quarter. With Dickens at my side, I traversed the ankle-deep gum of rotting straw and sewage covering the slippery cobbled streets. We hurried through the warren of damp brickwork until we arrived at King's Hill Road. From there it was no more than a few hundred sodden steps through the polluted slush, a few turns down God-forsaken alleyways, before we emerged into a square surrounded by warehouses. No, they might have been called by such an innocuous term by day, but as the last crescent of dull December sunlight vanished behind the grimy edge of London, the warehouses transformed. Red lights flicked on in windows, the hollow bass of music erupted from somewhere and was carried on the icy wind through each building. Doors clanged open and the square filled with people.

"A playground for those with money to burn," said Dickens, as we watched gentlemen shake hands with ruffians as if they were peers. "Behold, Scrooge, the Royal Quarter. From the stories I've heard over the years, this is where you'll find London's most depraved pleasure 'palaces,' each indulging in a different order of expensive sin and debauchery. The finest of opium dens. The greatest underground fight clubs and whorehouses. Each palace named after a current or past member of the royal family . . . and, yet, who knows what suffering lies at their foundations."

"It's business, Dickens," I mumbled. "London is a city of speculators, obsessed with gambling and risk. And money."

"Quite," said Dickens as he lit up a cigarette. The smoke swirled through the air and melted into the settling smog. "Not the business of humanity. This, sir, is the devil's own playground. Ask anyone if you don't believe me. . . ."

We drifted from doorway to doorway, where wretched men—dressed in fine suits, scarves, and hats—grinned to reveal missing teeth and rotting sores. They brandished walking sticks like swords.

"Peppercorn Jack they calls me," said the nearest, his breath quite possibly combustible. "Hazard a guess why? Don't strain your brain, I'll inform you presently. I'm the gent you call when you needs to spice things up!"

A man wearing the costume of an Indian swami vied for our attention. "You have a weighty aspect, my friend. A cloak of many worries, invisible to the eye, but not to mine, has been fitted upon your shoulders. Feel its weight? I can grant you blessed sleep—and such dreams! Elysium. Nirvana. Paradise. One pipe at a time."

A little man wearing a coat of many colors hopped

before us. "Ignore him! I can see you go a poppin', that's what I can do. Robin Roundabout, that's me. Oh the world poppin' with beautiful color. Bouncin' and flouncin'—"

I broke free of the lot while Dickens smirked. Another man peeled from the darkness of an alley. A young dandy. "No, no, no, sir. You have the bearing of one for whom only the best might do. Welcome to my emporium of exotic delights. Convention? Rules? Ridiculous! Cruel delight? I say nay! I have in my basement a child *with* child who is longing for your kisses."

"You disgust me!" I snarled.

The dandy took my words in stride. "I make no one do anything against their will. My girls are pampered princesses. A virgin, perhaps? Rare, but if you have the coin . . . ?"

We rushed ahead. Behind us he called, "I have twins! Triplets! *Triplets*!"

We hurried along a less-traveled street, avoiding more Haymaker Hectors, though I sensed such pimps were within reach throughout this hellish place.

Smithson resided somewhere in the Quarter, according to Dickens' "contacts." It made sense. A man of few or no morals would find the district a business bonanza, so no doubt he conducted his own dark undertakings from the depths of one of these palaces. There he could keep close watch on his enterprises and earnings. But how would we find the man? Where would we begin?

I spotted a young boy lurking within the shadows some way before us, crouching down behind an upturned barrel. He stole furtive glances at a gaggle of prostitutes laughing together outside one of the palace doors. His clothes were torn and filthy, the brown cap covering his head was a few sizes too big and kept slipping down over his eyes. He'd be in want of money, there was no doubt.

"You there, boy," I called. The boy looked up, startled, and caught my eye. His face was still bathed in shadow, and I could not make out his expression, but I guessed it was one of greed. "For a farthing, I have the name of a man: I need his location."

The boy half-stood, then froze, his brown cap sliding farther down his face.

"Well?" I pressed. "What of it? Have we a deal?" I reached my hand out to shake his, and took a couple of steps towards him, when suddenly he bolted. Weaving in and out of the heaving bodies of adulterers and gamblers, the boy vanished.

"They fright so easily," I noted.

"Even I myself find utterly petrifying your view on what can be considered a reasonable payment to a starving street urchin, Scrooge."

"If I were not so indebted to your damned charitable organizations, Dickens, I would have offered him a penny," I answered. "Put yourself to use and find Smithson."

Then Dickens nudged me and nodded towards the gilded warehouse door of one of the palaces. A man of oriental appearance, his silken black hair gleaming and reaching down beyond an impossibly tall top hat, approached the door with a woman on his arm.

"Shen Kai-Rui," I mumbled.

Dickens nodded, and added, "See the girl?"

I stared, incredulous. It was Nellie Pearl, the actress!

Shen knocked sharply at the door with the brass head of his cane, before turning to Nellie. Some soundless communication passed between the two before they grabbed each other and kissed with full abandon, hands fumbling in deep, dark places. The door opened and Shen presented his hand, the ring finger adorned with the very same type of heavy gold and ruby ring that I had seen on Fezziwig's corpse. Just as they entered, Nellie turned her face out towards the square, scanning the crowd. I frowned.

"See the scar running from her upper lip to her left cheek?" I asked Dickens.

"Nellie Pearl has no such scar," he said.

The woman—so like Nellie she could have been her twin—vanished into the building with Shen Kai-Rui. An impersonator? How odd. Yet she carried herself in the same distinctive way as Nellie did and wore a burgundy gown with gold partridge pin identical to the one Nellie usually wore in public. Even the imposter's hair, tumbling from a holly-appointed hat, was impeccably styled to resemble Nellie's lovely ringlets.

"What connection can there be between the Chinaman and this Smithson?" I asked Dickens. "This *is* Smithson's dominion, after all."

"Potentially thousands," he answered, dropping his cigarette to the ground and grinding it into the slush with the sole of his boot. "Or maybe he just prefers whores. There's a crowd of boys who might have a story to tell; let's start there. This time offer them more than a farthing."

They looked like rats and crows, plotting together, suspicious. Some were sitting on ledges of windows, others hunched over the slimy cobbles throwing hand-made dice. As we approached, the oldest of the boys, yet no older than fourteen, saw us and immediately stood up, squaring his shoulders and spinning a chain in his hand. He was followed by five or six others, while the rest maintained their positions, scowling.

We froze, but they continued to move towards us until they were flanking us like a pack of dogs. The clanking of the leader's chains sent ghostly shivers through me. One of the smaller boys behind him produced a short knife and began stabbing at the dirt. The fact that Dickens still hadn't lit up another cigarette betrayed that he too felt some nervousness.

"Lost, gentlemen?" asked the boy, his snub nose twisted in a mocking sneer. "Cor, what a jolly fine scarf you're wearing, sir. Silk, is it?" His own tatty top hat was resting on his head so lightly that I got the sense that if he had lurched forward to thrash me with the chain, the hat would not have joined him.

"Looking for Smithson," I said. "I'll make it worth your time."

The moment I mentioned Smithson's name the young scavengers and predators exchanged wary looks.

"And what is it you wanna know about Mr. Smifson, sir?" asked the lad in the top hat.

Dickens brushed by me, subtlety signaling me to let him do the talking. "We've been told he's the man to see if you want one of those pretty rings . . . and the delights that come with them."

A greedy grin etched itself upon the lad's grubby face. "'Ow do we know you ain't the filth?"

"Because we have money to spend tonight," I said. "And much more where that came from. You have a sense of that, I'm sure, as you haven't tried to part us from our gold. A long-term investment is how you're seeing us. Tell me if I'm wrong."

"Well, why didn't you say?" The leader laughed. "Always keen to aid a 'spectable gentleman, so we are! The name's Mr. Dawkins, but my chaps here call me the *Artful* Dodger, on account of my bein' an *artist*, you see."

The boys all laughed.

"And as you see, sir," the Artful Dodger continued. "As I'm sure you've noticed, I'm one of the very finest of Englishmen, just the very sort of business acquaintance you're looking for. Let me show you around. Come on, come on, don't dally!"

He and his mates suddenly transformed into cheery tour guides. The boy beamed and tucked his chain in his back pocket, the smaller boys towards the back hopped up and surged forward, all keen to get a look at us and to ask for change.

"Now just so you know," said the Dodger, "Mr. Smifson, then, he ain't no social butterfly. More like a spider in his web."

"Yeah, you see him, it's 'cause you're not long for this world," added one of his boys.

"Tell you what, let's find out what's your fancy, then we might set you up wiv a prince or a duke of the 'ouse. Cor, you might even get to see a king. But Smifson—"

"Why should we trust that you know anything?" Dickens asked.

Taking that as a challenge, the lads took turns introducing us to the various vice pits in the quarter, each in exchange for their own farthing until I felt, with grudging annoyance, my purse becoming quite light.

Hopping from building to building, climbing drainpipes, and scaling slatted roofs, they pointed out the gin houses, the opium dens, whorehouses, and fight pits. I could hear the scratching of Dickens' pen as we hurried along underneath them, struggling to keep up.

"This 'ere palace," said Dodger, pointing at a building as we passed, "is known as The Eighth, on account of Henry, of course, with all his wives. Eat like a proper fat man in there, you can, succulent foods they say, no 'bags o' mystery' sausages here, no sir! And all the bare-breasted maids you can fink of! And this one we call De Quincey's on account of a certain tome he wrote, you see, literary gentlemen as you surely are . . ."

"*Confessions of an English Opium Eater*," Dickens supplied.

"Right you are, guv!" Dodger knocked twice on a side door attached to the wooden building. Just as he reached for the handle, it swung open.

"Humperdink!" I exclaimed.

The fat constable stood at the doorway, gaping. His face was red, his eyes glassy.

"Just making inquiries, Mr. Scrooge," he offered, glancing between me and Dickens with a terrified look. "Better be on me way, nothing to report." He waddled off in haste, glancing back once before he vanished round a corner.

Then a plump maid in her fifties appeared in the doorway, saw Dodger, and beamed.

"I've saved you some scones, Dodger!" She pulled a small bundle out of her apron pocket, something warm that smelled of Christmas spices was wrapped in a napkin.

"Not right now, Princess!" exclaimed Dodger, pushing past the maid and beckoning us to follow. Dickens and I both squeezed past her, nodding politely as we brushed against her bosom. "I'm takin' these gentlemen to see the *Lycia*!"

"Ooh, Dodger, I don't think that's a good idea," urged the maid, scurrying along behind us as Dodger, Dickens, the boys, and I moved into a large, open room veiled behind a fog of sweet-smelling smoke. "I don't think Fagin—"

"Never mind Fagin, Princess, never you mind nuffin'!" sang Dodger happily. "You jus' leave business to us businessmen. These gentlemen are lookin' for the very best!"

The room was dark, with oil lamps veiled by colored shades casting ghostly shapes on the walls. Large oak beds were lined against the walls, their pale-faced occupants lying about each other on their sides. They limply sucked on tubes while exhaling thick rolls of smoke, muttering unintelligible imaginings as they did. One man sat up suddenly and laughed into the heavy air.

"Well!" I exclaimed when I recognized the haggard face. "If it isn't Greville himself! Or should I call you

Jasper? It seems neither our rail deal nor your choirboys are on your mind at present."

The maid rushed to his side, kindling a new pipe by blowing into it with short, quick breaths. "Have another, Mr. Jasper, here."

"Come on, then," called Dodger from a doorway. I left Jasper to his opium-induced stupor, but not before Dickens had completed a rudimentary sketch of the abysmal scene.

"Hold," I said, noting the gold and ruby ring on the fingers of Jasper and all the rest of Princess Puffer's "clients." I turned to the woman. "Do you know a man named Thomas Guilfoyle?"

She shrugged. "Can't say that I do. But it ain't all of my clientele what are so wholesome and honest as Mr. Jasper. Some don't even give their true names, if you could believe such a thing!"

I described Guilfoyle, said he might have been in the company of a certain Miss Annie Piper, and attempted to ply her with coin, but she refused my overture.

"Ain't that the gent they say killed that nice old fella in Spitalfields? Humbug they call him, yeah? Well, to be fair, I don't know you, sir. Perhaps if you'd sample my wares . . . ?"

"Another time," I said, and left it.

Dodger led us down a narrow corridor and out a back door, which opened into a dark court. The only light was streaming from a crack in the shutters of a building opposite.

"What's this, Dodger?" I demanded. "What are you playing at, bringing us here?"

"This, gentlemen," said Dodger, his teenage chest puffed out with pride. "This is *Lycia*!"

It was a tall, dark loading shed with a crane protruding from an upper window, and its windows were boarded up. The stream of light from behind the shutters betrayed life inside. I wrinkled my nose. A waft of some acrid stench drifted down, but it was faint, and I couldn't put my finger on its origin. Chemicals, I believed. But what kind, and why?

"What's Lycia?" I asked Dodger. "That building?"

"Don't know nuffin' about that building, sir!" said the boy unexpectedly loudly, with a broad grin and with a sudden twitch of his head to right the slipping top hat. Then he lowered his voice to a whisper. "But there's rumors, sir, not that I've 'eard any of 'em, that there's somefing new coming to the Quarter, snuggled away right 'ere, in this secret palace they call Lycia." He held his hand out, and I winced as I fished another coin out of my purse. "Remember this place when you return, sir," he continued, stuffing the coin in his pocket, "and mind you drop Princess Puffer there one of them pennies, too; she don't like her boudoir being used as no thoroughfare."

As the boys led us back through De Quincey's, where Princess Puffer was attempting to stoke life into her guests, I felt a ripple of unease. Whatever that building was that her opium den was being used to conceal, the strange smell and unusual description Dodger had provided left me with a sense of dread. Whatever Dickens was scratching in his notepad was undoubtedly of similar aura, for his face was dark.

"Now that building there," the boy said after we'd

circled back to where Shen had gone with the Nellie imposter, "that's the Doll House."

"A lock that those rings open," Dickens ventured. "Tell me, lads, does the name Thomas Guilfoyle mean anything to you?"

A sea of blank stares.

I went on to describe Guilfoyle, but to no avail.

"What about George Sunderland?" I asked. "Striking black whiskers, twice as wide as Father Christmas. Fancy dress. Or the Colley Brothers? Do they frequent—"

Dodger rattled his chains. "It's best not to be askin' such questions, sir. Healfiest by far to see to your own welfare and leave it as that. 'Spectable gentleman have needs, and the Doll House here is for it."

"A common whorehouse?" I asked.

"Cor blimey! I ain't never 'eard nuffin' so contrary! Ain't nuffin' common about that place. Seen any plays lately, sirs? Seen *Lady of Shalott*?"

"I haven't yet had the misfortune," I mumbled.

"Wrote a stellar review on it last week," said Dickens.

"You dream it up, any woman you could possibly want, you'll find her there."

"Or at least a woman who looks just like her," Dickens suggested.

"Just the way, just the way," boasted the boy about the palace Shen and the fake Nellie had vanished into. "Whores clad just like famous ladies of this or other times? Almost as delightful as Princess Puffer's scones. But nuffin' compared to what's coming. Somefing new, sir, not like nuffin' you've seen, sir! A thrill like no other, like magic, except it's quite real!"

I dug in my pocket for another coin. But instead of dropping this one into his dirty palm, I held it up. A tuppeny bit—shiny and new. Dozens of young, eager eyes grew wide and wet with greed.

"Find me Annie Piper. She has qualities I'd like to sample. Be back here within ten minutes with her location and you shall all have one." The words almost lodged in my throat, but business was business, and the sorry state of my purse was collateral damage.

The boys all scattered like cockroaches at dawn, all but one. One boy, taller than the rest but just as slight, remained behind in the shadows. I squinted into the darkness and spotted the large brown cap sliding off the side of the boy's head. It was the same lad who had run away earlier.

"Well?" I barked at him. "I need all men on the ground. Find the whore!" The boy looked around, clearly scouting for a getaway. But just as he was about to bolt off in the opposite direction from where the other boys had gone, the cap slid forward and a rich, chocolate curl fell from the nape of his neck. In fact, the "boy"—upon closer inspection—had curves even the baggy clothes couldn't hide.

My heart stopped as my eyes locked with an all-too familiar gaze. "That's Miss Owen!"

Realization dawned and Dickens beamed a most delighted grin. He flicked open his notebook and began to sketch the sight of the woman dressed as a boy. He would be of no help to me, so I moved towards the shadows, inching my way towards Adelaide.

She could tell I'd seen through her disguise. Her eyes

rolled, she got up, stuffed her hands in her pockets, and shuffled over to me, kicking pebbles.

"What by God's name are you doing here?" I hissed, grabbing her arms and giving her the slightest shake. She was unfazed.

"Looking for the prostitute of course!" she said. I released her, and she brushed off the enormous blue man's jacket she must have acquired from some charity shop.

"Of course," answered Dickens, still scribbling in that dratted notebook. "Makes perfect sense! She thought we were only interested in Smithson and would let the Annie Piper lead falter, so she came here to do something about it herself."

"Can you conceive of how dangerous your behavior is?" I asked. "That Shelley woman has put mad and dangerous ideas in your head."

"Don't be so soft," she trilled. "Women and children own these streets. Look around you! You're in the minority here, Scrooge. Ah, Mr. Dickens! I do beg your pardon, how very lovely to see you again. How do you do, sir?"

"Very well, thank you," answered my companion, removing a newly lit cigarette from his mouth just long enough to kiss her hand.

"You don't belong here," I interrupted. I spun Adelaide around so she was facing the square. Prostitutes cackled some way away. Vile hawkers pimped their disgusting services. A door opened, spilling light and music into the square, and a drunkard was thrown out, landing on his back with a sickening crunch. "These are not savory people."

But Adelaide turned back to me, her beautiful green eyes flaming under a tightly knotted brow. "I don't think you can know much about what is savory and what's not, Scrooge," she chided. "I have seen the world from both extremes; you will not educate me."

"Enough! You will leave this place immediately, or—"

"Or what?" came a voice, thin and chilling. I turned.

Before me stood an enraged man well past the prime of his years but not yet decrepit. His little eyes flashed and darted between me, Dickens, and Adelaide. His matted hair, of which there was a vast quantity, was as red as his pointed beard, and poking out from under his flat hat. His mouth was twisted into a villainous sneer.

The boys had all returned, but they were standing some way away, some of them sporting bloody noses and swollen lips. Dodger stood directly behind the man, a welt spreading across his eye and cheek.

"Is this gentleman bothering you, my dear?" the man asked. He unbuckled his belt, stripped it out of his trousers with a flourish, and wrapped it around his hand. "Bothering a nice young lad who might want to learn about the opportunities offered in joining my enterprise?" Adelaide's disguise had fooled him.

"That's gonna earn someone a batty-fang, it is!" He cracked the belt against the cold cobbles to underline his promise of a thorough thrashing. It rang out a sickening thwack and sprayed slush on my trousers. Adelaide backed away from him until she was pressed up against me. I could feel her warmth despite the chill. With one arm I swept her behind me and stepped forward. The man was grinning wildly.

"Easy now, Fagin," muttered Dodger. "Don't go gettin' yourself tangled up in noffin' serious, now. We needs you, Fagin. We needs our leader, can't have you taken off for the 'ang."

Fagin spun around and clocked Dodger in the face with the back of his hand, then immediately turned to face us again.

"Enough from you, Dodger, my dear," he said with a smirk, his eyes studying mine. "Giving strangers a tour of our world, telling our secrets, all without asking your master first. What if this man is a copper? Are you a copper, sir?"

Just as Fagin raised his arm above his head, Dodger reached up, grabbing the other end of the belt and yanking it. The man lost his balance, lost his belt. Quick as a flash, Dodger whipped the belt through the air like a lasso, and I caught the buckle end of it.

"Enough," I said, yanking the belt from the lad. I tossed it away. "You've saved Mr. Fagin here from making a terrible blunder. If he's wise, he'll thank you."

"Thank him for what?" Fagin demanded.

"Wotcher, Fagin," said Dodger. "These gentlemen are ever so wealfy! We've just been offering a service, just like you taught us, Fagin. Nuffin' more."

"Is that so?" said Fagin, his face twisting into a sickly grin. He climbed to his feet. "Well, then that changes the situation! That's a fine thing, a good thing, it's what we're here for, yes, we provide services. And coppers, no, they are not so quick to part with coin, not at all, so these 'uns, they're in the clear. But mind now, gentlemen, my dears, you had better be safe!" He put his hands together in prayer, like he was begging us, and his face was set in a sniveling humility that divulged no substance. "Pay my boys handsomely for their fine service, but pray, don't ask questions now. Don't ask about no Smithson, and you can have any girl you want, any at all."

"Splendid!" shouted Dickens, and slapped the old man amicably on the back. "We want Annie Piper. I'll have my assistant here pay your men presently. Well? Pay them!"

I did not share Dickens' sense of humor, so I shot him a glare as I grabbed practically the last coins in my purse and chucked them into the slush. Fagin and the boys dropped to their knees and started gathering up the cold money, not in the slightest ashamed.

"Oh, thankee, sir, thankee, yes, very good," groveled Fagin, still on his knees. "Any girl at all, except that one. Any at all!"

"We want Annie Piper," continued Dickens. "Only she will do."

"Right, yes," said Fagin, scratching his beard. "There would be considerable cost, my dears, quite a high price . . ."

"No obstacle. Arrange an audience with Piper, and my assistant here will pay you beyond anything imagined in your most colorful midnight trances."

"Lovely to hear, my dears, lovely to hear. I'll see about it, sir, you have my word." Fagin scrambled to his feet.

"How do we find you?" I asked.

"Oh, no, no need for that, good sir. I'll send a boy when Annie is ready for you, we provide services, you see. Yes, we know your faces, no worry at all, we'll find you." He turned to his boys. "Well? Off with you, my dears! Off and don't come back till your pockets are filled with treasures! Jewels, rings, coins, and brooches, go and find them, my good boys!"

The boys scattered to chimneys and open windows in all directions. As the Dodger vanished up an alleyway, he turned and gave me the slightest wink.

Fagin was about to leave when he eyed Adelaide once more. With a grunt, he reached out to fasten his claw-like hand on her arm. "With me, my dear. I will show you the way of things!"

Before I might even react, she ducked low, kicked Fagin in the shins, and ran for it. Her scarf billowed behind her as she darted down an alley, peals of laughter echoing in her wake.

I tossed a final coin on the groaning Fagin, who was now lying on his side in the snow, clutching at himself.

"For your trouble," I said.

Through gritted teeth he smiled—and thanked me.

"I almost admire his tenacity and focus," I reported to Dickens as he walked briskly from the Quarter. "A man of business, through and through."

"The business of misery," Dickens said darkly. "See that you never fall so far, Scrooge."

"Or what?"

"Or I'll be waiting for you. And your story shall flow from my pen in such a way it will live on for centuries after you are dust—and your very name will become synonymous with tight-fisted greed and a lack of compassion for your fellow man."

CHAPTER TEN

Wednesday, December 21st, 1833
Four Days to Christmas

I WOKE THE next morning with a start. Someone stood by my window, a silhouetted man peering out at the street.

Roger Colley, surely!

Grabbing up my cane from beside my bed, I sprang at him—

And froze as Dickens turned from the window and lit a thinly rolled cigarette. "What are you going to do with that?" Dickens asked, snatching my cane from me with his free hand. "Get dressed. We have an appointment, you and I."

"Shall we have breakfast first?" I asked, turning away, my cheeks hot from embarrassment. I didn't even ask how Dickens had gained access to my rooms. Surely, all it took was a smile and a kind word to Mrs. Doors.

"No, Mr. Scrooge," said the reporter. "I strongly suggest that, considering where we are bound, the less either of us has in our stomachs, the better."

Grunting with effort, I raced to keep up with Dickens' ridiculously long strides as we were guided through a damp, water-logged tunnel just off the docks. The raggedy man before us held his amber lantern high and grinned back. He had more scabs and sores on his leathery, weather-worn face than teeth in his head. His ancient clothing was a patchwork quilt of repairs.

"Who's this, then, Mr. Dickens?" he asked in a voice thick with a Scottish accent. "Cannae recall seeing this fine young man here in the deep dark boggin' 'afore."

"Nor will you again," I vowed. "Dickens, what is this place?"

"You'll see," the reporter said grimly.

"Aye, ye will!" cried the raggedy man. "Then ye'll wish ye had not!"

The tunnels leading from the docks had twisted many times, leaving any trace of bright sunlight behind. Amber light flickered in the shattered puddles at our feet. The familiar stench of the Thames rose, and I clamped my handkerchief over my face to save myself from catching the diseases suspended in the putrid air.

"These tunnels don't flood, do they?" I asked.

The raggedy man shrugged. Dickens strode on purposefully.

"Dickens," I said, "whatever's eating you must be suffering horribly!"

An echo of voices drifted from the next turn. We made it and a high cavern rose about us, a vault-like grotto with smaller tunnels of moist limestone creeping out in all directions like the bony, twig-like legs of a spider. A desk sat just ahead, manned by a thin-lipped police officer. A woman's horrible, grievous wailing assaulted us from one of the tunnels beyond.

"This the one?" the officer asked Dickens.

He nodded.

"This way. Keep that silk over your face," the officer said, nodding my way. "The smell doesn't get any better the deeper you go. That I promise you."

The raggedy man stepped back and began to inspect notices nailed to the walls. More of the missing women.

I followed Dickens down a narrow tunnel. As promised, a horrid smell rushed out at us. I coughed, spun, but Dickens grabbed my arm and dragged me through the dank and narrow passage. The distant wails of a woman in grief, punctuated by hollow drips echoing off the walls above and beyond, became a ghostly symphony of dread. Soon we found ourselves in a wide circular chamber lit by torches. Stone slabs divided the dark space into aisles.

Bodies covered in white cloths waited on at least half the slabs. Some full grown; others not.

"Why are we here?" I demanded, my voice muffled through the handkerchief.

"To make a point," Dickens said grimly. "That actions have consequences."

"That is the cornerstone of my business." I trembled at the sight of the feet and hands protruding out from under the white shrouds. Porcelain pale flesh, with green and blue veins. Bites taken out of many of them: some larger and more egregious than others.

"You wanted to find Irene and her friend, Miss Annie Piper," Dickens said. "We rushed unprepared into a place we knew next to nothing about, into the Quarter, and in our arrogance . . ."

I looked down at a pair of slabs where the shrouded corpses of two women waited. A shock of ginger hair poked out from the closest. I jumped back and accidentally brushed the hand of another corpse. Cold as ice. Impossible to believe it had ever been animate. Had that Miss Shelley visited a place like this when writing her *Modern Prometheus*? Though I would admit it to no one, I much admired the novel.

Dickens whipped the covering back—and I peered down at the naked form of a much older woman whose black and crusty innards had been chewed upon by something in the river's deepest murk.

"Cover her up! Cover it!" I demanded, holding back my most sincere urge to vomit, though I had nothing but a spot of tea in me.

Startled, the anger I'd seen in Dickens' eyes faded and he did as he was bid. He looked at the face of the other woman on the adjoining slab, then went round the room checking each body. He recoiled at a particularly disfigured brute. Half the man's face had been eaten away. Or had it?

"Did a fire do that?" Dickens asked, absently. "Or was he attacked with a knife? Old wounds, not new . . ." He shuddered and covered the body up. "It doesn't matter. They're not here," he said with relief. "Irene and Annie are not here. Oh, Ebenezer, I thought our inquiries had led to these poor women's deaths. But they are not here!"

"Then let's follow their example and be gone from this place as well!"

"One day, I shall use my pen to pull back the coverings off all this poverty and degradation for all of London to see," Dickens said with determination.

"No one will thank you for revealing this ugliness."

Dickens grabbed my arm and pointed at all the slabs of concealed corpses. "Do you think that the Humbug Killer is the only murderer in this city who walks free?"

I tried to shake free of his grasp, but the young reporter was stronger than he appeared.

"I'm not interested in just stopping one murderer or reporting on one injustice," said Dickens, still holding my arm. "I shall bring the light of truth to all the ugliness of this 'civilized' society—I will show all the ignorance and want that remains hidden behind our robes of prosperity."

"You're a fool," I said as I finally pulled myself free from his grip.

"Be careful, Mr. Scrooge, I could easily sketch you as such a villain that parents would tell stories about you to scare their children into being good at this festive season."

It did amuse me, the thought of children being afraid of me every yuletide season. At least it might keep the little brats from caroling outside my door every December. We marched back into the "fresh" air of London without another word passing between us.

Above, in the clean, fresh warming light of early morning, we walked together along the docks. Silence had passed between us long enough, so at last I said, "That is where the police take the bodies dragged from the river?"

"Limestone, I believe," he said, commenting on the cold, yellow tunnels we had left behind and their sour-milk smell. "Keeps them fresher longer."

"How very educational, Mr. Dickens. Are you having second thoughts about our arrangement?"

"I was," he admitted, "but seeing the glassy eyes of so many who have come to such a grim and sorry fate . . . No, if that note you received spoke true, Fezziwig was just the first. I would spare others the fate we just glimpsed. Present company included. I say only that we must be careful moving forward. Agreed?"

"Absolutely. Now, have your inquiries borne any other fruit?"

They had, it turned out. Though we had not yet heard from Fagin's boys about an engagement with Annie Piper, and Miss Nellie Pearl had been "too busy" to be interviewed by Mr. Dickens, those who worked in more menial positions at the theatre were happy to oblige. He spoke with some who had been at the place for decades, and from them he had gleaned the connection between Nellie and Fezziwig.

"Young Nellie had worked for Fezziwig as a spinner upstairs in the very room where he met his horrible fate," Dickens revealed. "She had often told him how much she adored the theatre. They went together many times, she said. He introduced her to the director at Garrick Theatre in Whitechapel, and she worked her way up to the Adelphi from there. She owed her career to Fezziwig, you know. So when he sent for her, she came. And unchaperoned, I might add, through this heaving cesspool of a London borough!"

I thought of the actress. A pretty thing. Soft, pink lips wobbling slightly, she'd been struggling to control her shock. Yet I had registered something else, too. A nervousness, something unsettling about the way she kept tapping her foot. She was hiding something, of course. They all were.

"Clearly, Fezziwig stumbled on to information concerning Sunderland and Rutledge," I ventured. "Shen and Miss Pearl, too, I would imagine, considering they were all summoned to meet him at the same time and place. The question is, what? I will never believe that my friend would stoop to base blackmail to line his pockets. Yet his offices were ransacked. No one seemed to know precisely what Mr. Fezziwig was involved in at the time of his death. It's all very puzzling."

Dickens lit a cigarette with trembling fingers. I steadied it for him, until it crackled into flame. "What about this 'Chimera,' whatever that is?" he said, exhaling with a relieved sigh. "That word put the fear of the almighty in the Colleys, and Roger and Jack clearly had some tie to Sunderland. And Jack is within our reach, at least for questioning."

"I doubt that Jack would say much," I told Dickens. "And there is that matter of actions having consequences. I would do nothing to have the Colleys think of me further. I regret mentioning their names last night when we spoke with those boys."

"Understood. The threat to Belle Potterage. Yes, yes, agreed."

"I have matters underway to press Rutledge for answers. Tonight, in fact, I should have my chance. For now, though, what of Shen?" I asked. "Clearly he has some fixation on Miss Pearl."

"Yes, he's often seen at the theatre. He is one of her most ardent admirers, though it is plain that she does not reciprocate his feelings."

"He frequents the Royal Quarter, he pays for the services of a whore who could be Nellie's twin. We need information about the whereabouts of a certain *other* whore, and the man who runs that place—"

"And Mr. Shen would not be pleased if Miss Pearl learned what he was up to in the Quarter."

"And who with. Come, Mr. Dickens. Let's visit the Chinaman straight away!"

Dickens had warned me that gaining an audience with Shen Kai-Rui at his offices within the East India Trade Company would be difficult, as his attempts thus far had proven fruitless. And so I was pleasantly surprised when a smiling bearded gentleman greeted us warmly and took us to see him directly.

"I thought you said you hadn't yet applied our leverage against Mr. Shen when you sent word we were coming," I whispered.

"I didn't," Dickens assured me.

I snorted with pleasure. Clearly, our easy access today was because *I'd* accompanied the annoying young reporter. My name had become associated with that of George Sunderland, after all.

If I was correct, then the unpleasantness we planned to unleash against our host might not be needed after all. Not that I would have minded making Shen squirm a bit. Until now, he hadn't revealed a polite or decent bone in him, and his lascivious fixation on poor Miss Pearl made my flesh crawl.

The bearded man, an usher, led us across the large, open atrium inside the opulent East India House. Pushing open the heavy doors to one of the many internal offices, he announced us.

"Yes, of course!" said Shen, laughing and smiling as he rose out of his leather chair. "Of course, do come in. Thank you, Fredrick." The usher nodded curtly and left, closing the doors with a thud behind us.

Shen strode to a marble mantelpiece at the back of the spacious office and removed the stopper from a crystal decanter. He filled a single glass with a smooth amber liquid and replaced the stopper with a clink. When he turned to us again, his expression had returned to the cold, angry glare I had come to associate with him. Now that we were away from prying eyes, he had abandoned the charming façade that had no doubt helped him rise so quickly in his company's ranks.

"Understand—you have ten minutes, not a second more," he said curtly, taking a sip of his drink and not bothering to offer Dickens or myself refreshment. "I'm only granting you this audience because the reporter's grating attempts to see me were becoming tiresome and I wished to put an end to them. What is it you want?"

A look passed between Dickens and myself. The choice had been the silken glove or the rusty gauntlet.

Shen had chosen.

The tradesman sat behind his desk, and we helped ourselves to his liqueurs. His frown deepened as I sipped the drink Dickens had handed me and shuddered as its warm spices scraped the inside of my throat. Dickens knocked his glass back and set the empty crystal to rest on the edge of Shen's desk.

"You will show us Fezziwig's summons," I told him. "And you will explain your connection to the man and to the others who received that summons. Then you will agree to make certain introductions on our behalf."

"Will I?"

I nodded. "You will."

Mr. Shen sat back down in his leather chair and pressed his fingers together in a spire. "I do not understand you British. You want your pound of flesh, which you tell yourselves is justice. Well, you will have it, and soon. I hear the police are satisfied and the trial against the murderer is to be expedited. A rational man would be satisfied with that. The reporter wishing to muckrake, that is unfortunate but understandable in this barbaric country. But a moneylender poking about in these matters . . . what is it, Scrooge? Did the old man die owing you money? I've heard you can be quite merciless in such matters."

Rage gripped me, but Dickens' firm hand on my arm steadied me.

"I can assure you," Shen went on, "you will find no transfers from Fezziwig's accounts to mine. Now if that is everything . . .?" He motioned to the door.

I shook my head. "You must have a low opinion of people if you think they're all your equals."

Dickens flicked open his notepad and poised a pen. "How do you think Miss Nellie Pearl would describe you, Mr. Kai-Rui?"

Shen rolled his eyes. "It is the other way about in my country. The family name comes first. Truly, I find England's system of education shockingly inept. For a country that would see itself the center of the civilized world, you're little more than pigs rooting about in shit, to use your vernacular. In fact, I would say—"

Unable to tolerate his smugness, I broke in. "We saw you with her last night. In the Royal Quarter. At the Doll House."

His hands tightened about one another, knuckles white, his shoulders hunched high. His face remained cold, his eyes suddenly distant.

"Where do you hide your ring?" asked Dickens. "Did Smithson give it to you personally? What filthy business did you and Miss Pearl get up to in the Doll House? Did you have Miss Annie Piper join you? Did she bring friends?"

Shen's breathing quickened, his nostrils flaring in barely suppressed rage. "Leave now or there will be consequences."

"Threats?" Dickens asked. "Now who is the barbarian?"

Dickens and I studied each other for a moment. We

had conspired to make Shen believe that we thought he had taken the actual Nellie Pearl to that whorehouse for God only knows what purpose. After all, we very nearly *had* believed it was her. He might have been willing to risk his own reputation being sullied, but not that of his obsession, Miss Pearl herself.

"You said you'd left the invitation here in your office," I reminded him, turning our talk back to less incendiary matters. For now. "Perhaps you can produce it?"

The Chinaman narrowed his eyes for a split second, then relented. "Quite impossible, I'm afraid! My desk is cleared every evening, paperwork not pertinent to the East India Trade is removed and burned. Nonetheless, I'm quite sure its contents would have been identical to that of the other summonses. You may have better luck with Lord Rutledge."

Abandoning his notepad, Dickens put one hand on his pocket and wandered over to the mantelpiece so he was standing directly opposite me on the other side of Shen. He'd assumed such a perfectly uncomfortable position for Shen that the Chinaman would need to keep twisting his head to switch between watching Dickens or me. I inwardly marveled at Dickens' choreography.

"Then perhaps you can indulge us with a little history lesson," Dickens urged. "Your connection with Fezziwig, what of it?"

Dickens moved slowly along the bookshelves behind Shen's desk, inspecting the spines, dusting off the surfaces. Every move he made was mirrored by a slight twitch in Shen's fingers.

The Chinaman turned back to me and smiled. His

hand moved to his belt, hovering slightly above it as if he were about to lunge for a hidden weapon. "I see. You seem to think I'm implicated somehow. The foreigner *must* be a villain. After all, he's a foreigner. What a cliché."

THUD! Dickens dropped a book on the floor and Shen leaped to his feet.

"Gosh," apologized the reporter. "Dropped *A Dictionary of the Vulgar Tongue*, by Francis Grose. Looks like it landed on *H*." He picked the book up before Shen could move from behind the desk. "Ah, yes. First entry, *Humbug*. What a marvelous coincidence! Say, Scrooge, isn't that just what was written on '*our friend's*' wall?"

"Fine," Shen said, settling into the leather chair and adopting a calm but stern expression. He glanced at a nearby clock. Our time was running out, which pleased him. "Though I'm afraid you will not find my connection to Fezziwig particularly illuminating, in fact I daresay it is nothing more than humiliating for me. But as you wish."

Dickens had flicked his notepad open again and began recording Shen's account verbatim.

"I arrived in England as a ship's cook when I was seventeen. It had been a rough year-long passage, via the Cape of Good Hope, in a trade ship that ironically belonged to the very company I now work for. I was granted a two-month furlough but could not face the prospect of returning to sea. So I decided to stay. I took to the streets, selling penny packets of incense to earn a living. It was a foul life, and with relations between England and China so tense, it wasn't long before I was attacked by ruffians. Hateful, angry drunkards. They focused their blows on my face, appalled by my appearance, you see, causing me severe concussion. The location of this assault was in Spitalfields."

"The millinery's quarter," I said. "Where Fezziwig was based."

"He found me badly beaten, left for dead, and hauled me back to his house. The concussion was so severe it left me in a semi-conscious state for weeks, and his wife, Jane Fezziwig, nursed me back to health."

I nodded, not at all surprised by Reginald's and Jane's kindness.

"There is little more to add beyond that," he continued. "Fezziwig showed me great kindness even when my own people cared little if I lived or died. He gave me strength, great strength, which I used to rise to my present position, now steering the very company that delivered me here in the first place. In fact, the whole company relies on my connections in Parliament. Thanks to Fezziwig, in part. So you see, when I received his invitation—which gave no particular reason for the visit yet stressed it was urgent I attend—I had no reason to hesitate to see him. As for my surliness, if you would, perhaps it is because I saw him as the one civilized man in this miserable country, and see where it got him. Now, as our time draws to a close, I trust you will keep any mention of an association between Miss Pearl and myself confidential. It would do her reputation no good to be associated with a 'foreigner.' "

"You mentioned Rutledge," I reminded him. "Know him well?"

"I see him at social events. And avoid the bore whenever possible."

"And Sunderland?"

Shen smiled. "Why, Mr. Scrooge, were you not his trusted yet secret confidant? Surely you would know if George had any dealings with East India. Which, naturally enough, he did. But I never dealt with him personally, just a certain Mr. Lazytree and other advocates of his."

Dickens stopped scribbling and flicked the pad shut, slipping his pen into his breast pocket, but I was not satisfied. "We seek an audience with a certain Miss Annie Piper. You may know her, you may not. But you possess a ring that grants you access to the most vaunted whorehouse in the city, from what I gather, and Piper is precisely that, a whore."

"A whore who has been recruited to the Quarter," Dickens added. He'd leaped to that conclusion in light of Fagin's initial hesitation to help us book time with the woman.

Nodding, I said, "You will arrange an audience for us with Miss Piper. It is vital that we—"

Shen stood up and slammed his fist on the desk, toppling an inkwell which spilled its contents over the face of a document. Dickens, forgetting to remain "in character" as it were, rushed to help. He lifted the ink-stained document, which Shen promptly snatched from him and pushed him back.

"Get away! I have answered your questions," he fumed, lifting the document by its corner and holding it over the wastebasket as black lines of ink dribbled across lines of penmanship. "As to your other 'request,' you both can go hang. Even if what you accuse me and Miss Pearl of doing was true, you have no proof. No one in that place would spill for fear of gaining a second smile, this one splitting their throats wide open. It would be your word against ours, and I assure you, the two of you would lose in such a challenge. The slander suits we would launch would then ruin you, be assured of it. Now leave!"

Dickens' eyes were fixed on the surface of the desk, at the spot that had previously been covered by the paper Shen was now holding. I tried to follow his gaze, but the dripping ink-stained paper was blocking my view and whatever had caught his attention was hidden from my sight. Where Dickens stood behind Shen, I saw him move a few inches closer and narrow his eyes, straining to read something.

"No, wait," Shen hissed, his brow tightly knotted and his brown eyes flashing. "I will give you one final nugget of information. Unless you promptly forget whatever it is you think you've learned about a certain Mr. Smithson, the Doll House, or any other establishment in that area of London, you will soon find yourselves plucked, gutted, and stuffed like a Christmas goose. Have I stated that matter simply and clearly enough for you *gwai lo*?"

Dickens smiled. He clearly understood the slight. "Foreign devils, yes, that is us."

I caught Dickens' eye, and he nodded.

"Please accept our apologies, Mr. Shen," I said, bowing in a sardonic and hopefully insulting manner. "Perhaps we have been a little over-zealous." I strode to the door. "Of course, I can't help but wonder, in your country, what do they call a man who, when he can't gain the attention of a certain lovely he desires, instead paints up a cheap tart to look like her, then parades her around a place like the Doll House, all the time smiling like a strutting goose?"

"Merry Christmas!" called Dickens over his shoulder as we left. We received no response.

Once outside, Dickens grabbed my arm. "So much for being careful. Did you have to say those things? He might be dangerous!"

"What was under that sheet of paper you spotted in Shen's office?" I asked.

He calmed, and excited curiosity burned in his eyes. "The envelope. The summons from Fezziwig."

"How can you be sure?"

"It had Fezziwig's monogram on it, of course. And there was something else, too," he said.

"Well?"

Quick as a flash, using a sleight of hand I had not seen the reporter display before, he produced a brass key.

"To Shen's office?" I asked.

"As likely as any other door," said Dickens. He lowered his head and ushered me into a shadowy alcove. He nodded to the company's front door, which Shen slammed behind himself as he stormed from his place of employment and stalked down the street away from us. "Hopefully he'll be gone long enough for us to put it to the test when we go back to get a better look at things."

"Breaking and entering," I mumbled. This was getting darker by the hour. Although Dickens might have been used to this kind of thing when pursuing a line of investigative journalism, I certainly was not. Yet, what other solution was there? Three *more* would die! And then me.

A furious drumroll erupted suddenly as horse hooves thundered towards us under a beast with steaming nostrils. I grabbed Dickens' jacket and yanked him out of the way seconds before we would have been pummeled to death, both of us slipping on the icy cobbles and landing painfully just as the horse's police wagon came to a stop.

"Watch it!" yelled a voice.

I detangled myself from Dickens' limbs and stared into the cold eyes of Constable Crabapple.

"What are you doing here, Scrooge? Never mind!" he shouted down at me. "It's an emergency, get in. You ain't going to like this, Scrooge, and neither is poor Miss Owen. It's concerning Thomas Guilfoyle . . . and it's most alarming!"

Dickens excused himself and I boarded the carriage.

"What's this all about?" I asked. I looked back, and Dickens was now following Shen, though at a considerable and discreet distance.

"The wages of sin," Crabapple said. "The very wages of sin itself! Our only viable murder suspect attacked at the courthouse by a figure out of nightmare. Right there in the holding cell! A black cloak, sir, black veil, white bony hands, exactly as Guilfoyle himself had described!"

And with that, we were off in a flash, the carriage bolting and skidding into traffic.

CHAPTER ELEVEN

OUR STEPS ECHOED off the cold stone walls as Adelaide and I were escorted down a narrow corridor to the ward where Tom was recovering. I could hear Adelaide's breathing, mechanical and composed, like she was consciously commanding each intake lest she lose control and crumble into fits of tears. "Her Tom" was locked in a coma, imprisoned in his own mind as his broken body attempted to crawl its way back from death.

Many more will die, then you, Ebenezer, Fezziwig's spirit had promised. I had thought Sunderland to be the first of these, but now I knew I'd been mistaken. His death had been misfortune, nothing more. And now Tom, yet clinging on to life. Humbug had clearly meant to butcher the poor boy; the word HUMBUG was half-written beside his twitching form, and in the victim's own blood.

Humbug had fled out another door, its work unfinished as Guilfoyle clung to life.

Because Tom was a murder suspect, and the prison hospital had no facilities to treat patients with such severe injuries, he had been admitted to a lunatic asylum near London Bridge. Here experimental technology was employed to aid medical progress and thus Tom would have some chance of a full recovery. The danger of hanging had not yet completely passed. Crabapple stubbornly assured me that there was still a chance that his neck, once fully recovered, would eventually be stretched for Fezziwig's murder. This second killer might be an accomplice, Crabapple theorized, who feared Guilfoyle would eventually break under questioning and reveal his name or other damning facts.

In direct opposition to Crabapple's view, headlines spurred by Dickens' take on things boldly proclaimed, "HUMBUG KILLER STRIKES AGAIN!" "INNOCENT MAN ATTACKED!" "POLICE MISTAKEN—CRABAPPLE LOSES FACE!" The articles sported sketches of the cloaked figure with its impossibly long, bony fingers. All it needed was a scythe and it might have been the Angel of Death itself. By late tonight, the penny dreadfuls would certainly be running lurid stories of the butcher of London.

My only surprise was that Crabapple had not yet asked me for an alibi as to my whereabouts during Mr. Guilfoyle's attack. But all good things to those who wait.

And as I looked to poor Adelaide, I could see that waiting, and the terrible anticipation of seeing "her Tom" maimed in some unspeakable manner that had not yet been revealed to us, was taking its toll. The matron of the institution scurried along a few steps ahead of us, a large ring of heavy iron keys clanging as it slapped against her swinging hips. The high-pitched piercing of a Christmas jingle she was whistling, seemingly oblivious to Adelaide's suffering behind her, mingled with distant wails and hollow groans coming from behind locked doors on either side.

"Now, you won't get no sense from the lad," she said suddenly. "He's fast asleep and will be for weeks, so say the surgeons. Miracle he survived. Still time for that to change, though; the infections may set in any time now."

Adelaide's breathing quickened, and she gripped my arm with such strength that I felt my muscles bruising under my thick jacket.

"Thank you, matron," I said. "We have no need for the details. We only wish to visit the man."

"Mind you, he got what he deserved, didn't he?" she continued. "Did the very same to another, didn't he? The '*Humbug* Killer' they call him. Our Good Lord delivers justice in balance, an eye for an eye, so they say."

So it seemed that not all public opinion had been swayed.

"Yes, thank you, matron." I glanced at Adelaide, her face set in an expression of strength and courage, though the trembling of her hands betrayed her true pain. I couldn't help myself. "Although, I scarcely think he could be the very Humbug that committed the foul murder of which he is accused, unless he has bravely and skillfully staged the savage attack on his own body. Do you?"

"Why, bless my cottons!" trilled the matron, stopping by a large locked gate. She turned to us and put her hands on her hips. "I daresay you're right! Well, that puts me at ease, it really does. You can imagine my anger when they brought a murderer to my ward. But now that he is innocent, well, I shall have the girls bring him fresh linens each and every day!"

"Yes, I'm sure that will be a great comfort to an insensate," I muttered. This was how our taxes were spent. Humbug indeed! Yet . . . Adelaide seemed comforted by the woman's words.

Clinks and clangs rang out as she fumbled for the key to the ward, her cheeks rosy and her broad smile bright and clear, until realization dawned. The smile vanished, her eyes became wide, and the key was left half-turned.

"Bless my . . ." she whispered. "But if this man is innocent, then . . ."

I saw the chance to avenge the pain the matron had inflicted on Adelaide with her thoughtlessness, and a twinge of pleasure erupted in my gut.

"Quite so," I said, raising my eyebrows to emphasize my deep concern for the matron's safety. "The Humbug Killer is still at large. Not one of us is safe this Christmas."

The matron went white as a sheet, and her trembling hands struggled to grasp the key and turn it. I glanced at Adelaide again. She had gone pale and stock-still, her terror over what she might soon witness paralyzing her.

The lock clanged open, the matron slid the heavy iron gates to the side, and I gently gripped each of Adelaide's arms and walked her into the ward as one might a child who was yet unused to walking and unsteady on her feet. Only one bed was occupied, a fact which the matron explained was caused by the typhoid epidemic just passed: all severely ill patients had perished months before. Foul air lingered, a sharp, surgical smell, but she assured us that no risk of contagion remained.

Tom's bed sat at the far end of the ward, and rows of steel cots marched up either side of us as we approached. Metal devices stood parked by the wall, novel mechanical applications with uses beyond my medical knowledge. A shaft for conveying the food from the kitchen and medicines from the laboratory clanked into operation, probably delivering gruel to the poor insane on other floors.

A policeman, one I recognized from the day Fezziwig's body was found, was dozing in a chair beside the patient, emitting occasional grunts as his hat slid down over his nose and he lifted a drowsy hand to right it.

Adelaide let go of my arm long before we reached the bedside, and the absence of her strong grip was a cool relief. She marched straight up to the bedside, pushing past the matron, and stood there staring at a body still as a plank, covered head to toe by a white sheet.

"Is he . . . ?" she gasped, quaking with fear that her Tom might be dead. Then the sheet rose and fell as the man beneath took a shallow breath.

"Covered up, yes. Constable Pepple doesn't like the sight, disturbs his constitution, so it does," said the matron. "Look away, Constable!"

The constable made no move, and with a flourish, the matron pulled Tom's sheet back, exposing his face and chest.

"Oh!" Adelaide exclaimed and pressed her hand to

her mouth. Bandages covered his face, neck, and chest, the white gauze now crusty and stained with gruesome yellow and brown patches seeping though.

"There, there, dearie," the matron said. "It's not so bad as it looks. You be a bricky girl, now. The cuts to his face weren't deep at all, the scars will be mild and perhaps not even visible should he grow a beard. His chest, his stomach, his arms, *they're* more of a right mess."

Adelaide wept silently, her shoulders shaking despite the lack of any other betraying characteristics. She stroked Guilfoyle's hair and caressed his hand, making soft soothing sounds with her mouth, as if her presence would be of any consolation to this man on death's door. I allowed myself to lay a hand on her shoulder, hoping it would give her some comfort.

"Well, just come and find me when you're done, then," said the matron, taking her leave. "Oh, wait!" She turned, cleared her throat, and recited something that sounded altogether outside of her character. "The cures have been numerous within the wall of our fine institution, thanks, in a great measure, to the bequests of benevolent individuals. Please consider, this Christmas season, the many—"

"Thank you, matron," I said again, this time with a sneer I made no attempt to hide. "We are here for Mr. Guilfoyle, *not* for your charity. Good day."

She huffed and scurried away, leaving me with a grieving Adelaide and her broken Tom.

"You must stay with him, of course," I said. "You won't want to come to the party tonight, I understand."

"Thank you," she whispered. "I may indeed choose to sit here with Tom tonight."

"I'm sure he feels most comforted by your presence."

I would need to attend the party by myself, though Dickens had expressed an interest in going and had mumbled something about having a well-connected contact, some widow who would be able to secure an invitation on his behalf. I shuddered to think how Dickens made his connections, but there was no doubt his insatiable curiosity and relentless investigating were of great benefit.

A woman in a blue nurse's uniform entered the ward pushing a trolley with a basin of warm water and some fresh bandages. She ignored Adelaide as she carefully removed the bandages, peeling them off his face to reveal that, indeed, his wounds there were mild. I expected Adelaide to look away when the woman went lower, but she kept her eyes firmly on everything the nurse did. She watched as the nurse washed his wounds, wiping crusty blood from seeping holes in his chest, applying a thick and smelly paste to the gaping gashes.

When the nurse had wound fresh bandages round the patient and taken her leave, Adelaide spoke without turning to me.

"This ball," she said absently, her voice dull, lifeless. "Where is it to be held?"

"Dyer Manor, I believe." I pulled the envelope from my breast pocket, still sealed, and handed it to her. She ripped it open and read it with wet eyes.

"Yes, the Dyers," she said finally, handing the invitation back to me. "I'll be there. I must be there. This has gone on long enough."

Before I might ask her what she meant by that, she lowered her head, took her Tom's hand in hers, and began to weep.

I left without looking back.

CHAPTER TWELVE

I RENDEZVOUSED WITH Dickens at the Cock and Egg shortly past one that afternoon, where we shared some mulled cider and traded information. He'd been most saddened (and not a little bit alarmed) by the news of the attack on Mr. Guilfoyle, and curious indeed at the showman-like nature of the killer.

"One could hardly just blend into a crowd dressed like that, now could one?" he jibed, smiling as he sipped at his flagon. But his hand still trembled despite his brave and dismissive tone.

"They're calling the masked figure 'Humbug' now," I added. "Ghastly. I didn't credit Guilfoyle's ravings, but it turns out . . ."

Dickens grunted, swallowed, and waited for me to toss a few coins on the table before we headed into the chill and back to the East India Trade Company's offices. "Poor Miss Owen. How is she taking it?"

"How do you think?"

We devised a plan along the way, and he became increasingly annoyed as I dismissed his ideas of procuring costumes and hiring accomplices to create diversions and other elaborate whatnot.

"Simple is best," I told him. "We sneak in, and if we are caught, we simply act like a pair of foolish and drunk occidentals who wandered in by accident."

"But we've been seen by the staff!"

"Don't be such a chocolate teapot, Dickens. It's unbecoming. We'll think of something," I said. My gloved hand shot out, and I arrested the progress of a running boy. He froze, terrified, looking up into my stern face. "Do you know what you've done?" I demanded.

Shuddering, the boy shook his head flicking the drips from his nose to either side.

"You've chanced on to the opportunity to make some money," Scrooge said. "That's what."

We paid the lad to walk an empty, unmarked envelope into the great offices and say that he must deliver it "all personal like, and in person" to Mr. Shen. He returned moments later to say that Shen had left for the day. Dickens wasn't surprised, as he had been following Shen and lost him in the early afternoon crowds while they were traveling in the direction of the Quarter.

The boy raced off, and I nodded to Dickens. "Let's be about it."

Wind-whipped sleet pummeled the back of my neck as we slipped behind the East India House and stole down the stone steps leading to below the street. Dickens crouched before a door marking the servant's entrance, his ever-present cigarette between his teeth, as he fiddled with a tiepin and a butter knife in the lock.

"I thought you said you could pick locks?" I said,

looking about anxiously. I held the brass key he'd stolen, which had not opened this particular door.

"I said nothing of the like," he mumbled. "I said I had a tie pin, which *might* work."

Actually, he had boasted of all he'd learned of the thief's craft from writing an article about the criminal plague on London and assured me he could pick a lock like this in his sleep.

"Good thing you brought that butter knife," I said, not even attempting to hide my sarcasm. "I shan't even ask *why* you carry such a thing about your person."

I heard the bolt shift slightly.

"For buttering toast," said Dickens, the bolt shifting slightly from his efforts. "Though I trust myself to always find bread to eat, I do not always trust that it will be under sanitary conditions. I also carry a clean napkin and a fork."

"Then at least we are prepared should we have to face armed guards," I said, squinting against the icy wind. "Particularly if they're in the mood for dinner service!"

I heard a further scraping as the tiepin forced the lock mechanism to loosen, and he wedged the butter knife against the bolt, scraping the paint on the molding. Almost there . . .

"The only weapon I brandish is my pen, Scrooge. Embellishing, conserving, and devastating in equal measures, limited only by my own will."

My heart lifted when he gave the tiepin a final twist and we heard the sharp snap of a bolt sliding free of its steel home. Dickens and I looked at each other and held our breaths. We listened beyond the howling wind, past distant hooves and the scratching of a city fox in a festering gutter nearby. We were alone. My companion reached for the doorknob. Exultant and terrified, I watched as he turned the knob, leaned all his weight inward, and flew inside, tripping down the unexpected set of half-stairs before us. I strolled into the dark hallway that smelled of polish and coal and eased the door shut behind us.

East India House was deceptively large, and the entire basement floor that we had just entered housed the many operations needed for the running of the administrative complex above. Navigating this floor would be challenging, though our earlier visit to Shen had at least provided us with a solid compass. His office was in the west wing, and the servants' entrance was east. We would need to find a stairwell and ascend to the ground floor as early as possible, for at the lunch hours it was more likely that the kitchen, pantry, or storage rooms would be occupied than the great halls and offices above.

Dickens led the way. Exposed water pipes jutted out of the walls at head height, iron hooks protruded a foot into the narrow corridor, and one had just narrowly missed my forehead but for Dickens' timely warning. A doorway opened up to our left, the earliest opportunity to move westward, so we entered cautiously. Foul smells of rotting food and soiled water seemed to thicken the darkness of the ill-lit rooms, and just as I reached up to cover my nose, I bumped into the back of Dickens.

"The scullery," he whispered. "There's no thoroughfare here, move out."

I turned to exit, but just then a sharp snort vibrated through the foul air, followed by a smacking of lips and an almighty belch and a cloud of stale beer and bodily gases contributed to the soupy atmosphere. Someone was sleeping in this horrible room! I froze, but Dickens continued, bumping into me and sending me crashing into the side, knocking a faltering stack of pans to the stone floor with a crash.

"Wha-what? Pardon?" came a slurred and drowsy man's voice. "Betsy?"

I squinted into the darkness and made out the shape of a man sitting on a small wooden stool, slumped against the stone basins at the end of the tight room, clutching a bottle and rubbing his eyes. The smell of his alcohol breath was poison, but at least it signaled that we were safe from immediate persecution.

"Jus' waitin' for you, Betsy," slurred the man, and belched again. "Think I love you."

"And I adore you, dear!" sang Dickens in an exaggerated female's voice, and my heart stopped with mortification and dread.

"Good, good, I knew it," muttered the drunk, and a thud rang out as his head fell, deadweight, against the sink.

Dickens tapped my shoulder, and I stepped over the mess of pots and pans and out into the corridor.

"Damnit," I hissed when we were clear of the scullery. "What were you thinking?"

"What harm? At least now the potboy knows his

Betsy loves him and he will sleep soundly through the rest of our mission. It'll be the next left now, if that was the scullery. Look for a tight spiral staircase."

Ducking under sporadic copper pipes, we found the staircase and ascended, clutching the banister as the steps twisted round. We were met at the top by a heavy door.

"We should try the brass key first," he replied, snatching it from my outstretched hand. I heard the scraping of metal on metal as Dickens fumbled with the key in the lock. "Doesn't fit. Time for the butter knife. . . ."

"Have you even *tried* the door?" I asked.

"No need," he said. "All doors leading to the basement are locked from the hall during this hour. It's safe to assume the housekeeper will not open them again for another—"

I reached past him and turned the knob, pushing the door open.

"Dickens, when I've funded your publishing venture and made a businessman of you, you should keep in mind to always attempt the simplest solution first. Otherwise, you will come to ruin, though I'd wager that's not unlikely either way."

The ground floor was airier, lighter, the ceilings higher and the air fresher. The building's floors were polished marble, forcing us to tread lightly lest our footsteps reverberate round the great hall. Bright, bracing sunlight streamed through the tall windows, was multiplied and reflected inside by the many shiny surfaces: marble columns, mosaic mantelpieces, crystal chandeliers. Vast paintings hung at every wall, dreamscapes of elephants and treasures, merchants in exotic places, and the quizzical eyes of King William following us as we snuck past Fredrick's empty post and to Shen's office.

"Well," I whispered, "our key will finally be of use." Facing the double door with elaborate golden painted carvings and a crystal glass doorknob, I grabbed it back from the reporter.

"Have *you* even tried the door?" Dickens said with a grin.

It slid open silently as soon as I turned the crystal knob. I felt both relief and annoyance as Dickens commented that he had noticed none of the internal office doors lining the great hall had locks, and that some housebreakers he had previously interviewed had testified that to be the norm in West End London. We were inside with the door closed behind us only seconds before footsteps rang out in the hall and a trio of laughing figures passed beyond us.

Sighing with relief, I hurried to Shen's desk, our footfalls sinking into the lush carpet. I rummaged through Shen's papers, taking care to note the position of each one.

"The envelope isn't here, Dickens," I said with a sigh.

"Check again."

"What did it look like?"

"Like an envelope."

He rushed to my side, overturning each paper I had carefully laid back in its place, but laying them back even neater than I had managed. No summons from Fezziwig, but whatever the papers contained had some value to Dickens, for he was meticulously copying words down in his notepad using one of Shen's dip pens and the remaining ink in the toppled inkwell.

Then I spotted the drawer in the desk, slipped the brass key in, and blissfully turned it with a near-soundless *clunk*. I pulled it open and grabbed its contents, flicking through each file. Nothing.

"Of course it's not in *there*," said Dickens. "How would he have got it in without the key? But look here." He reached past me and pulled a small velvet box from the drawer. "Hazard a guess?"

He opened it, and we leaped back with cries to the almighty. The ring—the key to the Doll House and the other great palaces of sin in the Royal Quarter—sat inside. It rested round a man's leathery and well-preserved severed finger. A macabre joke, perhaps. But it spoke with unquestionable authority as to the true and apparently deadly nature of Mr. Shen.

"I wonder," said Dickens, carefully closing the box and putting it back in the drawer. The color had drained from his cheeks.

"What?"

"Well," he said as he moved to the bookcase. "It seems our Mr. Shen likes his little jokes. So perhaps . . ." With fast-moving fingers he examined the spines and located *A Dictionary of the Vulgar Tongue*. It fell open in his hand, an envelope hidden between the pages at *H* for *Humbug*.

Dickens handed me the envelope, and I gently slid the flap open and removed the letter. My throat tightened as I read aloud Fezziwig's words, hearing his benevolent voice in my mind as clearly as if he were addressing me directly:

You must know that throughout our association, I have cared for nothing except preserving your utmost happiness and well-being. So please, heed me now when I tell you that I must speak with you on a matter of the utmost urgency.

Information has come into my possession concerning a threat to all you hold dear.

For fear of this missive finding its way into the wrong hands, I will say only that it concerns "The Lady." I think you know the personage to whom this nom de plume refers. Please attend me at eight in the morning tomorrow at my office.

I will tell all then.

Yours Affectionately,
Reginald D. Fezziwig

I folded up the summons and slipped it back in its envelope. Dickens flicked his notepad shut and put the envelope back between the pages of the book, then slid it into place in the bookshelf.

"The Lady?" I asked.

He shook his head. "I'm afraid I don't know. Considering he asked all four to meet at his offices on the same day, at the same time, I would think they all knew something of this 'Lady,' that she was the common tie between them."

"Some threat she held for each of them. How would Fezziwig know such a thing?"

"Mr. Scrooge, it appears there was much you didn't know about your friend." He was still scribbling.

I opened my mouth to agree but was halted by the sudden sound of muffled voices on the other side of the door. Shocked, I looked to Dickens, who was staring at his pocket watch.

"Lunch must be just about over," he mumbled. "Stewards will be in shortly to prepare the offices for their occupants. We need to leave, now."

"The window," I offered, and we moved to the tall panes and peered out. The street outside was clear, so I flicked the latches and slid the bolts to the side. Lifting the lower pane just enough for us to slide through, we stepped onto the ledge and hopped over the iron railing underneath. On the other side, Dickens gave me a leg up, and I reached up to pull the window shut just as I saw the crystal knob inside turning.

We huddled together over what was becoming our regular table at the Cock and Egg. My eyes were red raw from exhaustion, and a familiar ache in my legs closed tight round my calf muscles.

"What was all that you were copying down in your notebook?" I asked.

"Yes, about that," Dickens said. "I'd just have you read it, but shorthand, you know. Our foreign friend in there is hip deep in the underground opium trade. I suspected as much of course, rumors abound, but evidently, he's in command of shipments, had records of trade routes, the coded names of suppliers, receivers, and more. He may present himself to the world as a man of legitimate business, but his main trade is something else entirely."

"Do you think *he* could be Smithson?" I asked.

"It's possible, I suppose. And yet, I have difficulty imagining men like the Colleys taking orders from a foreigner, don't you?"

"I'd put nothing past them if money is in the game." I sighed. "We have no choice but to request an interview with the prisoner."

"An interview with Jack Colley?" Dickens mused. "Are you feeling suicidal, Scrooge? And what of Mrs. Potterage and her family? You're paying handsomely for their protection. Wouldn't it jeopardize them further if you antagonized that man?"

"Then I'll simply have to charm him," I said.

Dickens choked on his ale. "I'd pay handsomely to see you charm anyone. But yes, I suppose that considering the attempt on Mr. Guilfoyle's life and these startling developments about Mr. Shen, the days of caution are behind us, don't you?"

I nodded.

"Lunch at first, at least?"

"Sorry, Dickens," I said, eyeing the plates of salted ham that had just clattered on the table in front of us. "No time to waste!"

But my jovial tone was only to hide my terror at the thought of seeing the madman Colley once more.

"Well, then," Jack Colley said, fingers templed and tapping his lips, "to what do I owe the honor of this visit, Mr. Scrooge? Here to reminisce about old times? Hah! The last time we was face-to-face, you hit me right in the gob with a copper's baton, you did. But no hard feelings, eh? And by the way, how *is* that fine woman of yours. Belle, wasn't it? Belle Potterage, eh? Only, she's hardly yours these days, now is she?"

I thought I'd be prepared for Jack Colley's nasty tricks when I asked Inspector Foote to arrange this audience. But now, as I sat alone with him in this dingy "visitors' room," Jack in chains bound to a hook in the floor, I felt the heat rising in my veins. My hands wrung each other until my knuckles turned white.

"Still taste a bit of that porridge on the side, do ya?" Jack asked. "Naughty-naughty, hiring those bruisers to watch over her and that fool of a husband. The twins, though, they sound appealing. Perhaps Baldworthy might adopt them. Or make them into a tasty stew. Something. But those lads you're paying, war men, eh? Problem with blokes like that is they're used to having someone tell them what to do, and they operate by a certain code of honor. Roger and his lads . . . they don't."

"Do you want answers?" I asked, the words catching in my throat. "Or haven't you finished showing off?"

Lines crinkled about his eyes like spiderwebs as he smiled. "Just proving a point."

The point, of course, was that despite being locked up in here, Jack Colley had complete access to his brother Roger and others on the outside. Probably through notes and messages smuggled in and out via corrupt guards. It also meant that, as Dickens warned, my actions and words here and now with this thug could well have consequences for Belle, myself, Dickens, and Adelaide. Though I dearly wished to take advantage of Jack's "vulnerable" state—chained up as he was—and give him a fair thrashing for what he had done to me, I would instead need to employ thoughtfulness and reserve.

"The police make it sound as if they crippled your operations," I ventured. "I find that hard to believe. You may have suffered setbacks, yes. But with the right influx of cash and goods, I could see your empire rising again from whatever ashes Foote and the others would say it's become."

"Well, I never! Then you mean to be my benefactor, Mr. Scrooge. You fancy being business partners, just like you were proposing when you were, ah . . . hanging about with us at the docks?" He smiled, revealing gleaming teeth flecked with silver fillings.

I forced myself not to turn away, forced my expression to remain stony. "What if I might provide you with information about the opium trade? Very specific information. Arrival times, shipment weights, the names of those responsible on every side of the equation. Is that something that might interest you?"

"Never dealt with that stuff. Foul and nasty it is."

"Yes, but needs must, do they not? Even if all you did was seize those goods and sell them back to their rightful owners, the amount you stood to gain would be monumental. More than enough to rebuild."

"But I'd still be in here."

I snickered. "All you lack is the means to bribe a few well-placed judges. This would provide it."

Jack looked about suspiciously. "Trying to trap me, eh, Mr. Scrooge? I'd think you're more the type that if you came into the possession of information like that, that you'd turn it over to your copper friends, like the Inspector Foote. *Toot sweet.*"

I sighed. I had learned that the cornerstone of any great lie was a foundation of truth. And so I offered that now. "I am marked. The Humbug Killer is coming for me. Do you understand what I'm saying? My life is worth *nothing* so long as that creature is about."

He chortled. "The Humbug? You believe that's real? And old Saint Nicholas, too?" He winked at me.

I stared at him and let him read the dark truth in my eyes. At last he turned away, shuddered.

"All right, then," he said. "What's any of that got to do with me?"

"You admitted that you had something to do with Fezziwig's death."

"Nahhh," Jack said, shifting and testing his chains with a sharp jangling. He frowned with disappointment as he realized he was solidly bound and released them. "Just said that to put a fright in you, we did. News of what happened to that poor old man spread quick."

I leaned back and crossed my arms over my chest. I believed him, unfortunately. "Tell me what it was you thought Sunderland had cheated you out of. And what 'Chimera' means. How it connects to your enterprises."

He laughed. "So you were bluffing, too? Maybe you *are* fit for a partner after all!"

I shrugged. "It's all connected, Mr. Colley. Chimera, George Sunderland, that fool Rutledge, the Royal

Quarter, a certain Miss Annie Piper, perhaps even that Smithson fellow."

Jack Colley's face betrayed nothing but flickers of interest as I wove the tapestry before him.

"And 'The Lady,'" I added, pretending it was an afterthought. "We know of her, too."

At once his expression soured. I'd clearly touched on something with him, but he was not in a giving mood. Not yet.

Finally, I said, "And that means if I am on Humbug's list, you might be as well."

Jack's eyebrows flared with mirth. His dark eyes sparkled. "Let 'im try," he said, relishing the challenge. Then he sat forward, all smiles and laughter. "I'll tell you what, Mr. Scrooge. Because you've amused me, brought amusement to me, made me feel . . . amused, like. Because of that, and not that shite about the opium trade—leave that to the slanties—I'll give you this."

Closing his eyes, he rolled his head back, revealing a sore rash on his throat where his prison clothes were buttoned too tight, and began singing a nursery rhyme. At first I thought he was mad, but I knew the rhyme, knew it very well. *Mary, Mary, quite contrary, how does your garden grow? With silver bells and cockleshells, pretty maids all in a row.* He sang three traditional choruses, the final one replacing *maids* with *cuckolds*.

"There," he said at last. "That should do for you."

"You've told me nothing," I said, standing up and brushing the filth of this wretched place from my coat.

"Everything," he said. "Make that, 'everything.' Words have many meanings, Mr. Scrooge. And from innocent beginnings often comes hideous ends. Now, going back a final time to that other trade you mentioned, for your sake, steer well clear of it. I wouldn't want to see anything happen to you, Mr. Scrooge. Truly, I would not. You're so very amusing!"

"Well, in that very spirit, then," I said, "may I suggest becoming acquainted with soap and water? I've come across decomposing bodies that are less offensive than you are."

He laughed and laughed as I took my leave.

Trudging through the snow outside the prison some time later, I reflected on that rhyme. Like all good schoolboys, I was well aware that most such rhymes were thought to be allegories for religious or political matters in England's past. Some believed the pretty maids to be Mary Queen of Scots' four ladies in waiting or Mary's many miscarriages and her execution of Lady Jane Grey. Others that the rows referred to the execution of Protestants and that cockleshells suggested an unfaithful husband. Cuckolds one might leave on its own.

I cursed myself. I had risked much to come here and lay myself bare before that grinning lunatic. In return, it seemed, despite his assurances, that I had gained nothing at all.

Why had I done it?

Memories returned to me, visions of Adelaide weeping at the broken Guilfoyle's bedside . . . and layered upon them, the chill, dead look in ghostly Fezziwig's black eyes.

Later that evening, when I spoke with Dickens outside the gates of Lord Dyer's manor house, he rubbed his hands briskly and smiled ear-to-ear. "Ah, that is the way of these things," he assured me. "Information that at first seems meaningless later turns out to be the lynchpin to solving the entire mystery! Rejoice! Rejoice and be merry!"

The reporter threw his arms back, and the flaps of his jacket billowed open, revealing a silver flask.

"Are you drunk again?" I asked, adjusting the pressed white waistcoat under my jacket and checking that the brass buttons were still as brilliant as when I polished them.

"Inebriated with excitement," he said. "Ah, Mr. Scrooge, do not put a damper on this for me, I beg of you. It's Christmas, after all! And I have arranged quite the assignation tonight."

"A woman?" I cried. "Our lives weigh in the balance and your concern is with some woman?"

"No one's threatened *my* life," Dickens said, sneaking another gulp from his flask and screwing the top on tight. "Now, shall we wait for Miss Owen or go in?"

I checked my pocket watch. "No, if she was coming, she would have met with us by now."

"I hope Mr. Guilfoyle hasn't taken a turn," Dickens said.

And uncharitably, terribly, I know, I recognized that deep within that black bit of coal I thought of as my heart . . . a part of me would not have been unduly troubled if he had. Was it because I wished Adelaide to look at me with the kind, loving gazes she awarded "her Tom"?

To that, I could say only this:

Humbug!

CHAPTER THIRTEEN

"OH, EBENEZER!" DICKENS cried. "Did no one tell you the purpose of tonight's event? For shame. I can only imagine how all this must make you feel!"

I stood in the crowded, oppressive foyer where a placard boldly revealed the legend, "An Evening of Hope sponsored by the Haberdashers' Peacock Charity for Poor Debtors."

A charity for poor debtors, of all things. I shuddered. The party would be a frightful event, a terrible soiree of hypocrisy, with the wealthy classes of London, swollen with *noblesse oblige*, pretending to care for an instant about the plights of the less fortunate. My face contorted in disgust. "This is nothing but butter upon bacon!"

"Yes, it's a bit excessive," Dickens conceded. "I suggest describing yourself as an investment banker, if the question should arise, which it undoubtedly will. Somehow I don't think moneylenders are typically invited to these affairs!"

With that, he swept forward into the surging crowd

of expensively attired well-wishers, meeting each hand with a firm shake, each smile with a twinkle of delight.

I considered turning and fleeing into the chill night, but ahead, in the crowded main ballroom, I noted Lord Rutledge speaking with an elegantly dressed man wearing a gigantic top hat. Distracted for a moment by Rutledge's ludicrous periwig, a powdered hairpiece adorned by old-fashioned peacocks of his station, it took a moment for me to realize that Shen was his companion. Then harsh words appeared to be exchanged, and the Chinaman stormed away and disappeared into the crowd of hundreds who had arrived for the festivities.

I made my way through the wretched congregation of rich bigots, expertly evading those I recognized as chronic do-gooders who stalked the Exchange seeking contributions to various causes. I had stopped at the offices of the young clerk Billy Humble on my way here. He had provided most damning evidence on Rutledge that I hoped would secure a better result than my attempts at negotiation with Jack Colley. Now I just needed to speak with Rutledge, gain what information I might from him, and *leave*.

But the crowd pressed in on me. Fat women squealed and young ladies raised eyebrows. Enterprising gents surveyed me, appraised me. Was I someone who might help elevate them? Older gents peered at me with suspicion. Was I a threat to all they held dear?

Madness.

And the opulence of it all. The sickly sweet smell of the candied chestnuts, the garish holly wreaths hanging at every inch of wall not adorned with oil paintings of the wealthy, the songs, the lights . . . The isolated philanthropy that would evaporate as fast as the last falling snowflake soon after this wretched season of giving was over.

"Mr. Ebenezer Scrooge!" a cheerful voice called out. A hand landed on my shoulder and spun me about to face a rosy-cheeked man I did not know. "Merrick Lazytree, Esquire," he said, breaking into a shrill hyena-like laugh. "I am one of the chief solicitors for the estate of George Sunderland."

"Oh. I ah, well . . ."

"No need to be shy or modest, sir," Lazytree said. "Though no specific provision was made for you in Mr. Sunderland's will, I can assure you that he spoke of you often and wished to see you well taken care of. Oh! But that look of yours. I see you do not believe me. Well, I will say this. As he feared, a good deal of infighting has broken out among those in charge of his various empires. It has been kept out of the financial sections thus far, but . . ."

"Excuse me," I said roughly. "I fail to see what any of this has to do with me."

"He entrusted me with the duty of executing a scheme that might bring these various parties together in a manner that puts you squarely in the center. Your rail deal, of course. Let me introduce you to some fine fellows and you tell me what you think . . ."

I had come here to squeeze Rutledge, who was now entertaining a flock of impressionable young debutantes. He was going nowhere. And if I left here with even one sizable investor for the rail deal, then perhaps this "high society" whatnot would indeed prove to my tastes!

For the next hour, I met with one key member of Sunderland's various businesses after another. I expounded upon the virtues of rail, how it was indeed the portent of all things in our future. How the railways would expand our reach as businessmen and builders, and the fine, beautiful money that would be made by those strong enough and brave enough to invest now.

They listened intently. They took me into confidences, one, in particular, a portly man named Greenback, saying, "Have you seen in the papers all this nonsense I've been speaking about the import of saving the Brazilian razor-beetles? Hah! I'm only doing it because if I can have that land near Knightsbridge declared a preserve, then Henry Wartfellow will suffer and my wife will be most charitable towards me. She loathes his new wife and sympathizes with the old one, you see. The old one being not that old and still quite lovely to my eyes. My dearest dear has promised me a bit of French delight with her and her friend should I pull this off. What is the term for it, menagerie of three or some such? I only know that as the years go on, I find one too few, three too many. . . ."

Others laughed at the very charities to which they had generously donated this evening. They derided the halfways and "Social Houses" for the poor or addicted and instead backed the workhouses and prisons, for which we were already taxed so grievously. But it was popular these days to be seen as beneficial, and so the checks were written.

I had kept Rutledge in my line of sight the entire time, but now he was on the move. It appeared he had set his sights on the reclusive Lord Dyer, a white-haired gentleman who had put in a brief appearance and was now shrugging off the mob and retreating into the maze-like series of hallways beyond the ballroom.

After securing pledges for an astounding array of investments—my fortune would be made if even a single one materialized in proper funds—I happily grabbed a glass of champagne from the tray of a servant, ducked and weaved through the lavish crowd, and spotted Rutledge easing through what looked like a secret passage!

Squeezing past a group of gossiping ladies in vast bulbous dresses, I examined where my quarry had vanished. The wall in the corner had the telltale absence of perfect symmetry between two panels, betraying a passageway that must have been installed to allow servants to pass unnoticed between rooms. I tapped the corner and the panel slid open with a near imperceptible whisper.

I slipped through the passage.

It led from the ballroom to the great library, which was empty. It seemed that Dyer was leading Rutledge on a merry chase, and, by extension, me as well! The ceilings were high, and the murals depicted angels flowing from the heavens, bringing the gift of knowledge to mankind. *The first occasion of misguided benevolence*, I thought to myself. A globe stood in the corner, so I gave it a spin. It was heavier than I expected and barely moved. Yet I knew that with the rail deal assured, the globe was merely my next step in business: international trade!

The quiet, distant buzz in the next room became hypnotic and soothing as I took another sip of champagne and leaned against a leather chair while examining the spines of some of the library's books. Perhaps by dislodging one of these I'd find the next secret door.

Heavy footsteps approached the large double doors on the opposite side of the room. Without missing a beat, I jumped to my feet and dashed back to the secret passageway, but the panel had closed with a click and I couldn't get my fingernails to grip the crack. I tapped each corner, but the panel stayed closed. There was no other way in or out of the room but through those doors, and I would be seen the moment someone entered. It would not do for a party guest to be caught wandering about the private areas of this opulent abode. In fact, I might be publicly ejected and thus publicly shamed. And how might that look to my investors?

The footsteps stopped, and a muffled voice boomed out right outside the door, so I chugged back the champagne, bubbles bursting in my sinuses, and slipped behind the curtain.

Lord Dyer entered the room, closed the door behind him with a thud, and released a heavy sigh. He closed his eyes, pinched the bridge of his nose, and shook his head lightly. Then he went directly to the big globe, tapped the side, and the top half swung open, revealing a collection of bottles. He chose one, popped out the cork, and took a swig. The door opened again, and Lord Dyer slammed down the lid of the globe. A woman entered, with her rich chocolate curls tumbling over porcelain shoulders.

"Adelaide!" cried Lord Dyer.

I wondered quite how tipsy this bit of champagne

had made me. Were my senses playing tricks with me? Or did Lord Dyer actually know Miss Owen? What on Earth could be connecting these two?

Her hair was elegantly styled, and a cluster of sparkling crystals hung at the milky hollow of her throat. Her dress worth more than I might pay her in a year's time. She appeared more at ease with these surroundings than many I had brushed shoulders with in the ballroom.

"I thought I made it clear when we met at the servants' entrance," he said. "This conversation is over. And how did you get in here?" He sighed. "No, never mind explaining yourself. It's always been so. When you set your mind to a thing, locks and dismissals seem to you suggestions easily ignored."

She walked over to him and placed her hands on his shoulders, gazing directly into his eyes. "I hoped that was one of the things you admired about me. I learned it, after all, from watching you." Her eyes were wide and wet, and even through the slightest crack in the curtains I could see the sparkles from her diamond earrings reflecting in her tears. How did she even own such things?

"You must see him," Adelaide said firmly. "He might not last the night."

"To what end?" Dyer asked. "He wouldn't even know I was there, would he? But others would. And then the questions would start."

She took his hand, brushed it upon her cheek that he might feel the moisture of her tears. "Thomas would know. And so would I."

"I can't," he said firmly. "I've done everything I might

for him, and see where it leads us all." He shuddered. "A gruesome business. Is he . . . are his wounds . . ."

"Should he survive, he will still be presentable, if that's what you mean," Adelaide said, standing up and wrenching her hand from his. "He will not embarrass you in that regard."

"Adelaide, it was not what I meant! Please . . . tell me you have not inherited your mother's cruelty."

"No. But I've learned from yours." Skirts whirling as she spun, Adelaide hurried to the wall, pulled on a curtain hook, and the passage I had taken here opened. The sounds of the Christmas party swelled, and she rushed from the room, leaving Dyer to rise on uncertain legs and drag himself away out the double doors through which he had entered.

I waited a few minutes. Then, with my head swimming with new mysteries and unanswered questions, I crept out of the room and immersed myself back into the heaving fog of roast goose, brandy breath, mistletoe, and misplaced benevolence.

Altogether certain I had missed my opportunity with Rutledge, I returned to the party intent on collecting up Adelaide and questioning her about the odd business I had just witnessed. But in moments, I saw the solicitor snaking my way and, wishing to avoid another discourse with them until my head had cleared from the champagne and the startling scene I had accidentally witnessed, I put my hand on the shoulder of a lone woman and turned her to face me.

It was Belle. My Belle. As beautiful as the day she left me sitting on that park bench, though a few new lines had appeared by her eyes. Her cheeks were as pink as the rose detail embroidered into the band that secured her perfect ringlets to the side of her head. Not a hair out of place. No chocolate curl tumbling in front of a knowing grin. Belle was pristine, her expression polite.

We stared at one another in stunned silence, then she laughed, took my hand, and curtsied. A fit of madness must have then overcome me, because I felt my heart leap into my throat, my nerves burst to a tingling mass of needles. I cupped her face in both my hands and tried to press my lips to hers. So many things I wished to say, so much forgiveness I wished to beg, and all, all, I was certain, would be encapsulated in this magnificent gesture.

Our lips did not meet. She shrugged out of my grasp and shoved me away. I heard titters from the group of society wives clustered together under a rich sprig of mistletoe and sewn to the hip of the plump Lady Gertrude, who was clutching her stomach and looking mortified. But within seconds they had moved on to tastier nuggets of humiliation and gossipy ruin.

Belle's fury reddened her words. "Ebenezer, you can distinguish, can you not, between that which is past, that which is present, and that which is future?"

I could not meet Belle's gaze. "I apologize. I don't know what came over me. I am delighted to see you well."

I scanned the room and saw several bulky men in ill-fitting suits watching Belle from a distance. The guardsmen Dickens had hired.

"I would not see the light from your eyes extinguished," Belle said with a softness and generosity I did not deserve. "It is a fair and good thing to see. But the flames should not be lit for me. You know this." She looked to Adelaide. "What of that one? She hasn't stopped looking your way all evening!"

Adelaide stood gay and charming as ever, a shimmering star that had drawn the attention of many men and made satellites of them, Lord Rutledge included. Her misery of only a few moments ago had miraculously vanished. Though she made each of the men about her feel as if he had her complete attention, her gaze flickered back to me time and again.

I cleared my throat roughly. "Her? She's a . . . a business acquaintance. We seek to profit by means of a common end, nothing more."

"Profit, then? It is still all that guides you?"

"It does not betray me. *It* can be counted on to be fair and just."

"My hope for you has come to pass," she said distantly. "You are happy in the life you've chosen."

"Undoubtedly."

Her wan smile was the last I saw of her as she breezed over to a clutch of friends.

Dickens regained my side, a crystal tumbler of hot brandy in hand. "Is it not a curious thing?" he asked. "How much easier a lie passes one's lips, like a perfectly struck note off a finely-tuned instrument, than the flat and heavy thing that is so often the truth?"

"You're drunk."

He nodded. "Doesn't make me wrong."

"What of *your* conquest?"

He sighed and raised his glass in the direction of a radiant young lady whose circle of male admirers put Adelaide's to shame. "I thought there might be some future with me and that one . . . but, though I had been led to believe otherwise, that is clearly *not* how she sees things between us. She's nothing but a dirty puzzle." Under his breath he muttered, "Blast that Havisham woman!"

I nodded, but I could not share his current disdain of the other sex. I had deserved Belle's thorough rebuke. Perhaps, I thought as I gazed at Adelaide, it was time I looked to my future. . . .

"Blast that Havisham woman?" said a willowy voice at our backs. "I would second that—with interest!"

A handsome woman, close to ten and thirty in years, bore down on us. Dickens blanched at the sight of her.

"Miss Shelley," he said. "How very pleasant to see you again."

"Oh, Mr. Dickens, really now. You must know that my feelings towards you *entirely* mirror yours to me."

He frowned. "Delightful. Then we shall have no misunderstandings between us."

She smiled. "If that's everything?"

He breezed before her. "I understand we share a mutual friend. A Mr. Jingle?"

Her smile fell. "That reprobate. Why am I not surprised the two of you are acquainted?"

Shrugging, Dickens admitted, "We're not. I may have stretched the truth on that point. I have never met him."

"But you seek him out? For a news story, I presume?"

"A criminal exposé, yes."

"I suppose I should be grateful that you are not scurrying about my coattails seeking an endorsement for some ridiculous novel. How tiresome."

Dickens bristled, then caught himself. "Clearly not, madam."

I stepped back, unsure of what this exchange signified. Then I recalled Dickens' promise that he was nearing the whereabouts of Miss Annie Piper. He did not trust in the pledges of Fagin and his gang to arrange an audience, and Fagin's initial hesitation to set the meeting nagged at him greatly. This Jingle must hold important knowledge, I wagered.

"Suppose I help you? As our American friends might say, what's in it for me?"

"What would you have of me?"

"St. Raphael's Hospice for Paupers. Go there. Report on the brave men and women staffing that hellhole. Report on the wretched conditions that force fallen women and the helpless to go there. Promise me you will shine some light on that pit of darkness and perhaps assist in its desperate needs for funding by letting the public know what you see . . . will you do that?"

A strange look came into Dickens' eyes. Fortified steel. "Whether you help me or not."

She nodded and took his arm. "Come this way, I'll tell you what I know. . . ."

So intent had the two writers been on one another—and the clear spark that existed between them, despite, or perhaps because of, their evident friction—my presence had never been acknowledged. Though perhaps that was for the best, considering the mention of St.

Raphael's. I had been there numerous times attempting to collect what was owed me. . . .

"Mr. Scrooge!" Lord Rutledge cried as Adelaide led him straight to me. He was the tallest man in the room on account of his preposterous and frankly outdated wig. "I have heard of the successful outcome of your rail scheme. Congratulations are in order!"

"Not just yet," I said, nodding at Adelaide as she melted back into the crowd.

"Well, as I was saying to Miss Owen there, a delightful woman, I understand what you see in her . . . my country estate, you see, has become quite the bother. I've held on to it for sentimental reasons, but it is a sin to see such a lovely place sit empty. A new owner is in order, surely. You should see it, Scrooge. Newly fitted Doric columns, a hedge maze, and so much more!"

I shrugged. "What you call taste is living proof that nature does not abhor a vacuum."

Rutledge stiffened. "Sir?"

I smiled. "And here I might have thought your true motive for selling was because you're in debt up to your eyeballs, as they say." It took only moments for me to recount the information I had gleaned from young Billy Humble's research. Lord Rutledge was on the brink of complete financial ruin. And in his circles, that meant also social devastation.

"Oh, you tried to marry off your daughters, but the price you sought was too high, the dowry exorbitant for ladies a bit beyond the freshness of the ones you seem to like," I said, nodding at the clutch of debutantes who now looked his way.

"You're the devil," Rutledge murmured.

"Then fear me, because I could bring about your ruin with a few well-placed words. Do not even consider having me harmed or what I've learned will find its way to the press almost instantly."

Trembling, the blood draining from his cheeks until his face was as white as his hairpiece, he gripped his walking stick and nodded sharply. "What is it you want?"

I thought back to Jack Colley, and a mad gambit sprang to my mind. It seemed my group of suspects liked to use odd phrases to hide their secretive and dark dealings.

I began to hum the nursery rhyme. When I neared the end, I gently sang, "And pretty maids, all in a row."

He buckled, tears suddenly welling in the corners of his eyes. Through gritted teeth he said, "Ask . . . your . . . *questions.*"

"Tell me what you know of 'The Lady' and 'Chimera.' The connection between you and Sunderland and the Colleys. The rings, the Royal Quarter. Tell me all of it. And do not lie to me. I'll know if you're lying."

He snatched a drink from a serving tray moving at nearly a blur and downed it greedily. Wiping his mouth, he said, "Do you know one of the loveliest things about having a title before one's name? It frees you to speak simple unvarnished truth. Particularly to those who are lesser than you. Mr. Scrooge, I cannot possibly be the first to tell you that you are an insufferable bore. Worse, you are a conniving, clutching, cold-fisted beast whom I would see put down."

"But not today."

"No," he agreed in a trembling tone. "Not today."

"Out with it. Tell me. I mean to know why Fezziwig was murdered."

Rutledge stopped short at that, confused. He acted as if I had just completely changed the subject. Then he steadied himself and said, "I only know parts of it. 'Chimera' is simply something I overheard once, in somewhat low company, and when I inquired as to its meaning, my life was threatened by those I counted as friends."

"Like Shen?"

He shook his head. "Others. So I have said nothing of it since. The Lady, she is some kind of rival to Smithson and the Colley Brothers. She trades in the foreign, the exotic; that's all I know."

"How would Fezziwig have known of her?"

"I haven't the first notion," Rutledge said earnestly. "But it was the mention of her, in his summons, that prompted me to be at his place that terrible morning. If he knew of her, he might know of my other . . . pursuits."

"You feared he might blackmail you? Expose you?"

"No, no, never," Rutledge said. "I feared for him. I worried he had stumbled across something and did not understand its true nature. That he might unwittingly put himself in danger. And, now that I consider things in such light, you're right: that may be just what happened."

"I need more. This Humbug *will* strike again. First Fezziwig, now the lad we found and assumed to be the murderer. Sunderland is dead. Of the small group of us that were thrust into that room, the numbers dwindle.

Much as I normally admire the trait, now is not the time to be stingy, Lord Rutledge."

"Yes, yes . . . There is one who can illuminate these matters far better than I. He . . . It's just . . . You see, when one has the means afforded to me, the usual pleasures lose their luster. One seeks the new, the different, the perverse, to be blunt. I found a place that provides it. A person who provides it."

"Smithson."

"Yes. Smithson is the spider in the web, all right, but that's not his true name. Smithson is what you would call an alias. In truth, he is a man of business, much like you. Respected. Above board, so the world thinks. But the truth of it is he has his hands in every kind of filth you might imagine."

My heart raced as I pressed him further. "A name, Rutledge. Give me a name, and I will forget all I learned about your problems and . . . transgressions."

He quaked with rage, sweat beading on his forehead. Then his knees buckled, and I grabbed his arm to steady him.

"The wine, the wine!" he said jovially as others rushed to help and he dismissed them with a wave of his hand. Leaning in close to my ear, he whispered, "Marley. Smithson's true name is Jacob Marley. Now leave me and never speak with me again!"

Lord Rutledge composed himself, smiled, and waded back into the crowd, though his step was far less sure than it had been.

I too felt unsteady. Jacob? My once friend, my once partner . . . could he have truly fallen so? But then, his fortunes had risen dramatically since we parted, and he had expressed little hesitation in dabbling in wretchedness like the Black Trade.

Reeling from it all, I determined to flee this place, but a commotion at the edge of the room where the passage to the library resided caught my attention. Constable Crabapple was there, clutching a piece of paper, waving it in the face of Inspector Foote while Lord Dyer looked on in red-faced fury.

"Well, now, look at that!" Dickens said, swooping in beside me and clutching another drink. He looked about, took in the crowd's sudden fixation on the business ahead, and removed his flask. He emptied his drink into it and screwed on the top. "Might get chilly later."

"I think it is time we take our leave. Have you seen Miss Owen?" I asked, a terrible unease settling in as I thought of how easily she had hidden her distress earlier. She was an expert at hiding things, it seemed, and there were many things she'd hidden from me.

"I have not," he said curiously. "And in that dress she wore tonight, she is a bit hard to miss. Curious!"

We pressed towards the fracas and searched for Adelaide, but to no avail. Finally, I nodded to a side door, where we might make a discreet exit.

"I've learned much tonight," I said.

"As have I," Dickens said. "It seems our Miss Annie Piper is now the consort to Smithson himself."

"How—"

"I have my ways," he said, not even attempting to hide his smug expression.

Ahead, Crabapple was peering past Foote's shoulder

and waving a fist at the party's host. "Explain yourself, Lord Dyer! Why would my prisoner, Thomas Guilfoyle, the Humbug Killer his own self, be writing to you from his prison cell only hours before he was struck down? Why should he beg and plead for you of all people to save him? What's the connection? Tell me, sir!"

Pinpricks rippled through my flesh as I staggered back, physically struck by the revelation. I thought of Guilfoyle in his cell, madly certain that "he" would come and provide salvation. And later, Adelaide's teary story that Tom, in his drug-addled state, was referring to his dead father.

She had lied to me. Guilfoyle was talking about Dyer, and I had just caught Adelaide in an unquestionable untruth.

I looked about. Where the hell was she?

Inspector Foote motioned over a pair of bobbies, who roughly grabbed the belligerent, and now, I could tell, quite drunk Crabapple. They were about to haul him away as Foote made copious apologies to Dyer, when a sudden scream rang out. A woman's scream.

I whipped my eyes in the direction of the secret door. It was open now, and a terrified maid backed out of the library on legs as unsteady as those of a newborn faun and pointed within. "Humbug," she said, her voice hoarse from her sudden shriek. "In there, plain as life, the killer, black robes, bony hands, the angel of death . . . *HUMBUG!*"

Dickens sobered instantly—and ran for the doorway.

Shockingly, I was at his side.

CHAPTER FOURTEEN

LORD RUTLEDGE SAT in the leather chair in the center of the library, face slack, eyes unseeing, his fine suit ruined by a dozen slits, his white silk shirt and cravat now ruby red. His wig had slipped partly over his face, the bottom curls dark with the sticky blood slowly trickling from his gashed neck. Streaks of blood decorated the books, the ceiling, floor, walls. A figure I had first dismissed as a lunatic's ravings stood near the open double doors leading deeper into the mansion, one bony hand dripping with gore and blood. A painting had been torn from one wall, and the killer's signature now resided there.

HUMBUG

Streaked and dripping in blood.

I caught only a glimpse of the black-cowled figure before it whipped towards the door and fled into the darkened hall. A heavy black veil had obscured its face, and a blade the length of a man's forearm, flecked and still trailing red, was gripped in its hand.

No, not it, I told myself, my fear and disgust pressing down on me, threatening to bring me to my knees. Humbug was mortal. A man. Had to be.

And men could be brought low.

"After him!" Crabapple shouted from the door behind us.

Though the rational thing would have been to part for the police, let them do their jobs, Dickens and I sprang ahead, spurred by the command. We had only a short lead on the police, who trounced behind us, while ahead Humbug flew into the amber-lit main hall. A startled footman bearing a tray filled with wineglasses turned a corner, and the murderer crashed into him. The tray flew, glasses shattered, and the footman stumbled back and fell flat on his backside. Humbug whirled with surprising grace, spinning in mid-stride to avoid faltering. Regaining his footing, the killer sprinted ahead and leaped over a marble table to avoid two more startled servers.

"The last time I saw anything like that it was a troupe of Chinese acrobats," Dickens said, puffing, out of breath.

On we ran, following the killer up the main staircase, along the hall braced by the second-floor railing, through spacious and stunningly appointed bedrooms, and finally into yet another hidden passage, this one accessed by tilting a painting of a dour old man at a precise angle. Into the dank and murky darkness we ran, the sharp clatter of the killer's footsteps ahead. We wound down a spiral staircase with no thought to the trap Humbug might have set simply by stopping unseen at the first-floor landing and waiting for us blade in hand.

A door cracked open, light streamed in, and the man in black darted through it. We followed, Crabapple and his men laboring, shouting, cursing, but no longer at our heels. We raced into a main gallery and stopped dead, panting, clutching our knees. Humbug was gone. The walls surrounding us were lined with rows of portraits of those responsible for the mansion's history. They ranged over almost three centuries, with the emerald eyes of Lord Dyer staring at us from the end. Two heavy-paneled doors sat at the room's far end, but both were shut tight. The killer couldn't have had time to first escape through one of them and then quietly shut it behind him.

So where had he gone?

Dickens and I cautiously approached a secretaire and desk with tortoiseshell and brass inlay, the reporter snagging up a sharp blade used for opening envelopes. We approached from either side, determined to corner the monster who *had* to have been crouching behind it.

"Scrooge, behind you!" Crabapple called.

I spun to see Humbug rising to his feet, blade held high. The bastard had scuttled through the small passage under the desk and could have simply kept running, but instead, he'd come back around to take a stab at me.

I stumbled back and banged against the desk as the huge butcher's knife *whooshed* the air before me, its savage arc stopping and shifting with a masterful and blood-chilling swiftness and sureness. Dickens came around beside me and held his tiny blade in his trembling hand, looking as if he might faint.

Humbug's head angled to one side, a wolf taking measure of its prey. Then the black-clad killer darted away as the shouts and footfalls of Crabapple and the others rang out only a few yards away. He ignored the two now blocked doors but closed on a paneled wall where he struck just the right spot and slid inside another secret passage. Crabapple ran after the murderer, his men hot on his heels. Shots rang out from their pistols, misses one and all.

Chest heaving, breath labored, I exchanged looks with Dickens. He shook his head. We would not follow. Yet something gnawed at him. . . .

"That passage will come out somewhere," he said. "If we can get ahead of this madman . . ."

"Your flask," I said, reaching out with quivering fingers.

He accommodated, and the liquor helped bolster my courage and dim my good judgment. We prowled the halls, listening intently for the shouts and screams that had disappeared when the passage door had closed in the gallery behind Crabapple's people.

I cautiously passed wall hangings of crimson and green embroidered silk, fearful that the killer might be hiding behind any one of them. I studied the vibrant carpets for traces of blood still leaking from the blood-soaked blade.

We quietly stole through the drawing room, the ceiling adorned in an antique mosaic said to have been stripped from the Baths of Titus in Rome. From there we traced the length of the banqueting room, stopping to peer beneath the long central table, which might easily seat fifty, then on to the great conservatory. Statues of lions and other predators rose about us, peering from behind lush walls of exotic foliage, while carvings of Greek and Roman personages lazily peered down at us and gestured to the huge room's marble fountain. The conservatory, with its vast open globe of a ceiling and its many glass walls, led out to a spectacularly lit inner courtyard, where servants and workers were preparing for a night of fireworks under the stars.

I was about to say to Dickens that our plan had failed when a door creaked open and our black-garbed prey unceremoniously stumbled into the room. Humbug held his stomach, catching his breath. He hadn't seen us, and from the lack of footfalls and shouting at his heel, it seemed he had lost the coppers.

Then he looked up—and tensed, seeing us for the first time. The murderer's body coiled. Fevered intent seemed to reach into the shadowy figure. I could not see his face through the many layers of black gauze hiding it from view, but, in the pale, soft-blue moonlight, he could see mine.

Who are you? I wanted to ask. Why are you doing this? But terror stilled my tongue.

The killer was wordless as well, but not silent. His labored breathing assured me that the murderer was mortal, not some wretched thing that had shaken off the grave. It was small comfort. Humbug was shorter and slighter than I would have guessed. His cloak and hood had given the illusion that he was greater in measure. Tom, a specimen of a good six feet and four, would have towered over Humbug; no wonder the stab wounds had been concentrated on his chest and lower.

"There are two of us," Dickens said stolidly as he began to circle the killer. "We can do this!"

My gaze left Humbug for the briefest of moments as I scanned the room for anything I might use as a weapon. I heard a rush of fabric, like the exhalation of the reaper, and looked back to see Humbug leaping at me!

A glint of moonlight struck across the blade's deadly edge, scaling down it like a tear from heaven, and I was frozen with fear, a statue serving itself up for destruction. Then a shape smashed into Humbug from one side: Dickens, tackling the beast, and the blade fell, clattering to the polished tile. I kicked it away and dropped down upon the grappling pair. Dickens had pinned the killer, who was silently squirming and beating at him, and I fell to grasping the wildly kicking legs. They were leaner than I might have expected. The "monster" was hardly a brute at all!

And his white, bony hands . . . they were gloves painted to look skeletal, sharp, and fearsome.

Now all we had to do was hold the killer until Crabapple caught up with us. I shouted for help, hoping to gain the attention of the workers outside. The reporter, ever a slave to his insatiable curiosity, eased his grip on our prey and reached for the hood and veil that hid the murderer's identity.

Humbug's head flashed forward, striking that of Dickens with a hard, feral crack, and Dickens fell away. Startled, my hold loosened enough for the killer to spring back, then send a nasty kick at my face with his heavy, iron-soled boots. I grunted as stars exploded before me and groped madly, unwilling to lose the killer now, when we were so close—

But running footsteps sounded. I turned on my side and saw Humbug flee into the courtyard, racing past surprised workers in the garden, disappearing down the gravel paths and parterre beds edged with box hedges.

With a clatter, Crabapple arrived, Foote's goons close behind him. "Where?" he demanded, eyeing the butcher's blade the killer left behind and our sorry states.

I pointed to the garden and they ran into the night. Shots rang out again, but I had little hope that the killer would be brought low. Humbug might have been human, but he also had the luck of the devil.

Nearly an hour passed before Dickens and I were reunited with Adelaide, who stood by herself, hands crossed demurely, the pose of a serving maid. I could not bring myself to stand by her side, such was my fury at her betrayal.

Crabapple watched with glee as Foote suffered the verbal tirades of Lord Dyer and then a parade of his associates.

The Christmas charity ball had ended before the dizzying dances, before the fantastic fireworks. Nearly all the guests had been sent home. Rutledge's body had been left as we had seen it in the library. Dickens was anxious to return there with his sketchbook, but Crabapple was having none of it. We were material witnesses. We had stared into the dark face of the killer, we had laid hands upon him. Even if it took half the night,

Crabapple was determined to learn all we knew before we were allowed to be on about our business.

Soon, Dickens was huddled with Crabapple far and away from me, and Adelaide approached.

"Are you well?" she asked.

I made no pains to hide my anger. "Are you?"

She glanced at me with hollow, hunted eyes, and shot a look in the direction of Lord Dyer. "I would not have seen this happen here," she said. "I would not add to the suffering of this place."

"Where were you?" I asked, whirling on her, advancing with unmistakable rage. "When Crabapple was hurling accusations at Lord Dyer? When Humbug was putting the finishing touches on Rutledge?"

"T-taking *air*," she said, startled, but without hesitation. "I was . . . why do you ask?"

I stared into her dark eyes, trying to root out the madness and rage that the killer surely possessed in superhuman quantities. There was no hint of it. But, then, she was skilled at hiding her true feelings, was she not? Only instants after leaving Dyers' side in tears, she was in the ballroom laughing charmingly, holding court.

"Mr. Scrooge, explain yourself!" she demanded.

Humbug was small, athletic, and quick. Roger Colley was diminutive for a man, but I doubted his ability to remain so eerily wordless under duress as Humbug had. Dickens had mentioned Chinese acrobats, so that was one possibility. Another—and this connected to the mysterious "Lady"—was that Humbug might be a woman. And during all that had happened, Adelaide had been nowhere to be seen.

Yet . . . if Adelaide was the murderer, why had Fezziwig's spirit shown her such kindness?

Not wanting to "give away my hand," as a gambler might say, I shrugged and told her, "I was wondering if you had seen Shen anywhere," I said. "Or any of his entourage?"

She shook her head absently. "Why?"

"Later," I promised, unable to add even a trace of false pleasantness to my tone.

Dickens returned, Crabapple laboring to catch up to the long-legged writer, and, acting a bit more sauced than he actually was, giddily informed us of everything he had told the constable so that our stories would line up. He had played down our ongoing investigation into Humbug and instead focused on what he had learned about Miss Annie Piper, the woman who still might alibi Mr. Guilfoyle. He'd also spoken of Humbug's overall physique, so far as we might gauge it.

"You were seen speaking to Rutledge," Crabapple said, pressing his angry face close to mine. "First, you have a chat with Sunderland and he dies. Now the same with Rutledge. What did the two of you discuss, eh?"

"He was afraid," I said, which was true enough. But then my words and the truth parted ways. "He spoke of a man he had run afoul of. A criminal he believed to be a worse threat than the Colley Brothers and the illicit importers of opium into our ports combined. Someone he felt was pulling Humbug's strings, so to speak. But it had to have been nonsense, surely?"

Crabapple's hand gripped my arm. "Are you an imbecile? He says he's in fear for his life and then he's murdered? I think there just *might* be a connection. Did he name this man?"

"Yes, yes, he did," I said, shaking my head. "He said the man goes by the name of Smithson."

"There in the Quarter," Crabapple said. "The same man Miss Annie has taken up with. Makes sense. Only—no one has ever laid eyes on this Smithson. No one willing to talk to *me*, that is."

"He said that Smithson has another identity completely, that he is a respected man of business. But it could not be. It could not."

"The name!" he demanded.

"It is a man I once knew very well, or so I believed. Jacob Marley. And if you ask me, time is of the essence. Word is sure to reach him quickly, and that will give him time to hide his books, dispose of illegal goods and other evidence. . . ."

"It may take most of the night to get this arranged, but I know a few decent men I can trust for another raid," he said, looking away from Inspector Foote, who was still toadying up to Lord Dyer. "And I don't want *him* knowing about this." Ambition and greed danced merrily in the constable's eyes. A fine and gratifying sight.

"A wise move," I said. "Inspector."

He was about to correct me when my intent sunk into his thoughts and he grinned. Getting to the bottom of all this and dismantling a criminal empire would go a long way towards ensuring his rise to power.

Just then, an icy breath whispered in my ear. *Your turn comes soon, Ebenezer. Then you.*

Leaping to my feet, I cast my frantic gaze about for Fezziwig's specter, but I saw nothing in this lovely ballroom other than the grim sight of two men hauling away Rutledge's corpse, a white sheet tainted with crimson tightly wrapped about the body.

CHAPTER FIFTEEN

I RETURNED TO Furnival's Inn with no other plan than to fall into a dreamless slumber. With the strokes of two after midnight tolling from the clock tower near the inn, I ascended the staircase to my rooms. My footsteps dropped a concrete thud against the wooden steps, my joints groaned despite my youth, and my eyelids were half-closed under the weight of the night.

I yawned as I fumbled for my keys with numb fingers.

Then my heart stopped.

The doormat had been disturbed, and scratches had been etched in the paint around the keyhole as if someone had used a butter knife to force the lock open. Black and smudged fingerprints were smeared on the brass knob. The door was ajar, a faint glow from perhaps a single coal in the hearth, and a faint and deathly whistling.

Fezziwig? Absurd. Then a thought struck, winding me—could it be *Humbug*? No, more likely one of Colley's goons waited for me inside, with a clear order to bring back my eyeballs for Baldworthy. Summoning the last of my resolve, I gripped my cane, heaving it over my head, and kicked in the door.

"Ah, crikey, Mr. Scrooge sir!" cried a small lad in a thick green scarf warming his hands by my fire, a top hat falling off his head as he jumped. "Scared me 'alf out me wits, you did! Would 'ave fought a fine gentleman like you would fink to knock before bursting in!"

Dodger.

Relief washed over me, but the exhaustion in my body experienced it as a wave of hot ache rather than the pleasurable release of a fear that had, only seconds ago, been of a mortal nature. I leaned my cane against the wall, put my hat on the hat rack, and slumped into the armchair by the fire, right beside the one occupied by Dodger. Wearily and with heavy arms, I untied my boots and struggled to pull the wet leather off my feet. I chucked the boots to the side and sat back, feeling every vertebra in my back as I rested against the upholstery.

"Phwoar, sir! What a whiff!" laughed Dodger, pointing at the steam rising from my wet, darned socks as my feet were warmed by the fire. "Been out dancing till the wee hours? Good fing I lit the fire for you, warm this place right up, eh?" Yes, he had lit my fire. With *four* lumps of coal, no less!

The boy unwound his lengthy scarf and placed it absentmindedly on the side table. Without its bulk hiding his frail neck, I could see just how thin the young boy was.

I pinched the bridge of my nose and sighed. "How did you get in?" The boy was about to speak, and I raised a hand to stop him, thinking better of it. Stealing and picking locks were second nature to him, surely. I pressed my eyes closed, rubbed my temples, and observed the yellow stars bursting against a deep-red canvas on the inside of my eyelids.

"Why are you here?" I asked.

"I've got 'ere, upon my person, for you, sir, a treasure of great importance." His chest was puffed out, and with one hand he restored his worn top hat while the other retrieved a small velvet box, identical to the one housing Shen's ring in his desk. I knew precisely what was coming, though I tensed, remembering the horror that had unexpectedly resided along with Shen's ring.

"You, sir, are a gentleman of exquisite sensitivities and impeccable taste, the very characteristics we seek in our clientele. On account of bein' a high-class service, you see." Dodger drew his breath, then opened the lid with a slow, suspenseful movement. He held the ring aloft as if it were the Holy Grail, his wide eyes staring at me as if expecting a gasp or swoon, and his bottom lip sticking out when none came.

Relaxing—no severed finger this time, just a ring—I took it from him, turning it over, examining it. As I expected, it was a heavy-set gold and ruby ring in the very same style that Fezziwig, Thomas Guilfoyle, Shen, and who knows how many more had worn.

"If it ain't too much trouble, Mr. Scrooge, sir," said the young lad, assuming his exaggerated air of business acumen and credibility, "if it ain't too much to ask, you are to attend at the Doll House tomorrow at the request of the patron of this ring, and if it *is* too much trouble, I am to take the ring back and leave you with nothing but a solemn warnin'."

I smiled. Dodger was a keen businessman indeed, if his short stature and hairless chin could allow him to be classified as a man at all. With a little mentoring, he could easily fine-tune that rough commercial acuity and find a path in business, but such a commitment was not one for me to make.

I opened my hands solicitously. "And this, I presume, is regarding the engagement with Annie Piper that Fagin was commissioned to arrange?"

Dodger said nothing but grinned and held out his grubby hand.

I stared at it, unease forming like a lump of coal in my gut. "Well?"

"A tuppence, sir? As per our business arrangement?"

"So you have indeed secured an audience for me with Annie Piper?" I asked, studying the boy in the giant top hat.

"Indeed I 'ave, sir. Though officially-like, my function tonight is messenger only, a little under my station perhaps, but I takes what I can get!"

I fished a coin out of my leather purse, feeling its smooth, cold surface between finger and thumb, as I would with my Belle's locket. Parting with any amount of hard-earned, well-deserved money was no less agonizing than her departure had been. I flipped the coin to him, and he caught it handily, securing it in his ratty coat.

His expression changed suddenly, his eyes darkened, and he lowered his voice. "And I gets what I takes."

With that, Dodger pulled a thick envelope from inside the lining of his blue velvet coat and slid it across the side table between us, knocking his scarf to the floor in the process.

"I understands you're a man of business, just like meself," he said, his eyes set on mine like burning coals. I nodded. "Business is good in the Quarter, truly sir, but I wouldn't mind makin' a better future for meself, not that I need much. So I've got a business proposition for you . . ."

The tiredness was melting away fast. I sat up and leaned forward. Dodger took a deep breath and carefully opened the envelope. From within it he pulled a packet wrapped in tissue, a bundle of thin cards, with what appeared to be very detailed illustrations.

"It's magic, sir," he whispered. "Black magic. We could use it for good, you and me."

I frowned, taking the package from him. They were certainly illustrations, but clearer than anything I had ever seen, extremely realistic. Illustrations of women, doing . . .

My heart sank.

"See how lifelike, sir?" Dodger jabbed at one of the cards with a dirty finger. "See there? Like it's real. *Photography*, they call it. I knows it ain't magic really. I've seen the scientist they use. Ain't many people who know nothing about it yet, but this is what it's used for. Gentleman's Relish."

I flicked through the appalling cards, each depicting one woman or more, drugged or bound and to all appearances barely aware of what was being done to them. My stomach tightened and my head swam, and then I gasped. One of the cards featured Nellie—no, one of the

Nellie "dolls"—performing a degrading, explicit act in what appeared to be the drawing room of an upper-class home. Views of the sprawling countryside reached out through a nearby window. Her hands were bound behind her back. I shoved it quickly to the rear of the stack but was surprised to see an identical one underneath, and under the next.

"They're prints, they can do as many as they like of each image, hundreds if they wants. And there are a few select customers what buys them—guess what they pay for one of these prints . . ."

I shook my head. No price could be put on such atrocity.

"Forty pounds. *Each*!" Dodger took the photographs from me and carefully bundled them together, wrapping them back in the tissue and sliding them carefully into their envelope.

I gasped. Forty pounds was well over six months of my business takings, and it became crystal clear that the true "treasure" Dodger had brought was not the gold ring. This packet alone was worth the rail investment I was seeking.

"What is your proposition, boy?" I asked.

"They're right idiots, I fink. Not them poor women, but the men that run this operation. On account of them using this science for Gentlemen's Relish alone, you see. They keeps it right under wraps, very exclusive indeed, mind you. Keeps it special, and they can charge a king's ransom for each and every print. But I say, if proper businessmen like me and you was in charge, we'd see that every household in England could have real portraits done like this. Instead of paintin's. I bet anyone would pay something for a photograph of themselves."

The potential flooded my imagination. Parents and children, soldiers leaving for battle, distant sweethearts, architecture, crime scenes . . .

"I should say you were right, Dodger. It's remarkable technology. I've seen nothing like it."

The boy beamed. "Well, what if I told you I could get the secret of how this new technology works? Already told you I seen the scientist. I'll share it wiv you, Mr. Scrooge, honest I will, and in return . . ." He drew himself up to his limited full height and puffed out his chest. "And in return you'll make me an equal partner in the legitimate business. I'll make you rich, Mr. Scrooge, you bet your cotton socks I'll make you a fortune."

The ache once again began to creep up my legs and into my bones. A distant clock tower struck quarter past the hour and my headache reverberated with its hollow toll. I longed to be done with this gruesome Humbug affair, to escape the secrecy, the pursuit, and the terror.

"Thank you for your intriguing business offer, Mr. Dodger. It is a most fascinating idea indeed."

Dodger puffed his thin chest out even further, pursed his lips together in pride, and stuck out his hand for me to shake.

"But," I continued, "there is much to consider: What you have shown me is utterly horrifying. For example, it is impossible for me to judge whether these subjects have posed consensually."

Dodger averted his eyes immediately, which told me he knew something to the effect that they had not.

"And we would stand to make powerful enemies should we follow the course you suggest. Let's say you stole away the know-how. What would its current owners do to prevent us from ever capitalizing on it? These are dangerous people, are they not?"

Dodger shrugged. "Life's fulla risk."

He was right. I'd just seen a man murdered, I'd grappled with a known killer; certainly not the normal state of things for a man of business like myself. I considered the task I would be about in just a few hours: the raid on Marley's place. If proof was indeed found supporting Rutledge's claim that Marley was Smithson, then the entire criminal empire might crumble and this technology become ours for the taking.

"All right," I said. "For now, you must not show these to anyone else, to save the dignity of these poor girls. And let us not alert the police either, there are few within the institution I trust."

"Oh, right you are, guv'nor! I feel the very same!"

"How may I get in touch with you?" I asked.

Dodger named a particular inn just south of Whitechapel. "Ask for Nancy. You might 'ave seen her around, like, 'fyou've ever been to the Quarter. Shock of red hair, takes good care of me and me boys? No? You'd like her. A businesslady if you've ever known the like. She can find me anytime."

A businesslady? "Very well," I said, shaking his hand. Then I looked away, waved my hand absently as if what I was about to ask was of little consequence, a mere aside. "Speaking of ladies at the Quarter, young man. Do you know anything about a woman calling herself

'The Lady'? Does the title mean anything to you?" I studied Dodger's expression; it had become stony and calculated. I mentally crossed this Nancy off the list.

"Yeah, I heard of her," he said. "Scary sort. Talks funny."

"Funny?"

"Like she's a foreigner or sumfing."

"Chinese?" I quizzed him.

"'Ow would I know what a Chinese lady sounds like?" he retorted.

"But you've seen her. What does she look like?"

"Long hair, always wears dresses and 'ats."

"You couldn't perhaps be a little less vague? I could find women on every street corner in London that fit that description."

Dodger shrugged his slender shoulders.

"What connection does this Lady have to Smithson?" I pressed on, leaning in and locking eyes with him. The more dirt I might heap on Marley's grave, the better!

"Don't know nuffin' about that neither," he said.

I sighed. "And the Quarter? Is she somehow connected to this ring, the Doll House, the network of darkness in that God-forsaken district?"

"Tell you what," my potential business partner said, stuffing his hand in his pocket. "How about you fink on the matter and get back to me?"

There was no sense in pressing him further, his defensive stance and mineral expression spoke loudly that he would not answer any of my questions.

"I will send word to Nancy once I have fully considered the matter," I said, extending my arm in the exact manner he had just presented his hand to me. He shook my hand and leaped to his feet. His stomach growled. The poor lad was hungry, but how he acquired sustenance was up to him, the astute businessman that he proclaimed to be.

"You won't regret it, Mr. Scrooge!" cried Dodger, and sped out and down the stairs with a drumroll. I closed the door behind him, and my thoughts drifted back to the photographs, which he had taken with him. If I didn't regret it, somebody would.

Yawning, I turned to extinguish the fire and fall onto my bed in an unconscious slumber, but my eye caught something under the side table.

The boy's thick, green scarf. No part of me considered running after him into the freezing night; his little neck would have to endure the cold. I picked it up to hang it on the hat stand, but as I reached up to drape it over a hook, I was knocked awake by its acrid smell. The scarf stank, a biting, acerbic stench of the chemicals just like those I'd smelled drifting from the Lycia back in the Quarter. Screwing up my nose, I tossed it into the fire.

WHOOSH! A burst of light flashed and crackled, and bluish flames rose like an inferno for a moment, then subsided. I leaped back and dashed for the washbasin by my sink before dousing the fire with a hiss.

The blackened scarf lay in the hearth like a charred snake after a forest fire. What the *hell* were those villains doing at the Lycia?

Putting such thoughts from my mind, I stumbled to my bed and collapsed into the warm and welcoming arms of sleep.

CHAPTER SIXTEEN

Thursday, December 22nd, 1833
Three Days to Christmas

THE LACK OF sleep and terror from last night were a toxic combination, rendering my eyes sore but my resolve piqued. This time yesterday Marley was the last person I ever saw myself speaking with again. A mere year ago, I had broken off my referral relationship with Marley when I had caught him going through confidential papers on my desk. He stood there bold as brass, with a pad and pencil making notes of wealthy men that I had been developing as contacts. But now, with the chill morning air whipping my face, my head was poking out the cab window and I was clutching my hat, shouting and cursing at the horseman to drive his horses faster and deliver me to my former business associate.

"Sit down before you do yourself an injury!" called Adelaide from where she was sitting opposite me in the police cab. I could picture Crabapple rolling his eyes.

"Gossip travels faster than horses, Miss Owen," I said, angrily retreating back into the cab and adjusting my top hat. "We must beat the morning edition. If Marley gets wind of the murder at the manor, his storage rooms will be emptied faster than you can say 'Dickens.' "

I wasn't pleased to find Adelaide in Crabapple's carriage when it pulled up before Furnival's, but there was little I could say or do where that woman was concerned with Crabapple's watchful gaze upon us. Still, I noted with satisfaction the look of surprise and the sting with which she reacted each time I reverted to the formal "Miss Owen."

As soon as the cab drew to a full stop, I darted up the familiar stone steps to Marley's place and rained a deluge of staccato strikes at his door with the brass knocker. The handle of the knocker quivered when I released it, its head a snarling gargoyle that bore, I noticed, a subtle resemblance to Marley.

"Police!" shouted Crabapple as he rushed up behind me. "In the name of the law, open up!"

A gaslight was lit behind one of the upper windows, which slid open with a crash. Out popped Marley's enraged head, still wearing its nightcap over a shock of greying hair disheveled from its abrupt awakening.

"What's all this?" he shouted down. Then he saw me, and his face screwed up in distaste and fury. "Ebenezer *Scrooge* . . ." he snarled.

"Open this door immediately," demanded Crabapple, and Marley retreated. He slammed the window and the ghostly flickering of his gas lamp dimmed and vanished.

The metal clangs of bolts being drawn and locks being turned rang out in the cold, dark December morning. As soon as the heavy door opened just a creak, the host of policemen pressed past Marley and vanished inside his offices, which also served as his home.

"Oy!" he called out. "What's all this? What are you doing?"

"Jacob Marley," said Constable Crabapple. "We're investigating a series of offenses. Namely harboring stolen goods, dealing with known criminals . . . why, there's even the flavor of murder about you, Marley!"

Jacob Marley smiled. "I have no idea what this is all about, gentlemen, oh pardon me, and *lady* . . ." He gave Adelaide a nasty wink that was not lost on me. Adelaide a "lady"? *The* Lady perhaps?

I restrained my imagination from wandering further and focused on the task at hand.

"Please, come in," Marley said, "have a good look around, and then leave me."

Adelaide and I followed Crabapple inside. The hairs stood up on the back of my neck as I pressed past Marley. As soon as I was in the house, I turned to shoot him an angry glare, but he had descended his stone steps and was standing in the icy street, whispering something in the ear of a plump milkmaid. She nodded eagerly, and he pressed a coin into her hand before she peeled off, her milk jugs dangling as she slipped and slid across the ice. Marley turned back to the house, caught me frowning at him, and grinned mildly as he climbed each step to the front door.

"This is your doing, no doubt," he hissed at me.

"Come now, Marley," I said. "You're a man of the world—which explains the sad shape the world is in!"

Crabapple's men turned Marley's offices inside out,

sweeping clerks' desks, emptying filing cabinets, and pulling books from their shelves. Several of them stomped upstairs to his residence, and we heard the dull thuds of their heavy boots soiling his lush carpets.

I knew where Marley's storage room was; I used a similar setup myself to receive collateral goods from customers unable to pay their dues. So I nudged Crabapple and nodded towards the back of the office, at a heavy door adorned with a series of practically impregnable locks.

"What's this here?" Crabapple asked Marley.

"The vault," Marley replied. "The items stored within are of incalculable worth, and I'd beseech your men to—stop! You can't go in there!" He pushed past me and stood in front of the door, arms splayed to either side. "I'm appealing to your common sense, Constable; don't let your men raid my vault! There is nothing of use to you in there, I can assure you."

Unable to stop myself, I snickered.

"Open this door immediately, Marley," ordered Crabapple. Sulking, Marley went to his desk, unlocked its middle drawer. He removed it, scowling at me all the while. Secured to the underside of the desk was a small package with keys and combinations to the myriad locks securing the "vault" door.

"You'll pay for this, Scrooge," he said, glaring. "And you—what's your name, then?"

"Crabapple."

"Fitting. And you'll find your actions come at a high price, too."

"Not at all," I answered, taking off my top hat and

brushing the slush onto his carpet. I replaced my hat with a flick of my wrist. "It seems you are to pay today."

The vault door opened, and the policemen filed in, knocking over oil paintings and upsetting valuable porcelain vases as they did. Marley winced.

"Are these yours?" Crabapple barked, peering inside the vault his men were searching. "What proof do you have?"

Marley retrieved a thick book of ledgers from a safe and placed them with a thud on the desk in front of Crabapple.

The policeman flicked through a few pages. "I can't read this, it's all nonsense! Scrawls and scribbles."

"Let me have a look," Adelaide said, having until now been waiting in the reception area at the front of the office, watching and listening. Crabapple looked to me, and I nodded.

"Preposterous!" shouted Marley, as Adelaide took the ledger from the constable and sat down at Marley's desk. She took his magnifying glass by its ivory handle and began inspecting the contents, line-by-line. "Who is this woman? One of your whores, Ebenezer?" Adelaide shifted uncomfortably, said nothing. She continued to study the pages, but I could see pink roses forming on her neck and cheeks as she blushed.

"How dare you, Marley! To assault a lady's honor in that fashion, especially considering Miss Owen is now the only conduit between yourself and your freedom? Why, that is bestial even for you!" I cried, hot prickles of anger spreading across my scalp. I couldn't help myself.

"Besides, unlike you, Jacob, I can appreciate a woman for her mind as well as her loyal heart," I retorted.

"Only because you are so miserly that you no doubt confine yourself to cheaper, more solitary solutions," he said with a smirk.

"How dare you?" Crabapple fumed. "In front of a lady!"

"My dear gentlemen," said Adelaide with her nightingale voice and velvet smile. "It would be of such assistance to me if you'd please postpone your disagreement. If Mr. Marley is innocent, as he claims, then it is of utmost importance that I uncover, in these ledgers, the evidence to absolve him."

My former friend scoffed. He was about to open his mouth to release some acidic poison in Adelaide's direction when we heard a sudden crash from the vaults. Marley and I rushed to be the first through the heavy door, and I made sure to jab my elbow in Marley's side as I jostled past him. A wooden crate lay smashed on the floor, its contents spilling out over the booted feet of the policemen gathered round it: seemingly endless coils of chains and silver boxes.

"Had to smash it open, sir," said Humperdink to Crabapple. "It was nailed shut."

Crabapple grimaced. "Humperdink, if they made hats the size of your brain, you'd be wearin' a peanut shell!"

"What in God's name?" shrieked Marley, and pushed in, trying to scoop up the chains and wind them back into some order.

"What in the devil is this, Marley?" demanded Crabapple.

"A very valuable consignment of silver cruets," Marley wailed. "Collected from St. Savior's Church as security against a loan. Look, here!" He stood up, the chains draped over him and hanging from him like metal vines, and he pointed at a small dent in one of the boxes. "Look what you've done!"

I felt a ghostly chill at the sight of Marley weighed down with endless chains and boxes. As if it were a portent of some kind.

The policemen lost interest and continued their search, bringing cabinets and crates and boxes out into the office for examination and recording. I looked at Marley where he stood, tangled in his own chains. I tried to feel some compassion for him but failed. His expression changed from fury to something else, something far more pitiful.

"Look at these," he whispered, holding up the bell chains. "These great chains, designed to hold the weight of great crystal church chandeliers and never falter, never dropping their burden. Each link is like the bonds of friendship, formed laboriously. Yet so easily severed with the proper tools."

"Like betrayal," I interrupted.

"But, Scrooge, look here, see." He showed me a chain link with the telltale marks of soldering. "With a generous amount of heat and the right metal, they can be repaired. There's just a bit of *painful burning* to go through to resolidify those links, those bonds of *friendship* . . ."

"Your use of that word is an obscene exaggeration." I

shook my head. "Is there anything left in that dried up and rotten prune you call a brain?"

Another crash came from the office as a constable dropped a porcelain elephant. Marley cried out, pushing me over as he scurried back out, the chains dropping from him.

"Oops," said Humperdink, and Marley fell to his knees, scooping up the precious shards.

"You can cross that elephant off the inventory," Crabapple called over to Adelaide, who ignored him as she studied each line and entry in the book.

Marley yelped suddenly and stood up, sucking his thumb. Blood dripped from where he had sliced it open on a shard of broken elephant. He thrust the remaining porcelain mess into the hands of Humperdink.

"You'll do no such thing, woman," he barked, his chin wobbling. "Scotland Yard will be recompensing me for that item. Crabapple, I don't know what game you are playing, but you would do well to remove this little girl from my accounts. That is sensitive information, and by no means anything a woman can comprehend."

"Actually, Mr. Marley, the books are clean," she said finally, closing the ledgers and sliding them across the desk towards him. "Though your business dealings are murky at best, there is nothing in here that is incriminating in any way."

"Hah!" Marley yelled, triumphant.

Adelaide shook her head and muttered, "*Now* he thinks I'm competent."

"That can't be," I said. "Make certain you check again."

"So I have," Adelaide continued. "See for yourself. Marley has kept impeccable records. Each unit is accounted for and listed against value and debtor. Transactions are recorded thoroughly, and each month is summarized in a detailed cash flow statement. I can find no connection to the Rutledge estate or any of the other—"

"Lord Rutledge?" said Marley. "What's he got to do with anything? Never mind. It seems your judgment has once again been called into question, Scrooge. Not the first time you have been humiliated thusly, of course. You may leave presently—oh, unless, of course, there is more of my property you wish to have destroyed at the expense of Scotland Yard?"

"He would have traded through holding companies," I urged Adelaide.

"All traceable," Marley offered.

"They would have used pseudonyms."

"Each debtor and creditor is named with a supporting address," Adelaide admitted. "I recognize most all of them as reputable. I'd wager you would, too."

Marley scoffed at me, his nose twitching in a sneer, casting triumphant glances at Crabapple to ensure he was registering every word. He was.

"There must be other ledgers. Marley's mind for business is so hellishly astute he would have recorded everything, but I doubt even he would be thick enough to do so in open books." I turned to Crabapple. "Constable! Have your men found anything in Marley's residences above?"

"Quick as a corpse, that lot," I muttered.

At that moment a drumroll of heavy boots sounded out as Crabapple's men thumped down the stairs and burst into the office. Humperdink jumped and once again dropped the shards of porcelain elephant.

"Nothing, sir," said a constable from under a heavy moustache.

"Check again," I called out to him. The constable raised his eyebrows and looked to Crabapple. He said nothing but shook his head. His dark eyes were narrowed and bore into mine. His fingers twitched.

"Well?" shouted Marley, his voice thick with glee. "Pray, don't keep me in suspense any longer! What will you have me arrested for? The ownership of a porcelain elephant? Impeccable business records? Come now, Crabapple, tell me how you are to explain the coup of the century to Inspector Foote and Commissioner Rowan?"

A heavy knocking drummed from the front door. More voices, demanding entrance.

"*That* would be Inspector Foote, I believe," Marley said, raising an eyebrow to Crabapple. "The two of you are acquainted, I understand?"

"Humperdink," snarled the incandescent Crabapple. "You will remain here and take Mr. Marley's statement. Be sure to transcribe accurately the value of that elephant. All other men, off." His face was reddening, clearly visualizing the torment he would face from his superior.

I had no doubt that despite enduring a verbal thrashing from Lord Dyer and others of his station last night for "allowing" Rutledge to be murdered right under his nose, that Foote had, in the end, managed to lay all blame at Crabapple's feet.

I struggled to keep my breath under control, frustration and panic brewing in my gut. Then I saw Foote entering this chamber, and with him . . . Shen?

The Chinaman smiled thinly. Then I recalled the whispers that passed between Rutledge and Shen at the party. Shen had known I was coming after Rutledge. He had told the lord to give Marley's name and had engineered all of this!

"Perhaps Mr. Scrooge and I might take some air, as you Englishmen say?" Shen suggested. "We have much to talk about, I believe!"

Adelaide's eyes locked with mine and she nodded. "I'm sure Inspector Foote is going to want statements from all of us. I'm happy to give mine first."

Soon I was outside with Shen, clenching my fists against the nasty December chill. Morning carolers passed, heads popped out from a garishly painted wagon. They rang bells and pointed at the legends on the wagon, which promised "good and fair prices" for all one's Christmas needs.

"Now that's a humbug, wouldn't you say, Mr. Scrooge?" Shen asked.

The use of that word chilled me more than the cutting wind.

"What 'need' does one have for Christmas?" Shen asked. "Just a day to find yourself another year older and deeper in debt, wouldn't you say?"

"What do you want? Why did you do this?"

Shen's smile was a mockery of sympathy. "Even after

you were warned, you not only pressed on, you entered my premise illegally, rifled through my things when I was not there. That was ungentlemanly. Rude. I do not abide rudeness."

"I know about you and the underground opium trade."

"Knowing a thing and being able to prove it are two entirely different matters."

"What about 'The Lady,' eh?"

Shen shrugged. "Fezziwig's invitation, yes. I was most curious myself to learn what that was all about. Some woman in need of help, I assumed?"

"You're lying."

"Rudeness," Shen reminded me. "How much punishment do you really wish to endure? Particularly when vast pleasures may yet await you?"

I recalled the Colley Brothers making much the same offer.

"Your Constable Crabapple will no longer be willing or able to help you after this. Your Mr. Dickens will remain loyal only so long as he believes you are in a position to help him achieve his dream of becoming his own publisher."

I tensed. Shen must have overheard Dickens and me talking at the party.

"And poor Miss Owen. What do you really know about her? She arrives on your doorstep just as all this misery begins. A coincidence? I do not believe in them, nor should you. Perhaps she is this mysterious 'Lady' Mr. Fezziwig meant to warn all of us about. A warning you might consider heeding. But no matter. What is important is that you need money and I have money. Promise me now that you will put all this foolishness behind you, and I will see that you receive all the funding you might ever desire."

"From your foul trade."

"Does it matter where it comes from, so long as it comes?"

My hands balled into fists, I said, "I'd rather go to the poorhouse."

Shen bowed. "Very well, Mr. Scrooge. Perhaps when next we meet, I will draw you a map."

CHAPTER SEVENTEEN

THE COLD IN the air stung my cheeks. I pulled my coat tightly round my neck as Dickens and I walked against the icy wind back to our district. A carriage had been called for Adelaide, who wished to visit Guilfoyle before meeting me at the counting-house.

With lips numb from the chill, I told Dickens about the late-night visit from the young entrepreneur, even slipped him the ring I'd been given. He knew something of this strange photographic process. The camera obscura had been around for centuries, and a Frenchman named Niépce, who had only just died this year, had developed photo etching and a rough chemical process that might explain what I'd seen.

Little, though, could explain the base use that Smithson, whoever the bastard truly was, had come up with for the process. "Deplorable," I snarled. "It's one thing, a woman *choosing* to enter the world's oldest. But the listless expressions, the confusion, and even fear in their eyes, it's like they were drugged and dragged from their beds to perform in these . . . I don't know what to call them."

"You said there were elaborate sets and costumes," Dickens said, flexing his fingers through his fingerless gloves as he gnawed on these rough bits of information. "Perhaps a tie to the theatre?" He stopped to pull a cigarette from his breast pocket, lighting it against the howling gale.

"Anything is possible. All that said, the boy *was* correct, though," I said. "The commercial implications are staggering. Everyone with means will want one of these cameras, and the means to develop their own photographs. Whoever controls—"

"The word *camera* sounds an awful lot like *chimera*, doesn't it?" Dickens said, twirling the hand-rolled smoke between finger and thumb. I stared at him, but his eyes were fixed on the glowing end of his cigarette. "Chimera, the fire-breathing monster." He exhaled a swirling dance of grey air. "You see only profit, Scrooge. I see only misery. They're using children around these dangerous chemicals. It might be poisonous, for all we know."

"This city is poisonous. At least young Dodger is trying to make something of himself."

Frowning, Dickens spotted a woman, no older than twenty, standing only a few yards away by the entrance of a millinery. She was clutching at a filthy shawl barely covering her exposed skeletal chest. It was rattling with heavy consumption. Her dirty and tangled hair, which had the color and smell of a goat, poked from underneath a dirty head kerchief. With a jolt, I recognized her as the beggar woman outside Fezziwig's wake.

Dickens walked over to her, shrugging his coat off

his shoulders and draping it around hers, taking care to button it snugly around her neck. "Cover up, Rosie," he said, gently. "For the love of God, it's December. You'll catch your death if you haven't already. Christmas Day approaches. Have you anywhere to go?"

I stared at Rosie as she silently wrapped herself in the reporter's warm coat, *curtsied*, and scurried off down the street. In glum silence, the shivering reporter regained my side.

I opened my mouth, and he silenced me with a sharp look.

"What?" I asked. "I was merely going to—"

"Say one word about the pointlessness of trying to help someone who's beyond help by any measure, and I will cave your teeth in, Scrooge. That's a promise."

I shrugged.

Speaking loud enough to be heard over the roaring of the whipping wind in our ears, we discussed Shen's threats—and intimations—not the least of which implicated Adelaide herself.

Dickens dismissed the notion. "He's trying to get under our skins, that's all. He clearly knows that we broke into his office and found what we learned. That information about the opium trade is useless now. Deliveries, routes, couriers, even bosses . . . all will have changed at this point."

"So it's a good thing Jack Colley didn't take me up on my offer."

Dickens nodded.

We trudged past a frosted shop window displaying towers of Turkish delights and candied almonds. The door tinkled open to release a rosy-cheeked mother and her child. A waft of heavenly scents of fir, pine, hemlock, sweet spices of cinnamon, and cranberry rushed out with them, coupled with the woman's own rose perfume. The woman and her little daughter walked off in the wind, laughing.

I thought of Belle and her daughters . . . and turned away.

I steered our conversation back to Adelaide and told Dickens of the bold-faced lie I'd caught the woman in. And I described the manner in which she'd so quickly and icily gone from tears with Dyer to joyous laughter with Rutledge. I further reminded him that Adelaide had vanished before Rutledge's murder and not reappeared until sometime later, with only the flimsiest explanation for her disappearance.

"I hold to the notion that Humbug is a man," Dickens said. "Small, athletic, perhaps circus trained. As to Adelaide's ability to hide her sorrow after an ordeal, well, I think you're making too much of that. That she lied to you to protect Lord Dyer . . . yes, perhaps you should be cautious around her. Consider your words carefully before revealing what you've learned. But don't dismiss her; hold to the old adage of keeping friends close, enemies closer."

"Close is not where I wish to keep a knife-wielding killer, but I'll consider it. Another thing, Dickens, that rhyme . . . and Rutledge's reaction when I sang, 'Pretty maids, all in a row . . .' "

I noted that Dickens' face had hardened and he could no longer look me in the eye. "Roger Colley is still loose, there are Shen's threats, Humbug has killed again, now there's this Lady . . . I don't know that I can keep on with this. I'm a curious man, yes, but I also value my life, Mr. Scrooge."

My hand gripped my cane so tightly that it began to ache. "What of our deal? With the pledges I received at the party, I will be a rich man in a matter of weeks. A month, no more, and then it will be nothing for me to finance your publishing venture—"

"As I said before, it's not all about profit."

We stopped walking, stared into each other's eyes through the snow-laden wind. His dark and resolute. My own . . . I could only guess from his expression. But that changed as I spoke.

"I received . . . word . . . after Rutledge. Two more, then me. Please, Dickens. You know it isn't easy for me to ask. Any chance I might have had of the police helping me is gone now, after what happened at Jacob's place. And with Miss Owen proving herself untrustworthy . . ."

He lit another cigarette, looked about, took long moments considering what I'd said. "Fine, fine. You know, of all the odd things we've encountered, including those photographs you beheld, it's Dodger's scarf that gnaws at me. What could he possibly have come in contact with that would make the flames react so explosively?"

"I don't know," I said earnestly. "And frankly, I hope never to find out!"

Adelaide was in fine form at the counting-house. She had strung fragrant boughs and garlands from the mantle, framing a glowing fire of crackling pinecones. A weeping couple nearly bowled me down in the street as they hurried out my door, and a line of clients waited within.

After hanging my snow-laden hat and coat on the hat stand, I set about my own duties and did not disturb Miss Owen until the last of her visitors had flown. A common bond united them all. They had entered uneasily, filled with suspicion, and then, after unburdening themselves of considerable sums of real cash money in my unusually warm and atmospheric office, had fled with laughter in their hearts. The couple I had witnessed on my way in here, those were not tears of grief I had beheld on their faces; instead, they had been tears of relief!

"What scheme are you up to now?" I barked, counting the small fortune she had collected today.

"Well, you may want to sit down for this," she offered. Her gaze swept over my face, searching for signs of my continued fury at her.

Though I still felt flames in my heart, I focused on my genuine curiosity about her new scheme. Her hunched shoulders relaxed. My ploy to disguise my upset with her had worked. "I'll stand, thank you."

"Here it is, then: I sent word to each of these debtors that if they came and paid us a particular amount, different for each, of course, that we would never again hound them, never darken their doors. That their obligations to us would now and forever be at an end."

Outrage lit in my eyes. "You mean . . . you settled for pennies on the pound?"

Adelaide rolled her eyes. "Honestly, Mr. Scrooge, what kind of a businesswoman do you take me for? Look at the paperwork Mr. Snarkwick just signed."

I knew his account quite well. "There must be some mistake. This makes out that his total debt was the amount he paid. But I know for a fact he owed five times this!"

"And so he did, yesterday. Before I sold the rest of that debt to several of your competitors. They were most happy to take it on for the actual amount owed. Those amounts will grow substantially in the coming months of course as their own interest and fees accrue."

"Wait. You didn't tell our clients that you had sold the lion's share of their debts? They paid what they did *believing* they were leaving our company with a clean slate?"

"I said nothing that wasn't true," she told me. "It's not my fault if people don't ask questions, or if they make assumptions. They should know full well what they owe. They told me many of a story of you pounding on their doors, reciting amounts, demanding recompense. It is all perfectly legal; the paperwork will hold up in any court."

I rubbed my temple, a heat bursting within me that made our surroundings feel like they were warmed by the fires of hell. "I have to admit, I'm shocked."

She stared into my eyes, unapologetic, remorseless.

"Shocked I didn't think of it myself!" I cried, laughing and startling both of us by sweeping her up into my arms and locking her in the heartiest embrace I'd given anyone since Belle and I parted ways. "That's brilliant!"

She reared back, grinning, and nearly lost her balance. I held her tight, steadying her, all too aware of her wildly beating heart against mine. Her lips were inches from mine, her eyes and the promise they held intoxicating. Or was that simply the reflection of the crackling fire in her eyes?

"All right then," she said, breaking into peals of laughter while smacking my hands. "Let go!"

I did so, stepping back. "I'm sorry, that was—"

"It was hysterical," she said. "You . . . and me? The thought of it!"

She was right. The thought if it: me and someone who had broken trust and faith and thought nothing of it. Someone who kept untold secrets and, as Shen said, that I barely knew. "And there is 'your Tom.' "

Her laughter stopped dead away, and the breeching silence in my offices was broken only by the sound of her scooping up her dress, sitting back at her desk, and scratching away with her pen. "I don't understand you," she said at last. "One moment we are allies, respected confidants. The next you glare at me as if I were the architect of all your misery. I understand fully that simply because we have been thrust into this madness together, it doesn't mean we must also be . . . friends. But sooner or later you're going to have to give an accounting of the reasons behind your strange behavior. Otherwise, I will be forced to find employment elsewhere and endeavor to get to the bottom of this mystery on my own. I don't expect an answer now, but soon, Mr. Scrooge. I will not wait forever."

Clearing my throat, I asked, "Have none of the men from Sunderland's circle sent word?"

Adelaide shook her head.

"Well," I said confidently. "We have one more day. I'll call upon that solicitor first thing. He is probably coordinating all their bids. That was the point of it, to bring the warring factions together through profit."

"Um," she grunted, not looking up from her files.

"Damnit, woman, are you even listening to me?"

She grunted again, flipped a page. "It's the files Billy Humble sent over. Rutledge was on the brink, there's no denying that, but there's clearly more to it. If you look at the numbers, he should have lost his primary estate a year ago. There isn't a payment made for taxes in an age."

"But that wasn't one of his problems," I said.

"No. I have tax certificates here dating back a year saying he was now caught up and paid in full. Quarterly statements since then showing he had no worries along those lines."

"The endless cash draws, the succession of mortgages and loans . . ."

"All of which has been going on for years, mounting and mounting. And there were threats from the tax office of foreclosure, a number of them . . . but that stopped suddenly, even as the rest went on, unabated. Who has the power to forgive debts of this magnitude?"

"Someone in Whitehall, perhaps?" Like a certain Lord Dyer, I mentally added.

Adelaide opened another file. "Here, letters of thanks from the police superintendent for Rutledge's many donations over the past year. But he made none. It was as if someone were using him as a shill."

"For bribery?"

"Criminals need respectable types to 'front' for them," she said. "And Rutledge . . . his needs were vast."

"I must know more of this," I said, turning my back to her as I removed a certain ruby ring from my inner desk drawer and hid it in my fist. "Keep digging."

"Where are you going?" she asked. "No place dangerous, I hope."

"Certainly not," I lied. "Another possible investor."

"Good!" she said. "And don't think I've forgotten my promise to find you a few, oh, what do they call them? Whales, I believe. Big-time investors, that's what they are often referred to as, are they not?"

"They are indeed," I said with a bow. "Good hunting, Miss Owen." I dropped the ruby ring into my pants pocket while grabbing up my cane, hat, and coat.

"And to you," she said.

I slipped on my coat, popped my top hat firmly on my head, and hesitated. Perhaps I should just have it out with her, I considered. Vent my anger and get to the root of why she had lied.

Yet there was something so fetching about the confounded woman as she sat there, brow furrowed, blowing that lock of curls from her face and seeing it fluttering slowly back into place, that instead I spun and rushed out into the bracing chill of the snow-covered streets.

I passed a choir singing a carol I'd only ever heard in

the last few weeks, and hesitated despite myself as they joyously bleated:

God rest ye merry, gentlemen,
Let nothing you dismay,
For Jesus Christ our Savior
Was born upon this day,
To save us all from Satan's power
When we were gone astray:
O tidings of comfort and joy,
comfort and joy,
O tidings of comfort and joy.

"You'll never be led astray, so long as you're true to your nature," I said with a grumble, my cane digging into the snow as I whirled and stalked away. Thoughts of the money my house had just made by Miss Owen's ingenuity and guile warmed me, despite my rage at her betrayal. I laughed and hurled back at the rosy-faced cherubs, "And the devil, like Jesus, looks after his own!"

With a happy heart, I strode away, heading north to another hell entirely.

CHAPTER EIGHTEEN

I RETURNED TO the Royal Quarter alone. It was much changed by day, a desolate range of warehouses and tenements. But I could feel eyes on me. Shapes scurried behind shuttered windows. Whispers reached from darkened alleys. The stench of desperation whipped towards me on the cold breeze: gin, sweat, foul and diseased breath, unwashed clothing and flesh . . . Beneath it all lay need and want, those ever-present demons.

Clearing his throat, Fagin stepped from a storefront and presented himself with a ridiculous flourish. "Good sir, kind sir, my heart fills at the sight of you—and that tasty bauble you wear."

I peered down at the gleaming ruby ring perched upon my ring finger.

"Well, I must see what I can do to help you, mustn't I?" He groveled before me, touching my waistcoat like a fool until I smacked my cane on the cobbles and instantly arrested his attention.

"The Doll House," I said. "And be quick about it."

"Forthwith, my dear!" he cried, spinning and leading me through the maze of buildings to where I had glimpsed Shen and the Nellie look-alike. "Most haste! Without hesitation!"

I raced up the icy steps to the whorehouse as the grasshopper-like Fagin took them two or three at time, then burst into the warm but empty receiving hall before him.

"Fine treasures, sir. *Fine*," he promised and clapped his hands. Footfalls came from the corridor and the stairs as I looked about. Lining the hall's lush oak paneling were magnificent classical oil paintings of the biblical women of sin: Eve, Jezebel, Bathsheba, Tamar. Each had been mounted in her own gold-leaf frame, their bosoms bare.

Then the women appeared. A handful of prostitutes wearing elaborate costumes, makeups, and wigs lined up in the foyer, a parade of bare legs and full bosoms. Once I perused their ranks, I understood why this place was called the Doll House. I took in the living dolls before me: a busty Boudica, a jaunty Joan of Arc, a practically bare Eve and her equally revealed twin, a Lady Godiva, a dark-skinned Cleopatra, a smirking Marie Antoinette, a haughty Catherine the Great, even a forgiving Mary Magdalene and a sly Lavinia Edwards, a famous actress . . . who was clearly a man!

"Tell us what you desire," said the Cleopatra with a melodious laugh, breaking from her sisters to stroke my arm. She might have been a succubus for her deep yellow and red exotic robes, her dark haunting emerald eyes, and her rich mocha skin. She was the most striking creature I had ever seen. She promised me delights both cruel and kind, and assured me that any fantasy I might dream up could be made true in this place.

"Maybe another time," I said. "I have something particular in mind."

Cleopatra sighed. She exchanged looks with Fagin and nodded to the steps.

My hand slid smoothly along the banister as I was ushered up the wide staircase. A bronze gargoyle was perched at the top, grimacing. Fagin led me to a room with blood-red walls he called the Long Gallery. The familiar floral aroma of Indian tobacco whirled through the air and found my nostrils. From front to back the room was filled with laughing men sporting elaborate muttonchops, polished boots, and a surplus of swagger. These were not men one would expect to see at this end of town. Gentlemen gambled, drank, and conducted whatever business could not be dared anywhere else. Garlands of holly, mistletoe, and fresh evergreens laced the Long Gallery, hung high under the ceiling with deep-red ribbons. *So, the birth of Christ is celebrated even in the depths of Hell. . . .*

Business was surprisingly brisk for the middle of a work-afternoon. Every man here wore a ring like mine—except for those like Fagin and other servants who circulated, distributing liquors and exotic delicacies such as raw but seasoned fish in a bed of curry. I stepped out of the way of a serving wench adorned by a pearl necklace and nothing else, and bumped into a warm squealing mass that rewarded me with peals of giggles.

Peering down, I saw an odd little man cradled in a huge leather chair that enveloped both him and the half-dozen women pressed all about him. His clothing was ostentatious: a zebra-striped suit, crimson cravat with tiny white stars, glasses with little round lens tinted black as night. He patted bottoms with white silk gloves and tipped his stovepipe hat back in order to welcome kisses from his harem of admirers. Beaming a wide, greasy grin, he yanked off his gloves the better to feel the flesh of his admirers, and I saw that unlike all the other visitors, he wore no ring. He murmured something in a language not at all familiar to me, his voice deep, guttural. I turned away, wishing to see no more.

"A little shy, perhaps, my dear?" Fagin asked. "This ain't the place for lily-white hands, sir!"

"It's thorough repugnance that you mistake for shyness, Fagin. No matter—I'm here for Annie Piper," I said.

"But of course you are, sir, of course you are. Why, ain't no girl fairer than 'er. Fine gentleman like you, you likes 'em well-traveled, eh? Been all over the world, have you? Just like our Annie? Ah, a fair one is she. Speaks more languages than I can count, that naughty little ginger. Speaks them at just the right moment, if you understand me there, both of us being men of the world and such. You like girls with foreign tongues to flick, my dear?"

I recalled what Dodger had said of "The Lady," that she spoke with an accent that was "passing strange." Interesting.

"Get her for me," I insisted.

"Now there's the ever so slight chink in our agreement, Mr. Scrooge. Not entirely feasible, see? Seein' as how she has become the personal favorite of Mr. Smithson himself, you see . . . I just couldn't take you to 'er, no, don't make me! I'd be ruined, I'd starve, you'd find me lying in a gutter on Christmas morning!"

I swallowed hard as I slipped a small bribe into his grubby mitt. "I just want to talk to the woman. Surely your Mr. Smithson wouldn't object to that."

"Well . . . if you're sure?"

"It's why I'm here. The only reason, I assure you."

Fagin pocketed the gold and backed into a doorway framed by a crimson curtain. It parted as he disappeared within it, offering only the slightest glimpse of the corridor beyond. A golden corridor, marked with rooms stamped with elegantly drawn numbers.

Someone brushed against me and I tensed, then found myself staring into the face of Nellie Pearl!

No, not Miss Pearl. Her doppelganger. The one with the scar who had been escorting that devil Shen the other night.

"I'm one of the most popular dolls," she promised with sensuous, half-closed eyes. She brushed up against me, performing a sultry dance with very distinctive, sinuous moves. I considered pressing her for what she might know about the Chinaman, then thought better of it. I didn't want to see her end up on one of those slabs where the poor wretches whose bodies were fished from the Thames were displayed.

I dismissed her as politely as I could manage, but her gaze flickered to her modest cleavage and she assured me that I wouldn't soon forget her.

Someone tapped my shoulder from behind.

A lumbering brute stood before me, his hands stuffed in the pockets of a black velveteen coat. His filthy trousers were stuffed into grey stockings that had been pulled up over powerful calves. He stared at me, his face expressionless and his eyes deep and dark. In a rough, raspy voice he mumbled, "You're for Miss Piper, yeah? This way, sir."

He led me through the crimson veil and down the golden corridor. Muffled gasps, moans, and cries of pleasure or pain, I knew not which, burst from behind the doors bracing me. At the end of the corridor, he yanked open a door to a red bedroom where a couple writhed and ground together.

"Out!" he commanded, surging into the room and yanking the screeching woman from her paid companion. She was yet *another* Nellie! "Finish him elsewhere, ye slag!"

The man peered in shock at my guide, then skittered away, gathering up his clothes and racing bare-arsed from the room, inches behind the girl.

A four-poster bed rose in the center of the chamber, and to the side, a small table with a lamp and a pair of seats. He gestured at one and I sat, noticing an adjoining door at my side. An escape route, perhaps? My uneasiness was growing by the second.

"Hear you've been asking questions," he said, his face still stony. "Lookin' for an audience with our good Mr. Smithson hisself. Well, I'm here to tell you—rejoice! Your long difficult journey is at an end."

"You mean to say . . . you're Smithson?"

"I go by many names," said the man with his raspy

voice, the pungent fumes of beer heavy on his breath. "You like to think of me as Smithson, well, then, that's right, that's fine, that's fair as fair can be. Mind you, and count yourself privileged as I usually don't reveal this unless I'm about to slit a man's throat, my real name's Bill Sikes."

A rat raced by, hugging the floorboard. His hand shot out with surprising speed and he caught the vermin, his meaty fingers curled about its bloated belly. "Day in, day out, it's the rats this, the rats that. They frighten the girlies. They disgust the fine gentlemen. Myself, I quite appreciate the rats, sir. They teach us things, they do: How to hunt them. Lay traps for them . . ." The vermin squealed as the man's fingers closed even tighter and brittle bones crackled. It fell limp. "Lots of good things, they teach us how to do."

His meaning was clear. I was the rat and he the trapper. The limp dead thing had not even hit the floor when I ran, much good it did me. He was on me before I could open the door beside me. His huge hands slammed me face-first into the door. My head burst into a storm of fireworks, my thoughts suddenly a mass of confusion. He yanked the cane from my fingers, tossed it back against the table. His hands gripping me by the hair, he drove my skull into the heavy door a second time, and pain exploded with a frightful heat as something trickled down from my forehead. Hot and wet.

Then he hurled me back with a grunt. I stumbled until the edge of the bed struck my legs and I collapsed onto it, arms flung wide. A scratching came at the door, and he ignored me for a moment. He opened it and a white dog bounded into the room. The animal leaped to the bed and licked at the blood on my forehead. A great black splotch enveloped its right eye.

"Now you see that? That's Bull's-eye," Sikes said as he slowly closed the door again and stalked towards me. "You ask Fagin and he'd tell you, that's my dog. He ain't, though. No. Fagin . . . *he's* my dog. Now, you beat my dog, sir. I don't rightly mind, seeing as how he had it comin' and all. But Fagin was right to object, you askin' questions about Smithson as you were doing. Even when you were warned, you did it anyway. It's bad manners, sir. And bad manners must be punished, mustn't they? Worse, you asked about Annie. Kept askin' and askin', that's what you did. Why would that be? Even when you heard she was Smithson's woman, mine, if you take me as him—"

"You're not Smithson," I said, sitting up even as the world spun and swam about me. "You're the sweeper, aren't you? The one who disposes of messes? I could elevate you. I have money—"

"They all say that," Sikes said wearily. "And, 'You don't have to do this!' That's my favorite, it is. Because of course I do. It's my employment, and it's fun, yeah!" His fist clocked me square in the face, and stars burst into my vision; I felt the blood flood from my nose.

My hands groped blindly for anything I might use to protect myself as I swung my legs off the high bed and crumpled to my knees, another wave of vertigo seizing me. Sikes' footfalls echoed and crashed like thunder as he surged at me.

"I'm not sure you properly grasp your situation, sir."

His hand shot out with blinding speed and fastened on my throat. I tried to wrench my way loose, I beat at him, but he squeezed even tighter. "See this now? This is how I grasp!" With one hand around my throat, he brought the other to my face, wiped the blood from under my nose with his thumb, and made a circle of my own blood upon my forehead.

"There," he said. "A Bull's-eye. Now I know where to aim."

He raised me up until my feet were kicking, then he whirled me about and slammed me against the wall. Then he pummeled my forehead, and my skull cracked against the wall again and again until—

Nothing.

Darkness had me. Death, I might have thought, if not for the ringing in my ears and the commotion I heard all about me. How long had I been unconscious? And why wasn't I dead?

My eyes opened sluggishly and my mouth was slack, my breathing harsh and uneven, my throat swollen, irritated. The skin about my neck burned, and I reached up, loosened my tie, opened the top buttons. I lay on the floor of the wretched room where Bill Sikes had been about the mundane task of throttling me while bashing my brains in, and I gasped for breath like a transplanted fish.

Just as I forced myself to calm, a nearby explosion made the walls shake and a sudden thunder of running footsteps surged from the hall. Screams and shouts.

"What're you lookin' at? I'm Bill Sikes. *Nobody* looks at me!" the madman was shouting from a distance, his hideous dog barking from even farther off. Gasping, struggling to command my aching arms, I crawled until I heard rapid footsteps and saw two untidy shoes and stockings stomp across the floorboards to where I was, on all fours, blood dripping from my split lips.

"We must get out!" cried a woman's voice, and I raised my head to see, through the bursting stars on the inside of my skull, a shock of scruffy red hair framing a milky white face.

"The name's Nancy," she said. "There. Now I ain't no stranger no more, you can trust me. Come on!"

Another explosion, and we clung to each other as the house shuddered and something brilliant lit outside the curtained window, its glass crackling from the force of some unseen blow.

I let her help me, and together we joined the pack of men and women in various states of undress making their exodus from this sinful place. We passed through the Long Gallery, where Sikes was clapping his hands and screaming, "Bull's-eye! Where are ye, ye mongrel!"

But his back was to me, and he never turned. Not as my Nancy and I half-fell, half-dragged ourselves down the stairs, past the foyer, and out into the grey of a terrible, mad day.

The Lycia—the building that smelled of terrible chemicals—was now a blazing inferno. Men rushed this way or that, pistols drawn. I heard the jolting blasts, saw men jerk and fall.

I ran. The woman's hand had been in mine, then we pierced a crowd, were jostled and clawed at, and then she was gone, her fiery red hair swallowed up by the tide of madness all about me.

Two more buildings in the Royal Quarter were afire, and I saw a small man with wild eyes stand right in front of me, tears in his eyes, blood speckled about his face and hands.

Roger Colley.

"My brother! My *brother*, you bastards!" he said, firing a pair of pistols at some hard men who twisted and sagged. "Gonna have me a right *benjo* in his honor. Gonna see every one of you dead!"

He didn't notice me, and I kept with the crowd fleeing the Quarter.

Soon finding myself on my own, I made fast progress through the myriad of stinking, squalid blind alleys, courts, and passageways between tall and narrow houses. A dense fog gathered. A hazy orange color rose from the Quarter behind me, hellishly reflecting the moist windows of fetid gin-palaces and coarse eateries. I pushed my way past drunken scalawags, past women with heavy makeup and rotting teeth. I rushed past ovens with roasting chestnuts and baked potatoes sold to starving lads for a farthing. Finally, I swept through a narrow alleyway into the large open court.

Letting out a sigh, I wiped my brow and walked towards Furnival's Inn, above which were my rooms. Smiling, I was already embracing the sound of merriment and the wafts of kidney pie and mulled ale when someone cleared his throat behind me.

"Wotcher, Mr. Scrooge, sir!" called a guttural croak. Windows in the brick rows of houses and commercial buildings surrounding him were frozen on the inside. Gas lamps shone behind them betraying a rudimentary coziness, despite the smell of damp brick.

I stopped and sighed. "Good evening, Humperdink," I called back.

Humperdink, an example of what passed these days for a municipal constable, wheezed and reeked of gin as he waddled across the court. The tightness of his uniform caused Humperdink's body to release a vibrato of bodily gases as he walked. Yet he moved with surprising speed given his girth. "Mr. Scrooge, sir, so sorry to have interrupted your customary evening walk, sir. Most sorry indeed, sir. Oh, bit of a nasty bump to your lip there, sir?"

I wondered how this oaf might be so oblivious to the severity of my beaten state. Perhaps it was the dimming light as afternoon passed to evening.

"Unfortunate placement of a lamppost, Constable," I mumbled.

Humperdink cleared his throat. "Well, sir, and this is not a light matter in any sense, sir, but as a man of the law, it is my duty to protect the good people of London, sir, and naturally that would involve the sharing of the truth, as known by the Lord Almighty, sir."

Baring my teeth, I spat, "For the love of *God*, what are you on about, Humperdink?"

"Well, sir, as the protocols of the courts would have it, sir, I must inform you that a certain Mr. Jack Colley met a bitter fate in the prison yard but a few hours ago. Stuck and bled out like a pig he were. We knows you went to see him, and his brother Roger, well, he might be quite of a temper about this here turn of events, see. And Inspector Foote, he tasked me to find you and give you, the, the wotsit, the heads up, as it were."

With that, the portly man turned on his heels and waddled down the slippery lane.

I turned back to the inn, and a single thought burned in my aching skull: *Gin!*

But Adelaide was there, laying in wait for me at a table near the window, wearing a breathtaking floral-print dress and an elegant wide-brimmed hat that cast haunting shadows over her eyes. In her lacy-gloved hands rested a pair of theatre tickets.

"Aren't you the fright?" she asked, rising and taking my arm. "Let's get you upstairs, cleaned up, and ready for a night out."

"What? No!" I objected. And swirling in the back of my still aching head, Dodger telling me that The Lady always wore floral-print dresses . . .

"I don't suppose you're going to tell me what you were doing that led you to this sorry state?" she asked. "No, never mind. One of those wealthy investors didn't like the terms you proposed and got a bit handsy, did he?"

"None of your concern," I muttered darkly.

"Well, what is of our mutual concern is that Miss Nellie Pearl had her servant hand deliver these invitations to tonight's performance. She has Mr. Fezziwig's invitation; you see . . . and requests not just our company, but also our assistance in an urgent matter. This is what we've been waiting for, Ebenezer."

I was halfway up the steps when I looked over and

peered into her lovely eyes. In the span of just over twenty-four hours, I had found myself eye-to-eye with a trio of murderers. What had I to worry about in just confronting her about her lies?

Instead, I turned away. A night at the theatre it would be.

CHAPTER NINETEEN

THE CACOPHONY IN the Adelphi Theatre's main arena was like a roaring sea. Instruments were tuned as hundreds of people babbled and shifted, rustling into their seats and greeting one another. My head was still pounding from Sikes' treatment earlier, and the silk cravat Adelaide had picked out to hide the swelling marks on my neck where he choked me was a cool comfort against the pain. Having just survived a murder attempt and nearly becoming a casualty in what was clearly a war between Smithson and Roger Colley, I would have preferred an evening clutching a glass of brandy in the bath, but my reluctance had not been long lasting. As Adelaide had put it, this was what we had been waiting for.

I'd sent word to Dickens for him to round up a few more "war men" to keep an eye on myself and Miss Owen. Clearly, Smithson wanted me dead. All I could hope was that Roger Colley's assault on the Quarter would keep the crime lord busy until our protection arrived. I told him we would say nothing of this to Miss

Owen. I rather liked the idea of someone following her every move and reporting it back to me.

Although the Adelphi was a smaller theatre with reasonably priced tickets, its location off the Strand attracted the finer folk. The congregation ahead surged with shiny top hats and exaggerated gowns. Adelaide wore a crisp green dress with a floral pattern of delicate fern leaves, and she looked every bit as astonishing as she had at the Dyer affair. My stomach flipped. A woman of her station sliding so effortlessly in to such society functions . . . Suspicion brewed.

The narrowness of the atrium and the straightness of the sides rendered most of the seats completely comfortless, but the tickets Nellie had sent us secured us the very best seats in the middle, where we would be surrounded by London's rich.

With a smile and a twinkle of the eye, she caught the notice of a young usher to whom she presented our tickets. He burst into a flush of excitement when he spotted the backstage pass that Nellie had sent with the tickets.

"Well!" he exclaimed. "A rare opportunity to meet *The Lady*, eh? The star of our show must hold you in very high regard."

Shock hit me like a quivering arrow. "'The Lady?'" I asked.

"*The Lady of Shalott*! She is one of the very best actresses we have ever had on this stage, our Miss Nellie Pearl is. Have you seen her perform yet? You shall be astounded! Let me show you to your seats."

A stirring of unease snuck into the back of my mind. *Could* Nellie be the mysterious Lady?

Adelaide's arm was linked with mine as we made our way down the arena past rows and rows of lush red seats, the balconies all decorated for Christmas. Gold and green and red twinkled in the shiny surfaces of crystal chandeliers and polished brass railings. Adelaide was calm and poised, exchanging polite nods with wealthy patrons as we passed them. Her eyes met theirs with confidence, and she smiled. I felt my guard lowering as she brushed by me, filling me with tantalizing aroma of her rose perfume. But an image of *her Tom*, covered in my friend's blood, flashed into my vision, and I immediately shook myself back to awareness.

"You should simply tell me what's on your mind, Mr. Scrooge," she said without looking at me as we settled into our seats near the aisle.

"A great many things," I said, opening the program.

Her eyes flickered to something at my left, and her cold glare burst into welcoming warmth. "Oh, look! Here is a description of Nellie's role, *The Lady of Shalott*!" She leaned over me and pointed at the place in the program, her shoulder touching mine.

"Well, I never!" exclaimed someone in the aisle, loud enough for many heads in the rows in front and behind us to turn. Mine turned, too.

"Mr. Ebenezer Scrooge, how fortuitous to run into you here."

"Mr. Lazytree!" I said, jumping up to shake his hand. It was Sunderland's agent, the one who had only last night orchestrated all those interviews with potential investors. "Very good to see you again, how do you do?"

"Just out for a spot of entertainment with the missus, Scrooge. Loves the theatre, she does, don't you, Winnie? Haven't been since Villiers died, of course. Terrible."

"Villiers?" I asked.

"Indeed! Owner of this very theatre! Stabbed over a hundred times, they said, I'm sure you've heard. And his secret mistress, too, would you believe. Nobody even has the foggiest who she was." There was a gleeful flicker in his eye, and I could tell he was reveling in the gossip.

"Yes, Crabapple mentioned—"

"And I think I spotted this enchanting lady at the charity ball last night?" he said, delivering his hyena-like laugh and sending a cheeky grin in Adelaide's direction, to the obvious annoyance of his wife.

"Adelaide Owen," said my associate, rising beside me and extending her gloved hand. The man kissed it without breaking eye contact with her.

"Owen? Not Scrooge, then?" trilled Mrs. Lazytree with a smile that did not reach her eyes. "So you aren't married? And unchaperoned, I see! How very modern."

Adelaide smiled kindly.

"Thank you once again for orchestrating those opportunities," I said, lowering my voice. "The evening ended somewhat abruptly, so . . ."

"Not to worry, Mr. Scrooge," said Lazytree, with a conspiratorial wink. "You will be receiving *quite* the visit to your offices in the morning."

The Lazytrees continued on down the aisle and found their seats some rows in front of us, but not before Mrs. Lazytree could turn to send Adelaide an icy glare. I sat back down feeling thoroughly delighted. The deadline for the rail investment was tomorrow, and by the sounds of it, the funds would be secured with time to spare!

"Business looks to improve, Adelaide," I said. "We will soon have every penny we need."

She nudged me. "But what about all the capital I raised for you this week? It was already improving, wasn't it?"

Though she had no idea that the funds she had gathered were not even a tenth of what was required for the investment deal, she had certainly succeeded in areas I had not in that regard.

"A clerk worth their salt shouldn't need constant reassurance," I grumbled. "You know the books as well as I. A marked improvement, down to you. Which you already know."

Crossing her arms over her breasts, she said, "Pardon me, Mr. Scrooge. I didn't realize how much a kind word costs you."

The orchestra silenced their tuning, and the lighting flickered, signaling the imminent start of the performance. A hush rolled across the atrium. I heard Adelaide draw her breath, then she nudged me and pointed. A man in a tall top hat was late arriving, causing upset and annoyance as he squeezed past occupied seats several rows away. He was clutching white gloves and a program, and when his head turned towards me, I gasped.

Shen!

I looked away and brought my hand to my face. His warning this morning had been clear and, of course, I had not heeded. Had he already received word of my trip to the Quarter and come here to finish what Bill

Sikes had begun? My heart thumped against the back of my throat.

"He didn't see you," Adelaide whispered. "It seems he is here for his own enjoyment."

The Chinaman took his seat, and from that moment until intermission, he stared at *The Lady of Shalott*, transfixed.

The performance was mesmerizing. Unlike The Adelphi's usual melodramatic themes, this romantic interpretation of Lord Tennyson's poem had the performers sweeping across the stage in stunning feats of ballet-like nimbleness and grace. Actresses, each as beautiful as the next, dressed in pure white maid's costumes, swanned round Nellie as she cried on the stage, her character condemned to a lifetime of viewing the world only through a mirror.

"*I am half-sick of shadows!*" she cried, and from the shadows on the set, her maids mirrored her every move.

I sensed Adelaide glancing at me from time to time but did not turn my head to look at her. Instead, just as Shen, I stared at the stage, feeling each carefully choreographed step thud against the painful bump on my head. Adelaide eyed me. My companion was astute and sharp as the point of a dagger, and there was no doubt in my mind that she knew I was holding many things back.

A host of actors dressed as Arthurian knights thundered across the stage. The maids sighed and swooned over the handsome knights, their distinctive, sinuous moves expressing an infatuation *The Lady of Shalott* was succumbing to, falling deeper for Sir Lancelot and provoking a terrible curse. Nellie leaped up and caught a ribbon that descended from the sky, swirling round with absurd strength and a surprising athleticism. Her movements were quick, flawless, calculated yet natural. The dance of the maids was evocative, verging on sultry, and I heard collective gasps around me as impossibly graceful movements nevertheless signified deeper, darker meanings.

But wait—I had seen those moves before! As the girls bent into slow backbends and Nellie stretched her arms in intricate, flowing gestures, I caught myself predicting each move as they unfolded. How could I know this? I couldn't place it.

"The curse is upon me!" cried the Lady of Shalott, and the maids fell into protective positions about her, the middle one gazing out over the audience. And there, almost invisible under her heavy makeup, was the scar running from her upper lip to her left cheek. It was the "Nellie" from the Doll House! Her hair color was different, but she shared the same nose and haunting stare as her original. I had to speak with her.

As soon as the curtains fell at intermission, I snatched the backstage pass from Adelaide and made for the side of the stage, jostling audience members as they poured up the aisles to the bar. As soon as I had made sure Shen was nowhere to be seen, I hopped onto the stage, confident that the raucous activity throughout the atrium at intermission was enough cover for me to remain undetected. I slipped behind the curtain, keeping to the shadows.

The set was being torn down by stagehands, and they were not looking in my direction, so I hastened down the wooden steps to the backstage area. It was dark but alive, as actors, actresses, and crew jostled about one another to prepare for the next set.

"Excuse me," I said, tapping the shoulder of a confused and sweaty knight, who was promptly ushered away by a stage manager.

"You shouldn't be back here," he barked, leading me by the elbow to a door in the brick wall. I resisted and presented the invitation.

"It's imperative that I speak with a chorus girl," I urged.

"Not that kind of production, sir," he said sternly. "If Miss Pearl has indeed invited you to her dressing room after the show, then by all means return then."

I would attract too much attention if I argued, so I nodded and let him lead me to the door where I made to exit. A cry rang out suddenly as rope fell from a beam somewhere and the stage manager hurried off. I slipped back into the shadows to find the Nellie doll.

I spotted a woman across the room, with her back to me, dressed all in white. I drew a breath and made to slip across the room to her when I was stopped by nearby voices.

"No, not her," came a girl's voice, laughing. "It was Sarah he fancied. The one who looks just like Miss Pearl." I froze and listened. "Well, except for that scar, you know."

"Oh, *her*!" said another voice. Two chorus girls were approaching a bench near the darkened corner where I was hiding. They sat down and began tying their shoes. "Is it true he was all over her?"

"Obsessed. Saw it myself."

I tried to ignore them, yet I had seen Shen with Nellie's double. Were they talking about the Chinaman?

The women at my side babbled on. "And did she . . . you know?"

"She'd never! Not with an ugly brute like him, poor man . . ."

An ugly brute? No, certainly not Shen. So "Sarah," the Nellie look-alike, had another admirer . . . perhaps that nugget of information would prove useful if I ever caught up with her.

A strange movement caught my eye. I looked up and saw a familiar tall top hat moving through the bustling backstage. Shen had gained entry. Had Nellie invited him, too? More likely some weighty bribes had changed hands. He moved quickly and confidently between the cast and crew, heading for the woman in white. He grabbed her arm and she turned. It was Nellie, the real one, not the doll I was looking for. She looked furious, but he was talking to her resolutely; whatever words were being exchanged were impassioned. I strained my ears to hear, but their altercation was drowned out by the gossiping hens beside me.

"I reckon that Sarah fancies herself a bit of a prima donna, because of her resemblance to Miss Pearl. Treating the crew members like that. You know he spent hours working on her costume, fitting it for her just so, while the rest of us have to squeeze in to these standard sizes. Doubt she even thanked him."

"He's a bit of a monster, though! How did he get all those scars and horrible bumps and stuff?"

"*Damfino*!" she said, a low-class mumble that meant "damned if I know." "No, haven't the foggiest notion. Ain't seen hide nor hair of him in a week or more anyway. Probably curled up in a dark den somewhere, clutching an empty bottle or a pipe. This place is going down the sewer, I tell you, ever since Villiers popped his clogs . . ."

The gossiping girls continued speculating about the whereabouts of that tragic-sounding costumer and bemoaning the demise of their industry, and ahead, Shen was leaning in, placing a hand on Nellie's shoulder. Her expression flashed from anger to fear, when suddenly two or three stagehands appeared and pushed Shen off her. His hand moved to his belt, where I had previously suspected some hidden weapon.

He looked to Nellie, who was staring at him, and his hand stalled. The Chinaman drew a breath, composed himself, and bowed. Then he turned and walked away, his head held high as he passed right by me and through the side door.

"Places!" shouted someone. The girls hopped off the bench and darted off, the backstage became a flurry of activity, and I had missed my chance to speak with the Nellie doll. Cursing the gossiping chorus girls, I returned to my seat, where Adelaide greeted me with a scowl but asked no questions.

I paid little attention to the second half of the performance. Knights and maids jumped about and Sir Lancelot tossed the nimble Lady of Shalott some way into the air, but all I could think about was the series of suspicious incidents I had witnessed or been party to, including the strange interaction between Shen and Nellie. When the curtains fell at the end of the show, Adelaide and I went straight to the side door.

The stage manager led us to her dressing room, some way from the dark brick backstage where I had been skulking during intermission.

"Miss Owen, Mr. Scrooge!" exclaimed the star when we entered. She swept across the room and kissed us both. "Oh, thank you, thank you truly! I know how busy you both must be. Did you enjoy the performance?"

We both assured her that we did and were rewarded with a dazzling smile that was more teeth than soul. I couldn't help noticing in her dressing room that there were all the accoutrements for Miss Pearl to disguise herself as anything from a young lad to an old woman and all in between, but I kept these thoughts to myself.

"I finally found the summons from poor Mr. Fezziwig," said Nellie, pouting with sympathy. "Please do accept my apologies for taking so long, but oh! What a week it has been!"

She handed me an envelope and used the moment to gently stroke my hand as I grasped it. It was exactly the same as the one Dickens and I had discovered at Shen's.

The contents echoed verbatim what Shen's letter had said, with one exception. There was no mention of the Lady. That was strange. Why would Fezziwig omit something that had seemed of such great importance in Shen's letter? Crawling spiders of unease moved from my esophagus to my gut. I stared at the letter. For all my expectation leading up to getting hold of this summons, it had yielded nothing. But then . . .

Fezziwig would not have looped his *g*'s. I studied the letter. The handwriting was neat and tight, just like Fezziwig's, but a few technical differences betrayed the letter as a forgery. I had missed it when I first read the letter, for the quality of this counterfeit summons was almost impeccable. But I spent years as Fezziwig's clerk, I knew that man's hand, and this wasn't it.

"May I?" said Nellie, her hand outstretched. I handed her the envelope, finding myself disappointed that she didn't again touch my hand, and thanked her. Both Nellie and Adelaide watched me, waiting for my analysis, but my thoughts were racing. Adelaide raised her eyebrows at me, quizzically.

"Mr. Scrooge?" she tried. I snapped back into the present.

"Nellie, I do beg your pardon," I said. "I must say, it continues to plague me, the notion that Fezziwig chose you four in particular to receive this summons. Something must have bound the four of you. You truly had no connection to either Sunderland or Rutledge?"

Nellie shrugged, her smile vibrant as ever. "It's possible we met at some premiere or function. Beyond that . . ."

"Miss Pearl, tell me about the second matter you wished to discuss."

She sighed, adopting a mournful expression as she sat down by her dressing mirror and pouted at me through the reflection.

"I think you know," she said. "I saw you earlier. At intermission. You were hiding in the shadows."

I held my breath.

"You must have seen how he treated me."

"Mr. Shen?" I asked, relieved, and Nellie nodded. She turned to Adelaide and grabbed her hands.

"You know what it's like, don't you, Miss Owen? To be made to feel so vulnerable by a man?" Her voice became thick, and the pleading in her eyes was genuine. "We women are nothing more to them but playthings, isn't that so, Miss Owen?"

Adelaide gave Nellie's hands a squeeze, and the actress looked at me with wet eyes.

"I don't know who else to ask, Mr. Scrooge," she whispered, touching my arm. "I fear for my life. He is everywhere I go. I hear his steps behind me, I see him in the shadows. I am so very sick of those shadows. You have my word I have given him nothing to suggest that his obsession with me is anything but one-sided."

I nodded.

"Will you speak to him, Mr. Scrooge? As one gentleman to another? He will listen to you, I'm sure. He respects men of business. Doesn't respect me." Her voice broke and she began to cry, and Adelaide kneeled down by her and pulled her into a sisterly embrace.

"Of course, Miss Pearl," I said. "I'll see what I can do. But unfortunately I can make no promises; Shen and I are not currently in the warmest of friendships."

"Oh, thank you!" she sighed and gazed into my eyes with such fondness and gratefulness that I could see myself falling under her spell. "Thank you so much. Whatever help you can give me. You see, I could tell that you were a gentleman and would always help a lady in distress, I am so indebted. Just knowing you understand is a comfort indeed."

She rose to her feet and gave Adelaide a frank and tender hug, and Adelaide looked earnestly into her eyes as she curtsied. I bowed, replaced my hat, and Nellie's tears transformed into smiles.

Just as I turned to leave, my eyes fell on a side mirror, and my stomach tightened in surprise. Nellie's reflection was staring at me, her eyes filled with a longing and a desire. Then she turned her gaze in Adelaide's direction, her eyes darkened by a look of cold jealousy. Nellie was clearly not accustomed to competition for a man's attention—and woe betide the woman who got in her way!

CHAPTER TWENTY

"OH, LOOK," ADELAIDE said frostily. "A steam bus. How very interesting."

She was nodding across the street as we shrugged off the theatre's cozy warmth and stepped outside into the cold. Only pockets of attendees from the packed audience remained huddled on the sidewalk out front. Most had dispersed while we were backstage. I looked about, disappointed that Dickens was not waiting for us with guardsmen; I'd given him the address in the note I sent over.

I cast anxious looks about for Sikes, Shen, or any suspicious-looking types, then peered at the steel contraption that had arrested Miss Owen's interest. "The Silver Flash"—painted along its sterling flanks—was built to hold twelve, but the so-called engineers of these ungodly devices routinely crammed in twice as many to increase their profits. The engineer—or driver—stood next to the bus, which was left running, as he attempted to romance a pretty girl who might have been in the chorus.

"Come on now, let's go!" someone hollered. A crowd waited at the bus stop. Young lads with the look of Fagin's gang circulated among them, no doubt relieving them of wallets, watches, and whatever else the opportunistic urchins might nab. The well-dressed crowd was so intent upon the gleaming new vehicle that they paid little notice.

"Not time yet!" shot back the driver. He glanced to the empty cab where a gigantic wheel waited. Beside it, a steel column rose to the roof with a spout for venting smoke. It chugged much like a locomotive—or a panting beast readying to spring.

"How fascinating," Adelaide said, her voice surging with barely contained fury. "I've never been on one."

"An abomination," I grumbled.

"Really? This from the man who preaches about the future brought by technological advancement? How is this any different from the rails? Or is it just that someone beat you to it and peppered these through the city before you could?"

I leaned out into the street, waving my hand at the glowing lantern of an approaching horse-drawn carriage.

"So, you want to have this conversation now?" I asked.

She looked away, hugging herself against the cold. It was all the reply she would give. I grasped her arms, shook her, forced her to look my way. "Answer me."

Her eyes filling with dark bursts of anger, she cried, "I don't even know what 'this conversation' *is*! I've been *trying* to talk to you, but you keep shutting me out. So yes, Mr. Scrooge. By all that's holy, tell me why you're acting so cruelly!"

I snorted. "I'm not sure which performance was better. Nellie as the Lady of Shalott or you as the outraged innocent."

"You're a foul man," she said, her voice faltering as she stood with her back to me.

"And you're a liar!"

She whirled and slapped me, eyes flaring. I grabbed her arm and suddenly, the ruby ring was being waved before my eyes. I unhanded her at once. How had she gotten ahold of it? I didn't think even Dodger could have snatched it from my pocket without my knowledge.

"It looks like neither of us has been entirely forthcoming," she said. "A lie of omission is also a lie, or so I was always taught."

I snatched back the ring. "Perhaps you were right with what you said before. That we should pursue this matter separately."

"You coward," she spat. "You can't even say it, can you? You act high and mighty and level accusations, but when it comes down to putting some meat to the meal you—"

"It was Dyer!" I roared. "Thomas Guilfoyle was raving about Dyer coming to save him. Not some long dead and drowned father. Lord. Dyer. You broke trust with me. And if you lied about *that* . . ."

Trembling, she said, "Then I must have lied about everything. Tell me, am I the killer as well? At very least, the Lady?"

"You tell me."

The carriage drew up before us and the driver swooped down to open the side door. I gave him money and told him to take the young woman wherever she wished to go. I would get the next one. He flew back up to his perch, holding a lantern high for us. The nearest of the stallions was a nightmare black, the pair beyond a rich chestnut. They chuffed and wheezed, whinnying uneasily. They sensed something electric, some palpable danger in the air. As did I.

Lips pressed together tightly, she gave me an icy glare and took my hand as she placed one booted foot into the carriage's side stirrup. She settled onto the leather seat, and I was about to command the driver to remove her from my sight when heavy boots kicked at the snow behind me.

"Madam, Monsieur," said a heavy voice as a trio of men peeled from the shadows. "Have you the time?"

I sighed, fished out my pocket watch, and gazed at its face. Before I could speak, Adelaide gasped. My gaze whipped upward, right into the smiling faces of Roger Colley, Baldworthy, and the man with the claret mark. I should have detected his rough voice under the clearly fake French accent.

"You don't know dung from wild honey if you think you can escape us," Roger promised.

"Go!" Adelaide hollered as she held her hand out to me.

I leapt onto the stirrup and grabbed a leather strap above the open door, which waggled and creaked in the stiff December wind. The driver hooked the lantern in place on a sturdy golden pole, and with a crack of whips, we lurched forward, hooves stamping wildly to smash the ice already forming on the cobbles. Adelaide caught me by my suspenders as I bowed outward, nearly losing my grip as we barreled forward. Then I was scrambling inside, reaching for the open door even as a shot rang out and the flapping door's window exploded.

At the sound of the shot, the team of horses catapulted forward, and we nearly swept another hack.

"Sirruh, what's the meaning of this, eh?" yelled the driver.

"The meaning is be silent and drive if you want to live!" I yelled to him, and at that, he turned and smacked the whips again.

I heard distant screams and looked back to witness Roger and his boys driving off the crowd before the steam bus while ushering the terrified engineer up to his perch. Baldworthy and the man with the claret mark hopped inside.

"They can't catch up to us," Adelaide said, hope sparking in her eye.

"Not strictly true," I muttered, recalling an investment brochure I'd read from that annoying Frenchman who brought these monsters to our city three years ago. In seconds, the bus was barreling ahead spewing a giant plume of black steam into the air from its spout. White steam billowed from its flanks, firing then quickly dissipating. It chugged much like a Cornish steam engine and gained on us with merciless speed. "Twice as fast as a horse-drawn, blast it all!"

Our carriage swayed as our blurring wheels dug ruts in the street. We clung to each other, bracing ourselves in our seats as best we could against the mad jostling bounces, crashes, and thumps. The beasts were in a heavy lather, froth and sweat flying as easily as their spit.

"Lucifer!" the driver cried, whipping the horses into a gallop that was just short of a frenzy. "Belial! Azazel! Faster, or it will truly be the pits of hell for all of us!"

Buildings flashed past us. Brilliant lights blurred. Long-legged youths crossing streets ran in terror from our hurtling carriage. A bobby blew on his whistle and chased us, fast falling behind into the whistling dark abyss at our backs.

"Roger Colley?" Adelaide managed, barely able to catch her breath.

I nodded. Though why he should be after us *now* . . . I thought.

A golden light swept over us, twisting our shadows forward. Another shot struck the still wildly flapping side door beside me. I looked back to see the bus's lanterns burning a trio of suns at our back while Baldworthy hung half-out the vehicle's side flank, pistol aimed squarely at my head.

An old drunk stepped into the street, and the bus's engineer jerked the wheel, swaying the bus wildly to avoid him even as the shot was fired. I heard a window shatter somewhere, followed by a shrill scream.

"Turn there, turn there!" I hollered, pointing at a side street. I prayed the bus could not corner as well as a carriage.

We flew about the corner, and another flash of yellow light appeared from Baldworthy's hand. A surprised grunt burst from our driver, who had half-risen to guide the precarious turn. The carriage swung madly to one side and righted, jolting us and sending shrieks of exertion from the horses. The reins slipped from his fingers as he stood, one hand covering a nasty wound to his shoulder. Then the wheel closest to him struck a pothole and the carriage bounced, the shock of it sending him jerking fully upright and swaying off-balance. For an instant he looked like a teetering tin soldier, spine stiff and straight, as he fell from the cab and was swallowed up by the night.

The horses were runaways!

Trading desperate looks with Adelaide, I forced a thin smile into place, then climbed half out of the speeding carriage, my foot miraculously finding the stirrup, my hand the strap. Sharp stinging winds seared my eyes and cheek. My hat was picked off my head and flung into the black and frozen abyss. Adelaide surged forward, again grabbing my suspenders, helping to steady me as I tried to find purchase on the driver's box. Only the pole upon which our lantern was secured offered any chance at all if I was to wrap around and take the driver's spot—and the reins. Springing off the stirrup, I thrust my free hand up, missed the golden shaft, and hollered as Adelaide lost her grip on me and my foot missed the stirrup.

I held onto the strap, gripping it now with both hands, as my body was pounded by the swinging door. The carriage swayed as I was arced back and away from the carriage, then I was smacked against it once again with a fiery jolt, a macabre dance.

The steam bus whipped out from behind us, flew to our side, and, as the engineer yanked his wheel hard to the right, smashed into the side of the carriage. The impact was brutal, terrible, a hammer that smashed into my entire skeleton, sending a shattering vibration through my muscles, my brain, along with a shrieking shower of agonized sparks.

What happened next was a blur. I felt the strap yanked from my hand. The carriage angled crazily, the wheels on its opposite flank rising off the cobblestone street. Adelaide screamed and flew towards me.

Empty air, a floating, just for an instant, then impact with something massive and mercifully soft. A snowdrift? An ash pile? I didn't know. Adelaide and I spun and tumbled, arms and legs akimbo, and we heard a cacophony of thunderous crashes from somewhere near, coupled with cries of fear and pain.

My every nerve jangling, burning, I climbed onto my side, lifted myself up, and saw a horror unlike any I'd ever imagined: The carriage had drawn down the stallions when it capsized, and the beasts—those that survived, were a pile of screaming, quaking limbs. The carriage's lantern had set fire to the carriage's remains. Only a mercifully slight separation of the harness to the carriage's body—one wheel defiantly still spinning—kept the broken creatures from being roasted alive.

The steam bus had been knocked about. It was parked up onto a sidewalk beside an accordion-like array of tightly pressed together office buildings. Something seemed to be stuck half in the bus, half-smashed against the wall, and fully pulped into something that only vaguely resembled a man. Except for the face.

Baldworthy.

Another body lay in the snow past a shattered window. The glass shards dripped crimson. The dead man had been sliced to bits in mid-flight by the jagged jaws of shattered glass.

Roger hauled the engineer out of the bus, shoved him down on his knees. "My men—my only men left—both of them dead. This is your doing!"

"No, no, guv'nor, please, I did everything you asked," the engineer pleaded, his hands raised, his body shaking with fear. "Got a family, two little boys—"

"Stop bleatin', you bloody sheep," Roger replied. And he punctuated that reply with a single roaring gunshot that brought an end to the engineer's words—and his life.

I fell onto my side, searched for Adelaide. Found her near the curb, bruised and bloodied, her chest rising and falling in quick, frightened breaths. Still alive.

For now.

Screams sounded as men and women out for strolls scattered and sought refuge from the chaos and mounting horror as Roger Colley stalked towards us, smoking gun tapping the outside of his thigh.

"You two!" he yelled. "You two, then this is well and truly done!"

His boots crushed snow, smashed ice as he drew closer. I heard horses, running footsteps, carriages braking and skidding on ice. But all I could look at was Roger Colley as I climbed to my knees and crawled in front of Adelaide, attempting to shield her with my body should the madmen fire again. I acted on instinct, my fiery anger cooled by this mortal danger.

Roger raised his gun. "My brother Jack sends his regards, you *fucks*!"

I shook my head. "No! We had nothing to do with your brother's death."

"Everything!" Roger spat. "You had *everything* to do with it. I thought Smithson had betrayed me, that he'd got the filth to come raid us and bring us down. So I lashed out at him. Did things to hurt him; hurt his precious business. And in return, he had my Jack done like a filthy dog. But it wasn't him at all, was it? It was the two of you all along!"

"It was me," Adelaide snarled, shoving me away, rising to tottering feet. "I have no regrets. You'd have killed Ebenezer that night if I hadn't brought the police to stop you."

Colley's eyes were hollow and dark. He smiled slowly and waved his gun between us. "I wonder, should it be ladies first? Then I might see the fine gentleman's grief before I end his miserable life. Or I could let him die wondering what I might do with his fair bit of crimp before I send her down to hell for Jack to enjoy. That's agony, ain't it? The not knowing of a thing?"

A sharp echoing *CRACK* split the night, and I gasped, waiting to feel the searing pain of the bullet tearing through me. But instead, Roger was lowering his gun even as I heard the unexpected clomping of hooves through the snow as a spooked horse raced away. Roger's legs bowed as he took a step this way, then the other, a drunken stumble, while his head bobbed and wobbled. He exhaled deeply and dropped face-first into the snow, suddenly looking smaller than ever, a frail bird.

The back of his head was a reddened nest, a cavity that should not have been.

Shen Kai-Rui stood a half-dozen yards behind the dead man, a smoking pistol in his hand. The horse that I guessed he had ridden here was now racing down a narrow alley, vanishing past the moonlit cobblestones.

"Why would you save me?" I asked, my heart thundering.

He smiled. "If anyone is going to take your life for your transgressions, it will be me. I am not done seeing you suffer. As for my change of heart where your woman is concerned, well, all she's been put through since meeting you . . . She has suffered enough, wouldn't you say?"

A look passed between Adelaide and me. The chains of trust between us had been broken, yes. But, as Marley had said, links might be strengthened and repaired, though at a cost.

She nodded slightly, as did I. Our fates were again bound, it seemed.

"As for our business, I was following you so that I might catch you alone and tell you—" Shen froze, his gaze fixing on something on my coat.

Had I been wounded after all?

Shen stalked closer, his gloved hand pointing at my pocket. "I know that handwriting! The *Lady!*"

I looked down even as he snatched away an envelope that had been half-sticking out of my pocket. "I've never seen that before!"

He ignored me. Tearing open the envelope with shaking hands, he drew out a folded sheet and scanned its florid writing. Lips trembling, breath catching, he dropped the letter to the snow and fished about for his watch. "The time . . . the *time*! I must know!"

I snatched up the letter and read:

> *Sir,*
>
> *How does it feel to speak to a corpse? That is what you've just done, Mr. Scrooge. Think me and my words a Humbug, if you will. But the whore Nellie Pearl dies at midnight at St. Paul's Cathedral. Perhaps I'll see you there? The little slut always adores an audience.*
>
> *—An Admirer*

Shen was casting his gaze wildly about. His horse had bolted, and the cathedral was miles away.

A carriage stopped halfway down the street, the driver suspiciously eyeing the wreckage before us. Shen broke into a run, charging the surprised driver. He drew up his reins, as if to turn his alarmed horses and flee at once.

"One shilling!" Shen shouted. "I'll give you one whole shilling, but hold!"

The driver held.

"What is it?" Adelaide demanded. "What's happening?"

"Humbug," I said. "He's taken Nellie." He or *she*, I inwardly corrected myself. Was The Lady also Humbug? Or just the killer's sponsor?

More carriages drove into view. The police rounding corners, converging on us from all sides except the street ahead. There Shen was shoving coin into the driver's palm while eyeing me impatiently. I understood.

Humbug had slipped the letter into my pocket, had invited *me* to the latest performance. Shen must have worried what might happen to Nellie if I was not at his side when he reached the cathedral.

"Go!" Adelaide said. "I'll deal with the police."

I ran into the night even as the shouts of bobbies and blaring whistles were drowned out by the screeching wind at my back.

CHAPTER TWENTY-ONE

SHEN BURST FROM the carriage as it ground to a stop before the tallest and most striking building in England: St. Paul's Cathedral. Beneath its great dome—topped by a baroque lantern—stood the mourning stone figure of St. Paul flanked by St. John and St. Peter. A bell tower containing the Great Paul, a single sixteen-ton bell, speared the night sky on the southwest corner; a second empty and waiting tower the other. The statues peered down at two figures mounting the stone steps leading from the street to the column-strewn portico towards the propped-open center door. One wore a black cloak and veils, the other the same billowing white dress I'd seen her wear at the theatre only an hour ago. The murderer hauled the stumbling, dazed, yet oddly compliant Nellie Pearl into the darkness; I trailed behind Shen in his mad dash to catch them.

I found him inside the dull, featureless nave, panting, pistol in one white-gloved hand, whipping his head about as he searched for any sign of our quarry. But Nellie and the killer were nowhere to be seen. Great stone arches towered above us, and the long aisle stretched with endless shadows towards the vast central crossing. White bolts of thin cheap fabric hung down over the abandoned stepstools, ladders, planks, platforms, and scaffolding left over from the recent rounds of repairs done here.

Darkened doorways and niches taunted us with a wealth of shadowy hiding places. The choir with its great organ was housed in the eastern apse, beyond the central crossing. I knew that the morning congregation at St. Paul's faced east for the sunrise, a metaphor for resurrection. Before resurrection might be possible, though, there must first be death.

"Can't have gotten far," Shen whispered, teeth gritted. Sweat beaded on his forehead. His breath was ragged. Rage and fear danced in his dark eyes.

"Miss Pearl was drugged," I said, panting. "She is outside herself. Compliant. Humbug was practically dragging her. The killer used chloroform on Fezziwig. A small enough dose . . . ?"

"No. An opiate, surely." Shen's voice was cold, distant.

"Shen, is this one of yours?" I asked. I'd recalled Dickens remark that the killer moved much the same as a Chinese acrobat. Was it not possible that we had all become caught up in some power play between Shen and a rival opium dealer? That Fezziwig had been silenced for information he had innocently stumbled upon and it was our connection to the kindly old man that had marked the rest of us?

He stared at me as if I were an insignificant gnat that had suddenly gained the power of speech. "Enough." He stepped away from me and called out, "Miss Pearl! Miss Pearl, if you can hear me, say something! Make a sound. Do it now!"

A candelabra teetered and fell a dozen yards ahead. We were in motion before it toppled and spilled an armful of three-foot-long candles across the floor. The robed murderer broke from behind a pillar, and Nellie shrieked as she was pulled along. She looked like a rag doll, legs wobbly, hair flopping over her face.

Shen raised his weapon, cursed, lowered it. He could not chance hitting Nellie.

It would be over in seconds, I knew. The killer could not move quickly enough while pulling the drugged actress along.

"Let her go!" Shen screamed.

Humbug obeyed. The cloaked figure darted from Nellie, leaving her hunched forward and teetering like a puppet hanging by a single frail thread, arms sweeping this way and that. Shen rushed for her—

And Humbug dove into another alcove and yanked at a rope. I heard a mechanism whirl above me, a hard, ratcheting sound. With a sudden rush of air, a steel boxed lantern nearly eight feet high flew down and crashed to Shen's side. Glass shattered and rained upon me as I flung up my arms and spun to protect my face. A few tiny stinging glass splinters dug into my arms and I heard footsteps, a woman mumbling, muttering confusedly. I turned back to see Shen crawling and dazed, groping for his pistol.

It was no coincidence, I now realized, that Humbug appeared yanking Nellie onto the steps after our carriage arrived. It wasn't just that we had been given a set time for this "performance." The killer had been waiting for us and had waited for our arrival as the cue to begin. This had all been carefully planned.

"This is a trap," I said hoarsely.

"Fool. You think I don't know that?" Shen said. He found the pistol under a chunk of fallen wood and pried it loose. We heard a door creak in the distance, an echo from the central chamber. "Nellie!"

He shrugged off my hand as I tried to help him to his feet. Glass crunched beneath our boots as we flung ourselves ahead, passing through a carefully arranged gauntlet of shrouded platforms and the like. Why put on a show like this? Why not just kill Nellie and have us arrive too late to do anything about it?

Wide arches and coffered vaults flanked us, buttresses and saucer-shaped domes were all about us. We reached the central crossing, where it appeared—though it was not so—that eight corridors connected it like spokes jutting from a wheel. Four were mere illusion. I flicked my gaze high, to the very inner core of the dome, and my breath caught at its magnificence.

"There!" Shen commanded. I followed him to a heavy wooden door. We passed through it into a narrow winding stone staircase. He vaulted up the steps, and I followed behind: we could go but one at a time. The stones were narrow, the ledges high. The cold and uneven walls to either side of us were barely wider than my shoulders. Up we ran, while above, a woman's sobbing and the echoing of footfalls mockingly drifted down. Only an occasional shaft of blue moonlight caressed the way. Otherwise, it was black as pitch, which retarded our movement.

Ours, but not that of the killer. I smelled oil and guessed that Humbug had an already burning lantern waiting at the top of the stairs.

Incensed, Shen shouted Nellie's name again and again. He threatened the killer, he screamed and bartered and pleaded, but the only voice that ever met his was that of the confused and near-breathless actress.

"Why?" Nellie asked piteously. "What harm could I possibly . . . You . . . ? You!"

She recognized the killer!

Clattering footfalls, more sobs, our own labored breathing. A hundred steps, I was sure. Two hundred. The muscles in my legs were on fire. I could barely breathe!

Then, finally, we heard Nellie's echoing cries from somewhere ahead, and we climbed out through a passageway, down two more steps, and stood upon the Whispering Gallery. We were on a small circular walkway that hugged the inner dome well into its heights. The tight circular railing stood out only a few feet from the wall. It rose to my mid-chest, and peering down past it was like looking down a near incalculable height to the very hall in which we'd stood minutes ago. A fall from this height would smash any man to pulp.

But where was our prey? And Nellie?

"*Please . . . help me, please!*"

Who is it, who has you? I wanted to yell, but Shen put a finger to his lips for silence.

Nellie's whisper drifted from our left. We whirled,

chased the sound, ran a quarter of the way about the circle, and stopped as another whisper came to us from the spot we had just vacated.

"*I'm sorry, I didn't know . . . I couldn't . . . don't . . .*"

This was why it was called the Whispering Gallery. Whispers from any point about its radius could be heard at any other point, but one never knew quite where the sounds originated.

Shen whipped his gaze from side to side. In the dim light, we could not see Nellie or the monster that held her. Had the killer wrapped them both in that infernal nightmare-black cloak and crouched low to hide them away?

A sharp gasp of pain from the far end of the gallery drove Shen into a frenzy. He flew forward, racing for where he'd heard this sound land, unmindful of the many doorways lining the round gallery. Winded from the sharp climb and aching from the bruises and bumps I'd received during the madness of the carriages and the harm I'd endured in the Quarter yesterday, I could not keep up with him.

But I saw the danger as, in the pale light, he passed one of those doorways and the cloaked killer sprang out behind him, knife raised high.

"SHEN!"

My shout thundered through the gallery, echoed off the walls, and he stopped, startled, and turned slightly in my direction, an act that saved him. The blade came down and bit into his shoulder instead of the nape of his exposed neck. Shrieking in pain, he nevertheless spun in his attacker's direction, reaching out for the killer. Humbug was too quick, withdrawing the blade and darting back into the doorway, vanishing into the black beyond.

I reached Shen even as his knees threatened to give. My hand went for the wound, but he was already clutching it, staunching the flow of blood, at least for now, the pistol tucked in his waistband. An amber flicker caught my eye from the door before us, and footsteps scraped more steps.

His fingers tightened about his shoulder, his left arm dangling uselessly. He launched himself ahead, drops of blood marking his passing. He took a sharp turn in the direction from which the light had lapped out at us—the killer's lantern—and cursed as he stumbled over another trap: an array of bricks and debris piled about the base of a second flight of curving steps. By the time I had him back on his feet, I saw how Humbug could easily have stepped over these. The drugged Nellie must have already have been deposited on the next landing, then the beast had doubled back.

Freeing a path, we climbed upward once more, the killer and Nellie far enough ahead of us that we heard only the scraping of footsteps and labored breathing. The sound of something being dragged.

Then the amber light brightened, creeping like skeletal fingers across the curved walls to either side of us. Shen let go of his wounded shoulder and drew his pistol from his waistcoat's pocket. He stumbled, light-headed as blood flowed at a steadier trickle now, and called, "Let her go! I command you, do it and I'll let you live. Harm her and I'll harrow you to the gates of hell and beyond!"

The creaking of metal rungs sounded above the December wind. Unmindful of further traps, I pushed past Shen and stepped onto the roof. A merciless fist of cold propelled by a swift and heavy wind struck us, nearly driving the air from our lungs. We were in a long rectangular gallery and far ahead and another story higher than us jutted the empty tower we'd spied when we first arrived. I stepped out and heard metal groans and the clatter of the same steel-heeled boots that had kicked me square in the skull back in the manor house. They clanged while something *thump-thump-thumped* up behind them.

Shen stumbled out next to me. The empty tower's spire stabbed at the full moon and was kissed by the drifting clouds. The sounds were to our right, and we crept out until we saw another flight of metal steps. They led up to the slightly arched roof nestled over the long alley we had run through downstairs.

High above, the killer hauled Nellie from the steps onto the slanted rooftop. A long, narrow walk beside it acted as a gutter leading back to the west façade through which we had entered St. Paul's. Hooking gloved hands that looked pale and sharp as bone under the actress's arms, Humbug dragged the apparently unconscious woman towards the trio of waiting saints.

Shen and I exchanged worried glances, then we reached the metal stairs and climbed. I helped the wounded man as best I could, steadying him as his left arm dangled uselessly. By the time we reached the top, Nellie and the killer had vanished, or so it seemed. Then Shen grasped my steadying arm so tightly I might have cried out from the pain.

The robed figure stood from a crouch and revealed itself next to the statue of St. Paul. The saint's back was turned to us, and he was framed by a burning white moonlight. The murderer stood at the very center of the rooftop's two slanted panels. Shen tried to climb onto the arching roof but could not.

The killer's arm was around Nellie's waist. Her hair flowed down past her face, but her arms were moving, her hand touching her skull. It came away bloody. The monster had clubbed her to unconsciousness when the drugs had begun to wear off back at the Whispering Gallery.

Beyond the ledge on which the killer stood, carrying the now weeping Nellie, the woman's body convulsing with terror, was a sheer drop to the steps. A long fall nothing could survive.

We edged closer, and Humbug made no move to stop us. Clutching the cold railing to my left with one hand, steadying the weakened Shen with the other, I watched for any sign that our movements displeased the maniac. There were none. This was what Humbug wanted.

A great distance still separated us from the killer and the girl. We carefully trod along the rooftop's angled flank, Humbug still and quiet as the statue of St. Paul. Nellie started to struggle. Humbug leaned in close and whispered something in her ear, then turned her slightly. She peered over the ledge to the terrifying fall awaiting them should they lose their balance and tumble from their precarious perch.

Then the beast fixed its veiled eyes on us once more. And waited.

Humbug dressed as the spirit of death itself, the ghost of the future that would come for us all in its good time, and I thought to flatter the maniac beneath those robes. Anything to buy us time and the chance to reach the pair now a dozen yards before us.

"Spirit, what would you have of us?" I asked, my exhaustion and the sting of the bitter cold putting a plaintive quaking into my speech. "What is this 'humbug' that drives you? What lie was told, what duplicitous act are you punishing? What is it that binds all of us to you in such a hateful way?"

The face beneath the veils lifted with interest. I thought perhaps the killer's mouth opened, that speech might betray the killer's hidden identity. Then the figure went still again.

I stepped closer. "Do you seek to bargain? What do you want?"

Slowly, inexorably, the murderer's bony hand rose and a single incredibly long finger pointed first at Shen, then at myself. Ice drained down my spine.

"No," I whispered, remembering Fezziwig's promise. "It's not yet my time . . ."

"Coward," Shen snapped, dropping the pistol and shrugging off my helping hand. A trail of blood in the snow behind us marked our path like crimson tears. "Monster, take me. Let her live and I will go to the deathlands with you."

Humbug's head angled quizzically.

"I love her," he said, in response to the unasked question. "She is light and life itself. I would give up all for her, and be glad. That is a bargain I am happy to make."

His voice hitched, his throat constricting with emotion. Tears glistened on his cheek.

He waited.

In response, Humbug loosed the grip about Nellie's waist—and seized her by the throat. The actress was lifted up until she balanced on her toes. We were close enough to see ice on the stone ledge beneath them. They could not dance long or well upon that spot without slipping back into the abyss.

Nellie was turned ever so slightly until she faced the street, her hair billowing behind her.

I had thought the killer might be a woman, but the sheer inhuman strength now displayed made me question that theory.

Do not do this, I begged in my mind, even as Shen fell to his knees and moaned similar pleas.

Humbug looked our way a final time. An instant before the deed was done, understanding crept into our bones, our blood, our flesh. We could not stop this. We had been powerless from the start.

Then, with a jerk of one hand, Humbug shoved Nellie out into empty space. Her hand shot out for the statue, as if to find a hold to arrest her flight. Her nails scraped the statue's robe, one bending, flicking off.

Her scream as she disappeared from sight was quickly drowned out by Shen's horrified wailing.

Humbug watched us, stared with what I could only construe as delight, feasting on Shen's misery and my growing fear.

A ghostly hand rested on the nape of my neck. *One more, Ebenezer. Then you . . .*

"Bastard!" Shen cried. He groped for the fallen weapon. The murderer stood beside St. Paul with nowhere to go, no means to escape justice. Or revenge.

Not unless the mad thing intended to join Nellie in oblivion.

Heat rose in me with the desire to avenge not just this innocent woman I had wrongly suspected, but my old dear friend Fezziwig.

"We end this, now," I snarled.

Then I heard a clanging.

The killer sprinted across the center join of the gently steepled roof. Black cloak whipping in the freezing, bitter wind, Humbug passed us even as Shen snatched up the weapon and aimed it with a trembling hand. Inhumanly quick, Humbug dropped and slid down the far side of the roof. Shen fired, but his arm was unsteady, the bullet sparking a good yard beyond the killer, who flew over the edge and down into the opposing gutter from us.

On trembling legs, my companion trod upward on the icy roof. A single misstep might have spelled disaster and death, but his eyes were hollow, beyond caring. I rubbed the numbness from my limbs as I followed him, cutting glances back to the silent saint that had stood by and watched as yet another soul was consigned to the void. I knew that a horror waited below and was in no hurry to take it in.

We found a rope dangling from where Humbug had slid over the ledge. The rope led all the way down the two stories to the flat floor of the workman's gutter between the cathedral's high outer walls. Far beyond it was a propped-open door, through which Humbug had again escaped.

There was no chance of catching up now.

We found our way down the many winding staircases, through the great nave, then out to the freezing night. A crowd was gathering; children were running to find the nearest bobby.

Nellie lay on the steps, a crumpled, shattered doll, limbs twisted unnaturally, her head caved in. Her face—what remained of it—was a bloody red shattered mess of protruding bone and teeth with only a single eye.

There was one thing more. A task the killer had managed to perform before fleeing into the night:

The word "Humbug" had been written on the steps in the shattered woman's blood.

CHAPTER TWENTY-TWO

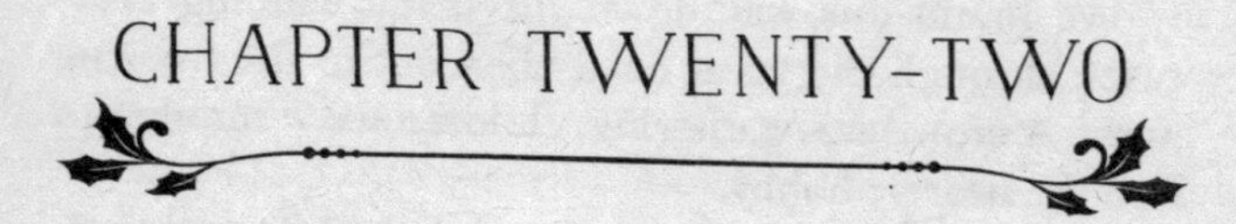

Friday, December 23rd, 1833
Two Days to Christmas

I WAS RUNNING.

Running through twisting paths within dark abbey ruins under a gibbous moon, whispers caressing me from every side. A giant bell tolled a series of slow, deathly clangs, and the darkness and mist obscured my vision. My legs were heavy, and each step was like trudging through coagulated blood while the hollow steps of Humbug came ever closer.

Panting, I turned a corner and stopped. Humbug rose up and towered before me, a ghost shrouded in black clutching a bloody knife. I squinted, trying to recognize him, and just as I feared the knife would be plunged into my heart, a lock of chocolate hair tumbled loose from inside the hood. I gasped. The killer raised a bony hand and combed back the veiling hood.

The visage before me belonged to *Adelaide*!

I woke with a start and sat up, clutching my chest and gasping for air. The window was cracked, the curtains fluttering gently in the frosty Christmas breeze, and the bell in the clock tower was striking the hour. Four in the morning. Still dark. I sighed and ran my hand through my sweat-drenched hair, an icy droplet trickling down my spine.

Suddenly a gust burst into my room and blew out the candle by my bed. A shadow whipped wildly, then another, and I felt the icy droplet trickle back *up* my spine. Shadows began to form, emerging towards me, taking shape until I saw Fezziwig's pale ghost before me. His white and grey spirit contrasted against the blackness of the night. He rasped and stretched a bony finger towards me, accusing me, warning me: *One more, Ebenezer, then you. Then you!*

Then he leaped and *flew* at me, deathlike hands outstretched—

With a painful gasp, I shot up in bed, morning sunlight glowing all about me. I scanned the room. I was alone—no ghost, no killer. I felt my face, pinched my own cheek, threw off my bedcovers, and swung my feet round to touch the cold floor. I was no longer lost in a waking dream state; this was real. The clock tower tolled. Seven strokes this time. It was morning, and the faint light of winter dawn streamed through the windows. Breathing out and rubbing the exhaustion from my eyes, I let out a little chuckle. I should not be surprised at my own foolish imagination considering the week I'd had.

At the washbasin, I doused my face in the freezing water and peered at myself in the mirror. Bags under my eyes, unshaven . . . then my heart stopped. For in the reflection behind me . . .

I spun round. The word HUMBUG was written in blood-red paint on the wall opposite.

The wind seemed harsher and the grey daylight dimmer than was normal for the hour as I trudged through the snow to my office. Wary of spying Sikes or another of Smithson's men, I tipped my hat at a woman I passed, but she scowled in return. A few paces on and a gentleman avoided my eyes, sending only a fearful glance as he passed me. One after the other, the normally cheerful Friday morning Londoners were giving me odd looks as I walked along the icy cobbles. Fearful. Angry. *Disgusted.* Confused and concerned, I rushed to my office.

A mob was waiting for me outside the counting-house. Scores of men, angry faces.

"There he is!" cried one of them, and they collectively turned my way just as Dickens appeared from behind me, grabbed my arm, and rushed me into the building.

Where the hell have you been? I wanted to ask. *And what happened to the guardsmen I requested for Miss Owen and myself?*

I slammed the door and locked it behind us against a roar of accusations and questions, then tweaked the curtain and peered through the windowpane. From their ravenous demand for "statements," it was apparent that the mob was a crowd of other reporters on a feeding frenzy, the taste of blood on their lips.

Dickens slammed a folded newspaper on the desk beside me, and I jumped, turning to see my office already occupied. A trio of stern-faced and expensively dressed gentlemen stood there with folded arms, and behind them Adelaide, Constable Crabapple, and Shen. Their expressions were dark, their looks grim.

I glanced at Dickens, quizzically, but he too was staring at me from under a heavy brow.

"What have you to say for yourself, Scrooge?" he said. "Did you do it?" Then he chuckled and unfolded the newspaper. Beneath the headline "HUMBUG STRIKES AGAIN" and a drawing of poor Nellie Pearl sat a story about me. The title read, "IS HUMBUG THE ONLY KILLER?" My image was crammed beneath it, next to that of George Sunderland.

Just as I opened my mouth, a shocking whirlwind of accusations and angry statements spun round the room, led by the three gentlemen. They were solicitors, it emerged, associates of Lazytree. One of the men handed me a large brown paper envelope. "I am officially, and in the presence of witnesses, serving you with court papers, sir . . ."

Civil proceedings were being launched, they said, by the heirs of the Sunderland estate. The administrators were accusing me of besmirching the reputation of the estate by allegations of an ongoing association, as well as fraud on account of using those claims to further my business ends. They then made it very clear that any offers of funding for the rail deal from Sunderland's people had, naturally enough, and with extreme prejudice, been withdrawn.

To cap it off, they pointed to the newspaper story

suggesting Mr. Sunderland did not fall from that bridge, that instead, he was pushed. By me.

I sank into my office chair.

"You'll be hearing more very soon," promised the lead solicitor, "on *all* accounts!"

He turned and gave a short bow to Adelaide, and the three of them left the office. A roar of voices rang out as soon as the door opened, the solicitors pressing their way past the protesting reporters. Dickens locked the door again. I caught his gaze and could not mistake the silent apology in his eyes. Capitalizing on my time with Sunderland had been his idea. I turned away but not before awarding him a quick shake of the head and a stiff raising of my lower lip. He had forced me into nothing. My own greed had been my undoing.

"Well," I said, "Lazytree, that sly bastard, told me I would receive *quite the visit* this morning. I certainly have!"

I turned to the constable.

"What are *you* doing here, Crabapple?" I asked, but before he could answer, I spotted something past him and shouted out in surprise. The door to my vault was wide open, a ransacked mess spilling out on the floor. I jumped to my feet to rush over, but as I passed Adelaide, she put her arm out to stop me.

"We've been robbed, Ebenezer," she whispered. "It's all gone. All your money, all your valuables." I stared at her, her green eyes glistening with sorrow. "All I collected for you, all our hard work, for nothing." Her voice cracked and she looked away.

Ruined.

I was ruined. The blood drained from my face, and I had to lean against the desk to steady myself.

"There were services you requested," Dickens murmured, clearly referring to my need for more protectors. "But I had not the coin to put them into effect. I'd hoped to receive an advance this morning, but . . ."

My head was swimming. The worst had come to pass. This feeling was much like the day Belle broke off our engagement on a chilly park bench, and that wound had never healed. I had lost it all—all my money, my very purpose.

"They left a calling card," said Dickens, handing me a small piece of paper that I now saw had been shoddily hammered into my plaster wall. I looked at it. A bull's-eye had been crudely painted on it, in what looked like blood.

"Bill Sikes," I fumed. "Delivering a warning."

"Or a promise," said Dickens.

"Just here to get a statement, Mr. Scrooge," said Crabapple, chewing a toothpick. "In your own time."

"And you?" I raged at Shen. "What is your purpose here? Come to gloat over what you and Marley promised would happen? Well?"

I stared at him, and finally it registered that Shen had changed. The fire had gone from him, his back was bent under an invisible weight, and his once dashing face was pale and tired. He lifted his eyes to meet mine, and I was startled to see a cobweb of blood red vessels creeping over his eyeballs. He had succumbed to grief.

"I have little left to offer the world, Scrooge," he said, with a voice that was dry and hoarse. "But I can yet offer you my apology." He moved towards me, his feet shifting on my dusty floor like those of an old man, cautious, fragile. I saw his left shoulder twinge from the stab wound inflicted by Humbug, but his hand was planted in his pocket and he said nothing. Instead, he reached his right hand out, and I shook it.

"I did not look deep enough in your eyes before I judged you," he said. "For your valor last night I release you from the bonds of oath. You owe me nothing, nor I you."

I nodded.

"Last night?" asked Crabapple, spitting the toothpick onto my floor and perking up. "What, you mean that raucous display with the carriages and that bus? I thought only Miss Owen had been there when Roger Colley's past caught up with him."

Adelaide had told the police that men who claimed to be former victims of Colley and his boys had ended him. She'd left Shen and myself—and the business at the cathedral—out of her account.

"So you were there, then?" Crabapple asked. "Both of you?"

A dark look passed between me and Shen, a moment so tense that I felt the room pressing in on me. I had little left to lose and gave him a sharp nod.

"Exactly so, Constable," said Shen. "Exactly so. . . ."

Then, with the arm that still worked, he reached into his jacket and withdrew a thick, brown envelope. I had seen its twin before: Dodger had presented it the night before last. I pictured its contents and shuddered.

Shen handed the envelope to Crabapple, and Dickens and Adelaide sent each other looks of confusion.

"This may be of use to you, Constable," said Shen. "I believe it might be connected to Miss Pearl's death." Then he sank to his knees on the cold floor, and Adelaide rushed to his side.

Crabapple opened the envelope and withdrew the packet. His eyes were wide and his mouth agape as he flicked through the images, one by one, the series of ill-used women. Shaking his head, he stopped when he arrived at one featuring the fake Nellie. He dropped the photographs on the desk and rubbed his forehead. Dickens saw the motifs and drew back horrified before grabbing his notepad and pen and beginning to scribble.

Slowly, Crabapple raised his head and looked at me. "You *knew* about this!" he shouted. "It's written on your face, as clear as 'Humbug' in blood!"

I simply nodded. There was little else I could say. Adelaide pulled herself up from where she had been comforting Shen, frowned at me, and went over to the desk to see what Crabapple was talking about.

"Don't, Adelaide!" said Dickens, but she lifted a card and then immediately dropped it as if it were acid.

"Oh!" she said, her hand to her mouth. Her soft and pretty features were twisted in an expression of utter disgust. Her green eyes flashed at me. "*This* is what you were keeping from me?"

"In part," I mumbled. "Yes, I have seen these monstrosities before."

"Hang on," said Crabapple, lifting one of the cards

again and examining it closely. Then another. "I know this girl. Oh, Lord above! The missing-persons cases—right here, this very girl, and this one, too!"

I suppressed a feeling of nausea. The blood drained from Adelaide's face. Dickens helped Shen to his feet, dumped him in a nearby chair. The loss of Nellie Pearl had devastated him.

"Pretty maids all in a row," I muttered. Feeling a burning threat in the back of my throat, I bit my lip to stifle the erupting emotion. Rutledge had flared when I sang those words to him.

Realization dawned on me, and the fog lifted like dawn mist.

"Let me see those photos," I urged, reaching over and gathering up the vile things.

"Take them," said Crabapple. "Remove them from my sight."

"Adelaide! Rutledge said he was trying to dispose of his country estate, didn't he?" I asked her, studying each card, searching past the women, my eyes squinting to discern the detail behind the deplorable acts frozen in time.

"Yes," she said. "That's right . . . he said it was becoming a burden."

"And he went on about some recent addition to the house, didn't he?" I went on.

"The columns. He had lined the great hall with Doric columns, some homage to an architect or something. And he said something about having a hedge maze, too. But why?"

I stopped flicking as I reached the photograph of the

Nellie doll, her hands bound behind her back, her neck tied with rope to a squat, white, Doric column. I sat down and handed the card to Adelaide. Fat tears rolled down her cheeks as she looked at each of the cards. Columns in each of them, some shrouded in shadow, some obscure in the background, but this was no coincidence. Other details of his country house that Rutledge had coughed up also matched, including the hedge maze, though it was hardly new from the look of it. The backdrop for these hideous images was his remote estate.

Adelaide drew a deep breath and stood tall, dropping the photographs like dead rats. "He was taking payments for the use of the estate," she deduced. "All under the table. It explains much about his finances."

"These are sold to wealthy men at forty pounds apiece," I told her, and everybody except Shen gasped.

"Wealthy and *powerful* men . . ." said Dickens, scrutinizing the images.

"Powerful enough to settle a man's tax bill and make contributions to the police," Adelaide added.

Just as I was about to agree, a thud sounded as Crabapple slammed his fist on the desk.

"That's it!" he fumed. "Enough of all this! What the *hell* is going on here? You'd better tell me everything, Scrooge, like I've been warning you to do right from the day we met. What's all this? Well?"

I exchanged looks with Dickens, Shen, and Adelaide. Collectively, we silently agreed.

"Crabapple, a few days ago I deemed you deserving of no more respect than the fleas in poor Rutledge's wig," I said. "It is clear I underestimated you, for you deserve at least the same level of respect I show the moths in Dickens' coat, if not more. I shall tell you everything. It began on Monday. I was here, in my offices, entertaining a man who wasn't quite what he seemed. . . ."

Crabapple dropped his elbows onto the desk and his head into his hands. Between Dickens, Adelaide, and me, we had told him the whole story, from Fezziwig's ghost to the soul-destroying chase on the top of St. Paul's. Shen had only looked up briefly to nod a short assent when we disclosed to Crabapple everything we knew about the Chinaman's criminal endeavors. A silence fell over us as we watched the story sink in.

The constable drew a breath, then stood up. "Why didn't you tell me this before?"

"We didn't think you'd believe us," Adelaide said.

"Nor could we trust you as far as we could spit a dead rat," I said flatly. "Besides, you like things simple, remember? The truth isn't always like that."

Dickens lit up a cigarette. "Really, Scrooge . . . ghosts? You're a curious man!"

Crabapple eyed him angrily. "I've seen things. Things that can't easily be explained," he said to the reporter. "I know darkness in all its forms, and I know it better than to dismiss any possibility because it upsets your way of thinking."

Shen cleared his throat. "There is something more." He produced a smaller envelope. At first I thought it The Lady's invitation from last night, but his name had been etched on its surface in the same florid handwriting.

Crabapple snatched it up, fished out the sheet of parchment within, and read the summons aloud:

> *Sir,*
>
> *I bet you'd love to avenge your tasty crumpet's death. Wasn't her scream hysterical? Bit of a pulpy mess when she hit, though.*
>
> *Well, do meet me at the party tonight. You know me as a most colorful type. I'll be adding a splash of red to the festivities. Death by the dozens, I expect.*
>
> *You could not protect your lady, but there is still a chance to safeguard her honor. And do tell Mr. Scrooge to join us. He and I have unfinished business. I'm sure he will know of what I speak.*
>
> *I trust you can find out the where and the when all on your own. As for the how, well . . . as your shoulder can attest, it's not just my wit that's sharp. And that is no humbug.*
>
> *Though I am.*
>
> *—An Admirer*

"So you weren't involved in these depravities?" demanded Crabapple of Shen.

Shen shook his head. "My only involvement in this putrid web of corruption is the one the killer has clearly already guessed. I loved Nellie. As unrequited as my love was, I adored her like my own. And whatever score the killer had to settle with my pretty pearl, he has decided to extend the suffering to me as well. This letter, it was with that filth." Shen gestured at the package of photographs. "The meaning is clear: either I go and confront Humbug, or those photos will be shared with vultures like that one." He nodded towards Dickens.

"Rather think of myself more as a noble eagle, but fair enough," Dickens agreed.

And now I knew why Shen had come to me. Humbug had left him no choice.

Crabapple handed the note back. "And this is like the one you received last night, Scrooge? Warning that Nellie was in danger?"

I nodded.

"So we're running out of time."

I studied his face. The man had changed, his usual sneer and cynical squint had gone, replaced with a look of concern. Why was he now, so suddenly, willing to help us? "What game are you playing?"

"No game," he said. "I've only ever asked you for the truth, Mr. Scrooge. Seems like I finally got it."

"Then you believe us?" Adelaide asked.

"Insofar as select bits of this mystery, I believe that *you* believe," he said, "and that's plenty for now. Insofar as the rest, 'death by the dozens'? I can't ignore a threat like that, even if I don't yet know what it's all about."

He marched over to Shen and dragged him to his feet, brushing off the Chinaman's jacket and giving him a series of quick slaps across the face.

"Focus, man!" he barked. "This 'Lady.' You said you recognized her handwriting. Who is she? What do you know of her?"

"An importer, an exporter," Shen mumbled. "Exotic goods and services. Powerful. And clearly . . . quite mad."

Crabapple smacked his own forehead. "Have none of you considered that there may not even be a Mr. Smithson? That the 'chimera' business might all come down to her and the three faces she wears? First as herself, then as 'The Lady,' and lastly as the always unseen 'Smithson'? And what was your connection to Rutledge, anyway?"

Shen drew some strength and was about to reply when a sudden pounding slammed against the locked front door, and a note slid under the threshold. Fear simmered up in me again: What word would be scribbled on that paper?

Adelaide ran to the door and picked up the note.

"It is a summons from Lord Dyer. He has been to see my Tom. I *have* to go," she said, gathering up her coat.

I objected, but Adelaide pushed past me and went for the door. She only stopped when Crabapple said, "Guilfoyle's benefactor? Yeah, I would like to know more of how he figures in all of this. Go on, then. Scrooge, you go with her. None of you should be out and about on your own with this murderer still on the loose. Dickens, Mr. Shen, you two stay right where you are. We have more to discuss. A lot more."

"You want to know why I lied to protect Lord Dyer," Adelaide said as she gripped the doorknob. "You're about to get your answer."

CHAPTER TWENTY-THREE

A BLACK CARRIAGE waited for us at the entrance to the Dyer manor. The white beast harnessed to it—almost invisible against the idyllic winter backdrop—stood calm and confident, snorting steam into the frosty air. Thoughts and questions tumbled one over another in my mind as to Adelaide's connection to a man of such wealth and power. *Powerful enough to settle a man's tax bill*? Adelaide's earlier words resurfaced in my head. My stomach tightened.

"Who's this?" barked the voice of Lord Dyer as our crunching footsteps approached. "Certainly not a chaperone, for you would perish before suffering the protection of someone assigned to you, isn't that so?"

Adelaide said nothing but took my hand and stepped up into the carriage. I followed.

She settled into the leather seat opposite Lord Dyer, and they both watched me as I took my place beside her with an awkward huddle. There was tension between them, between us, and Lord Dyer's eyes narrowed as they bore into me.

"Well?" he said, not for a second easing his gaze. "Our conversation is to be private!"

"Mr. Ebenezer Scrooge," said Adelaide, "has been much support to me during Tom's ordeal, considering there has been little support to gather from *elsewhere.*" She said the last word with palpable bitterness. "And yes, he *was* sent along by Constable Crabapple to protect me, because for lack of much action on the part of those with power, there is still a murderer on the loose, so it is the wish of the London Metropolitan Police that he remain with me. And I trust him."

I stared at her. Her audacity towards this man was baffling, quite contrary to her normally beguiling character, but he did not evict her from his carriage as I would have thought. Instead, he sighed, his eyes looked away, and he tapped on the side of the carriage with his cane and called to the driver to take us to the lake.

We trundled into motion, the carriage wheels crunching frozen gravel, and thick snowflakes began to fall. I stared through the carriage window at the bare, white trees, their naked branches reaching towards, pointing at me like bony fingers.

"You're known to me, Mr. Scrooge," Dyer said at last. "You contributed to that article that wretched Mr. Dickens wrote about our Tom. I wouldn't have expected Adelaide to suffer your presence at all after that, yet here you are, with her staunch defense. But understand, I do not share her affection for you."

"Understood," I said. I held my tongue at any more.

"How is he?" Adelaide asked suddenly.

"Thomas? There are no infections," mumbled Lord Dyer. "He may yet live."

Adelaide turned her gaze to the passing whiteness outside and released a sigh, breathing a frozen lace across the carriage window. Then she whispered, "Thank you, Father."

Father? I stared at Adelaide, whose steady gaze signaled that this was no slip, she had meant for me to know this. Lord Dyer was a marquess, which made Adelaide . . .

"No," she said bluntly. "I am no lady." She took a deep breath. "But do allow me to introduce my father, Lord Dyer, Third Marquess of Dyer Haven."

"And you?" I whispered.

She turned to me, her emerald eyes sparkling. There was some deep look of sadness, but also of pride.

"Miss Adelaide Owen," she said. A wheel hit a stone in the path and the carriage jumped, I involuntarily reached out for balance, and she grabbed my arm to steady me. "Just that and nothing more."

"This is not seemly," barked Lord Dyer. "And it is none of this man's affair. Adelaide, you are not only disclosing your secrets, but mine!"

Adelaide ignored his fuming and took my hand. "When I first came to you, I considered my parentage irrelevant. I made my own way in life through hard work, just like you, Ebenezer, and do not need my place in this world to be defined by the stations of those who brought me into it."

I shifted in my seat, feeling the warmth of her hands through my leather gloves, the pressure of her fingers against mine. Lord Dyer said nothing, but an air of sadness rose about him.

"Your parents were not married," I surmised. Lord Dyer twitched and stared out of the window. The implications of illegitimacy rolled in like a white winter storm and crashed into my mind in great drifts.

"My mother raised me and my brother by herself, in the country. For all of Lord Dyer's financial contributions to our life, she had to work hard, endure gossip and prejudice and the toll of two children." She withdrew her hands and again looked out of the window. "Not that life for me."

"You were always determined to make your own way, Adelaide," said Lord Dyer suddenly, his moustache twitching as he pressed his lips together.

"Well, what should I have done?" she said firmly. "You left us to fend for ourselves!"

"What should *I* have done?" her father said, an unexpected passion rising in his voice. "I loved her. Beyond measure, I adored her! We wanted to escape, go away, and forget the world and all its squalor. Deny such mundane things as servants and lords, maids and masters, duty and expectation. How I hated it all, all but her." The marquess inhaled sharply and cleared his throat, I heard the telltale shake of emotion threatening to upset his lordly façade.

He composed himself. "I was born into a cruel world, Adelaide. Far crueler than the one you were raised to know." He looked to me and said, "We should continue this privately."

"No, Father. I promised Mr. Scrooge no more withholding, no more lies."

"So be it, then." The ugly look in his eyes signaled that should I breathe a word of this to anyone, particularly a newshound like Dickens, the consequences would be dire indeed.

The carriage ground to a halt under the white and weeping locks of a frozen willow, and I followed Lord Dyer and Adelaide into the snow. An ornate bench, covered in frost, overlooked the frozen lake. The two sat down, but I stood witnessing their exchange.

"It was on this very bench she told me she was expecting you. Twins! A happier moment never occurred to me since." Lord Dyer reached into his jacket and pulled out a small brown bag. Reaching into it, he gathered a small handful of breadcrumbs and scattered them onto the hardened snow. Two identical robins fluttered down and began pecking.

"My father's advisors made it clear that day. Any public knowledge of illegitimate children would put the family in peril, jeopardize the estate, ultimately damage the credibility of king and country. And for a future marquess to *marry* a handmaid? A terrible 'accident' would surely have befallen her if we had attempted to elope. What could I do, Adelaide, against the force of such responsibility? But I tried to do well by you, I truly did. Especially when your mother died. How many times did I try to recruit your brother to a better station? I tried to mentor him, to lead him up through business so that he might yet succeed despite his class, but he just *kept on* sabotaging himself. Alcohol. Drugs. Women. Gambling. Time after time, chance after chance. He would not be helped. Didn't I do all for him?"

Adelaide's face reddened with anger. She chanced a look my way, studying my face to ensure that I was fully understanding the scene being performed before me. I was.

Thomas Guilfoyle, "her Tom," was her twin brother. I had mistaken her familiar love as something very different.

"Of course you did, Father," she murmured. "You did all you could . . . for *him*! But what for me? What opportunities came my way? I would not have squandered any of it!"

Lord Dyer stared at her, hurt laced across his face. "Oh, Adelaide! Your brother should have been born the girl, and you should have been my son. I always admired your strength. Courage. Thirst for knowledge. But more than anything, so much more attention was lavished on your brother because he needed it. He was weak. But you! Strong! Self-sufficient."

Adelaide looked down, a tear dripping into her lap.

"And now . . ." Lord Dyer lowered his voice and his head. "I fear I may have ruined it all. One final project I gave him, one last chance that would legitimately give him control of one of the companies. To secure the land for one of the fabric importers in our supply chain, you see. Said he knew of property would put us in a favorable position."

"Then Piermont and Piermont Acquisitions is one of your companies," I supplied.

"Many times removed, but yes," Lord Dyer admitted.

"The owners of all the surrounding properties agreed to sell, but not Fezziwig," I said. "Not so long as there was breath left in his body. Tell me, Lord Dyer. How go negotiations now? With his widow, Jane?"

Dyer glared at me. "You're every bit the cruel and heartless type I might have expected."

"Then you deny that the acquisition proceeds apace?"

He hung his head, and Adelaide wrapped her arms around his broad shoulders, which began to shake. The robins took flight, soaring back into the willow above us, which rained icy fractals as it was disturbed. I looked at father and daughter, joined in grief and sadness, and at once, as the mist on the frozen lake cleared with a sudden gust of wind, realization dawned.

Rutledge had claimed that Smithson was a great man leading a double life, a man of business with a reputation beyond reproach. An apt description of Lord Dyer. But Rutledge had also been coached by Shen to say what he did.

I thought it over as above a stream of sunlight broke through the thin cloud cover. Twinkles fell over the park like heavenly angel dust sprinkled across the lake, the trees, and every blade of grass as the sun caught the icy crystals of each frozen dewdrop. My skin tingled from the freezing air, and my stomach tingled, too.

"Father," Adelaide said at last, oblivious that this was a new and happy revelation. "The monster that butchered poor Tom, who killed Mr. Scrooge's dear friend Fezziwig, Lord Rutledge, and Nellie Pearl, has vowed to kill one more, then Mr. Scrooge. The next one . . . it could be me. Or even you."

"Do you know of any ties between George Sunderland and the Colley Brothers? Some enterprise they may have shared?"

"I know they're all dead," Lord Dyer said darkly. "Beyond that, no."

Adelaide took up the charge. "Father, do you know anything of the Royal Quarter and the evil they get up to there? Smithson? The Lady?"

Lord Dyer stirred. "The Lady?" He looked up, his eyes flickering as if he were recalling earlier conversations. "Tom spoke of The Lady. Some woman with a scheme that would ensure that we would pick up Fezziwig's land for a fraction of what it was worth. I thought little of it. Tom was always coming up with this scheme or that. I assumed this 'Lady' was some patron. Perhaps a wife if God was kind, as Tom would have excelled as a kept man. . . ."

"But there must be more to it?" I interjected. "We must examine his paperwork, study the business of the proposed acquisition of Fezziwig's land."

"If you wish. My men retrieved Tom's belongings after the attack. There are boxes of the stuff stored in the gamekeeper's lodge. Adelaide can show you the way through the gardens. Myself . . . I'm feeling quite tired. Some days it is like all my sins weigh me down like chains posed to drag me to perdition."

As Adelaide and her father kissed good-bye by the doors of the stone lodge, and the carriage trundled back towards the splendor of the manor, I bit my lip to calm my beating heart. We were close to a new revelation. I could feel it!

In the dusty, freezing gamekeeper's lodge, we dug together through boxes of Tom's paperwork and belongings that had been removed before the police could get their hands on anything that might embarrass the house of Dyer. Some of it would have: journals filled with senseless rants, many aimed with fury at Adelaide and their father. Their family secret would not have lasted long in the hands of Crabapple.

"You lied about who Tom prayed would save him because of a prior pledge," I said at last. "Your promise to Lord Dyer to keep your lineage—and Tom's—secret."

She shook her head. "It's tempting to let you believe that. The truth is . . . selfishly . . . I just try to have as little to do with that man as I can."

"But perhaps, considering the things he told you today, those old wounds, the rift between you, it could be repaired."

A thin smile etched itself upon her pretty face. "Are you talking about my father and me . . . or us?"

I thought of all I had learned of this strange woman; she was so unlike my Belle. But something in me felt drawn to her. Was it merely a respect for someone else who had to make their own way in the world? But no, I felt it was more than that, there were other feelings . . . but this was neither the time nor place for these complications. The killer had to be the priority and anything else was unimportant . . . for the moment.

Adelaide gave a cry and revealed a box stuffed to the brim with paperwork. Contracts. Ledgers. All from Fezziwig's offices.

"But Inspector Foote firmly assured us that all of

Fezziwig's most recent ledgers were there and were in order," I said. "Nothing had been taken from Fezziwig's establishment. He was quite certain."

"Well, you were his clerk once—are these written in Fezziwig's hand?"

I nodded.

"Then we should see the ledgers left in his office," she said. "In fact, I need to see them for myself!"

CHAPTER TWENTY-FOUR

BEHIND US, CRABAPPLE locked the front door to Fezziwig's former office, stifling the sound of a nearby newspaper boy calling "*Fire! Fire! Great fire in London only yesterday! Read all about it!*" The stench of smoke and burning chemicals still impregnated my hair, yet so was the horror from the clock tower chase, the confusion following Adelaide's abrupt revelations about her lineage, and the exhaustion from the most harrowing week of my life.

We crept through the front room, passing the rudimentary fireplace and a mahogany pedestal desk that now bore wilting sprigs of holly and cards of condolences. The building was unoccupied; Fezziwig's body had been transferred to a funeral home after the wake, and Jane Fezziwig had escaped the morbidity by packing up her daughters and travelling to family in York. I presumed that Dick Wilkins would help Jane deal with Dyer's overtures, but even he was not here.

A dark atmosphere lingered, and we treaded gingerly and cautiously as if evading the sudden horrors of death. Laughter, scurrying, jokes, and parties had once been the music of this place; now there was only the silence of the grave.

Shen ascended the fragile staircase to the workroom, followed by Dickens and Adelaide. Each step groaned like the undead. As Adelaide reached the top, before she vanished through the trapdoor, she turned and sent me a sad smile and the slightest nod. She sensed that my soul was wailing with painful nostalgia. I took a deep breath and placed my foot on the bottom step.

The spacious workroom was dusty and forgotten, and it appeared Mrs. Fezziwig had not stepped foot up here since the police had ended their investigation. The crime scene had been swept clean, but the sickly smells of death still lingered as subtle as a ghost's footprint.

Adelaide and Dickens were already rummaging through the cases holding Fezziwig's books and ledgers; Crabapple and Shen heaved the looms and spinning wheels away from the floor to make space to splay out the papers. Soon the wooden floor was carpeted with records, and Adelaide was scanning them, quickly and efficiently, her eyes working like the automatic needle of a sewing machine.

"Oh!" she exclaimed suddenly, jabbing her finger in one of the archives. "Pass me the set of Tom's accounts, please!" I handed her the package I had been clutching, the roll of papers we had retrieved from the gamekeeper's lodge. With her head flicking between the two like a metronome, she compared the records meticulously.

"Well?" barked Crabapple, but I lifted my hand to silence him. Adelaide was both quick and thorough, and she deserved her concentration.

"There are many discrepancies, Constable," she said, running her finger down line by line as she crouched on the floor of the workroom. Dickens helped her by studying figures and names and making notes of every point of inconsistency. "Entire pages with certain entries missing, other names and addresses have been replaced with what looks like nonsense. Made-up names? Code? All recorded in a hurry, it seems."

Then she got up, dusted off her dress, and sighed. "Tom forged these. I know his hand." In that moment, her eyes seemed dark with a profound sadness.

"But how was he able to switch the ledgers?" I asked.

"He must have come here often," said Shen. "Different ink, different day."

"He was letting himself in and out as often as he liked," said Dickens, calling from the window at the far corner of the room. "Look." With a smooth and soundless movement, he slid the window open and leaned out, feeling the sill with his fingers. "It's been prized open from the outside so many times the latch mechanism has snapped. Nobody would know unless they opened it, which I doubt has been necessary since summer."

Crabapple started pacing, scratching his moustache and making nasal noises as he thought. "He was setting something in motion, then. Needed to cover his tracks as he went along. Stay where I can see you, Shen! You are still a fugitive criminal as far as I'm concerned! Your grace period lasts only as long as you help solve this abomination."

Shen had been moving to the window to see what Dickens had discovered but turned and sat down. He didn't care about the man's threats. He sought only to get to the bottom of this and do what he might to protect Nellie's legacy.

"Stellar policing, Crabapple," I scoffed. "London's underground opium dens may rest safely yet another night." The constable ignored me, snatching away the papers Adelaide had been comparing and scanning the leaf from top to bottom.

"This entry here," he said, his nose almost touching the paper, "is a farm complex up in Essex. It's not in those copies. How many times does it turn up in that book you've got there?

Adelaide checked. "A lot. Only in the originals, though. In Tom's forgeries it has been replaced with . . . I don't know that address. I doubt it exists."

"Criminals often hide their wrongdoing in plain sight," Shen mused, staring into the space of the room as if he were counting dust flecks dancing in the afternoon light. "I do it all the time. The Colleys certainly did as well. Co-opting legitimate businessmen to use their offices as fronts for whatever they need, money laundering, you name it. It's so simple to arrange. Yet . . . not with a man like Mr. Fezziwig. Too honest."

"Unless it was being done without his knowledge," Crabapple said.

A sudden chill shuddered through my body as a ghostly finger traced my spine all the way to the nape of my neck. "We need to see what's on that farm," I whispered. "And something tells me we should go now!"

Two hours later the police wagon Crabapple had commandeered veered round a gravelly corner and sped up the driveway to the farm complex, nestled in a remote valley between white hills in Essex. I had been here once before, with my former mentor, many years ago. It was a non-operational farm on land now derelict and untended that Fezziwig had held on tight to as a security asset. He had collected several such spots around the country, never selling them despite their value; he kept them for his daughters.

The stone farmhouse stood empty, with black windows staring at us like dead and hollow eyes. Parts of the roof had caved in under the weight of snow and neglect. The adjacent farm buildings, spread out across at least an acre, consisted of cowsheds, stables, and barns. It would take us hours to search them all.

Adelaide sighed, steam bursting from her red lips and into the frozen air. Just as I was about to suggest starting at the farmhouse, a horse snorted. The beast was tethered to a broken winnowing machine outside a threshing barn; its trotting tracks led right from where we stood. Someone was here.

With hushed whispers and exaggerated gestures, Crabapple indicated that Shen and Dickens should creep round to the back of the barn, avoiding the horse lest it got startled and alerted its rider. The two of them would block any exit from the back while he and I snuck in from the front. Adelaide was ordered to stay safely hidden in the wagon, a suggestion she bore with a tense and reluctant obedience.

"Wouldn't it be safest to alert your men, Constable?"

she asked with a palpable irritation. Crabapple's face grew dark.

"No time," he answered. "And there ain't no one left that would help me these days. Not even Humperdink, and if that don't show how a man has fallen, nothing will."

The heavy padlock securing the front door was smashed and hanging limply from a broken hinge. I pushed the door gently. It creaked, so I stopped, slowly prying it open just enough for us to squeeze in through the crack.

As soon as we set foot in the barn, we were accosted by an almost impenetrable darkness and a stench so foul and evil that I had to fight to keep from doubling over in nausea. I had smelled this macabre miasma of decay before, deep in the limestone tunnels where Dickens had forced me to confront our recklessness.

"Handkerchiefs, now," whispered Crabapple as he finished silently loading his gun. We pressed our silk handkerchiefs against our noses.

As my eyes adjusted to the darkness, I noticed that the space had been converted into something of a labyrinth by a series of tall three-panel room dividers. We moved into the first space as quietly as we could with our footsteps shuffling through frozen straw. My foot brushed against something, and I crouched down to examine it. A chipped plate. Looking round, I made out the silhouettes of several more plates and bowls dotted in the corners of this room. Rancid bits of food still festered despite the freeze. Bread, meat . . . human food. What humans had eaten off the floor like animals?

I pointed it out to Crabapple, and he nodded solemnly. We rounded the side of the first divider, Crabapple's gun leading the way. We used quick, silent movements to dodge any sudden oncoming assault. None came but the assault on our eyes by the horror laid out in the dark space.

Thick iron rings were bolted into the walls in long lines, chains hung down weighted by heavy metal shackles. Rough blankets were crumpled under each one, dried bloodstains speckled across several. Unemptied piss pots stood in the corner, their contents frozen yet putrid.

I nudged Crabapple and pointed to a small table in the corner. Empty tincture bottles lay toppled, bloodstained surgical knives tossed carelessly onto the surface, as if thoughtlessly discarded once used. I picked up a bottle and read the label. Laudanum. Another—industrial ether.

Against my will, my imagination began painting a vivid and gruesome picture of what this place was. The missing women imprisoned here, tortured into submission and drugged, chained—waiting for the sweet release of death. I pressed Crabapple on; I needed to leave this room.

We inched our way to the second divider; Crabapple stopped to check the gun was cocked and then nodded. We rounded the corner and stopped dead.

The decomposing body of a girl no older than twenty was laying on the ground, her foot still shackled to a chain—and a man, with his back to us, was towering above her with an axe held high above his head.

"Feelin' a bit contrary, are you, Mary?" he gruffed

and sniggered to himself. He was just about to bring the axe down to sever the foot and free the body. I recoiled in horror, stifling a cry, but as I stepped back, I rattled a piss pot.

The man turned, gasped, threw the axe at us! It spun through the air, the handle striking Crabapple's elbow just as his gun went off, the fiery burst carving the darkness but missing the man. His shadow vanished behind the next divider.

Someone pushed between me and Crabapple and surged after the man. *Adelaide!* But instead of rounding the corner, she threw herself at the divider, bringing it crashing down on the man, pinning him to the ground. Adelaide let out a cry of pain as she landed on top of the pile, a sharp edge stabbing her side.

I rushed to her aid while Crabapple yanked the wriggling man free from under the fallen wall, jamming his gun into the man's bleeding mouth.

"Are you all right?" I asked Adelaide, checking her side for signs of impalement. "Are you hurt?"

"I'm well, thank you, Ebenezer," she said cautiously. She studied my face, looking, I gathered, for some sign that my continued anger at her betrayal—despite its understandable cause—was beginning to subside.

I looked away.

She dusted herself off, wincing slightly as her hand brushed her bruised side.

"We're going to have a little chin-wag, you and me," said Crabapple to his prisoner, shaking the gun so the metal barrel ground and crunched the man's teeth. "You'd better start talking!"

The man emitted a pained squeak and a series of terrified, unintelligible mumbles. Tears, snot, drool, and blood were mingling about his mouth as Crabapple stared furiously at him.

"Well?" barked Crabapple. "Talk! Oh, right you are, my apologies." He removed the gun from the villain's mouth—and punched him sharply in the gut.

Dickens rushed in shortly after the gun had gone off and helped to drag the whimpering man to the previous pen. We shackled him to one of the posts. Shen wandered in, glum and glassy-eyed just as Crabapple moved off to continue to search the premises while I interrogated the brute. Though bruised and broken, the man remained tight-lipped, though I could not tell whether it was from defiance or shock.

Crabapple returned shortly, reporting to have found three more bodies, two of the women appearing to have died from starvation, one from injuries following a beating. According to the constable, only one of them was on his missing-persons list, the other two were not. The case was clearly far bigger than we had thought.

Adelaide's knees buckled, and I caught her just as she sank. Steadying her, I looked into her eyes. "Adelaide," I whispered.

"My Tom was mixed up in all this," she whispered, her lips trembling. "All these poor women . . . Tom . . . could he have known about this? Could he, really?"

I stared into her big green eyes, the pain and grief

coursing through her at the thought of how far her brother might have sunk was pushing her to the breaking point. We needed answers.

The man beside us sniffed pitifully, and my patience cracked. I snatched Crabapple's gun and cocked it, pointing it directly between the man's eyes. "Enough. Talk now."

Whether it was the sight of the gun's dark, merciless barrel or the embarrassment of having soiled his trousers that finally broke the man, I shan't guess. But when I pressed the barrel of the gun hard into his forehead, he confessed to being a lowly clean-up man, hired by nameless criminals across London to remove evidence and dispose of bodies. He had been called out here before, he said. Some girls had seen fit to die from exhaustion or infections. He claimed that many were brought in by boat from foreign places, kept in pens like this until they were needed. Drugged into submission for ease of control. When Crabapple asked whether they were raped, Adelaide pressed her face into my chest, but the man shook his head. If one like him did that, he said, he'd wake up with bits of him gone that he'd never want to lose. That was how The Lady did things.

"But I never seen what happened to none of them lasses after they left here, I swear," he continued, his desperation finally releasing his voice like a deluge. "They emptied this place this morning, took 'em all away. Well, except the dead 'uns. Which is why I'm here again."

The man's lip began to wobble again and he sniffed.

"Who sent for you? Who runs this scheme?" Crabapple barked at him. "Roger and Jack Colley?"

"No, no!" the man cried, shaking his head. "Well, I mean, it's odd. Like, they did have something to do with it, then all of a sudden, we was told never to associate with them dark, bad men again. I got the word that if I so much as spoke with demons like the Colleys, I'd have me throat slit!"

"The world suffered a great injustice that you never did," I said.

Shen shifted, his eyes flashing with anger as he stared at the man. His lips were curled in disgust and fury. "This is all connected to those photographs," he said, the sound of his voice laced with poison. "They have defiled Miss Pearl's image, her legacy, and you—you have allowed it!"

"I never did nothing!" cried the man.

"Thomas Guilfoyle!" Adelaide shouting, rounding on the villain. "Do you know that name?"

The man shook his head.

"Why this place?"

"It's all complicated like, now inn't it? I mean, half the time they just find places like this abandoned and the like, and just take 'em."

Crabapple chewed on a toothpick, working it out. "So Guilfoyle knew this place would be used for no good, but it wasn't likely he'd been told specifics."

The fury went out of Adelaide, but a fierce determination filled her. "All right. All right, I can face it now. Whatever comes next. So long as he wasn't a partner to this depravity."

"I'd like a quiet word with this man," Shen said, back straight, feral smile flashing.

"Well, well, well, Mr. Shen," said Crabapple. "Finally some flames stoking you back to life, some passion, eh? Well, yeah, sounds good. See to this man, will you?"

"No!" cried the man as we left him, broken and shackled in the shadow of a grinning and vengeful Shen.

"Don't kill him, we need a statement," Crabapple called back as we walked past the dead bodies and towards the barn doors at the back. "But he don't need to be able to walk for that, now does he?"

Fresh air rushed into my lungs as we emerged out of the dark hell of torture and death and into the crisp winter countryside. Adelaide was pale, but some of her strength returned with the breeze. Still she avoided my eyes and kept herself a few paces away from us.

"This is clearly all connected," I said. "We need to speak with Sarah, the Nellie doll from the Quarter. She could tell us more."

"Oh yeah, now there's a good idea," Crabapple said. "How many times has it been that Smithson's tried to have you murdered?"

Dickens shook his head. "We don't know if any of these women ever returned after being used like this. They might have been shipped off to other lands or dumped in the Thames."

"But the Quarter is a part of this," I insisted. "The boy said as much. And that smell, the flammable chemicals at the Lycia—"

"The what?" interrupted Adelaide, suddenly raising herself up and standing tall, a new surge of interest running through her. I raised my eyebrows and repeated the word.

"That's their lair. Their headquarters. The Chimera, the three-headed, fire-breathing monster, born out of the fires of Lycia. A female monster. The Lady."

"With a head of a lion. The king of the Royal Quarter—Smithson, of course," added Dickens, drawing sketches of the beast around his elaborate notes.

"The Colleys knew of the place, knew it well enough to know it would go up in a blast," I said. "They were an integral part of the enterprise. The third head, I'd guess. The women were nothing but goods, shipped like cattle. I'd wager the words Colley sang, '*Mary, Mary, quite contrary, how does your garden grow? With silver bells and cockleshells, pretty maids all in a row,*' was code to signify the arrival of a shipment. The women, they were what the Colleys claimed had been stolen from them. But why in the deuce would they have thought Sunderland had them?"

Adelaide sighed. "Something went rotten in this devil's trinity," she whispered. "They turned on each other."

Crabapple nodded, his moustache twitching. "Yes, yes. That's why the gorilla in there was warned not to have anything to do with Roger and Jack or their boys. But where are the women now?"

The doors to the threshing barn burst open, and pitiful sobs rang out from inside. Shen marched out, his knuckles bruised and torn, but his face alive again, a glint sparking in his eye.

"Right, then," said Crabapple. "There's enough here to get me back on track. I'll head back to Scotland Yard and alert the force. I'll need copies of your notes, Dickens. We'll get to the bottom of this, though will I get any credit for it? No, I will not, Inspector Foote will see to that."

Shen's smile widened. "You may decide not to alert Scotland Yard yet, Constable," he said quietly, replacing his gloves finger by finger. "Before I turned his knees to dust, he claimed he was protected, insured via his employers. In fact, he evoked the name of a certain Inspector Foote as the one to call if there was trouble."

Crabapple spun round, his hands clutching his hair, furious curses and profane obscenities streaming from his mouth like bullets.

"Well, I never!" chuckled a cheeky voice behind us. "Fruity language like that in front of a wee child!"

And from round the corner of the shed poked a top hat, then a ruddy face with a snub nose. Dodger's grin was wide, and he was chewing the end of a pipe.

"What the hell are you doing here?" I demanded.

"Whas' wiv 'at one?" Dodger demanded, looking over at Shen. "He's got a right case o' the morbs, he has!"

"Don't worry about him. I ask again, why are you here?"

"On account of needin' to speak wiv' you, Mr. Scrooge, sir! Urgent business, you understand; businessmen like me and you often have urgent meetin's like this. Spotted your wagon trundling off from London, so I caught up and hitched a ride. Thought I'd wait until you was done playing on the farm, but you're taking such a frightful long time."

"I said I'd get back to you when I was ready." I sighed, rubbing my temples. "This is dangerous, Dodger."

"Very dangerous, Mr. Scrooge, sir!" the boy agreed, his head nodding eagerly and his top hat slipping backward and forward as he did. "And you see, I would have waited for you, but an opportunity has arisen, and I'm the sort of very finest businessman what takes risks and jumps at a chance for profit! Just like you!"

"What the devil are you talking about, boy?" shouted Crabapple.

Dodger looked indignant for a moment, like a crucial business meeting was being interrupted by a tea lady, but cheered right up. "The time is now, gentlemen! Oh, excuse me, and lady. But we 'ave to move fast. It's a ways from here, see, down in Temple Brook. I never thought you'd come all the way into Essex! My fingers were right frozen clinging on all that way!"

"Temple Brook?" Adelaide asked.

"Rutledge's country house," I said. "Of course. Of course that's where they'd take them."

The lad continued to boast that he had thought of a cunning plan. Scowling at Crabapple suspiciously from time to time, he explained that he knew exactly where the magician, the photographer, would be tonight, and that the very best way to secure the secret to photography would be to kidnap the scientist. He even offered to overpower the man himself and tie him up.

"It'd be easy," he boasted, describing the man as little and funny, always wearing white and black stripes with silly round glasses tinted dark as night: he'd never see Dodger coming, the boy theorized.

My heart jumped. I'd seen that man. He had been the one man in the Doll House receiving the "specials of the house" without benefit of a ring. The same little man in the zebra suit.

"We'll get our hands on him, Mr. Scrooge," Dodger said with a toothy grin. "We'll get him to teach us and others how the magic works, and we'd be set for life on account of being extremely rich, you see! Bob's your uncle!"

A lifetime of fortune and prosperity flashed before my eyes but in a split second had been replaced by the darkness of the hell I had just left.

"No," I shook my head sadly. "This is beyond the worth of any profit margin."

"But he's up there right now!" cried Dodger. "With all them ladies! Chance of a lifetime, see, Mr. Scrooge! And by tomorrow, well, it'll all be over, see. They're shipping him elsewhere. It's what The Lady wants. She'll be there, just to make sure it all goes off right smooth. . . ."

The first person I looked at was Adelaide. Her face sported an expression of urgency, her eyes wide and her lips slightly parted. Dickens was nodding. Shen might have had steam pouring from his nostrils at the chance to further avenge his Nellie. If not now, then when?

The time had passed four in the afternoon, and the drive to Temple Brook was five hours. That didn't take into account how long it might take to stop and find a few honest men—and men of that sort were fewer by the hour as Shen's revelation about Foote had revealed. And God forbid, there were snow drifts on some of the narrow and winding country lanes.

By tomorrow, all the women could be dead. Any chance of solving the hideous mystery would be wiped like melted snow. Still, who knew how many men might be patrolling the place? The handful of us against what nature of a beast?

"Look, I knows what I'm talking about," Dodger assured us. "Ain't never been a sneak thief like me. I sneaked about the Lycia, hitched rides and sneaked about that fine house, and ain't never any o' them punters *ever* had a clue I was there. I know the secret ways in and out. You needs me!"

A howl whistled through the bare branches in the surrounding woods as a frigid gust swept snow across the fields. "*It's there*," whispered the distant and frozen voice of Fezziwig. "*Humbug is waiting. The next, then you, Ebenezer. Unless you stop it.*"

I stamped my cane on the icy ground. "I'm going. Any of you have the courage to follow me, come along. Otherwise, rot in hell."

One by one, the others followed.

CHAPTER TWENTY-FIVE

WE STOPPED A mile outside Temple Brook and stepped upon the moonlit road leading to Rutledge's country estate. The rushing breath of the ocean lapping onto jagged stones greeted us as we removed lanterns and other provisions from our carriage's boot. An icy wind kicked up as Shen dug into his flush pockets and paid our driver a handsome sum to wait here for us until morning. I turned to Adelaide and made one final appeal.

"Miss Owen—Adelaide—this is far too dangerous," I told her. "Even young Dodger saw the sense in staying behind. Take the carriages and go, I beg you."

"And Ebenezer Scrooge is not one to beg," she said distantly, her gaze fixing on a reddish glow in the distance and the sounds of revelry accompanying them. "Not even if the hounds of hell were scratching at his door. Why would you think me any different?"

"There is bravery and then there is madness," Shen said as he joined us. "For once, I'm in agreement with Mr. Scrooge. Quite enough of you have taken leave of your senses by getting mixed up in this. I have one woman's blood on my hands. I would not have another's."

"Not even The Lady's?" Adelaide asked.

Shen turned away. A good deal of his strength and swagger had returned. He and I were decked out in our finest suits. Adelaide was once again dressed as a lad, but not the sooty-faced beggar she'd pretended to be in the Quarter. Her hair was slicked back, her bust strapped, and she wore the clothes of a young footman.

"What happens to her is on your head," he said, looking back at me.

"I'll look out for myself, thank you," Adelaide assured him.

"You may have to."

The ruby rings we had acquired in our adventures set firmly on our fingers, we walked ahead towards Middlehays, the country estate Rutledge had inherited, then put out to let. The isolated house was perched on a rise overlooking the ocean. A frozen fairytale wood reflected the silver-blue moonlight to our left as the ocean lazily lapped at the shoreline far below to our right.

"How do you think the constable and Mr. Dickens are faring?" Adelaide asked. She hugged herself against the frigid winds, which caressed us like invisible hands.

Though Crabapple was woefully lacking in compatriots he might draw into our madness tonight, Shen and Dickens were not. Shen had quickly drafted instructions for Crabapple to take to one of his key agents in the drug trade, while Dickens—now weighted down with Shen's funds—went to pull away the security detail he had assigned to Belle and round up even more protectors. With any luck at all, they would join us within the hour accompanied by a score of hard, dangerous men.

"I have no doubt they will be here presently," I lied. For I had every conceivable doubt.

"The two of you," Shen said without looking back at us. "You are clear on our objective?"

We'd talked about little else. Dodger had explained that the photographer—the only man who knew the secret process that made his miraculous image-taking possible—considered himself quite pious. Part of the allure of Rutledge's country estate had been its chapel. Though the foreign gentleman had accepted that he was damned, he would not begin or end his photo-taking festivities without a private moment of prayer in a sanctified space. No one knew if this was to cleanse himself or to spit in the eye of God, but it was his ritual.

Guards were stationed at the two main doors leading in or out of the chapel, but there was a secret door hidden behind one of those newly placed Doric columns. That door led to a stone stairwell and a series of underground tunnels coming up into open air far from the house.

"We hide in the chapel and lay in wait for the photographer," I said wearily. Shen had made me repeat our plan countless times since we'd left London. It had almost taken my mind off the distinct possibility that once we reached our destination, Miss Owen would give a command to the scum within for our capture, thus revealing herself as The Lady. The chains of trust were not yet secure. "We knock him senseless, bind him, and kidnap him. Later, we offer to trade him for the release of the women and—"

"Be *quiet*," Adelaide hissed. She nodded ahead. The house was in sight, and we dared not risk being overheard by the men standing outside the well-lit front entrance.

The crimson glow we had glimpsed in the distance now lay far to our east, beyond the house and along the cliffside. We could not see what cast it.

Rutledge's house was a modest affair, at least when contrasted to the magnificence of Dyer Manor. We passed a hedge maze that had fallen on hard times, an iced-over fountain sitting smack in the middle of the rounded front drive, a pair of stone lions beside the steps leading to the porch, one cracked so badly half its face had fallen off. A pitiful forced attempt at opulence made the recently added Doric columns stand out in stark contrast to the rest of the house. Two columns bracketed the front double doors where a pair of valets stepped forward and greeted us. They were impeccably dressed—and armed. Masks rested upon red silk pillows cradled in one man's arms. I might have thought the masks a fortuitous turn, but Shen had been confident they would be presented to us. The men in the photos always wore them.

No one questioned that we had strolled in from the darkness with no carriage in sight. From the jaundiced look in their eyes, I wagered they had seen far stranger things tonight. One look at the ruby rings adorning Shen's hand—and my own—settled any possible raised eyebrows. Except one.

"What's with the boy?" the nearest valet asked.

Smiling, Shen draped a casual arm about Adelaide's shoulders and winked. "We like to have him about when we . . . watch. He serves our purposes."

Adelaide, remaining perfectly in character, regarded the men with a ruddy sneer and knowing nod. The men shrugged and turned to one another.

"Does he get a mask?"

"I suppose."

We three were swept into the warm and noisy antechamber, where a pair of handsome young women rushed at us. Sparkling green and brown wood nymph costumes barely covered their comely bosoms and striking legs. Laughing and frolicking, they relieved us of our hats, canes, and heavy winter coats. My cheeks blazed with a sudden heat as I realized their "costumes" had mainly been painted on, the green and amber leaves glued strategically in one place or another.

This pair must have been from the Doll House, I reasoned. Those poor women who'd been drugged and held against their wills in their pens at the warehouse simply could not have managed such smiles and unspoken promises of delight. We passed another of the great Doric columns, and my gaze rested upon hooks that had been driven into its side. One thrust out at waist level, the other slightly over my head. Looking about at the low-hanging chandelier, the paintings, and gilt-covered woodworks, the ornate resting couches, I knew that I was walking through a spot used for the terrible photographs.

I felt as if I were striding through a particularly deep, dark, and inescapable level of hell.

The women opened a pair of doors, and we strode confidently into a whirling mass of decadence and vice. Dozens of finely-appointed gentleman wearing outlandish masks laughed, ate, and drank to their wicked hearts' content. Shen was already making small talk with one of them, his grotesque "plague doctor" mask with its birdlike beak drawing little attention. His mouth and chin were yet uncovered, revealing his bright white teeth and perfectly chiseled chin.

Christmas, now only days away, had hardly been forgotten in this wretched place. A perverse bacchanalian twist had been thrust upon what might have otherwise been a genteel Christmas get-together. The air was thick with myrrh, which smothered all other fragrances, including sweat. Whole hogs had been slaughtered and carved to perfection, served on great tables with orange rinds and deep, delicious-smelling gravies. Joyous music sprang from tautly-tuned instruments as a string quartet supported a stunning cellist. Fires sizzled and gaslights whispered. Staggeringly beautiful women circulated in various states of undress and pagan excess, jewels glittering on naked flesh. Men and women danced in the center of the vast banquet hall. I found myself taking in the sight of a woman whose entire derriere had been adorned in ringlets of bouncing white cream.

"Remember, no sampling before the main event," a man in a lion's mask said, nudging my arm knowingly. "Save it up, you're going to need it!"

Across the room, a man with a familiar laugh held court. He was dressed as Father Christmas, perhaps, the founder of the feast. His bare chest shimmering in the glow from the fire, his red velvet coat swept to the floor, gold and purple sashes adorned him along with glittering chains. A crown of wild holly sat on his head. He was masked, like all the fine gentlemen here, but I knew that hyena-like laugh.

"What an absolute gigglemug," Dickens said. "Worse than that Pickwick, even!"

I knew the man. It was Lazytree.

My mind reeled and hauled me back to the Colleys' warehouse, where I was tortured and prodded to reveal what Sunderland had done with Roger and Jack's property. Sunderland as much as said that his many companies were infested by scoundrels, like ships overrun by rats.

Was I standing in the very presence of Mr. Smithson himself? Was it Lazytree?

"Friends, eat, drink, be merry!" Lazytree invited, silencing the music with a brief flash of his gloved hand. "Your Christmas presents wait outside. They are being carefully prepared against a spectacular setting to best immortalize this evening's incredible nature. Dozens of gifts we present you with from all over the world, all waiting to be unwrapped with rising excitement. Will you tear at them a bit at a time, greedily, passionately? Or rip them open and see what they contain with no further ado? Whatever your choice, we will immortalize your passions on film. Have no fear of discovery; your masks will protect you."

Lazytree signaled the players, and the music resumed. He was immediately ringed in by anxious men who clearly did not appreciate being kept waiting. "Soon,

soon," I heard Lazytree telling them, then the sounds of the party drowned out further intelligence.

Adelaide grasped my arm. "It's happening outside," she whispered, her chest rising and falling with sharp quick movements. She was nearly breathless with worry. "The women aren't even here."

"Quell your panic," Shen said in his most reasonable voice. "All that matters is that it has not yet begun, and this means that most of their goons are certainly arrayed elsewhere, to prevent the 'presents' from wandering off. All we must do is avoid Lazytree and wait for our opportunity. The moment the crowd is sufficiently distracted, we will leave here and take up position in the chapel. Don't forget why we're here and don't forget Humbug's promise."

"Frankly," I said, "if these men are to be the dozens that were threatened, I think I'd just as soon let carpets run with their blood before lifting a hand to stop them. We both know what they're going to do with these women."

To our right, a man holding court with several of his fellows asked, "What do you call a pearl that's been dropped from the roof of St. Paul's?" The jokester smiled. "Nellie."

The crowd about him burst into raucous laughter, and my gaze whipped to Shen. I expected to see him tremble with barely controlled rage, teeth grinding, hands ground into fists. But instead, he was detached, smiling thinly, exhibiting no sign of distress other than some drops of perspiration on his forehead.

Lazytree's great crimson robes flashed as he made

his way through the crowd. Sooner or later, he'd come our way.

"Should we do something?" Adelaide whispered. "We can pretend to fight and draw all eyes to us while Shen gets away."

"No . . . that would draw Lazytree, and we would be found out."

"We have to do something," she said, her voice hitching.

Just then, fate took the matter out of our hands. A pair of double doors leading to the garden swung in, and a small man flanked by a handful of armed guards was pushed through the crowd. Lazytree did his best to push and shove people out of the way. The diminutive fellow was scowling, intent on something of great import, frustrated that he could not simply avoid attention. I remembered him by his round spectacles and their tinted black glass.

The photographer, surely!

"The time is nearly upon us!" Lazytree called out. "This is Mr. Gustuv Bleier, and all of you are, of course, well-acquainted with his miraculous science: photography. He will be immortalizing your stag-like prowess with our vast selection of Christmas nymphs out by the abbey. Now if you would simply be so kind as to make way, make way, yes, there's a good fellow, he will complete his final preparations and the night's true entertainment shall soon commence!"

I had spied the door Dodger had described, the one leading to a hall at the end of which resided the chapel. Now was our chance to slip away unnoticed, except—

Shen was surging ahead, moving to intercept the photographer.

"Ebenezer?" Adelaide asked, her voice laced with worry.

There was nothing either of us could do. Shen surged with such inhuman speed that I barely registered that he had cracked the nearest guard's nose with his elbow and relieved the man of his pistol before the shot rang out and the little man crumpled to his knees. A neat little red hole had burst into existence upon his brow, and a spray of blood had speckled several men who'd stood behind him.

Shen lowered the gun, staring down as the little man sank to one side. Women screamed as a pool of crimson spooled out onto the hardwood floor. The Chinaman's expression was curious, even a bit perturbed, as if the experience had been less than he'd anticipated.

"Do you know what you've done?" Lazytree shouted, grinding the heels of his hands into his temple and screwing them about so tightly I thought his eyeballs might pop out. Face beet red, veins bulging, fit to burst, he studied the other guards, who now stood with their weapons all pointed at Shen. Eyes popping, mouth frothing, Lazytree raised his hands high, balled them into fists, and he loosed his incredulity at his men. "What are you waiting for!?"

In the moment before they all opened fire on my companion, I was certain that Shen's serene smile returned.

Amidst the blaze of gunfire and Shen's dying screams, Adelaide grasped my hand and hauled me to the hall door. She yanked it open, shoved me ahead, and we were running, following the plan as if it had not just been literally blown to hell.

We raced down the corridor that we had been told would lead to the great chapel and never learned if that was true or not. Behind us exploded cries of, "Those two were with him" and "Kill them." My hand grasped the handle to the door at the end of the hall and found it locked. Adelaide hauled on another door, mercifully open, and we darted inside a small, darkened study, slammed the door shut, but did not have a key to lock it against our pursuers, whose footsteps echoed in the hall.

We upended a towering bookcase, bringing it crashing down in front of the door just as someone shoved it open. A sliver of harsh yellow light from the hall sliced in, but the door was jammed long enough for us to find an open window and slip outside and race into the night.

We ran back in the direction of the carriage road; teeth chattering, the heat sparked by terror offering precious little defense against the chill of the evening. The guards from the front of house whipped around before us, no doubt drawn by the sounds of gunfire. Shouting bolted outward from the way we'd come. For an instant, I thought we were trapped, but Adelaide grasped my hand, and together we flew towards a gazebo and beyond it, a romantically-lit trail through the woods.

We skidded on ice, tumbled, and that alone saved us as shots bit into trees that had been at eye level a moment before. I grasped Adelaide by the shoulders, propelled her further down the twisting path, and only the constant sudden sharp turns kept our pursuers from firing again.

Any notions I yet held that Adelaide was the mysterious Lady were well and truly gone.

We drew up as a pair of costumed gentlemen shrieked in surprise at the sight of us, preventing a collision as they strolled, cigarettes in hand, back from wherever this path led. Adelaide and I brushed by them, swung them back and away from us, ran on, taking another sharp turn, then another. Our masks kept slipping as we ran, obscuring our view, and we threw them down as we raced on.

"There!" someone yelled. And without thought, a hailstorm of gunfire exploded at our backs coupled with shrieks of surprise and agony.

"Don't stop!" Adelaide hissed. I did not. I surmised that the men we'd passed had been mistaken for us and shot down in our place. I also guessed that our pursuers' blunder would only keep them from us a short while.

We burst from the path carved among the trees and saw moonlight tinge the ocean ahead and far below. We'd been harried up along a road paralleling the coastline, and the path had spilled out onto a ruin-littered glade where towering abbey walls flickered with crimson light. In summer, this would be a rich, welcoming meadowland. In winter, it was a frozen waste.

We could barely take in the madness before us. All activity was centered in the great cradle of the abbey ruins. Fifty people, if not more, had set about the most peculiar industry I had ever witnessed. Cauldrons so great they might have made Macbeth's witches weep in envy burned with crimson flames. A boy trudged back and forth between a dozen or more of them, examining them, chugging bucket loads of a thick powder onto them when they threatened to burn clean to yellow once again.

Dozens of women lolled upon stones or incongruously placed velvet chaise longues. Others stood with shackles upon their wrists, easing out from chains leading back to half-destroyed walls. Though thin and weak, the women had been bathed, their hair washed. They wore translucent gowns of teal, emerald, gold. Attendants, both men and women, circulated among them, painting their cheeks with rouge from palettes they held or placing flowers in their hair. The cauldrons provided not just a gaudy theatrical reddish glow that had suffused the sky even from miles away, but precious heat that kept the barefoot women from freezing to death.

Guards stood at the perimeters, just as Shen had predicted. They were at every doorway, looking inward, watching the women for any sign that they might escape. And at the heart of it, a half-dozen odd contraptions set up on tripods with cloth hoods, accordion-like extensions, rectangular glass eyes. Long steamer trunks filled with supplies for the strange machines sat nearby. What would happen to these women now that the night's "festivities" had been spoiled?

Voices rose at our backs, and Adelaide pointed upward. "We can hide up there," Adelaide commanded.

We passed near enough one of the many open steamers to snatch blankets we might use as cloaks against the icy winds as we fled back into the chill. I followed her up a brutally steep winding stone path that cut right through the heart of the ruins to the only structure that had not been razed in whatever attack leveled the abbey. We soon found ourselves in a high tower overlooking the hellish pit below.

Adelaide sank into my arms, murmuring something about needing the warmth, and I held her tightly. We were both shivering.

Why had Shen done it? What madness had overtaken him?

Perhaps I had just answered my own question. And perhaps further, the madness had been upon him far longer than had been evident to my senses.

Something behind us caught Adelaide's attention. She pressed a finger to her pursed lips, and I saw the camera I had not noticed when we'd first stumbled in. Of course, it had been placed to peer down at the "Christmas gathering," as we were now doing, and capture the entirety of the depraved scene set to go off below. Footsteps scraped along stone steps and we pressed against a wall as a pair of young men trudged inside. They complained about the "wretched fur'nor" and wishing he'd take a slow boat off to hell. We snuck down the steps as they set a heavy trunk next to the apparatus and cracked it open.

We fled the ruins entirely, ran up along a narrow path to a hillside, and stopped as three figures stepped out in front of us, onto the plateau we thought might lead to freedom. A short, squat man flanked by tall, brutish-looking men who reminded me of Bill Sikes. The fat man stepped into a pool of moonlight, a silver glow tracing along the barrel of his weapon.

George Sunderland smiled.

"You're Smithson," I said, ice flowing along my spine.

"I suppose I could explain it all to you," Sunderland said, leveling the pistol at my heart. "But what does it matter now?"

A sudden wind struck his back, buffeting him, and he rocked slightly, shuffled on the rock, but I'd had no chance to run; his aim had remained true. I blinked— and one of the goons next to Sunderland was no longer in place. A trick of the moon, I told myself, a drifting cloud had darkened my view, surely.

I said nothing. My gaze was riveted to the pistol held firmly in the fat businessman's gloved hand. I edged my way in front of Adelaide, praying that when the bullets struck me, she would flee into the night and perhaps lose herself in the darkness.

Sunderland's smile widened. "Mr. Scrooge, you surprise me. Not going to try and bargain for your life? Chivalry, even? Ah, this will make a fine tale with my boys. A fine one!"

A grunt sounded behind him, to his left, and Sunderland stood alone. The second thug was now removed from my sight.

Sunderland spun, forgetting us, aiming his gun with shaking hand, sweeping it this way and that. A woman's insane laughter echoed on the wind that again punched into him, making him sway.

A voice echoed on that wind. "Well, well, Mr. Sunderland . . . or should I say Smithson? It seems we have something in common after all. The world thinks we're both dead!"

A black wind whipped forward and a blade sank into the side of Sunderland's neck.

"Only in your case, it's true!"

CHAPTER TWENTY-SIX

SUNDERLAND FELL, SPASMING, hands flopping, fighting his own attempts to grasp the blade that had sunk cleanly through his neck and severed his windpipe. Gasping for air, mouth flapping, he mercifully twisted onto one side and hid himself from our sight as the horrible wet gurgling sounds went on, but only for a short while.

Humbug stood before us. Cloak, veil, skeletal hands. Yet—unarmed. Now was the time to flee. I could smell the sickly odor of chloroform she'd used to render Sunderland's men inert when she'd come at them from behind. Yet I had heard her voice. Knew exactly who was under those veils and still thought it impossible, though the sudden resurrection and second death of George Sunderland should have prepared me for anything.

A ghostly chill settled on my neck as the voice of my one-time master whispered, *No more, Ebenezer. Just you!*

"Nellie Pearl," Adelaide said beside me.

With another peal of laughter, the actress tore back the veils and stared at us with that same malevolent gleam I'd seen in the mirror the last time we'd visited.

"Nellie Pearl's dead," she said. "Don't you read the newspapers? Hmmm . . . I will say, I can't help but be curious: how long will it take people to start wondering what happened to Sarah?"

"The chorus girl, the one who looked so much like you," I said. "She was the one you were dragging around in St. Paul's. You kept us far enough away so that we would not realize she said nothing the entire time, the voice we heard was yours."

Adelaide shivered. "You had to be sure her face was destroyed so no one would see her scar and know it wasn't you."

"Aren't you two the clever little ducks," Nellie said. "Quacking away. I meet so many of your kind. Like dear, disfigured Crisparkle. The greatest costumer I ever had, though it was Sarah he loved. I suppose he thought that little scar of hers made them alike. But his wounds, hideous."

"He made that for you," I said, pointing at her costume and gloves, assembling the pieces of the puzzle strewn before me. Then I recalled the man with the torn-apart face that Dickens had gazed upon in the underground chamber where the bodies fished from the Thames were stored. "Before you killed him."

"Clever, clever!" Nellie said, beaming. "I'm so very proud of you both. I've slaughtered so many stupid animals. Stupid and trusting. It'll be a pleasure to gut you both and send you to your reward."

Adelaide stumbled back. "Why? Why my poor Tom? Why all of this?"

"Well," Nellie said as she bent low, working the blade

free of Sunderland's now-still form. "I could say it dates back to some of those awful Bible lessons Jane Fezziwig would give, 'do onto others *before* they can do onto you' or whatever it was. . . ."

Dipping her hand in the spray of blood from the wound in the fat man's neck, she wrote HUMBUG on the flat stone.

"But at the end of the day, I think this one had it right. What difference can it possibly make to someone who's about to die? Just one thing: where is that bastard Shen, anyway? He should be with you."

"Dead," I told her.

She blanched. Shook her head. "No . . . No, *I* kill him. I get to see his face when he realizes who is stabbing the life from him. He followed me constantly, everywhere I went. Do you know how many times that infernal foreigner nearly discovered my secret? I couldn't let that happen. The play had to be allowed to continue until the final act, the final scene. That was going to be my greatest triumph! The show must go on!"

I said nothing, simply prayed that Adelaide, still behind and off to one side of me, could see my hand as I motioned her to back away.

"You're lying!" she screeched. Her eyes blazed in the moonlight.

"I'm not."

Bounding to her feet, she rushed at me, blade slicing the air. I flew at her, whipping the stolen blanket from over my shoulders. Half-stepping to one side as the cold steel rushed past me, I flung the blanket over her head and wrapped my arm about her. We went off balance and tumbled down the path in a mad tangle. I heard running boots—Adelaide's, I prayed, then was jolted as the side of my head struck a heavy stone jutting up from the path. Dazed, I lost my grip on Nellie, who spun far from me.

Head throbbing, dizziness threatening to take hold, I rose and stumbled in the direction of the running footsteps I'd heard earlier. The footfalls doubled back, and I fought against the throbbing in my skull long enough to lift my head and see Adelaide rush towards me. She cast an anxious look towards the snowy hill at my right, then silently hauled me back down the path to the ruins.

The crimson glow beyond the great walls made its remaining windows look like the devil's eyes, fixed and watching us. From the screams and commotion on the other side of that wall, where the women were being held for the foul pleasures of the masked men at the country house, chaos had finally erupted.

Lazytree was bellowing orders. Whips snapped and piteous wails rose up. Echoing voices, guttural laughter, prideful boasting, frightened screams, all bounded from beyond the crumbling walls where the red flames were stoked and cracked and licked the blackened sky.

Hell indeed.

"This way, this way!" Lazytree demanded. "Put that unpleasantness behind you and see the delights you have in store!"

Even without the photography, the night of cruel use and abuse of the stolen women was proceeding.

Panting, desperate to catch our breaths, we looked

about for Nellie. We saw nothing. I felt my boot pressing against something and looked down to spy another of the large trunks. This one was pressed up against the rear of the great wall. So far as I could see in the dim light, it was but one in a series, a link in a chain that stretched all about the cradle.

I opened it, praying I might find a weapon, and a familiar stench of chemicals punched up at me. All I could make out was blankets, towels, food, yet as I rummaged I found, buried beneath all the rest of the supplies, jugs of the chemicals that had brought down entire warehouses in the Royal Quarter when they had combusted.

Humbug had promised death by the dozens. How many men and women had now been herded into the cradle of the abbey ruins?

"Tsk, tsk," came a bit of nastiness carried on the whipping breeze. I heard the blade whoosh down instants before I felt Adelaide yank me back and out of the way. We turned and ran deeper into the ruins before Nellie could try again. Her cloak made her melt into the night, but I had to remind myself that she was as mortal as Adelaide and me. The idea that she was an unstoppable spirit, *that* was the true humbug.

We ran along a narrow pathway, cold stone at either side of us. My boot kicked bits of debris, we stumbled along at sudden sharp turns, the moon rose overhead then blinked away. Patches of ice cracked under our feet, we rose up a flight of half-steps and leaped into the unknown, miraculously gaining footing while scrambling ahead, through an archway.

I stole a glance beside me. Adelaide was no longer

at my side. I turned back, hesitating for only an instant, which proved long enough to summon death's avatar.

Nellie surged from the blackness, blade held high, a chilling banshee shriek torn from her lungs. I stepped back, stumbled on a ragged stone, fell, and she threw herself on me, straddling me as the blade sliced down with chilling finality—

CRACK!

Her head jolted to one side, Nellie dropped on me, the blade scraping the rock to the left of my ear. She was surprisingly light, but far from frail, my hands finding the great masses of muscle she'd developed in her years of study as a dancer as I shoved her from me. Adelaide stood over us with a heavy stone tinged with red and bits of blonde hair. A crimson wound marked Nellie's skull where Adelaide had struck, apparently after she had flattened by the archway to wait in ambush as I served as bait.

I couldn't tell if Nellie was yet breathing or not, and cared even less. I managed to get to my feet and held the quaking Adelaide, who had carefully set down the chunk of rock.

As I held her, so many of the answers I'd been seeking came clear in my thoughts. George Sunderland, on the bridge, and his sudden burst of madness as he demanded I tell him what secrets of his Fezziwig had revealed. My sudden uptick in fortune at the Dyer affair when Lazytree secured all the investors I could possibly need for the rail deal, and their crashing reversal just this morning. All meant to control and distract me, to bring me bit by bit under Sunderland's—Smithson's—sway.

"Ebenezer, we should go," Adelaide said softly. "There's little we can do for anyone here if we tarry any longer."

She was right. Nellie—Humbug—might have been subdued, but Lazytree would still have his men searching for us.

"We need to find something to bind her with," I said, nodding down at the madwoman.

But Nellie was gone.

We raced about through the ruins, even climbed once more to the high stone keep and looked out onto the crowd. Back where we'd seen the trunks filled with the strange flammable chemicals, someone drifted about hauling a lantern.

"She's going to kill them all," I whispered.

"What?" Adelaide asked.

Taking her hand, I raced for the great stone steps. "I'll explain on the way!"

"Bankers," a man groused as he untied his boots. "You know what they say. Give them an inch!"

Beside him, the jokester from the party laughed. "Really, Henry? From what I've been told, an inch is all you *have* to give!"

We crouched low outside the abbey walls, looking for Nellie. Seven of the trunks now lay open, the chemical jars discarded, their contents soaked in the foul-smelling rot.

"Those women," Adelaide whispered. I could see from her expression that, like me, she wouldn't have cared if these walls caved in and flattened every one of the wretched bastards who'd organized this night or who had paid for a place in the "festivities." But the women did not deserve to share that fate.

"We have to stop her," I said, looking for anything I might use as a weapon. When I looked up again, Adelaide was gone.

I crept to the edge of the nearest towering abbey wall and peered through a narrow, ragged opening. I couldn't fit through it, but Adelaide already had. Taking advantage of her footman disguise, she made her way through the sweaty, stinking orgy of debauchery, a key she had evidently lifted from one of the guards in her hand. She unlocked a woman's shackles while pretending to be about some other business. Yet the doe-like, uncomprehending looks of the thin, exotic women brought here to act as slaves gave me little hope that even if the sky split above them and an angel thundered down from heaven to order them to run, that even half of them would make it to their feet before judgment rained down on them.

"You!"

Nellie's voice tore a chilling gash through my nerves. I saw a whip sitting on a boulder just inside the ragged gap and reached in even as Nellie charged me. My fingers were not quite reaching the whip, tapping it away—

Then I had it, yanked it out, and cracked it once while Nellie was still a dozen paces away, knife at hand. It bit into the icy range between us, and she darted to one side, stopped short. Blood-matted hair blew before her face and she twitched it away, panting, snarling, her gaze darting all about.

"You sent her to warn them? Idiot, they won't listen to her. They'll just cast her onto the pile!"

Meaning they would treat her as another vessel for their lusts.

"What do you care?" I asked.

Tossing the knife from one gloved hand to another, hunching forward, locking gazes with me, the madwoman blew me a kiss—then ran at me again.

CRACK!

Frankly, I was lucky I hadn't put out my own eye with the whip. But the threat of what I held had been enough to make Nellie pause. She backed away, slipping the blade back in her cloak, and reached for the lantern she'd set down on the ground.

I raised the whip, hoping the threat alone would stop her. She raced back for the lantern.

CRACK!

This time she shrieked in pain, a red welt forming on the side of her perfect face, a bleeding fissure not unlike the one her fallen look-alike Sarah had sported. With trembling fingers, she reached for her face, caressed the stinging welt, and surveyed her bloody fingers.

"I thought I could get my life back," she whispered. Her teeth flashed as she lost herself in a mad smile. "Who would pay to see me now?"

Suddenly, a cacophony of outraged voices exploded from within the crimson-lit chamber. Pistol shots rang out. Screams.

"Get them out of here!" Lazytree yelled. "Get them out!"

A burst of shouts in a rapid-fire foreign tongue joined

the unmistakable shouts of Constable Crabapple's "Here now," "Watch that," "You lot are under arrest" as well as Adelaide's warnings that the walls would soon come down.

"Run away, Mr. Scrooge," Nellie urged, edging again towards the lantern. "You won't stop me."

I tightened my grip on the whip and chanced a look inside the cradle. The jokester had raised a bloody fist to strike at Adelaide. But she was too quick for him. In a flash she snatched up an urn filled with the material used to make the fires burn red and emptied it into the man's face. Startled, he stumbled back and fell into a cauldron, where his screams joined a sparking plume of flames that consumed him. She turned from the grotesque sight of his wildly thrashing limbs even as Shen's people rushed into the midst of the scene, pistols and swords drawn.

I heard a rustling, looked back—

Nellie held the lantern. She had only to throw it and we would be at the apex of the destruction. The initial explosion would reach the next trunk and the next, igniting a ring of explosions that would bring the walls down.

Every second I delayed her meant more might be rescued from the pit beyond the abbey walls—including Adelaide.

"Why all of this?" I asked. "The others I think I might understand. They were hip-deep in all of this. Why poor Fezziwig?"

"You have an eye for detail, Mr. Scrooge. Think back to those photos of the Nellie dolls. Did they all bear Sarah's scars?"

I blanched. "They were real."

"They took me one night. Drugged me. Brought me . . . I didn't know where, not then . . . But I remember the humming. They would snicker and cheer as they sang. *Pretty maids all in a row*. Even now the tune haunts me in my sleepless states. They showed me the photographs. I was to keep on with it, to give one spectacular private performance after another, and so long as I did—"

"The images would be sold only to trusted private buyers. Talk and they would go to the press."

She nodded. So they all had to go, clearly.

"But why Fezziwig?" I asked. "Why me?"

Before she could answer, a man waving a pistol staggered down from the hillside where George Sunderland had met his death. One of the guards Nellie had chloroformed. He shouted something guttural, the gun barrel wavering madly, capturing my full attention—

Nellie threw the lantern upon the chemical-soaked trunk.

CHAPTER TWENTY-SEVEN

Saturday, December 24th, 1833
The day before Christmas

A BLINDING FLASH and a roaring thunderous crashing. Stone sentinels of impossible, towering heights falling down upon us, knees buckling, torsos ripping to pieces, dust and snow, screams and a crushing, horrible weight dropping towards me, amused by my insignificance even as it perished—

Startling pain. A chaser of darkness, oblivion, death.

Then a sliver of light, pure, merciful morning light. Shafts tearing open as silhouetted figures worked to drag heavy flat sheets of stone from my moaning, complaining form.

"Over here! Found him!"

Crabapple's grinning face loomed over me as the man hauled me from my makeshift crypt out into the blinding cleansing light of day. Head light, the world lazily whirling, soot and a low-laying bed of smoke twisting about the wreckage and the chaos of dozens—or was it a hundred or more—men surging all about the place, all I could think of was one thing. A name. Through a throat full of ash I croaked, "Adelaide."

"Here!" she called. Her voice was reassuringly strong, and she joined me, taking one of my arms as Crabapple led me out of the small mound of debris where I'd lain to a plateau near the cliffs. Sunlight sparkled like a sea of diamonds over the distant waves.

"Merry Christmas," I muttered, taking in the ruination about me.

"It hasn't been that long," Dickens said, looking up from his sketchbook. He sat upon a nearby rockfall. The remains of the fallen towers and abbey walls stood out upon the snowy waste like spent coals soiling white sheets. Men moved about the ruins, poking about, rattling sticks into the debris, then listening, praying perhaps, for a response.

"Who are all these people?" I asked, shivering. Adelaide waved her hand, and someone brought a pair of heavy blankets that I snatched away and hugged about myself. Before I could even form the thought that I could murder a cup of tea, one was brought to me, hot, steaming, heated by one of the few cauldrons not swallowed up by the abbey's fall.

"Local townsfolk, mainly," Crabapple said. "All the ruckus drew 'em."

"How many?" I asked, my tone dark as the weight settling over my heart.

"How many did we lose?" asked the constable. "Or how many did we manage to save?"

Shuddering, I asked, "How . . . *many*?"

Adelaide told me. Roughly two-thirds of the women

had been dragged from the hellish "set" Smithson and Lazytree had conceived and constructed in this spot before the last of the abbey walls had come down. Five of the women had been found dead, thirteen were yet unaccounted for. She had come to such a precise accounting from Lazytree, who'd been captured, thrashed, spilled all, and thrashed several more times for good measure.

Only three of the wretched punters—the fine clients—had perished.

Someone called, "She's coming around!"

Crabapple and Adelaide rushed towards the voice. Dickens and I followed. We stared down at a familiar-looking ginger who sat up, coughing.

Miss Annie Piper!

It didn't take long for the prostitute—still drenched in clove perfume—to understand what had happened here. She told her story with little urging. She had indeed been recruited to the Doll House, as we had heard, and into Smithson's bed. But he tired of her quickly and had her drugged and cast her in with the rest of the women in the cradle.

Adelaide pressed the woman about her association with Thomas Guilfoyle, and a fuller picture quickly emerged. The mystery of how Fezziwig knew of The Lady and why he had sent invitations to Sunderland, Rutledge, Shen, and Nellie turned out to be remarkably simple: "Tom took me to the old man's place one time," Annie revealed. "Where he was doing his scribbling on the man's books. He explained it all to me, though I have to admit, I was a bit distracted. While he was going on about The Lady and how she was connected to Sunderland and them others, I was realizing we weren't alone in the room. Old Fezziwig had fallen asleep in a chair in the corner. I thought him asleep, at first. Then I came to see he was listening to all of it."

"And you said nothing?" Adelaide asked. "Not to Tom, not to anyone?"

Annie shrugged. "Didn't see how it was my business, so long as I was getting paid."

The prostitute was taken off by a pair of volunteers, and we returned to the cliffside.

"The truth of all this will never be told," Dickens said ruefully. "I'll never be allowed to print any of it."

"He's right," Crabapple said, spitting out the toothpick he'd been chewing on. "The whole lot is whinnying for their solicitors like screamin' babies wantin' Mama's tit."

"Nellie?" I asked.

Adelaide gestured back to the mound where I'd been found. Workers continued to excavate.

I was about to sigh with relief when icy fingers strummed along my neck. There was no ghostly whisper, nor was one required. A shout of surprise rose from those sifting through the ruins where I'd been found, and a dark-cloaked figure climbed into view.

Nellie was stooped, bowed, slack-jawed. Dark hollows half-mooned under her eyes, and one of her bony gloves had been lost, her hand scraped raw and bloody to the bone. Slowly, she straightened her spin, removed her cloak, flipped it about. The lining had been bright red, reversible. No wonder she'd been able to be Humbug so easily one moment, then lost in a crowd, just another onlooker, the next.

"Miss Owen told me, but I didn't fully credit it until just now," Crabapple admitted. He raised his pistol and aimed it at Nellie's heart. "Bloody hell, what does it take to kill you?"

Shaking, moving unsteadily, she made her way towards the cliff's edge, turning her back on Crabapple's orders and threats. We gathered about, along with the local workers, forming a crowd as Nellie suddenly whirled and bowed, her hands describing exaggerated, theatrical flourishes, her face now mined by the blue-black ragged whip scar, cracking into a satisfied smile.

"Oh, my dears! My precious, devoted followers, my cherished audience, come to witness our last performance of the season," she called, her voice loud and clear to soar above the waves crashing below. "I promise you surprise and delight, intrigue and madness, and most of all, I pledge to curl your toes and quicken your pulses with my tale of murder. And sex, of course. Lust and betrayal and the foul stench of death, a heady brew, my beloved fans, that is what I have blended for your rarified tastes. A warning though, my darling dears, if you've come for the sweetness of love, then I'm afraid you'll have to look elsewhere. That is a nectar I have never tasted and its sweetness will not be found in this play. . . ."

"She's mad," Dickens ventured. Then he caught himself, considering the woman had been off her head for some time now. "All right, *madder*."

"Why doesn't someone grab her?" I asked.

Adelaide shook her head. "She's too close to the edge, she'd fall right over. It's thirty yards to the rocks, at least."

"I was once but a girl working for a generous old man. Not a letch. Though his skin was withered and his ivory hair falling out in clumps, he sought not to regain lost youth by lusting after pretty young things like me. He had eyes only for his beloved Jane, who had weathered just as many winters as he. An orphan myself, I felt as if I had finally found a loving home."

"She's talking about Fezziwig," I whispered. Crabapple nodded.

"And when I confided in him my dreams of one day becoming an actress, he simply said 'no time like the present' and whisked me off to the Adelphi where he introduced me to its owner, Anton Villiers, a man who would change my life. I gave myself to Villiers in every conceivable way, and he pulled strings for me, helped me get auditions. Before long, I was Nellie Pearl, the ingénue and talk of the town. And he was what he was . . . what he'd always been, but I'd been too besotted with the possibilities of everything my life might be to see him clearly: A gambler. A drunk. A 'pimp' as they call it, who'd never expected me to succeed. When I did, he bided his time to let my fame grow, all in the cause of his own ambition. . . ."

She hesitated, began to sway, dance awkwardly, horribly, on the cliffside. She nearly lost her footing, once, twice, but caught herself and did not fall. Striding from one end of the cliff to the other, she continued her soliloquy. "Finally, when he was desperately in debt, in danger of having his neck wrung by the vile sorts in the Quarter, he came to me with his demands. I would be his whore after all, servicing the richest men in London.

All very discreet, of course. Hush-hush, don't you know. After all, I owed him. When I refused, he attacked me. I'd never harmed a living being in my life, but when he attempted to force me to my bed, my hand gripped a glass, shattered it, and ground it into his face. He fled, covering one eye, bleeding, cursing, promising revenge. I waited night after night for his return until finally my dear Crisparkle dragged my sad tale from me as I wept in his arms. He promised I would never see Villiers again. That he would 'see' to the man. I believed him. And for many years, it proved true. Ah, for many years . . ."

Nellie tottered on the edge, one boot sliding, then regained her footing. I looked to Adelaide, who stared at the madwoman with the coldest and most piercing gaze I'd ever seen. Then Nellie went on.

"But months ago," Nellie said, "I knew the truth of it. '*Mary, Mary, quite contrary*' they sang of me, before my punishment was issued. Punishment for what? I don't know. Being a woman, I suspect." And she recounted the horror of waking to strange men on every side of her bed, of being dragged, beaten, drugged, and taken in the night to this place, where we had seen but a fraction of what was done to her. Villiers had engineered all of it. Her precious costumer, Crisparkle, had paid the man with his life's savings to leave London and allowed Nellie to believe Villiers was dead.

"So that's why you killed the costumer?" I asked. "After he made that hideous costume for you?"

Nellie laughed. "Oh! Questions from the audience. Yes, yes, please! And yes, that is exactly so."

"And I'd wager you took care of Villiers as well," Crabapple added.

With a sigh, Nellie said, "Yes, well, and that's where the twist comes into the tale. I had no idea when I cut him to bits that anyone else was with us in the villa. Then I found his whore, alight in an opium haze. I could not take the risk that she might have seen, might remember, so I cut her, too. It's surprising how easy it is, once you've done the first one. I gathered up Villier's correspondence, anything that might help fill in the gaps of his story. Oh, yes, I see, I left that bit out. I went there this time with Crisparkle, and he helped me grind the truth of things from Villiers. He had left London and in France fallen in with a trafficker of the exotic who called herself The Lady. The Lady had the little photographer in her employ and had already begun her great and ambitious enterprise, supplying ladies from every port of call for Smithson and the Colleys. In fact, they had forged a three-way partnership, with Smithson remaining in control of vice in the Quarter, the Colleys lording over the docks, and The Lady supplying her particular goods and services. They even had a name for it."

"Chimera," I said.

"Well!" Nellie clapped her hands together. "Very good, my darling dear, quite wonderful you are. The Lady was Greek and had grown up with all those ancient legends of three-headed beasts. The Colleys added to the Greek mythology with their despicable use of our own English children's rhyme."

I took a step towards Nellie, who drew back, nearly

falling. I stood rock still. "*Mary, Mary, quite contrary . . .*" I sang. Nellie winced.

"*Pretty maids all in a row,*" she continued, her voice choked. "They used it as a code to alert the other factions of the trinity to any new shipment of women. Telegrams and message boys delivered the rhyme, the men themselves sang it while they . . ." She stopped suddenly as the memories darkened her face. "Even waking moments were shrouded in shadows. I grew so sick of shadows."

"Killing Villiers wasn't enough," I said, giving the poor killer some solace from her haunting memories. "The Lady had those photos and wanted more."

"Tut-tut," Nellie said, raising a finger to object. "Smithson, by way of his lackey Lazytree and that fool Rutledge. Villiers had been The Lady's lover, he was quite astounding in that regard, even I must admit, and through her, he had known of Sunderland's double life. But you see, what kicked off all the ruckus was that the whore I had slain along with Villiers actually *was* The Lady! He had plenty of her photographs, examples of her writing, and so on. So, because I'd removed both those foul beasts from the face of our Earth, she vanished just after the latest delivery had been made to that warehouse where the girls were stored. Oh, what a mess I caused, quite outside my intention! You see, I finished her before she could tell the Colleys where to take ownership of their delivery! Whoops!"

Adelaide was nearly out of breath with worry as she asked, "Then my Tom, he knew none of this terrible business?"

"Just a pawn. He knew something illegal was being delivered to those warehouses, and he was handsomely compensated for his services, but the details, no, I don't think so. Thinking back on it, though, I can't help but surmise that he had planned to bring about old Fezziwig's ruin. I think he was going to, ah, 'tip the coppers' to the idea that something illegal was in Fezziwig's remote warehouses, then be on hand to pick up the pieces somehow when the old man was dragged through the courts."

"The land deal," Adelaide said, lost and saddened. Her hand brushed mine—and I took it.

"So that was what did it for poor Fezziwig, then," Dickens said, rubbing his journalist's brow. "You assumed the worst when you received Fezziwig's invitation mentioning The Lady, that he was a party to what had been done to you."

Nellie scampered about, tempting death. "When I received it, I thought back to the day he introduced me to Villiers—"

"And you decided that Fezziwig might have known the kind of man Villiers really was," I said. "He clearly knew *something* of all this. And that's why you killed him. You sent him an anonymous letter promising a repayment for an earlier good deed, and when he met you, you delivered."

"Clever duck," Nellie said, "so clever."

"But he just wanted to warn you. To warn all of you, people he had helped in the past. I'd wager that there was even something he had done for Sunderland before, though that fat, lying bag of filth went to his death denying it. You thought Fezziwig the liar, the Humbug, but you were wrong."

She laughed. "I took that word from some of his correspondence to you!"

Yes, Fezziwig's offices had been ransacked. She'd gone through his papers trying to understand what he knew and how he'd found it out.

"You didn't have the heart to do to him what you did to Villiers and The Lady," Crabapple said. "You still had feelings for the old gent. It's why you put him out, slit his throat while he slept, and then went about your business."

She nodded, unashamed at the retelling of her barbaric acts. "As for your involvement, Mr. Scrooge, I found your card and tried to, ah, frame you, as they call it. If you had not meddled, had not continued to poke and prod at things that did not concern you, I might have let you go . . . or I might not. After all, you were clearly close to the old man. What might he have told you? No, in truth, I'd have come for you eventually. So I slipped you a letter, like I did for that *dreadful* Shen, just to aid you along a little. You see, sometimes the supporting characters need a little prompt, just to keep the play going smoothly. I almost had you. The final victim of the Humbug Killer. I wanted to be sure this was done. I wanted my life back. . . ." She touched her scarred face. "Just a dream, I see that now."

"Enough of this," Crabapple said, stalking towards her. "You're coming with me."

"I have a prior engagement. . . ." Nellie perched one teetering foot over the void.

"No!" shouted Adelaide. Wrenching her hand from mine, Adelaide ran at Nellie, approaching at a sharp angle. Even the actress gave a sharp, startled cry as Adelaide flung herself at the woman, pounding into her, and together they fell from our view.

I ran ahead, heart in my throat, waiting to hear their screams or the horrible impact of their bodies being smashed below. But instead, there was only a low, soft weeping.

I peered over the edge and saw Adelaide with one arm around Nellie, the other holding onto a solid perch on the sole outcropping just past the cliff's edge. I grabbed her arm, pulled her up, and Crabapple took custody of the crying, broken young Nellie Pearl. Humbug no longer.

"Stop crying," Adelaide snarled. "You're not getting off that easy."

"Let me die, let me die . . . ," Nellie pleaded.

"Soon enough," Crabapple said. "After your trial!"

The carriages pulled away. As the snow settled in their wake, I spied an old man watching me from behind the skeletal branches of a frosty willow tree. Though he was some ways off, I could not mistake him for another. It was Fezziwig, his hands in his pockets, a warm smile spread across his elderly face. As our eyes met, a soft breeze picked up, breathing relief and calm into my broken body. Now that the episode had passed and the mystery had been laid to rest, my old friend's spirit that had haunted my conscience expelled its last breath down my spine and dissolved into the swirling snowflakes. Like morning mist, I felt the tension leave me, and at that moment, it became clear to me that no spectral visitation had taken place that morning six days ago. No more than a blot of mustard, an undigested bit of beef at the most curiously placed moment. Although the week had been short, it had been the longest week of my life. I welcomed normality with open arms.

The gentle movement of the carriage started to lull both myself and Adelaide into a desperately needed slumber. We sat close together in the small carriage, huddling together partly for warmth and partly . . .

But just as I was about drift off, I heard a gentle voice calling to me.

"Ebenezer," Adelaide whispered in my ear.

"Yes, Adelaide."

"I need you to understand that this must never happen again."

"What are you talking about? What must never happen again?"

Soft hands cupped my face and Adelaide's rose lips met mine. Leaning into the kiss, I wrapped my arms around her and pulled her closer. Her lips were so warm, despite the cold, and their warmth spread to my heart in a way not even Belle had induced.

Then, just as quickly, she pulled herself away.

"You know what I am, Ebenezer. I'm the illegitimate daughter of a nobleman. I have a brother who is an opium addict. He is weak and needs to be cared for. I'm no fit wife for any man who plans to rise in the world of business." Her words were direct, focused, and enunciated. She had rehearsed them well.

I tried to argue, but she held up her hand.

"My family will always come first for me," said Adelaide, with tears in her eyes. "As your business will always come first for you."

CHAPTER TWENTY-EIGHT

Sunday, December 25th, 1833
Christmas Day

I WAS SPENDING the holiday alone with a dust-covered bottle of cheap gin. My feet rested upon my desk, my offices were cold and dark. Since Sikes robbed my offices, I could no longer afford coal for the fireplace, let alone oil for my lanterns. It would be a long time before I earned the money back, and in the meantime, I would certainly mind each penny with more frugality than even before.

I might have parted my curtains, it was early enough, sunlight still played about the laughing, singing children as they breezed down the street. I would have none of it. I was aching from my many wounds, only a handful of them visible upon my flesh. Adelaide and I had barely spoken a word since the nightmarish events at Rutledge's country home. Even now, she sat at the side of her sleeping brother, her father with her. She would forgive Tom any sin, it seemed. But I could not. Had it not been for Thomas Guilfoyle's weakness and guile, my oldest friend, Reginald Fezziwig, might still be alive.

Even after that warming embrace, we had argued over this and parted not on the best of terms. Yet I was still haunted. Not by spirits—Fezziwig's ghost had of course not reappeared given that it had merely been a symptom of stress, indigestion, and woman's folly—but by the lingering feeling of Adelaide's hand in mine, and Belle's suggestion that perhaps my only hope at future happiness lay in that bold young woman's direction.

"You're a sinner, Ebenezer Scrooge," I told myself in the distorted reflection cast upon the smoky green bottle I'd held. "A prideful beast. And an absolute fool!"

A knock came at my door. With shaking hands, giddy as a schoolboy, I hid the bottle, wiped my mouth on the back of my sleeve, and bounded to the door.

Adelaide! It had to be her.

I hauled open the heavy wood door—and found myself confronted by a woman I'd never seen before. Her age was difficult to discern. She was handsome enough, not quite comely, perhaps one and twenty, perhaps one and thirty, I simply could not tell.

Her wealth, however, was instantly apparent from her stunning dress, fine jewelry, and near regal carriage. "Excuse me, hello, is this the counting-house of Mr. Ebenezer Scrooge?"

"Madam, I believe *that* is what's written on the sign upon the door you've just come through. Perhaps you could set my mind at ease to that fact, as you walked through it more recently than I. Now, if you are seeking a charitable contribution—"

"I am not," she said swiftly and decisively. "I am here on a matter of utmost urgency. A fiduciary matter, in a way, as I certainly intend to compensate you for your time."

I spied beyond her a gentleman standing on the street before a carriage. He frowned openly in my direction.

"Wait for me out here, Mr. Pocket," she commanded. "My cousin, you see. He's quite protective."

I showed her in, gestured at my finest visitor's chair, yet she simply stood. The woman gazed into my eyes as if mirrors lurked behind them, and in whatever reflection she beheld, she might take full measure of not only the man I was, but the one I would be.

A thin smile etched firmly in place, she said, "I was referred by a former associate of yours. A Mr. Jacob Marley?"

I reeled, thunderstruck. Surely this was another blow, another move in my former associate's game of revenge?

But what if it was? I wasn't exactly busy, and there was no further I could fall. I was ruined financially, my life in all other regards equally in tatters.

"Perhaps you might sit," I said, gesturing at the leather chair, "and tell me how I may be of assistance?"

"My name is Miss Havisham," she said, rushing forward, taking my hand, and squeezing it with surprising fierceness. "And you must save me. You see—I think I just *killed* a man!"